THE GHOST WAR

GORDON ANTHONY

The Calgacus Series:

World's End
The Centurions
Queen of Victory
Druids' Gold
Blood Ties
The High King
The Ghost War

Britain
c. 80 A.D.

Smertae

Carnon

Decantae

Vacomagi

Creones

Taexall

Caledones

Boresti

Caligacus

Tava

Venicones

Bodotria

Gludi

Votadini *Trimonium

Damnonii

Oba

Selgovae

Novantae

*Dun Brigantia

Carvetii

Brigantes

* Isuria

* Eboracum

Parisi

Cornovii

Deva

* Lindum

Deceangli

Coritani

Ordovices

* Viroconium

Iceni

* Durobrivae

Demetae

Silures

* Dobunni

Catuvellauni

Trinovantes

* Glevum

Verulamium *

* Camulodunum

Atrebates

* Londinium

Calleva

Regni

Dumnonii

Isca

*

Note on Place Names

The following list provides details of the places mentioned in this story, along with other principal places in First Century Britain. Most of these are marked on the accompanying map.

Bodotria
The River Forth.

Camulodunon / Camulodunum
The Celtic / Roman forms respectively of a settlement which occupied the site of modern Colchester. The name means, "The fort of Camulos". Camulos was the war god of the Catuvellauni. The original, Iron Age settlement was reputedly founded by King Cunobelinos (Shakespeare's "Cymbeline") when he conquered, subdued or assimilated the neighbouring tribe of the Trinovantes. The Romans regarded it as the "Capital" of the Catuvellauni and established their own colony there soon after the invasion.

Clota
The River Clyde.

Eriu
The Celtic name for Ireland.

Giudi
One of the ancient Celtic names for the modern town of Stirling, more properly linked to the fortress rock which is now the site of Stirling Castle.

Hibernia
The Roman name for Ireland.

v

Ister
The Roman name for the River Danube

Iova
The island of Iona, off the west coast of modern Scotland.
There is some evidence that suggests the island was home to
a druidical sect long before the arrival of Columba and
Christianity.

Londinium
A Roman port and trading settlement built on the site of
modern London.

Tava
The River Tay.

Trimontium
A Roman fort and supply base built near the site of modern
Melrose.

Prologue

The man screamed as the nails were hammered through his hands. Agony seared through him, filling his world, blinding him, making him deaf to the taunting shouts of the men who crowded around, delighting in his torment.

His arms were draped behind the heavy wood of the cross, his hands fixed to the back by long, iron nails that were as thick as his forefinger. His body sagged, making it almost impossible to breathe, but his captors placed his feet on a block of wood so that he would remain alive longer, prolonging his torture.

On either side of him, the other victims were moaning with the pain of their own torture, pleading to be released, but he knew there was no escape, and he would not give his captors the satisfaction of hearing him beg for mercy. He hung there, naked, while his tormentors laughed and jeered at him. Then he screamed aloud as they took turns to cut his flesh.

Sharp knives sliced at his skin, not cutting deeply, but drawing blood from his chest, his arms, his thighs and his calves.

"Cut his balls off," someone suggested.

"He'll bleed to death too quickly," another voice replied. "Just nick him. Make him suffer."

Another blade burned across his thigh but he was in so much pain, his nerves sending so many signals of agony that he could no longer differentiate one hurt from another. His entire body was a mass of unbearable, agonising misery.

"You brought this on yourself," a man informed him, his voice harsh and uncaring.

Somehow, the man on the cross managed to raise his head. He looked into a face that was as hard as the voice, a face that was utterly devoid of compassion.

"You will share my fate," the prisoner gasped, coughing blood as he forced the words out. "The Emperor will demand your deaths."

Mocking, scornful, hateful laughter greeted his defiance.

"The Emperor," his chief tormentor replied, "is a stuck-up, pampered, perfumed piece of shit who is more interested in whoring and drinking than in ruling the Empire."

Another voice called out, "So am I!"

Yet another man mocked, "What? A piece of shit?"

"No. I meant the whoring and drinking."

The crowd laughed heartily at the joke. Someone shouted, "Maybe you should be Emperor, then."

Hating them, the prisoner spat, "You will all be crucified. You cannot escape."

Jeers and taunts, accompanied by more slashes with knife blades drowned out his protests. His head slumped again, his chin resting on his bare chest. Through the blood-red pain that engulfed him, he heard a more serious voice, Saying, "He is right. The Emperor is far away, but his army is not. How can we return home? They will not let us live when they learn what we have done."

Dimly, the prisoner heard the leader say, "Don't worry about that. I have a plan. We will leave this miserable dump and go back home, far away where the Romans will never find us."

"How?" the serious voice persisted.

"Wait and see. By the time this man dies, we will have our means of escape."

The prisoner thought he must be dreaming. He knew he would die, but he also knew that he would be avenged. His captors would not escape retribution. It was impossible for them to march the length of Britannia and cross the sea without being caught. No, he must have imagined hearing the man say they would escape.

But that did not matter. All that mattered was to die well, to show them that he despised them for the barbarian scum that they were.

They were still there, still crowding round, still clamouring to see a Roman die like a thief, but he could no longer hear them, could not even feel the knives that continued to cut his bare flesh. His last thought was that he would soon meet them again when they joined him in the Underworld.

Chapter I

The air was still, not so much as a zephyr rippling the morning calm, while the sun hung like a bronze lantern, low in the southern sky. The river, broad and deep, was a silver mirror, reflecting the cloudless, icy blue heavens. On the far bank, tendrils of smoke drifted lazily into the chilly air, evidence that there was a barbarian village concealed somewhere among the dense woodland that lined the river valley.

Glumly, Lucius Anderius Facilis wondered how likely the savages were to maintain the peace they had promised. Not very likely at all, he concluded, although they would probably confine themselves to small raids in search of plunder rather than wage outright war. Most of the hostiles had retreated further north rather than live so close to the Empire's encroaching border, but Facilis knew that a small convoy such as his might provide a tempting target for some young warriors who could cross the river in their light, animal-hide boats, spring an attack and be back across the water in less time than it would take Antonius Pulcher to eat one of his ample dinners.

Facilis glanced across to his companion, the Quaestor, wondering how the man had ever managed to be appointed to the position. Pulcher was more suited to a comfortable, luxurious life in Rome than the more demanding post of a military Quaestor. He was one of the fattest men Facilis had ever seen, his body bulging and flabby, his face heavy with multiple chins and fleshy jowls. Quite what he was doing out here on the fringes of the

Empire, Facilis could not fathom. Perhaps, he mused, the man was in disgrace, seeking to avoid some scandal at home, or perhaps he thought there was money to be made in the military. That was a possibility, Facilis decided. Quaestors were responsible for the army's supplies and pay. If anyone could make money in the middle of a campaign, it was an unscrupulous Quaestor.

Pulcher was not the only person who seemed out of place. Not for the first time, Facilis wondered about his own position. Why had the Governor sent him to be Pulcher's assistant? It could have been merely a way of finding a job for a displaced former Tribune who needed something to do or, knowing Julius Agricola, it could have been because the Governor suspected Pulcher of corruption and hoped that Facilis would find some evidence of malfeasance. Not that Agricola had said anything when he had authorised the posting, but the Governor was a circumspect man and would expect Facilis to work things out for himself.

Facilis shook his head. His imagination was running away with him. He had only been Pulcher's assistant for three weeks but, as far as he could see, the man's principal vices were an inflated opinion of his own importance, and a tendency to hedonism. Pulcher enjoyed fine food and plenty of wine, which he was in a position to obtain before the best quality supplies reached the legionaries, but that seemed to be as far as his ambitions went. Where the money was concerned, Antonius Pulcher appeared to be scrupulously honest.

The fat man twisted in his saddle to look at Facilis.

"A fine day," he declared, his breath forming swirls of steam in the chill air. "Still cold, but perhaps we shall see a good summer this year."

"Perhaps," Facilis agreed with little enthusiasm.

"Is something bothering you?" Pulcher asked sharply, his voice displaying more irritation than concern for Facilis' welfare. "You seem even more depressed than usual."

6

Facilis, who had actually been wondering how Pulcher's horse managed to carry the man's enormous bulk without collapsing, responded with a weak smile. He could not deny the truth of the Quaestor's jibe. Facilis had always been a serious individual, but the events of the past few years had resulted in him sinking into a despondency he often found difficult to shake off.

He said, "I was just wondering whether the Britons might try to intercept us."

Pulcher's flabby face wobbled as he chuckled, "I doubt that, Facilis. We have enough armed men to ward off anything less than a small army."

Facilis looked back over his shoulder. Winding along the narrow path that ran parallel to the river, he saw the ox-drawn wagon bearing the iron-bound pay chests. Behind the wagon rode a dozen soldiers, carrying shields, lances and heavy swords.

Pulcher continued airily, "You should worry more about the Usipi."

"The Auxiliaries? I thought we were going to deliver their pay. They should be pleased to see us."

"They'll be pleased to see the coins," Pulcher grunted. "But, if you ask me, they're almost as savage as the Britons. They're always fighting among themselves, you know, and they're usually drunk. But what can you expect from Germans? You know what the Emperor Tiberius said about them? There is no point in trying to conquer the Germans. Leave them alone and they'll destroy themselves sooner or later."

Facilis did not bother answering. Like most Romans, Pulcher had a dim view of anyone from outside Italy. A lot of Germanic tribes had provided soldiers for the Empire and Facilis knew that the German auxiliaries were as tough as any. What he also knew was that they liked a drink and could be volatile if not kept under close discipline. Which was why the Governor always tried to ensure that they were paid on time; hence this latest trek out to the western edges of the army's sprawling chain of camps that lined the southern bank of the river.

"What can you tell me about the Usipi?" he asked the Quaestor, more to distract himself from brooding over his personal worries than from any real desire to engage in conversation.

Pulcher was always happy to display his knowledge. He explained, "They're quite new up here. They only arrived last year and they didn't see much action."

Facilis could not resist smiling to himself. Pulcher spoke as if he were an experienced soldier, a man who had fought in several campaigns, rather than a semi-civilian who had never ventured within twenty miles of a fight.

Expansively, Pulcher continued, "They were posted out here to guard the fleet's ships. We have a small naval force on the west coast of Britannia, and they've established a base on the southern bank of the Clota. The Usipi are here to deter the natives from raiding the base."

"Sounds like an easy job," Facilis observed.

"That's part of the problem," grunted Pulcher. "They have too much time on their hands. They're a fractious lot and the Centurions have a lot of trouble keeping them in hand."

Seeing through Pulcher's bluster, Facilis doubted whether the Usipi were any more of a problem than any group of soldiers. They would be tough, hardened men who were used to using violence to get what they wanted, a trait that would be held in check by the knowledge that they were only one small group within the great host of soldiers that Julius Agricola had led into the north of Britannia. Roman discipline was harsh, and the Usipi would know that they could not afford to step out of line.

The way Antonius Pulcher spoke, the auxiliaries sounded like a band of barely civilised savages, who drank blood and ate small children for breakfast. Yet Pulcher, a

8

man so unwarlike that he had never donned armour, was seemingly prepared to venture into their camp with an escort of only a dozen men. Facilis had come across such blowhards before and he was not impressed by Pulcher's gleeful assertions concerning the barbarity of the Usipi.

"A wild lot," the Quaestor concluded. "Watch them carefully, Facilis. They are not to be trusted."

"Yes, sir," Facilis acknowledged, resorting to meek acceptance rather than become embroiled in a pointless argument. He knew Pulcher was not a man who would change his mind unless someone of greater authority disagreed with him, in which case the Quaestor would immediately alter his stance. Facilis had little time for such fawning sycophancy. In his younger days he had often been forced to agree with senior officers and officials, although he prided himself that he had never been one who nodded agreement simply because an important man held a certain opinion. That, he supposed, was why his career had stalled. Now, back in the army after an absence of nearly twenty years, he had decided to do no more than his duty. He would keep his head down, would not argue with anyone, not even a bumptious fool like Pulcher.

Slowly, the convoy wound its way along the southern bank of the wide river, plodding at a pace determined by the stolidly docile oxen who pulled the creaking wagon that carried the heavy pay chests. Facilis shivered slightly, for although the sun was slowly climbing into a cloudless sky, the earth had not yet shaken off the chill of winter. Early spring flowers were tentatively peeking out from the thawing soil, the trees were clothed in greenery again, and birds were filling the air with their mating calls, but there had been a frost that morning, a reminder that this northern land, so far from the balmy warmth of the Mediterranean, could be an unforgiving place.

"There's the naval base," Pulcher announced, gesturing with one pudgy hand towards a small inlet in the

9

river bank where a handful of galleys had been drawn up onto the shore.

Facilis studied the place Pulcher had indicated. He could make out the dull shapes of four small galleys, their prows nudging the river bank. With their masts lowered and oars shipped, the boats reminded him of beached whales, stranded out of their usual environment.

He frowned, "I don't see anyone working on the galleys. The place looks deserted."

"The sailors are probably sleeping off their hangovers," muttered Pulcher. "Don't worry, they'll wake up as soon as they know their pay has arrived."

As they rounded another stand of trees, Facilis saw a stockade which stood on a low rise overlooking the tiny bay, the interior space crammed with long, low barrack buildings which Facilis presumed were home to the sailors of the Imperial Fleet and the Auxiliary troops who garrisoned the fort. Together, the wooden ramparts of the camp and the galleys on the river bank represented Rome's power in this part of the world, but Facilis could not help thinking that, surrounded by endless miles of rugged countryside out here on the western fringes of the northern frontier, they looked puny and inconsequential.

Pulcher, though, gave a satisfied smile.

"Magnificent, isn't it?"

"Sir?"

Pulcher gestured towards the fort.

"We bring civilisation to this wilderness, Facilis," he declared pompously. "The sailors told me that the savages ran away, wailing in terror, when they saw our galleys rowing up the river. They are so backward that they'd never seen large, wooden ships before."

"I'm sure they hadn't," Facilis replied, although he was privately certain that, if the barbarians had fled at the sight of the galleys, it was probably because they thought they were about to be attacked.

Pulcher, who seemed prepared to believe any tale about the ignorance and foolishness of the barbarians, went on, "Mark my words, Facilis, the Governor will complete the conquest of the entire island this year. Britannia is an island, you know. Some of our ships sailed all the way round the northern edge last year."

"Yes, I'd heard that."

"So, the savages have nowhere to run. They will submit, or they will be destroyed."

Despite himself, Facilis challenged, "I thought the aim was to incorporate the local people into the Empire so that we can raise taxes from them?"

Pulcher snorted, "You can't treat with the Britons, Facilis. They are utter savages, completely beyond redemption, with no trace of civilisation whatsoever. Believe me, we will need to crush them. When you have been here as long as I have, you will come to understand that."

"Perhaps I will, Sir," nodded Facilis, struggling to conceal his contempt for the Quaestor.

Pulcher misinterpreted his tone. The fat man retorted, "Cheer up, man. We are on the verge of greatness here. You could show a little enthusiasm."

This time, Facilis could not help himself. He replied, "If I may say so, Sir, dishing out the pay hardly seems an action worthy of being described as great."

Pulcher's rotund face flushed as he shot back, "We are part of a great enterprise, Facilis. A vital part, I should remind you. If we do not ensure that the troops are properly equipped, fed and paid, there would be no campaign at all."

"Yes, Sir."

Facilis was annoyed with himself. He had vowed not to become involved in such petty arguments but a few bombastic comments from Pulcher had broken his resolve. It was, he thought glumly, not a good omen.

Pompously, Pulcher went on, "I expect you to display rather more commitment to your duties, Facilis. I need an assistant who understands the importance of our task here."

"Yes, Sir."

Pulcher huffed at that, shifting in his saddle so that his horse almost stumbled under the movement of his immense weight.

He asked, "You were in commerce before you came here, is that right?"

"Yes, Sir. I ran a construction business."

"Well," Pulcher lectured, "you must forget that. You are in the army now, and you must act accordingly. I suppose it must be difficult for someone of your age to adapt after so many years of civilian life, but things are different out here."

Somehow managing to keep his words free of scorn, Facilis replied, "I understand, Sir."

"I'm not sure that you do," sighed Pulcher. "How old are you, anyway?"

"I am fifty seven, Sir."

Pulcher, who was, Facilis guessed, somewhere in his mid-thirties, gave him a sharp look as he asked, "May I ask why you decided to join the army at that late stage of your life?"

"It's a long story, Sir."

Pulcher waited expectantly for Facilis to continue, but the older man refused to divulge any more about his past. Much as he wanted to put the Quaestor in his place, to deflate his overweening ego, the man was his superior officer, and venting his frustration would serve no purpose. All it would accomplish would be to make life even more difficult than it already was. With an effort of will, Facilis remained silent.

Pulcher, as he had expected, was too wrapped up in himself to press the matter any further. The Quaestor merely shrugged his enormous shoulders and muttered, "Suit yourself, man. Just try to appear a little more keen on your duties. That way, we'll get along fine."

12

"Yes, Sir."

They trotted down to the stockade. A lone sentry stood on the earth wall behind the wooden palisade. As they drew near, he signalled down to the fort and the gates were pulled open. Facilis saw four more soldiers, big, long-haired men wearing chainmail coats over tunics and trousers. They held the gates open, grinning fierce welcomes as Pulcher led the convoy into the fort. One of the soldiers said something in his native German, a short, guttural remark which Facilis could not understand but which brought low chuckles from the other men who held the gates open.

Facilis gave the waiting soldiers a courteous nod, but their eyes were hard and hostile, their humour vanishing as soon as he looked at them, replaced by stares of stony contempt. He began to wonder whether Pulcher's warnings about the Usipi might be more accurate than he had believed.

The interior of the stockade was much the same as any military base Facilis had ever seen, except that it appeared remarkably deserted.

"Something's wrong," he whispered to Pulcher.

The fat man frowned, "What are you talking about?"

"Where is everybody? It's the middle of the morning. The place should be heaving with soldiers."

"Perhaps they are out on patrol," Pulcher replied dismissively.

"Why? Their job is to protect the ships."

"And your job," Pulcher snapped in response, "is to do as I say. Now be quiet."

Behind them, the gates were slammed shut and the great locking bar, a huge plank of oak, was dropped back into place by the four burly auxiliaries. By that time, Facilis and Pulcher had reached the main square at the centre of the camp. They stopped abruptly at the sight that met their eyes.

"Immortal Gods!" breathed Facilis.

"What is that?" Pulcher asked, his eyes wide with frightened horror.

13

Facilis struggled to take in the awful sight that met his eyes. At the far side of the central square, three large, wooden crosses had been erected. On each one, a naked man hung, arms draped behind the cross-beams and long, iron nails driven through the backs of their hands, through the thick wood where the points had been bent over to prevent them being pulled out.

Blood dripped from the awful wounds and from the men's mouths. Their heads hung low on their chests, unmoving. Even from a distance, Facilis could see that the bodies had been slashed repeatedly, leaving them a mass of red gore. A large, black bird perched on one cross, pecking at the face of one of the dead men.

"What on earth is going on?" Pulcher protested loudly, at last realising that things were not right.

Facilis breathed, "They've been crucified."

They stared in disbelief at the three victims. Facilis looked all around, then felt his stomach lurch in panic as more men began to appear.

Doors opened and soldiers scurried into the open, quickly fanning out to surround the Quaestor's small convoy. Like the men who had opened the gates, they were dressed for war in chainmail and helmets. Most of them, Facilis noted, had long hair that cascaded down to their shoulders. All of them were grinning triumphantly and holding their swords in eager hands.

Facilis glanced at Pulcher, but the man's face was rigid with shock, his eyes gaping incredulously. Facilis turned to wave a signal to the riders of their escort, who were looking around apprehensively, gripping their lances uncertainly and trying to control their nervous mounts.

"Wait!" Facilis shouted to the commander of the escort who was preparing to strike out at the soldiers who were closing in around the horsemen.

"Very wise," called an unfamiliar voice.

Facilis saw a huge man stepping to the fore, dressed, like the others, in chainmail and wearing a bronze helmet on his head. Long, fair hair draped his shoulders and his eyes were as blue as the frosty sky, with no warmth in them at all.

The man called, "I suggest you lay down your weapons."

He paused, gesturing towards the three crucified men as he added, "Unless you want to end up like our former Centurions here."

Facilis felt helpless. There were more than a hundred armed men surrounding Pulcher's small convoy. In the confined space of the camp, the horsemen would have no chance of outfighting the grim-faced auxiliaries, and with the gates barred, there was no way of escaping.

Pulcher had still said nothing. He seemed frozen in place, his eyes fixed on the gruesome sight of the crucified officers.

Wearily, Facilis turned to look back at the cavalrymen of the escort.

"Lay down your weapons," he told them.

"Very wise," the big Auxiliary approved.

"Who are you?" Facilis asked him.

Eyes gleaming with triumph, the man laughed, "I am Fullofaudes of the Usipi and you are now my prisoners."

Chapter II

As the days lengthened, and the frosts of winter gave way to the gentle warmth of spring, the time for sowing seeds arrived. The end of winter brought the hungry months, when the grain stored from the previous year's harvest was running low, and the new year's crops would not be ready until late summer. There was fresh meat, because lambs and calves had been born, but grain, fruit and vegetables would be in short supply for some time. This was the beginning of a period of hard, unrelenting work in the fields, a time when every man, woman and child was required to contribute to provide food.

Broichan the druid knew all about the cycle of the year, but he also knew that this year was different. This year could see the end of everything, because the free tribes faced the greatest threat to their survival that they had ever known. The Roman Empire had come north, extending its reach as far as the southern banks of the two great rivers, the Bodotria in the east, and the Clota in the west. Soon, inevitably, the legionaries would cross the rivers, bringing death and destruction in their wake.

Broichan understood death. He did not fear it, but he feared the coming of Rome because it signified the end of his people's way of life. That could not be permitted. So, this year, when the tribes should be working in the fields and meadows, he had summoned them to war.

Clutching a long staff in one hand, he stood on the side of a low hill. Tall, lean and angular, his long, grey hair and beard fluttered in the breeze while he watched the war host assemble. It had taken many months of travel, of talking to Kings and chieftains, of encouragement, persuasion and even the occasional threat, but it had been worth it. For the first time anyone could remember, the tribes had agreed to set aside their animosity, to forget their ancient feuds, and had come to this sacred site, a neutral place on the borders of several tribal lands.

Many small war bands had come, and three of the largest tribal groups had arrived. Now Broichan was waiting for the fourth. He saw them ambling into the wide plain that was already occupied by thousands of warriors and long lines of tethered horses. Around the hill where Broichan waited, the meadows were covered by newly-constructed shelters, the land sparking and smoking with more camp fires than a man could count.

The new arrivals came in a long line, most of them riding short-legged, shaggy-coated war ponies, but some trudging wearily on foot. Most of them carried long spears made of ash, tipped with leaf-shaped iron blades, and they carried shields made of wicker covered by animal hide. Some, the wealthy, carried swords and a few even wore chainmail armour.

Broichan watched with approval as the new arrivals made their way to a wooded slope near a wide meadow where they set about making camp. He estimated that there were more than two thousand of them, mostly rough-looking, hardened warriors, although, as with the other tribes, there were some women among them. Some of the women came because they wanted to accompany their husbands. Some would act as cooks, or would tend the sick and wounded. Others would take up their own spears and fight alongside the men.

While the new arrivals set about making camp, a small group of men left the main body and walked towards the slope where Broichan waited. Most of this group was made up of followers, warriors pledged to defend their chieftain. One of them held a long, wooden pole to which was affixed a boar's skull. Broichan did not need the symbol to tell him that these men were of the Boresti, a small but

17

important tribe who lived a little way to the north. These were the men he had been waiting for.

His eyes scanned the three men who walked at the head of the delegation. The first, squat, ugly, with a squashed nose set above a mouth that was full of crooked teeth, wore a sleeveless leather jerkin that was open at the front, displaying a host of tattoos that covered the man's chest. Broichan recognised Bridei, King of the Boresti, a man who rarely seemed to take anything seriously except his favourite pastimes of hunting and fighting. He was a King, but Broichan dismissed him after only a cursory glance.

The second man was even shorter, his head balding, but his eyes alive with intelligent humour. He wore two short, Roman swords, one at either hip, a habit that Broichan knew was more than a mere affectation. The man may have been slight in build, and over fifty years old now, but he was a renowned warrior, still feared by his enemies. His name, Broichan knew, was Liscus, although most people knew him as Runt because of his diminutive stature. He never seemed to mind the pejorative nickname, wearing it with the same self-mocking pride with which he wore his twin swords.

Again, Broichan acknowledged Liscus' presence, then discounted him, because it was the third man he needed to speak to.

Tall, broad-shouldered and massively muscled, this man was a giant, towering over most men, especially his two companions, who were both much shorter in build. He wore a tunic of chainmail, and carried a huge longsword on his back. He had removed his iron helmet, leaving his long, straight hair to fall down around his shoulders, a raven-black mane that was now tinged with hints of grey at his temples. He walked, Broichan thought, like a cat; always confident, always prepared. He was unmistakably a warrior, even to those who did not know him. Those were few, Broichan mused, and even people who did not know him were aware of his name and reputation.

This was the man Broichan was waiting for. This was the warrior who would lead the great alliance of tribes against the invaders. This was the exiled King who had made a home among the Boresti and who had turned that small, insignificant tribe into a power to be reckoned with. This was the only man among all the Pritani who had ever defeated the Romans in battle.

This was Calgacus.

Calgacus saw the druid watching him and braced himself for their meeting. They were reluctant allies, with little in common except their opposition to Rome. Calgacus had no great liking for druids at the best of times, and very little for Broichan at any time, but he knew that he needed the old greybeard.

The power and influence of the druids had waned in recent years, their numbers diminished as the Romans hunted them down and slaughtered them, but Broichan was determined to reassert that authority. He was an imposing figure, stern and fierce, vehement in his arguments and never slow to put forward his own point of view.

"He's not coming to meet us," Runt observed quietly. "He's waiting for us to come to him."

"What do you expect?" Calgacus replied. "He's a druid. He counts himself above Kings and War Leaders."

"He's a hard man to like," Bridei observed.

"You'll get no argument from me on that," Calgacus agreed. "We couldn't have built this alliance without him, but that doesn't mean I trust him any further than I could throw him."

"Best not to upset him, though," warned Bridei. "Don't get in the way of a druid or an angry bear, as the saying goes."

"Bears are probably easier to deal with," Calgacus agreed. "At least you know where you stand with them."

They climbed the lower slope of the small hill, stopping in front of the old greybeard. He regarded them haughtily, looking down his angular nose at Calgacus.

"You are late," he stated stiffly.

"We're here now," Calgacus shrugged. "Wherever this place is."

He nodded his head, indicating the slope behind the druid. The hill was low, a ridge of elevated land little more than forty paces above the surrounding plain at its summit, but it dominated the land around it, not because of any natural advantage, but because it wore a crown of dead trees. Set in rings around the hilltop were tall columns of wood, branchless pillars that had been planted in concentric circles like sentinels, screening the summit from view.

"What is up there?" he asked the druid.

Broichan frowned, but if he had been thrown off balance by the unexpected question, he concealed it well.

"It is Cingel's tomb," he replied gruffly, as if the answer should explain everything.

"Who was Cingel?" Calgacus persisted.

Bridei chuckled, "Don't you know? I thought everyone had heard of Cingel."

Calgacus shook his head. "I haven't."

Broichan shot him a disbelieving look. With a weary sigh, he explained, "Cingel was one of the Old Ones, from the days before men learned the secret of working metal. He was a great hero. I thought everyone knew his story."

"I don't," Calgacus shrugged.

"It is a lengthy tale," Broichan informed him, clearly impatient to discuss other, more pressing matters.

Calgacus told him, "Give me the short version. If this place is important, I want to know why."

Frowning at this disrespect to the art of story-telling, Broichan recounted, "Cingel was blessed by the Gods, but he and all his neighbours were plagued by an army of bandits who raided their farms and stole their crops and livestock.

20

The brigands murdered and raped, taking whatever they wanted by force."

"Things haven't changed much," Runt observed quietly.

"Is this the short version?" Calgacus asked pointedly.

Broichan sniffed his disapproval before continuing, "Cingel decided that something must be done, but there were too many bandits for he and his fellow farmers to oppose, and they did not know where the brigands' camp was located. So Cingel decided to join the enemy."

"Not the noblest plan," Calgacus remarked.

The druid exhaled loudly, clearly annoyed at the interruption.

"Do you wish to hear the tale or not? We have more important matters to discuss."

"Yes, I want to hear it. Carry on."

Frowning even more darkly, Broichan went on, "The tale relates that Cingel took with him a magic cauldron. It was a wondrous thing, always full of whatever food or drink its owner desired."

Calgacus raised his eyebrows sceptically, but made no comment, allowing Broichan to continue his tale.

"The bandits found Cingel wandering in the woods and were going to kill him until he showed them how he could control the cauldron and give them whatever they desired. He assured them that, if they permitted him to live, they need never go hungry or thirsty again, so they took him back to their hidden camp. Once there, Cingel sent word to his people, telling them where the bandits were based. Then he ordered the cauldron to produce strong beer and he gave drinks to all the bandits. Soon, they were all drunk. When they fell asleep, Cingel called his people and led them to the camp. They fell on the bandits and slaughtered them. Thus did Cingel save his people."

"That's it?" Calgacus asked, shaking his head.

21

"It is an instructive tale," Broichan insisted. "Cingel used his brains to defeat a stronger enemy, which is what we must also do. That is one reason why this is a significant place for us to meet. The Kings will not be unaware of that. Stories have power."

"Only for those who do not question them," Calgacus grunted.

"It is not our place to question the ancient tales," the druid informed him icily.

"Why not? How else do we learn except by asking questions until we are satisfied with the answers? I mean, if this Cingel was alone, how did he send word to his friends? And what happened to his magic cauldron? We could do with it to help feed our men. Come to that, if he lived in the days before men knew the secret of working metal, where did he get a cauldron from?"

Bridei laughed, but Broichan scowled at the questions.

"We are wasting time, bandying words over an ancient story," the druid said impatiently. "The other Kings are waiting for us."

"Are they all here?"

Broichan's nose wrinkled as he replied, "Most of them. There are small groups from the far north, although they are few in number. Of the other tribes, the Caledones, Venicones and Damnonii are here."

Calgacus nodded, but there was one major omission from the list of tribes the druid had recounted.

"What about the Taexali?" he asked.

Broichan's steely gaze did not falter as he said, "They are not here yet."

Bridei spat his disgust. "Bloody Maelchon! I never trusted him."

Broichan shrugged, "They may arrive soon. Maelchon of the Taexali is a man who is aware of his own importance. He may wish to arrive late, to make an entrance, as it were."

Bridei grimaced, "Maelchon of the Taexali is a sadistic bastard who cannot be trusted."

"Forget him," Calgacus interjected. "At least the rest of them have come. Let's go and speak to them."

Broichan nodded, "I will take you to them." He gave a warning gesture as he added, "Be sure you show no weakness. They must believe you can lead them to victory. Bringing them together has not been easy and there is still mistrust between them. There have been several arguments already."

"Andraste preserve us!" muttered Runt. "Is there any good news?"

Broichan regarded him with a cold stare before silently turning away and heading up the low slope towards the forest of pillars.

"I didn't think so," sighed Runt.

Following the druid up the gentle slope, they emerged from the forest of dead trees into a sunlit space at the top of the ridge. Calgacus saw that there was a wide expanse of grass in front of a low mound. The mound, he realised, must be Cingel's tomb, a pile of rocks and stones, bleached white by the years, with grass growing between them, giving the mound a mottled appearance. It was, indeed, an ancient monument, a grave of the Old Ones. Whether the man whose bones lay beneath the mound had really been named Cingel was, he thought, less important than the story. The people believed it, and they maintained the forest of wooden pillars to watch over this sacred site. Some of the branchless trees, he had noticed, were worn and weathered while others appeared to have been placed quite recently.

The hilltop was an important place, but Calgacus had no time to appreciate its majesty, because the open space in front of Cingel's tomb was filled with men, all of them turning to look at him. The low murmur of conversation that had filled the meeting place died away as Broichan led him into the enclosure.

Calgacus took a deep breath, calming himself. He had waited for this day for years, and now it was here. Today, he must convince the Kings of all the tribes to follow him. Too many times in the past, he had tried to unite the tribes. Too many times, he had failed. He could not afford to fail now.

Show no weakness, Broichan had said. Remembering, Calgacus strode out to face the assembled chieftains.

The waiting men were gathered in groups, each one under a standard that proclaimed their identity and independence. He saw the eagle of the Caledones, the stag of the Damnonii, and the bull of the Venicones. There were other symbols he did not recognise, the emblems of the smaller tribes from the far north, tough-looking men who had travelled a long way to join this alliance. Broichan had permitted them to attend the meeting, but Calgacus knew it was the leaders of the three largest tribes he needed to convince.

The boar standard of the Boresti was now added to the assembled display, its supporting pole planted in the earth, two burly warriors standing protectively beside it, while Bridei stood proudly in front of it, his arms folded across his tattooed chest.

Each King had brought a retinue of followers, the leading chieftains of his tribe, together with an escort of warriors. Kings always wanted to bring a large band of guards because the more men they had, the more important they would seem. Broichan, however, had insisted on no more than the traditional twelve. When a King left his home, he walked or rode with three warriors in front, three behind, and three on either side, a protective ring of men who were sworn to die for their Lord. Here in the open space beside Cingel's tomb, those guards stood behind the chieftains, casting suspicious looks at their counterparts who watched over the rival Kings.

Broichan wasted no time. Striding to the centre of the meeting place, he summoned a younger druid, one of his acolytes, who took the senior man's staff and replaced it with a large clay beaker.

Everyone watched in silence as Broichan held the beaker aloft in both hands, presenting it to the sky.

"The Cup of Peace," he intoned in a loud voice. "Every man shall drink as a sign that he will not draw blood while this gathering lasts. Any who break this oath will be cursed by the Gods."

He paused, his dark eyes scanning the crowd, checking that he had their attention. Then he tilted the cup, pouring some liquid onto the grass at his feet.

"For the Gods," he intoned as he made the libation.

"For the Gods," the assembled men chorused.

"Now, be seated. The cup will be passed among you."

The men sat on the grass, spreading their cloaks beneath them.

"Sensible," Runt whispered to Calgacus. "Sitting men are less likely to start a fight."

Calgacus nodded, watching as Broichan took a sip from the beaker before passing it back to his apprentice and reclaiming his staff. The younger druid walked carefully towards the group of men closest to Broichan, offering the cup to the first of the Kings.

Broichan announced, "We welcome Drust, King of the Caledones."

Drust, a big, middle-aged man, running to fat, with a nose mottled by a web of red veins, drank from the cup, then passed it to his chieftains.

"Drust looks half drunk already," Runt observed in a low whisper. "I'll bet that's not his first taste today."

"I heard he's often drunk," Calgacus nodded. "It seems he dislikes the responsibility of being King."

"Can we rely on him?"

"He will do as Broichan tells him," Calgacus replied. "And we can trust his men to fight for us. That's what matters."

Once each of the Caledones had drunk from the cup, the young druid re-filled it, then moved on to the next group.

"Gabrain of the Venicones is here," Broichan boomed.

Gabrain was a young man, little more than twenty years old. Slab-jawed and sharp-nosed, he was a tough-looking character of imposing height. He also exhibited a surly attitude, casting a cold look at Bridei as he drank from the large beaker.

Recognising his traditional enemy, Bridei whispered, "That bastard will probably spit in the cup."

"We'll drink it anyway," Calgacus hissed back.

The third King was Ebrauc of the Damnonii. He was an old man, his hair completely grey, his limbs thinned by age. Calgacus had noticed that he walked with the aid of a long, knobbled stick of hazel, and he frequently accepted support from a powerfully-built, slim-waisted young man who was in constant attendance on him. Calgacus knew that Ebrauc always rode in a chariot because he was too frail to sit on a horse, but the old man held his head high, and his eyes were clear and bright.

The cup came to Bridei, then to Runt and Calgacus. They all drank, taking the sips that confirmed their oath of peace.

Finally, the cup was passed among the minor tribes, the war bands who clustered at the rear of the crowd.

Broichan nodded his approval. He raised his staff, calling for attention.

"I thank you all for coming," he told them. "We are here to unite against the invaders who threaten us. Under Calgacus' leadership, we will drive the enemy back and preserve our way of life."

26

Broichan was an imposing figure, but bringing the tribes together had created a volatile mix. Calgacus sensed trouble brewing almost as soon as the cup of peace had completed its circuit.

It was Gabrain, the young King of the Venicones, who caused the first stir. He rose to his feet, claiming the right to speak.

"It was my father who agreed to this alliance," he declared belligerently. "But he was an old man, weighed down by his fears. I am King now, and I demand to know by what right Calgacus claims to lead us."

Broichan's brow furrowed. He answered, "I would have thought that the Venicones, of all people, would know of Calgacus' skill in war. He has defeated your warriors often enough."

Gabrain bridled at the less than diplomatic remark. Casting a furious look at Calgacus, he shot back, "That was before I became a man. I lead the Venicones now, and we do not need lessons in fighting from an old man who wears armour to protect himself."

Bridei snorted, "Sit down, puppy. Your yapping is giving me a headache."

Gabrain's young face flushed angrily. He jabbed a furious finger at Bridei, snarling, "You are no King! You hide behind Calgacus, letting him do your fighting for you."

"That's because he's the best there is," Bridei retorted. "But if you want to test my skill, I'm ready whenever you are."

"You are an old man!" Gabrain sneered. "And Calgacus is even older. I could beat both of you."

Calgacus knew a challenge when he heard one. Holding out his arm to restrain Bridei, he pushed himself to his feet, confronting the young King of the Venicones.

Speaking calmly, aware that the eyes of every man were on him, he said, "We are not here to fight one another.

That has been our problem for too long. We are here to join together to face an enemy who threatens us all."

Broichan butted in, "All the tribes have come here to aid you, Gabrain. Your lands will be the first to suffer when the Romans cross the river. You need allies if you are to defend your people."

"I do not dispute that," Gabrain snapped. "But I should be the War Leader."

He cast a mocking gaze around the assembly, looking at each King in turn as he went on, "Of all the Kings here, who else should it be? This is an assembly of old men and drunkards."

His words caused an angry stir among the tribes, causing Broichan to call for calm. Facing Gabrain, the druid insisted, "It was agreed that Calgacus would be War Leader. He has fought the Romans before, and won."

"Much good it did," snorted Gabrain. "They are on our borders now. He has been unable to stop them."

Ignoring Runt's soft hiss of caution, Calgacus stepped towards the young King.

He said, "All right. You have made your point. Now, we must decide this. Why don't you show us how you would kill a Roman?"

"What do you mean?" Gabrain asked suspiciously.

"Let us have a demonstration. Take your sword and show everyone how you would kill a Roman. As you say, I am wearing armour, just as the Romans do. It is not easy to kill a man who wears armour, so I will let you have one attempt to strike me."

A murmur of surprise swept round the enclosure. Men grinned, keen to witness a fight. A challenge had been issued and must be accepted, or Calgacus would lose the respect of every warrior, but his offer was unprecedented.

Gabrain said, "We swore an oath of peace. I might kill you."

28

"I doubt that," Calgacus smiled. "But we need to settle this. If you can drive me to the ground, I will agree that you should be the War Leader. In turn, if I down you, you must swear an oath to follow my command. Is that agreed?"

Gabrain gave a fierce grin. "Agreed!"

Ignoring a disapproving glare from Broichan, Calgacus gestured an invitation.

"Go ahead, then. Use your sword to drive me to the ground, Show everyone how you would kill a Roman."

"Aren't you going to use your sword?" Gabrain frowned as he drew his weapon from its scabbard.

"I don't think I'll need it," Calgacus replied evenly.

"You are a fool, old man," Gabrain smirked.

Calgacus waited, standing motionless. He could hear the murmurs from the watching men as they whispered their opinions. Gabrain was powerfully built, not as tall as Calgacus, but stockier. More importantly, he was thirty years younger, with all the energy and stamina that brought. Calgacus knew he must win a quick victory, because he would tire much sooner than Gabrain. But if the young man had youth on his side, Calgacus had experience.

Gabrain held his sword ready, raising it across his body. He took a step forwards, but stopped when Calgacus held up a hand.

"Wait a moment! If we are going to do this, we should at least do it properly."

Gabrain hesitated, frowning impatiently.

"What are you talking about?"

"You are holding your sword the wrong way."

Gabrain looked at his sword, a double-edged, round-tipped blade as long as his arm, a weapon that could smash through flesh, muscle and bone, inflicting death and awful injury. He blinked, as if expecting to see something other than a killing weapon.

"Let me show you," Calgacus offered.

29

Too late, Gabrain realised he had been tricked. He had relaxed when Calgacus called a halt, and he was unprepared for what happened next.

Calgacus stepped close, hand outstretched as if to offer guidance, but he suddenly grabbed Gabrain's wrist, yanked hard and pulled the young man off-balance. As he did so, his right knee jerked up to catch Gabrain in the groin.

Gabrain gasped in pain, doubling over and letting his sword fall. As he collapsed to the ground, Calgacus deftly caught the tumbling sword, cutting down to plant the blade in the ground beside the writhing figure of the Venicones' King.

"That," he told the watching crowd, "is how we will beat the Romans. We will not fight them fairly, standing in an open field and taking them on face to face. They have all the advantages if we do that. Instead, we will cheat, we will trick them, and we will kill them. We will be like ghosts in the night, striking terror into our enemies' hearts. They will die before they even see us."

Laughter and cheers met his words. The Venicones, angry at the humbling of their King, scowled and muttered, but made no protest.

Calgacus told them, "Help your King. He is a brave man, and I hope he has learned from this. He could beat me in a fair fight, but I fight to win, and I don't care how we achieve that."

While Gabrain was helped back to his place, Broichan declared, "Calgacus will lead us in this war."

Calgacus was annoyed that it had been necessary to make an example of Gabrain, but he knew he had proved himself to any who doubted him. For a brief moment, he allowed himself to believe the alliance could work.

Then the Taexali arrived.

There were twenty of them, all sword-bearing warriors, led by a burly, bull-necked young man with a hard face that was dominated by a nose that had clearly been broken at some time in the past. He swaggered into the enclosure, his attention fixed on Calgacus and Broichan.

"I am Algarix," he announced. "Shield-bearer to King Maelchon of the Taexali."

"You are welcome," Broichan responded. "Where is Maelchon? Is he here with you?"

Algarix's cruel eyes sparked as he replied, "No. He has sent me to tell you that the Taexali will not join this alliance unless his conditions are met."

"Conditions?" Broichan demanded angrily. "What conditions does he dare place on us?"

Calgacus had been uneasy ever since the Taexali had entered the sacred arena. Their leader's attitude was arrogant, and the man's cruel smile betrayed that he had a shock in store. Based on his past dealings with Maelchon of the Taexali, Calgacus felt his heart sink at the mention of conditions. Even before Algarix spoke, Calgacus knew that Maelchon's messenger was about to ruin his dream of a united tribal alliance.

Aiming a sly look in Calgacus' direction, Algarix sneered, "My King has been misled by Calgacus once before. There has been a feud between them for many years. My King is willing to see an end to this rift, but he demands a price before he will seal any agreement."

Calgacus heard Runt mutter, "By Toutatis, I knew we should have killed that devious bastard."

Algarix shot a venomous look at Runt, although his frown suggested that the words had been spoken too softly for him to hear.

Calgacus felt his own temper rising and was about to step forwards to confront the Taexali spokesman, but Broichan sensed his movement and, without turning round, stopped him with an urgent wave of one hand.

Icily, the druid asked Algarix, "What price does your King seek?"

31

Algarix returned a smile like that of a fox among chickens. He said, "My King wishes to aid you, but Calgacus has wronged him in the past. If you wish our help, Calgacus must atone for this by coming to him in person and begging for his assistance. If he does not do this, the Taexali will not join your alliance."

Chapter III

"It's a trap!" Bridei declared. "Don't go. We don't need the Taexali, but we need you."

Calgacus looked around the other faces of the men he had asked to become a Council of War. The main meeting had degenerated into a squabble, with everyone shouting at once, each man trying to drown out the others. Through it all, the Taexali warrior, Algarix, had stuck to his demand.

"I am not here to negotiate," he informed them. "I have delivered my message. I leave it to you whether to accept my King's terms."

He had stalked out of the meeting, gathering his men and riding away, not waiting to hear what Calgacus intended to do.

Now, only eight men remained in the sacred enclosure, discussing what should be done.

Drust, King of the Caledones, sat staring morosely at the ground, his eyes half closed, apparently paying little attention to what was going on. He had, though, insisted that one of his chieftains, a dark-haired man in his mid-twenties, with an intelligent face and a calm demeanour, should take part in the discussion.

"Bran is my most trusted adviser," Drust informed them.

Bran smiled, but there was no humour in his first question.

"What is the cause of your feud with Maelchon?" he asked Calgacus pointedly.

"There is no feud on my part," Calgacus replied.

Bridei asserted, "Maelchon is mad."

"No," Broichan put in. "He is not mad. I spoke to him last year, when I was trying to arrange this alliance. He is eccentric, perhaps a little irrational, and given to violence if he does not get his own way. That, I believe, is the root of the problem."

Addressing Calgacus, The druid went on, "Is it not true that your daughter refused to marry Maelchon?"

"That was twelve years ago!" Calgacus protested.

"She ran off with one of his followers on the night before she was due to marry Maelchon," the druid persisted.

"Better than running off after she'd married him," Calgacus pointed out.

"Be that as it may, Maelchon was slighted, and he still harbours a grudge against you."

"That is ridiculous," Calgacus spat. "He married someone else, didn't he?"

"Yes," the druid agreed. "He married a woman of his own tribe. But she died last year. Some say Maelchon beat her to death when she displeased him in some way."

Bridei grunted, "I told you he was a vicious bastard. Don't go. He's likely to feed you to his dogs."

Calgacus said bitterly, "I paid him a handsome compensation when Fulvia ran away. I didn't need to do that. She was free to marry whoever she liked."

"Nevertheless," said Broichan, "he has obviously not forgotten. It is probably the only time in his life that anyone refused him anything."

"He's waited a bloody long time to do something about it," Calgacus grumbled.

Smiling, Bran remarked, "There are many who believe that revenge tastes sweeter if it has been brewed for a long time."

"It is not that, I think," Broichan answered. "Maelchon only became King last year, when his older brother died. I believe his principal aim was to assume the kingship, so his attention has been focussed on that. Now that he has fulfilled his main ambition, I suspect he has decided to concentrate on avenging other perceived slights."

34

Calgacus declared, "Whatever he is trying to do, I am the War Leader. The war is here, and I should not need to go grovelling to anyone."

Runt murmured, "You've never grovelled in your life, Cal. I can't see you starting now."

Bran ventured, "There is a more important issue we should discuss before deciding whether anyone should go to Maelchon. To my mind, the real question is whether we can defeat the Romans without the Taexali."

Gabrain, who had sat sullenly, still nursing his injured groin, muttered, "Without more men, we will need a lot of tricks."

Broichan agreed, "The Taexali are a numerous tribe. They could bring another five thousand spears."

Smiling smoothly, Bran said, "By my reckoning, we have around fifteen thousand fighting men at the moment. I have not seen the Roman army, but I believe they have almost twice that number. How can we defeat them without the Taexali?"

"We can try!" barked Gabrain. "Or die trying!"

"An admirable plan," Bran nodded, "but hardly likely to succeed."

"Numbers are not everything," Calgacus told him. "I was at the Battle of Caer Caradoc, where my brother, the Great King, Caratacus, led an alliance of nearly forty thousand warriors against three Legions. We had as strong a defensive position as you could imagine, yet they still beat us."

"Which proves my point, does it not?" Bran challenged. "We also face three Legions, plus all their Auxiliary troops. How can we succeed with fifteen thousand fighting men, when your famous brother could not with forty thousand?"

"We will not stand and face them," Calgacus replied. "I told you that."

Old Ebrauc, who was leaning against his young assistant for support, spoke for the first time. In an aged, cracked voice, he said, "Five thousand extra men would be a great help, though."

"I still say it's a trap," declared Bridei. "What if Maelchon has taken Roman gold? He might want to hand you over to the Romans to curry favour with them."

Bran quickly put in, "If Maelchon has joined with Rome, we have a serious problem. With the Legions to the south and the Taexali to the north, we would be caught between them."

Broichan argued, "The Taexali are a proud people. I do not think they would make peace."

"Why not?" Bran argued. "We have all had visits from Roman emissaries. They promise gold and silver if we become their allies."

He gave a faint shrug as he added, "If we are outnumbered, perhaps it would be wise to accept such offers."

Not bothering to conceal his contempt, Gabrain rasped, "I came here seeking allies, not cravens who want to talk peace. We are warriors!"

"What do we gain by fighting when we cannot win?" Bran persisted.

Broichan waved Gabrain to silence. He said, "Perhaps Ebrauc should tell us his story."

Ebrauc inclined his aged head. In faltering tones, he recounted, "Last year, the Romans invaded my people's land south of the Clota. They had offered us peace, but they learned of our mines, where we dig for gold, coal, lead and iron. We would have been happy to trade with them, but they demanded that we surrender control of the mines to them. When I refused, they attacked us."

He paused, making a visible effort to contain his emotion as he explained, "I lost both my sons in the fighting. My children and grandchildren have been taken from me by the greed of Rome. I have nobody now, only those of my tribe who escaped north of the river." He fixed his gaze on Bran as he added, "Whatever Rome says, you cannot trust them. We must fight or become slaves."

Broichan declared, "You see? It is not what you might gain, but what you might lose. If the Romans take over, whether through war or peace, they will steal your freedom. They will take your women for their wives and concubines, they will take your young men to join their army. They will destroy our sacred places, will deny our Gods and steal everything that makes us Pritani."

Bran gave a slight bow as he said, "I hear you, Revered One. I was not advocating peace. It is just that I think we should understand all the issues that face us. And there is one further thing I must point out."

Gabrain rolled his eyes, snorting his impatience, but Bran merely smiled and explained, "Let us say that Maelchon has not taken Roman bribes. We still have a problem. If he does not join us, we are severely outnumbered. Not only that, our homes are unprotected. The Taexali lands border those of the Caledones and the Boresti. Maelchon is an ambitious man. He may not be able to resist the temptation to enrich himself by plundering our villages."

Bridei muttered curses under his breath, recognising the truth behind the young chieftain's words.

Calgacus said to Bran, "You have a lot of questions, but do you have any solutions?"

Bran returned a soft smile as he answered, "I think you must do as Maelchon demands. We need to know what he intends to do. Also, I think we need his warriors. The Taexali are fierce fighters and we could do with their help."

"I will not beg him," Calgacus asserted firmly. "Who would respect a War Leader who crawls before another man?"

"I would not expect you to beg," Bran agreed. "But you could at least talk to him. What harm would that do?"

"It's a trap," Bridei insisted.

Broichan held up a hand. He said, "This is an alliance of equals. We agreed to follow Calgacus in matters of war, but this problem must be decided by the Kings. Answer me now, should Calgacus go to Maelchon, or should he remain here?"

"Stay!" snapped Bridei instantly.

Drust looked up for the first time, his eyes heavy and somnolent. He said, "I think he must go. Bran is right. We need to know what Maelchon intends to do."

Calgacus felt the jaws of a trap closing in around him as he looked at the other two Kings.

Gabrain said, "I agree. You must go."

Calgacus held the young man's gaze, realising that Gabrain was exacting some revenge for having been humbled in front of the chieftains. With Calgacus gone, he would have a chance to stake another claim for the leadership of the alliance.

Ebrauc nodded slowly, saying, "I think I must agree. We need the Taexali. Swallow your pride and do whatever is necessary to bring them to join us."

"So be it," declared Broichan dispassionately.

With those words, the trap closed around Calgacus. Almost before it had formed, his great alliance was already crumbling. To save it, he must grovel before a man who hated him.

Chapter IV

Calgacus was still angry when he reached the woodland where the Boresti had established a camp. Temporary shelters had been constructed from branches, turf and spare cloaks, fires had been lit in hearths made from circles of stones, and pots of gruel were already being stirred in readiness for the evening meal, but none of that could ease Calgacus' sour mood.

"You don't need to go," Bridei told him.

"Yes, I do. I may be the War Leader, but I don't rule the tribes. If I don't do as the Kings ask, they'll soon elect someone else as War Leader."

"Gabrain wants the job," Runt observed.

"That's why he wants me to leave," Calgacus grumbled. "He's probably hoping Maelchon will kill me."

"Aye, you've not made a friend there," Bridei grunted. "Gabrain's a hothead."

"He's young," Calgacus replied evenly. "At least he wants to fight. I didn't like the way Bran kept talking about making peace. He seems to want me out of the way, too."

"He's a cool one, isn't he?" Runt observed. "We'll need to watch him. He's too clever by half. Maybe that's why Drust let him do the talking."

Calgacus nodded, "I suspect Drust put him up to it."

"You think Drust wants to make peace with Rome?"

"I wouldn't put it past him. He only wants a quiet life."

"The Caledones won't stand for that," Bridei put in. "Whatever else you can say about them, they're always ready for a scrap."

"Which is probably why Drust let Bran do the talking," Calgacus ventured. "He doesn't want to be seen to be pushing for peace."

Bridei snorted, "He won't be King much longer, if you ask me. Someone will take his place. Probably Bran."

Calgacus nodded thoughtfully. Among the northern tribes, Kings ruled with the consent of their people, and there was no automatic right for a son to inherit the rule of a tribe. Instead, the chieftains elected the man they thought best fitted to govern. In practice, the Kings tended to be chosen from among the leading families, and sons often followed fathers or uncles to the kingship. But the position of King was a dangerous one. A weak or ineffective ruler could easily be deposed, either by the leading men of his tribe combining to oust him, or sometimes by more direct means, such as a knife in the back.

Calgacus sighed, "I feel sorry for Drust. He was pushed into being King. But the truth is that we need the Caledones, whoever leads them. They are the largest tribe."

"Broichan will keep them in line," Runt asserted. "He has a lot of influence with them. And he has a vested interest in opposing Rome."

"Aye," grinned Bridei. "The Romans kill druids on sight. That's a powerful incentive for him to make sure this alliance works."

Calgacus nodded, "That's why he wants me to persuade Maelchon to join us. He knows we need their warriors."

"It won't be easy," Bridei mused. "Maelchon is a twisted son of a bitch. He'll probably cut your balls off and feed them to you."

"Whatever he intends to do," Calgacus stated, "I need to go and talk to him."

"I think you're making a mistake," Bridei told him.

"We all make mistakes," Calgacus shrugged. "All we can do is what we think is right at the time, and live with the consequences."

"Or die because of them," muttered Bridei gloomily.

Calgacus spent most of the evening talking to the Kings, making sure that arrangements were in place to gather food, to maintain scouting patrols, and to send women and children further north to places of relative safety.

Gabrain was still in a belligerent, uncooperative mood, complaining bitterly that his people's settlements were being abandoned to the enemy.

"We cannot defend every home," Calgacus informed him. "Better to lose a few villages than to lose everything."

"You are a vassal of the Boresti," Gabrain spat. "That is why you are happy to abandon Venicones' settlements."

"I have no tribal allegiance here," Calgacus responded. "We are trying to protect you. It would be easier to withdraw to the north, where there are mountains and forests that are better suited to setting ambushes for the enemy. But if we do that, all your lands would be surrendered. None of us wants that. We will fight them, but we will do it my way. Do you understand?"

Gabrain gave his sullen agreement, but he was not the only person who was unhappy.

Bridei grumbled, "What do we do if the Romans cross the river while you are away?"

"I don't think they will. It's still early in the season. They'll want their horses to feed on fresh grass for a bit longer. We'll only be away for a few days. It's a three-day ride to Maelchon's home. We'll be back in plenty of time for the Beltane festival. In the meantime, make sure you don't start any trouble with Gabrain."

Bridei gave him a hurt look of innocence.

"Me?"

"Yes, you. Your lads are a rough lot at the best of times, and there's bad blood between you and the Venicones. Just stay away from them, and keep the peace."

"My lads won't start anything," Bridei huffed. "But we won't walk away if the Venicones provoke us."

"Yes, you will," Calgacus said firmly. "We are here to fight the Romans, not each other. If I can go to Maelchon and ask for his help, the least you can do is stop your squabbles until we've beaten Rome."

He placed the same injunction on the other Kings, and pleaded with Broichan to maintain order while he was away. It was, he knew, an almost impossible task, because the tribes had always fought one another, raiding cattle, stealing women, ransacking outlying villages. War and plunder were an accepted way of life, a habit that could not be cast off in an instant.

"We need to get back as quickly as we can," he told Runt.

They set off at first light the following morning, accompanied by the thirty-strong escort of warriors from Calgacus' own village. These were men he had trained himself, men he could rely on. Many of them wore chainmail tunics and carried short, Roman swords in addition to their traditional, long, round-tipped blades. Calgacus had taught them how to fight like Roman legionaries, acting in unison rather than fighting as individuals. Most of them had never seen a Roman soldier, but they all knew how the legionaries fought, and how to counter them. These men were, Calgacus knew, the finest fighting men among the free tribes.

They were led by Adelligus, Runt's twenty-year-old son by his first wife. Adelligus had inherited his mother's tall stature, and his father's once-renowned good looks. Tall, handsome, dark-haired, with a scar on his right cheek that only added to his rakish good looks, he was also Calgacus' son-in-law, having married Calgacus' youngest daughter the previous year. But his command of the bodyguard was not

42

due to his family connections. Despite his youth, Adelligus commanded the war band because he was the best warrior among them.

Now, as they rode north, Adelligus moved his pony close to Calgacus.

"We are being watched," he reported, speaking in a matter-of-fact voice that held no trace of alarm.

"Bandits, you think?"

Adelligus shrugged, "Possibly. Or it could be Maelchon's men, watching to see whether you are riding north."

"How many?"

"We've only spotted half a dozen so far."

"However many there are, they'll think twice about attacking a strong group like this," Calgacus said. "But keep an eye out for trouble."

"I always do," Adelligus grinned.

Whoever the watching men were, there was no further sign of them. They were left far behind as Calgacus' war band forded the upper reaches of the Tava, then turned east, following the northern bank of the ever-widening river towards the great estuary where it joined the sea.

The light was fading when they caught sight of their home silhouetted against the darkening evening skyline. It was a fortified hilltop stronghold perched on a steep hill that overlooked the river to the south.

Calgacus felt the familiar sense of peace as he approached his home. On the northern side of the ridge, where the terrain sloped more gently into fertile farmland, was the village where his people had made their homes for the past twenty years, following their long trek from the south to escape the encroaching Roman Empire. It was, he thought, a good home, a place where they had been safe, where they had raised their families, and where they had been happy.

As a boy, he had known another place, far to the south, where he had also been happy. That place, Camulodunon, the principal town of the once-mighty Catuvellauni, was gone now, obliterated, like so many Pritani settlements, by the Roman conquerors. He whispered a soft vow that he would not let that happen again.

"We'll go north in the morning," he told Runt.

"We'll be ready," the little man promised.

Calgacus signalled to his men to disband. Most of them had families in the village, and they hastened to return to their homes, leaving Runt, Adelligus, and a handful of warriors to accompany him up to the hilltop stockade.

It was almost full dark by the time they reached the gates which swung open to admit them. Flaming torches lit the open yard and illuminated the collection of roundhouses that provided homes for Calgacus and his household warriors.

A tall, grey-haired man stood inside, waving a hand in greeting and reaching for their reins.

"Welcome back," he said. "There's supper ready if you're hungry."

"Thanks, Garco," said Calgacus as he swung himself gratefully down from the saddle. "I'll be glad to get this heavy chainmail off. It's been a long day."

"You're getting old," Runt told him.

Garco, prematurely grey and half crippled by a wound to his left foot, was one of their oldest companions. He gave them a wary look as he said, "We weren't expecting you back. Is something wrong?"

"Come inside and I'll tell you all about it."

Calgacus saw the spilling light as a door opened. He turned to see several shadowy figures hurry out to meet them. Even in the dark, with only a handful of blazing torches to shed light on the scene, he recognised the people who emerged from the house.

His daughter, golden-haired Fallar, hurried outside, running to Adelligus, her movement hampered by her swollen belly. Her child, Calgacus' grandchild, would be born before mid-summer. The thought added weight to Runt's jibe about his age.

Beside Fallar came another young woman, carrying a small girl in her arms. Tegan, Runt's second wife and Adelligus' step-mother, was younger than Runt's son, an arrangement that somehow never seemed to bother any of them. Runt grinned as he embraced Tegan and his young daughter.

Calgacus accepted a soft kiss from Fallar, but his eyes were drawn to Beatha when he caught sight of her framed in the firelit doorway. She was still beautiful, he thought, tall and elegant, although she claimed her blonde hair was greying and her figure was sagging in too many places. He did not agree. For him, she was still the young woman he had rescued from a life as a Roman.

She smiled and kissed him, holding his arm. He had expected her to ask about the meeting but, as soon as he felt her touch, he knew that something was troubling her.

"What's happened?" he asked in an anxious whisper.

Beatha replied, "We had a visitor while you were away."

"A visitor?"

"A Roman."

Calgacus stiffened. He looked past Beatha to see his son, Togodumnus, watching him intently. The slender young man was hovering nervously, biting his lip as if expecting a reprimand.

"What did this Roman want?" Calgacus demanded harshly.

Togodumnus met his question with a stare of defiance. The two of them had rarely seen eye to eye on anything, and where the Romans were concerned, there was a gulf between them, a rift that had widened as Togodumnus had grown to manhood.

Refusing to be intimidated by Calgacus' barely suppressed anger, Togodumnus explained, "He was an emissary. Like the ones who have come before. He came to offer peace."

"I expect he came to offer a bribe," Calgacus spat.

Beatha tugged at his arm. She said, "Cal, it's not what he said that's important. It's who he was."

Calgacus could hear the warning contained in her fearful voice.

Frowning, he asked, "What do you mean? Who was he?"

His blood ran cold when he heard Beatha say, "His name was Venutius."

Chapter V

Sdapezi should have been happy. After twenty years of service in the ranks of the Auxiliaries, he had attained the rank of Centurion, a position that was as high as the illegitimate son of a tavern keeper's daughter could ever have dreamed of reaching. He also had a duty that was important but relatively easy, with little danger attached. He should have been content, but he was not.

For the past two years, Sdapezi had commanded a *Turma* of thirty men whose sole task was to watch over the hostages who were kept close to the Governor. All he needed to do was make sure that the captives remained safe while also keeping them under close scrutiny to ensure their good behaviour.

For the most part, it was a task that was simple and straightforward. There were five hostages to be watched; the young princeling from Hibernia, two southern nobles who were no trouble at all, and the girl who was kept away from the others, as much for her own protection as anything else. Those four, Sdapezi had no concerns over. It was the fifth man who worried him.

He sat opposite Venutius now, waiting patiently in the antechamber of the Governor's headquarters, while messengers, scribes, secretaries and Tribunes dashed in and out, all of them intent on urgent business.

Venutius, Sdapezi reflected, was the cause of his unease. He disliked the man intensely, yet he was compelled to spend more time with the former King of the Brigantes than with all the other hostages combined. Somehow, Venutius had persuaded the Governor that he would make a perfect emissary, an ambassador to the savage barbarians of the north. With golden coins and a silver tongue, Venutius had promised to smooth the way for the final stage of the conquest of Britannia.

That new role had meant that Sdapezi had been forced to accompany Venutius on his forays into the wild lands. Those journeys had been made by sea, sailing or rowing up the east coast, visiting Kings and chieftains, dispensing gold and honeyed words. Sdapezi disliked the work, for it was potentially dangerous, carrying the risk that the barbarians might not respect the position of an ambassador. That never seemed to bother Venutius, who regarded the northern Britons as ignorant savages.

"They are easily dazzled by displays of wealth and power," Venutius insisted. "They run in terror when they see our ships. Your swords are enough to petrify them."

Sdapezi was not convinced by the emissary's smooth words, nor by his use of the phrase, "our ships". Venutius may have displayed all the outward signs of being a loyal ally of Rome, but Sdapezi had known the man when he was the self-proclaimed ruler of Brigantia, and he distrusted every word that Venutius uttered.

Sitting on a low bench opposite the Centurion, the renegade Briton now waited patiently, a secretive smile playing around his lips. He was, as always, dressed in British clothing; a shirt and trousers topped by a warm jerkin and a thick, hooded cloak. What differentiated him from the other natives was the quality of his clothing and the array of jewellery that he wore. Rings adorned every finger, a large, golden brooch fastened his cloak, a silver buckle gleamed on his belt, and the small knife he was permitted to carry had a red garnet stone embedded in the silver hilt. The only ostentation denied him was the right to wear a torc around his neck, because he was no longer a King. If that restriction annoyed him, he masked it well. He was the model of a subservient ally, a man who had decided to throw in his lot with the all-conquering Empire. In itself, that was not what bothered Sdapezi, for many Britons had seen the wisdom of siding with Rome. No, what concerned the Centurion was the sly, self-seeking mind that lay behind Venutius' hazel eyes. The man was too clever, too cunning, to be trusted. He was in his fifties now, and had spent most of his life plotting against and betraying anyone who had befriended him, his sole ambition to gain power and wealth for himself. However much he proclaimed his allegiance to Rome, Sdapezi could not trust him.

Now, the Briton had some new ploy. Their last trip had been routine, another short voyage up the coast, another visit to a barbarian stronghold, a lengthy discussion with a young chieftain, and a gift of silver coins.

Sdapezi had been uneasy, as he always was on such missions. He was a cavalryman, used to being on horseback, but Venutius' role required them to travel by sea. Sdapezi disliked the sea, so he never enjoyed these voyages.

This trip, though, had been odd. Sdapezi was used to a degree of hostility and distrust from the chieftains they visited, but the hilltop stockade they had found had been even more daunting than most. The barbarians who had gathered in the chieftain's roundhouse had seemed more belligerent than usual. Even the women had given Venutius a frosty reception. Some of the men had fingered their knives and swords in a threatening manner, and Sdapezi had braced himself for an attack. Fortunately, the young chieftain restrained the warriors, but the meeting was a tense one, and Sdapezi was relieved when the discussion ended and they were able to leave the hilltop stockade.

He had expected Venutius to display some signs of agitation at their reception, yet the emissary had seemed inordinately pleased with himself as they descended the hill and returned to their ship.

"I must speak to the Governor," Venutius had stated emphatically, a spark of excitement in his eyes.

"Why?" Sdapezi had enquired. "What happened?"

"I have discovered something important," Venutius grinned.

Sdapezi frowned, "What have you learned? All I saw were angry faces and a lot of swords."

"You were not paying attention," Venutius smirked.

"You know I don't speak the language," Sdapezi retorted. "But Hortensius didn't notice anything unusual."

Hortensius was one of Sdapezi's troopers, a Briton who had joined the Auxiliaries to escape the poverty of his home village. Now, his role was to listen to what Venutius told the Britons he visited in case the emissary deviated from the pro-Roman stance he professed to hold.

Venutius snorted, "Your pet Briton wouldn't understand. It was what was not said that was important."

"What do you mean?"

Venutius had merely laughed, "You will find out when I tell the Governor."

Which was why the two of them were sitting in the small antechamber, watching the bustle of activity as men dashed in and out of the Governor's office. Several times, Sdapezi attempted to question Venutius but the Briton was determined to keep his knowledge to himself until he spoke to the Governor in person.

At last, after more than an hour of bored waiting in the antechamber, a Tribune came out of the Governor's office. He was a young man, dressed in immaculately polished armour, and a red cloak that was spotless, showing no signs of the mud that spattered most men's clothing. The Tribune's name was Aulus Atticus, and he was another man Sdapezi disliked intensely. The Tribune came from a wealthy family and had been appointed to the Governor's staff only the previous year. Despite his inexperience, he had adopted an attitude of superiority that rankled the Centurion. Atticus had probably never drawn his polished sword in anger, yet he acted like a twenty-year veteran, talking down to men like

Sdapezi who had spent years in the army. Atticus was so determined to be the epitome of a Roman officer that he had refused to don trousers during the coldest spells of winter, going bare-legged when even the Governor himself had acknowledged that keeping warm was the sensible thing to do.

True to form, Atticus beckoned Sdapezi and Venutius with a haughty finger.

"The Governor will see you now," he informed them grudgingly.

Sdapezi stood, adjusting the heavy cavalry sword at his hip before following the Tribune and Venutius into the inner sanctum of the building, from where the Governor controlled the vast army he had brought to this northern extremity of the world.

This was a temporary fort, constructed to provide winter shelter for the Legion. The wood and plaster buildings were purely functional, with no decoration or luxury. The Governor's office was no exception, with bare walls, a row of high windows to provide light when it was not too cold to open the wooden shutters, and an iron brazier filled with charcoal to provide some warmth. The charcoal was unlit now, and the windows were open, admitting the late afternoon sun. Its brightness revealed that the only furniture was a wooden table and a handful of stools.

The table was stacked with writing tablets and bore a large map that had been spread to show the island of Britannia. Sdapezi could not help noticing that the northern part of the map was mostly blank. Apart from what had been gleaned from forays such as those Venutius had undertaken, what lay to the north was *terra incognita*, unknown land.

Two men had been studying the map. Sitting on two of the stools, they now faced their visitors.

"Centurion Sdapezi and the Emissary Venutius!" barked Atticus unnecessarily as he threw a dramatic salute before stepping to one side.

The two men nodded a welcome. The younger of them, in his early forties, was Marcus Licinius Spurius, Legate of the Ninth Legion. Dark-haired and handsome, he was nevertheless a man who had a talent for saying and doing the wrong thing. His appointment to the command of the Legion was a political one, and Spurius had, so far, displayed no great aptitude as a soldier. This, Sdapezi mused, was rumoured to be the reason that the Governor had based his command centre with the Ninth. Some men said that he did not trust Spurius enough to leave him unsupervised. That, Sdapezi thought, was a harsh judgement, because Spurius was far from stupid. It was just that he was not a soldier, and showed little inclination to become one.

There was a great deal of speculation as to why he had been sent to take command of the Ninth *Hispana*. The whispers on the army's grapevine claimed that Spurius had a young, attractive wife who had caught the eye of the Emperor. This story was fuelled by the fact that Spurius' wife had not accompanied him to Britannia, preferring to remain in Rome. Whether the story was true or not, Sdapezi had no idea. Personally, he thought Spurius' wife had shown remarkable good sense by choosing to remain at home. If he had been given a choice between living in an army barracks in Britannia or a large villa in Rome, he knew which one he would have chosen.

Whatever the background to Spurius' appointment as Legate, he was an important figure, although not as important as the man who sat beside him. Older than Spurius, he was lean and fit, his eyes sharp and challenging. Dressed in a short-sleeved tunic with a broad, purple stripe denoting his senatorial rank, he exuded an air of command and authority. This was Gnaeus Julius Agricola, Governor of Britannia and General of the enormous army that was poised to bring the whole island of Britannia under the control of the distant city of Rome.

Agricola's gaze fixed on Sdapezi.

"You wanted to speak to me about something important?"

Sdapezi had spoken to Agricola several times, yet he always felt nervous in the Governor's presence. His anxiety was not helped by the knowledge that the immaculate Tribune, Aulus Atticus, was standing to one side, watching him. Sdapezi was all too aware that his scratched and dented breastplate looked shabby compared to the Tribune's gleaming armour. His tarnished helmet with its tattered cross-wise plume was equally unprepossessing. Feeling like an errant child about to be scolded, he threw a hasty salute, removed his helmet and tucked it under one arm before flicking a gesture towards Venutius.

"Our hostage claims to have learned something important during our last voyage, Sir. He has refused to tell me what it is, but I thought it best to let him inform you."

Agricola's eyebrows rose in question as he regarded Venutius.

"Well?"

Venutius gave an obsequious bow, refusing to show any irritation at being referred to as a hostage.

He said, "Sir, I have located Calgacus' home."

The Governor leaned forwards, his face alive with interest.

"Indeed?"

Smoothly, Venutius explained, "I knew he lived somewhere on the east coast, but I was not sure of the precise location. Today, I found it."

He moved forwards to tap a finger on the map.

"We are here, on the southern bank of the Bodotria. Some way north is another great river, the Tava. Calgacus' home is on a steep hill overlooking the estuary."

"You saw him?" Licinius Spurius interrupted.

Venutius told the Legate, "I doubt whether I would be alive if he had been there, but my information was correct. He has gone to join this alliance the tribes are forming."

53

"In that case, how do you know it was his home?"

Treating the Legate to a condescending smile, Venutius replied, "Because his wife was there. I have never met her, but I know her description. The name fitted, as did his son's name. The young man pretended to be the chieftain, but that was merely a ruse. It was Calgacus' home. I am sure of it."

Spurius observed, "You seem to know a great deal about Calgacus' family."

"The man is my enemy," Venutius explained tersely. "I make it my business to know about him."

Waving an impatient hand to silence the discussion, the Governor asked Sdapezi, "Can you confirm this?"

Shuffling his feet slightly, Sdapezi answered, "No, Sir. All I can say is that, apart from the young chieftain, the people in that village were not overly friendly."

Unexpectedly, Agricola asked him, "What was the woman's name?"

Sdapezi faltered, searching his memory. After an embarrassingly long silence, he was forced to admit, "I don't recall, Sir."

Smugly, Venutius announced, "Her name is Beatha. She is the sister of one of your client Kings from the south."

"I know who she is," Agricola stated coldly.

Sdapezi realised that the Governor had not trusted Venutius enough to believe him and had wanted independent confirmation. Sdapezi, though, had failed. He felt foolish, knowing he should have been better prepared for this meeting, wishing that he had forced Venutius to reveal his discovery rather than springing it on him like this.

Seeking to redeem himself, he blurted, "Her son's name was Togodumnus."

Thoughtfully, Agricola nodded, "That fits."

He paused before asking Venutius, "So, what do you propose that we do with this information?"

"Launch an attack," Venutius declared instantly, jabbing a finger at the map to emphasise his point. "Send ships to destroy Calgacus' home and kill his family. That will show everyone that he is unable to protect his own people. The damage to his reputation will destroy his alliance at a single stroke."

"A bold plan," the Governor reflected. He looked at Sdapezi once more. "How strong was this place?"

"Very strong," Sdapezi replied, feeling more confident about offering an opinion on military matters. "The approach is steep, through thick woods, with a killing ground having been cleared in front of the walls. The stockade is strong, with a ditch. I also saw some signs that the barbarians had constructed traps on the hillside. The path through the trees follows a zig-zag route, and there are piles of rocks stacked behind felled trees that are held in place by ropes. If the ropes are cut, the tree trunks and rocks will sweep down the slope like an avalanche."

"Are there any other approaches?"

"We could not tell," Sdapezi admitted.

Venutius put in, "There must be."

"How many men defended the place?" Agricola continued.

"Not many," Sdapezi told him. "It was a small place, barely ten roundhouses inside the stockade. I counted fewer than half a dozen armed men, and most of them were past their prime."

Venutius added, "They said there is a village further inland where most of their people live. But that is unimportant. Calgacus will have taken most of the warriors with him. The place is virtually undefended. It could be taken easily by a determined force."

Sdapezi could tell that the Governor was tempted. Agricola was a first-rate General but he was not averse to taking risks. Sdapezi recalled how the Governor had sent a small force across the sea to Hibernia, hoping to capitalise on

55

a civil war that had broken out between rival claimants to the High Kingship. That expedition had been a failure, principally because Calgacus had also been in Hibernia and had led the tribes against the small Roman invasion force. That memory rankled, and Agricola was clearly attracted to the idea of taking some revenge on the man who had thwarted his plans.

But recollections of the failed expedition to Hibernia sparked another concern for Sdapezi. Unfortunately for him, Agricola noticed the involuntary frown that creased his brow when he recalled the memories.

"Something else bothers you?" the Governor asked.

Sdapezi felt even more foolish as he mumbled, "It's nothing, really, Sir. But there are rumours about Calgacus."

"He is a man who attracts all sorts of legends," Agricola said dismissively. "He is notorious. But he is just a man."

"Yes, Sir."

The Governor continued to stare at him, then gave a resigned sigh.

"You are speaking, I presume, of the tales of sorcery?"

"Yes, Sir," Sdapezi admitted.

"What are the men saying about him?" the Governor wanted to know.

Sdapezi did not like telling tales, but the Governor was no fool, and Sdapezi guessed he had a fairly good idea of what was being said around the camp. Besides, Agricola's insistent stare demanded an answer.

Sdapezi gave a reluctant shrug. Resignedly, he explained, "They say he is a giant who possesses a magical sword."

Venutius, unwilling to have his proposal rejected, hurriedly put in, "He is a big man, but he is not a giant."

"And I doubt very much whether his sword has any magical properties," Agricola added. Then he pinned Sdapezi with his iron gaze once more and demanded, "But I expect the rumours are of what happened in Hibernia, are they not?"

"Yes, Sir," Sdapezi admitted. "They say he died and was brought back to life by a sorceress."

"I have heard that tale," the Governor agreed. "It is not true."

"No, sir."

Sdapezi held his tongue, fearing he had already gone too far. There was more he could have said, for the stories surrounding the ill-fated Hibernian expedition had grown in the telling. Men said Calgacus had been sacrificed by druids, had been butchered as an offering to the bloodthirsty British Gods, his guts ripped out and his head cut off. Then a witch woman had resurrected him, and he had taken up his magical sword, using it to single-handedly slaughter an entire Cohort of legionaries.

Nervously, Sdapezi glanced at Spurius and saw the Legate frowning. It was a Cohort of the Ninth which had been destroyed in Hibernia, and Spurius knew the tales of witchcraft as well as any of them, for the few survivors who had escaped the slaughter had returned with stories of sorcery and a giant warrior who could not die.

Agricola slapped his palm on the table, demanding their attention.

"The rumours are untrue!" he barked insistently. "I want no more talk of this. Is that understood?"

"Of course, sir," Sdapezi nodded dutifully.

The other men remained silent in the face of the Governor's anger, but Agricola continued, "Calgacus is a man, nothing more. He is clever, and he is cunning, but he has no special powers. Make sure the men know this."

Spurius muttered his agreement, and Sdapezi nodded his understanding.

"Besides," the Governor went on, "Calgacus is not at his home, so attacking it now presents us with an opportunity to strike a blow which will show that he is fallible."

Venutius beamed in satisfaction as Agricola, having made up his mind, gave his orders.

"We will send five galleys," he decided, "with a full force of Marines. That ought to be enough. If most of the warriors have left, taking this place should be straightforward."

At the side of the small room, Tribune Aulus Atticus stirred.

"Sir! I would like to request the honour of leading this assault."

Agricola seemed amused. He smiled, "Is there a particular reason for this request, Atticus?"

"I would like the opportunity to prove myself, Sir. This seems ideal. Especially if it gives us a chance to strike a serious blow against the barbarians."

Agricola made up his mind quickly. He nodded, "Very well. You will command the expedition. But I'll send an experienced officer with you."

His eyes fixed on Sdapezi as he went on, "Centurion Sdapezi has seen the place and knows how to fight the Britons. He will go with you, Atticus, and I urge you to listen to his advice."

Sdapezi was not sure who was more disconcerted by the Governor's decision. He had not been engaged in any fighting for two years and had hoped that state of affairs would continue. His only consolation was that his dismay was matched by that of Atticus, who had been ordered to listen to his advice. The pompous Tribune clearly did not like that at all.

Agricola's next decision held another shock for them. He jabbed a finger at Venutius, saying, "You will go too."

For the first time, Venutius' veneer of calm deserted him. He gasped, "Me? I am no fighting man."

"No. But you can identify Calgacus' wife, Beatha. Her brother wants her back. Jupiter knows why, after all

58

these years, but he's a King, and an important ally, so I'd like to send her back to him if I can."

Venutius nodded sombrely, trying to overcome his surprise. He observed, "From what little I know of him, Cogidubnus is a proud man. His sister disobeyed him when she ran off with Calgacus. I expect that is why he wants her back. He will punish her, no matter how long ago she defied him."

The Governor shrugged, "I have no interest in his motives. Just bring her back alive and unharmed. Is that understood?"

"Yes, Sir."

Agricola nodded, "Then it is decided. Gather the ships and the Marines. Be on your way tomorrow if possible. Burn Calgacus' home, and bring me his wife. That, as Venutius has suggested, will destroy the myth of his invincibility."

"What about the other barbarians?" Atticus enquired.

"I really don't care what happens to them," Agricola shrugged, his mind already moving on from this discussion. He nodded to Sdapezi and Venutius.

"Thank you. You may go."

Venutius bowed, while Sdapezi saluted. Atticus showed them out, then closed the door.

"Thank you for this opportunity, Sir," he beamed.

"I have every confidence in you, Atticus," Agricola assured him. "Now, there is one other thing I would like to discuss. Is there any news of the Usipi?"

"The German Auxiliaries who mutinied? No, Sir. All we know is that they murdered their officers, took some hostages, then stole three ships and sailed away. We have heard nothing for more than three weeks now."

"Let us hope they sank and drowned," Agricola murmured. "It will save us the bother of crucifying them."

Atticus nodded, "They have certainly disappeared, Sir. None of our ships have seen any sign of them."

Licinius Spurius said, "Perhaps they have joined the barbarians."

"I hope not," Agricola frowned. "But we cannot have Auxiliaries murdering their Centurions and deserting. If one group gets away with it, others may copy them."

Spurius asked, "What can we do about it, though? They are beyond our reach, whatever has happened to them."

Agricola smiled, "What we must do is convince the rest of the army that something dreadful has befallen our erstwhile auxiliaries."

"How?"

"By starting some rumours of our own. Let us give the men something else to talk about other than Calgacus. Atticus, I'd like you to mention to some of the Centurions that you've heard the Usipi were caught by the Britons. Say we believe they were beheaded or shoved into cooking pots and eaten. That should start tongues wagging."

Atticus' expression was puzzled, but he nodded his agreement.

"Of course, Sir. Is this an official report?"

"Certainly not. The official report will say that they are believed to have drowned when their ships sank."

"I see," said Atticus uncertainly. "But you want me to start a rumour anyway?"

"That's right. The more horror stories about the deserters' fate, the better. I don't really care what happened to the Usipi. I just care that none of our other troops emulate them. We must spread tales of terror to prevent another occurrence. Do you understand?"

Atticus saluted primly. "Yes, Sir."

"Excellent. Thank you, Atticus. That will be all for now."

The Tribune threw another salute, turned on his heel and marched out. Once he had closed the door behind him, Licinius Spurius asked, "What do you think really happened to the Usipi?"

"I have no idea," Agricola sighed. "I hope it was something unpleasant. They killed some good men, and they betrayed us."

He shook his head sadly as he went on, "I do feel sorry for poor Anderius Facilis, though. He was a good man who deserved better. The Gods have not been kind to him."

Chapter VI

Salt spray splashed over the deck, soaking the prisoners who sat with their hands tied behind their backs. The ship was pitching and rolling under assault from waves which were growing in height and intensity, driven by a cruel wind that had swept in from the west, driving heavy, rain-laden clouds that gradually covered the blue of the sky.

Facilis closed his eyes, spat away salt water from his face and shivered in his wet clothes. He had lost count of how many times the ships had been caught by the weather. All he knew was that each time the wind and waves buffeted the three vessels, he felt sick, cold and wet. The ropes that bound his wrists were sodden now, chafing his skin. He shifted uncomfortably, bracing his heels against the wet wood of the deck, and pushing his back against the low rail behind him, trying not to think about the depth of the water that lay just beyond that slender barrier. The sea, he thought, was determined to sweep him overboard.

Beside him, Antonius Pulcher groaned as the huge bulk of his body wobbled in time to the rolling of the ship. Pulcher retched, but could only muster a small dribble of sticky phlegm; he had already emptied the contents of his copious stomach, leaving his clothing stained and filthy. Fortunately, the constant battering of rain and spray had washed the worst of the vomit away. The way the voyage was going, Pulcher would have little opportunity to re-fill his belly, because the Usipi had not stored much food on board, and most of what they had brought had been ruined by rain and salt water.

"When will this end?" Pulcher groaned desperately.

Facilis did not answer. He was no augur, nor was he a sailor, but he knew there was no point in railing against the weather.

It was Ambrosius Thrax who answered. Sitting on Facilis' left, he was unaffected by the weather or the wild-horse bucking of the ship. If anything, he seemed to take a perverse pleasure in his companions' discomfort.

"This looks like a big blow," he announced in a matter-of-fact voice. "I'd guess it will last for the rest of the day."

"Will these storms never end?" Pulcher moaned.

"I warned them it was too early in the season to make a long voyage," Thrax grinned. "But this is nothing. I've seen worse. We should survive this one. With luck."

Pulcher groaned again, moaning that the Gods had abandoned them.

Facilis, annoyed at the fat man's continual complaints, snapped, "At least we are still alive."

That, he thought, could only be because the Gods were still watching over them. But the Gods had been cruel to Facilis all his life, and he suspected he had only been saved because The Fates had something worse in store for him.

It was a miracle they were still alive, he reflected. They had almost died in the small, naval stockade. Ignoring Facilis' advice, the commander of their escort had drawn his sword, jabbed his heels into his horse's flanks, and lashed out at the nearest auxiliary, smashing the man's shoulder into a mass of blood and ruined bone. The officer had not lived long to celebrate his small victory because the Usipi had launched themselves at him with a furious howl, dragging him and his men from their horses. There was no room for the riders to manoeuvre, no space to wield their long swords effectively, and they were overwhelmed by over a hundred roaring, vicious soldiers. Dragged from their saddles, the cavalrymen were slaughtered mercilessly.

Only the intervention of the giant Fullofaudes saved Facilis and Pulcher.

"Keep those two alive!" the big German roared as men swarmed to grab the two Romans.

Facilis did not resist as one man seized the reins of his terrified horse and two others hauled him to the ground. His knife was taken, he was punched and kicked, and his hands were hurriedly tied behind his back, but the blade he had expected never struck him.

He heard Pulcher shouting terrified protests, demanding to be released, protesting that he was a Quaestor, a man of importance and that they should not dare lay their filthy hands on his person. Facilis saw the huge figure of Fullofaudes stride over to the Quaestor, raise a club-like fist and deliver a punch that silenced Pulcher instantly.

Facilis could not bring himself to look back at the remnants of his escort. He could hear the triumphant yells and laughs of the Usipi, and knew that the fight, such as it had been, was over.

The wagon-driver, a small, terrified man, had surrendered to the mob. They threw him to the ground, laughing, not bothering to waste their energy killing him.

Fullofaudes had found the keys to the money chests, ripping them from the cord that hung at Pulcher's waist.

"Let's see what we've got, boys!" he shouted gleefully, barrelling his way to the back of the wagon.

He clambered up, fiddled with the keys and threw open the lid of the first box. A loud cheer greeted the sight of its contents. Fullofaudes opened the other chests, then stood and held his arms wide, demanding attention.

"I want it shared equally," he boomed. "Any man who takes more than his fair share will lose his right hand."

The Usipi jostled one another as two of them took charge of counting and dividing the coins. Leaving them to the task of distributing the pay, Fullofaudes jumped down and shouldered his way back to face Pulcher and Facilis.

"So you're the Quaestor?" he snarled in coarse Latin.

Pulcher, supported and imprisoned by two burly soldiers, his mouth bloodied and bruised, could only whimper an incomprehensible reply.

The big German waved a hand in the direction of the three men who dangled lifelessly from the wooden crucifixes.

"That's what we do to Romans," he leered. "What do you have to say to that?"

Pulcher closed his eyes, unwilling to look at the awful sight.

With a snort of disgust, Fullofaudes slapped his face, bringing a yelp of pain from the fat Quaestor.

Facilis shouted, "Leave him alone. He has done nothing to you."

Fullofaudes turned to him, his brutish face twisted into an amused smirk.

"And who are you?" he demanded.

"His assistant."

Facilis braced himself to receive a punch, but the big German studied him for a long moment before remarking thoughtfully, "You have the look of a man who can think."

"I think you have made a big mistake if you believe you can get away with this," Facilis answered, surprised at how calm he felt. Perhaps it was because he was resigned to his fate. Whatever the Usipi did to him, it could not be worse than he had already been through. Death, even a painful one, held no fear for him. He had lost everything else, so what use was his life?

He stared at the big German who loomed over him, waiting to hear what the man had in store.

"Our mistake," Fullofaudes informed him, "was to join this bloody army in the first place. Now, we are leaving it."

Facilis regarded the big man closely. The words were folly, he knew, but he saw only confidence in the man's eyes.

He said, "You think keeping us as hostages will prevent the Governor sending legionaries to crush you?"

Fullofaudes' mouth opened in a cheerful grin.

"They'll have to catch us first."

"You're going to desert to the barbarians?" Facilis guessed.

"Oh, no!" laughed Fullofaudes. "We're going home to Germania."

Facilis had thought the man was mad, but Fullofaudes was, at least, prepared to let them live. Many of the other Germans were in favour of killing them. One in particular, a small, dark man with a pointed chin and a manic gleam in his eyes, had jabbered away furiously, pointing at the two Romans.

Grinning, Fullofaudes informed them, "Necrautis thinks we should crucify you, but I've told him that important men like you could be useful as hostages. Still, you'd better do as you are told, otherwise I'll let him nail you up."

Pulcher had moaned in terror, much to the disgust of the Germans, who scorned such cowardly behaviour.

"What do you want from us?" Facilis asked.

"You're valuable," Fullofaudes informed him. "You might be worth a ransom if we run into trouble."

Privately, Facilis doubted whether anyone would pay a ransom for him, but he was not inclined to admit that to the German. He decided a little exaggeration might help.

He said, "I know the Governor personally."

"Is that so?" Fullofaudes grinned. "In that case, you are even more valuable than I had hoped."

He chuckled happily to himself as he signalled to his men and ordered, "Lock them up."

The sailors who manned the ships had been locked into their barrack rooms. The wagon driver was thrown in with them, but Facilis and Pulcher were taken to a low, wooden building that comprised smaller rooms, the officers' quarters. The room they were bundled into was already occupied by a bow-legged man with short hair and burly arms. His face was weather-beaten and tanned, scoured by years of standing on a ship's deck in all weathers.

"Tiberius Ambrosius Thrax," he introduced himself. "So the bastards caught you just like they planned?"

Pulcher collapsed, moaning loudly, onto a chair, paying no attention to Thrax, so Facilis introduced himself.

"What's going on here?" he asked. "Do you know what they are planning to do?"

"I'm afraid so," Thrax grunted. "The daft buggers plan to steal our ships and row themselves back to Germania."

"How? The fleet will intercept them as soon as they reach the south coast."

"That's what I told them," Thrax sighed bitterly. "But the stupid bastards think they can escape by sailing all the way round the north of Britannia. That's why they need me. I've done the trip in the opposite direction, so they're going to take me along as their navigator. They think they can sail into the Northern Sea and cross to Germania without going anywhere near the Imperial Fleet."

"You don't sound confident about their chances," Facilis observed cautiously.

"They haven't got a hope," Thrax grunted. "There's not a seaman among them. They'll probably sink before they get half way."

"But there are trained oarsmen here," Facilis frowned. "The sailors who normally man the ships."

Thrax shook his head. "The Usipi won't take them. They'd need more than a hundred rowers, and they're worried so many sailors would be able to turn the tables on them. Like I say, they plan to do it themselves."

He grinned as he added, "It's complete madness, of course. I hope you can swim. If not, you'd better learn fast."

Pulcher let out another soft moan, dabbing at his blood-smeared cheeks.

"They cannot do this," he wailed.

"They're doing it," Facilis replied impatiently, irritated by the fat man's constant complaints.

Glancing at Thrax, he asked, "Can we escape?"

Again, Thrax shook his head.

"There's only one door out of here and there's a guard on it. Our best chance is to wait until we're at sea. We're bound to get an opportunity once we're on the way because they'll need to put into shore at night. You may as well make yourselves comfortable until then."

While they waited helplessly, Thrax explained what had sparked the mutiny.

"The Usipi were reluctant soldiers in the first place, but the Centurion and his men who had been sent to command them were stupid. They treated them like second-class scum, called them barbarians and dished out as many punishments as meals. When they tried to flog Fullofaudes for giving them some cheek, he decided to take things into his own hands. You saw the result outside."

Facilis nodded, recalling the gruesome sight of the three naked men who had been nailed to the wooden crosses. Crucifixion; a Roman punishment for Roman criminals.

"They knew you were due to bring their pay," Thrax continued. "So they decided to wait for you. Germans love silver coins, you see, and Fullofaudes thought having some important men as hostages might be useful. Also, he didn't want you turning up and finding them gone. You'd have raised the alarm too soon. This way, they'll get a good head start before anyone learns about what they've done."

"He has it all worked out, doesn't he?"

"All except the important part," Thrax agreed. "He'll soon learn there's more to rowing a galley than he thinks."

They could see nothing of what was happening outside, could hear only shouted orders, the tramp of feet, and the babble of guttural, German voices. They were left alone all day but, late in the afternoon, six men of the Usipi came to take them to the ships. They did not resist as they were shoved out through the riverside gate and down to where three galleys had been manned by the mutineers. Oars were waving clumsily from the portholes in the lower deck, and they could hear the sound of raised, argumentative voices. Glancing to the fourth galley, Facilis could see dark smoke beginning to rise from its hull, and caught a glimpse of flickering tongues of fire.

They were led up a narrow gangplank onto the deck of the first ship, where Fullofaudes stood, legs braced, smiling hugely.

"Welcome aboard," he boomed jovially. "We are just about to depart."

Pulcher made an effort to draw himself up to face the big German. In a cracked, fearful voice, he blurted, "I am a Quaestor of the Imperial Army. I insist that you release me. If you let me go now, I will ask the Governor to be merciful."

Fullofaudes shot the fat man a look of disgust. Jabbing a finger at him, he snapped, "Shut your face, or I'll shut it for you."

To the men who had brought them from the stockade, he said, "Put them by the back. Check their bonds and one of you keep an eye on them."

They were bustled to the far end of the open deck, where they were shoved roughly down to the wooden boards. The Usipi made sure their wrists were tightly bound, then five of them returned to Fullofaudes while the sixth loomed over them, eyeing them threateningly.

"This should be interesting," observed Thrax with what sounded like a hint of amusement. In response to Facilis' enquiring look, he explained, "These idiots don't know anything about boats. He didn't even know enough to call this the stern. It'll be fun to watch how they cope with the oars."

69

Facilis knew little about ships either. Rome was essentially a land power, with its navy being subservient to the army. Many of the sailors who manned the fleet's galleys were from Greece or other nations who had a nautical history, because most Romans viewed the sea as a strange, dangerous environment. Rome may have conquered the Mediterranean, but few Romans enjoyed venturing on the waves unless they had no alternative.

Facilis knew enough to recognise the three galleys as liburnians, lightweight vessels about eighty feet long, with two banks of oars on either side and a single mast which was usually lowered and stowed on the deck when the oars were in use. The Usipi, though, clearly did not know this, because the masts of the three galleys they had commandeered now towered above the decks like enormous versions of the crucifixes that the Roman officers had been nailed to.

"That just makes the ship less stable," Thrax snorted, shaking his head. "They could go faster if they lowered it. Mind you, speed won't matter much seeing as they've set fire to the other galley. There aren't any other ships near enough to catch us."

Facilis twisted to see the fourth galley, now wreathed in swirling, oily smoke, with hungry flames leaping up from below decks. The fire had a good hold and the boat would soon be burned to the waterline. Thrax was right; even if the sailors in the fort freed themselves, they would not be able to pursue the Usipi.

Resignedly, he turned his attention back to their own vessel. The deck, twenty feet broad, stretched out in front of them like a wide roadway, smooth and clear. Fullofaudes stood near the mast, calling encouragement and issuing orders. One man stood at the tiller, gripping the steerboard anxiously, while others moved around the deck, brandishing weapons as if expecting to be called upon to repel boarders.

Below the deck, the men who manned the oars were sitting in cramped gloom, thirty men on either side. Facilis reckoned the ship held around eighty men in total, which meant that, with three galleys, Fullofaudes commanded at least two hundred men. From what he could see, every one of them was eager to set off on this mad venture to circumnavigate the wild island of Britannia so that they could return to their homeland in Germania.

He said to Thrax, "I thought liburnian galleys were designed for coastal work. Can they cross the sea?"

Thrax pulled a sour face as he replied, "In good weather and with an experienced crew, yes."

He fell silent, leaving Facilis to draw the obvious conclusion.

Liburnians were small, lightweight ships, nimble and agile. Most of the Roman fleet comprised liburnians or the slightly larger triremes because the Romans disdained the huge quinqueremes which they considered too bulky and cumbersome in battle. The quinqueremes, with their five banks of oars, were only used as flagships, for display, while the navy relied on the liburnian biremes for most of their work. The liburnians could follow rivers deep inland thanks to their shallow draught. They were small enough to go where larger ships could not, but big enough to carry a decent complement of sailors and marines. Now, these three would carry the Usipi into the unknown.

As the evening wore on, Thrax became increasingly scornful of the Usipi's efforts to control the galleys. They managed to haul up the great, stone anchors but, below decks, in the dark, cramped confines of the rowing benches, they struggled to control the long, heavy oars. Their first attempts to row were laughable, with oars smashing together and becoming tangled, others waving uselessly above the surface of the river, with only a few biting into the water, and none of them pulling at the same time.

"It takes a lot of practice," Thrax remarked scornfully.

71

Somehow, with Fullofaudes shouting what sounded like dire threats in German, the Usipi managed to coax the galley into a lurching, awkward motion that was generally forward. Aided by the river's current and what Thrax assured Facilis was an outgoing tide, the three galleys drifted slowly towards the sea.

"At least they are keeping well apart," Thrax commented. "Otherwise we'll have a collision and we'll all end up at the bottom."

Pulcher, who was sitting disconsolately by the rail, groaned, "When are they going to feed us? I am starving."

"Be grateful we're still alive," Facilis told him.

"Aren't you hungry?" Pulcher asked querulously.

"I've been hungry before," Facilis retorted. "Haven't you?"

Pulcher regarded him with hurt surprise and Facilis realised that the Quaestor probably had never missed a meal in his life.

Pulcher shouted to their guard, asking for food and wine, but the German gave no indication that he understood what was being asked. He simply growled a throaty warning and kicked Pulcher's leg with a vicious swipe of his booted foot.

Some time later, Fullofaudes appeared from the lower deck where he had been trying to organise the rowers into some sort of cohesion. He stomped back to stand beside the steersman, another brawny, fair-haired man who was clutching at the long steerboard as if his life depended on it. After the two of them had held a brief discussion, Fullofaudes came to stand over his three prisoners.

"This sailing business is not so difficult when you get the hang of it," he remarked jovially.

Thrax grunted, "It's a flat calm, and we're not out at sea yet. Wait until you try putting up the sail."

"You can help us when we need to do that," Fullofaudes told him. "More importantly, when we reach the sea, you are going to make sure we don't get lost."

"What if I refuse?" Thrax shot back.

Fullofaudes grinned evilly as he replied, "Then we will torture these other two until you agree."

"Go ahead," invited Thrax. "I only met them this morning. They mean nothing to me."

"You are not a good liar, Captain," smirked Fullofaudes. "You are not the sort of man who would stand by and watch fellow Romans be skinned alive."

Facilis made an effort to keep his face impassive. He knew beyond all doubt that Fullofaudes was not bluffing, but he refused to show the giant Usipi that he was afraid. Pulcher, though, whimpered in terror.

Fullofaudes grinned at Thrax as he added, "If killing those two doesn't make you do what we want, I'll feed you to the fishes, one small piece at a time. You know, I'll cut off your fingers, then your toes, then your ears, and nose. I'm sure you understand how it will go."

"Do as he says," pleaded Pulcher. "For the Gods' sake, do as he says."

Thrax shot the Quaestor a sour look before glancing at Facilis.

"They are going to try to sail away with or without your help," Facilis told the Captain. "If they run aground or sink because they don't know what they are doing, we'll be dead, too."

Thrax gave a resentful nod. Looking at Fullofaudes, he sighed, "All right. Untie my hands and I'll do what you want."

Fullofaudes reached out with a meaty hand to haul Thrax to his feet.

He said, "You don't need your hands to tell us what to do. Besides, I don't want you jumping overboard and swimming away. Your hands will stay tied."

Reluctantly, Thrax guided the three galleys downriver, making sure they did not run aground. By dusk, they had almost reached the sea. Under Thrax's instruction, they found a small cove where they beached the ships for the night.

"Bloody clowns," muttered Thrax when he was returned to the rear rail. "They've brought all that silver you had in the chests, but hardly any food. We're going to be hungry."

Pulcher looked appalled.

"Can't they buy food from the natives?" he implored.

"That's what Fullofaudes thought, but the locals won't stay around when they see Roman ships. They'll run and hide."

"How much food have we got?" Facilis asked.

"Enough for two or three days. Maybe five if we go on short rations."

"And how long will it take to sail round the island?"

"It's a bloody big island," Thrax replied. "But it depends on the wind and the tides. At least a couple of weeks, though. Probably longer. At this time of year, there will be squalls coming in off the ocean, and we won't be able to sail far at all."

There were more arguments among the Usipi that evening. The swarthy Necrautis led the opposition to Fullofaudes, but the big man retained enough command to settle the confrontations without blood being shed.

"What are they fighting about?" Pulcher wondered.

"The food situation, I expect," Facilis guessed.

The next morning, Thrax told the Germans how to raise and furl the sails. Using long ropes, blocks and tackles, and with some men clambering precariously up the mast, they eventually managed to set the huge sheet in place. The task was not without cost, though. One man lost his grip and fell from the top of the main spar, killing himself when he thudded onto the deck and broke his neck.

"Let that be a lesson," Fullofaudes barked callously as he ordered the corpse thrown overboard. "Be careful."

After several practice attempts, Fullofaudes declared that they had mastered the task, but there was no wind, so the three galleys set off under oars, the Usipi straining blistered hands and aching backs as they struggled to drive the ships out to sea.

"They seem to be getting the hang of it," Facilis observed.

"Wait till we hit some waves," grunted Thrax.

They did not have much longer to wait. Now that they were beyond the relative shelter of the wide expanse of the estuary, tidal flows from the sea met the river current, creating eddies and swells that made the deck cant from side to side.

"This is nothing," said Thrax in response to an agonised groan from Pulcher.

There was a stiff sea breeze now, a salty tang in the air. Gulls soared and swept the sky overhead, and the land drew further and further towards the horizon.

Using the oars, they rounded a wide headland, then headed north, guided by Thrax, who was frequently consulted by Fullofaudes. The big German seemed happy with progress despite Thrax's scorn.

"The oarsmen are pathetic," the Captain complained. "A proper crew would have covered this distance in a quarter of the time."

"No matter," chirped Fullofaudes. "We are beyond the Empire now."

Pulcher moaned, "The Governor will send ships after you. You cannot escape."

Fullofaudes laughed at him. "Even if those sailors break out of the barracks, it will take a day or two for the news to reach the Governor. By that time, we'll be well away. Besides, there are few ships on this side of Britannia, and they are all well to the south of here, so we don't need to hurry."

"Just as well," muttered Thrax.

The day was uneventful, but progress was slow. Following a course set by Thrax, they edged northwards, moving through the maze of islands that lay off the western coast. They found another sandy beach late in the day where they pulled ashore for the night.

The Usipi staggered onto the beach, grumbling loudly about the effort that was required to row the galleys. All three crews were sore and exhausted.

Sitting on the smooth sand, Thrax whispered to Facilis, "That was an easy day. It will get worse before they go much further."

Facilis did not care. He was tired, sore and hungry. Their bonds were untied, allowing them to rub some circulation back into their wrists and hands, then they were given mugs of beer while the Usipi lit fires and cooked a meagre meal of gruel with strips of salted meat and dried vegetables.

The prisoners were given wooden platters and used their fingers to scoop the food into their mouths. Even Pulcher was so hungry that he barely made a protest before devouring the food, much to the amusement of the watching guards.

After they had eaten the sparse meal, Facilis whispered to Thrax, "Every day takes us further from safety. If we want to get away, we'll need to do something soon."

"If you have any suggestions, I'm happy to listen."

Pulcher frowned, "Perhaps we should do nothing. They will ransom us when we reach Germania."

"You, maybe," Thrax conceded. "Personally, I doubt whether we'll get that far. Even if we do, the best I can hope for is a life of slavery. They won't ransom me."

He looked at Facilis, who shrugged, "All we can do is stay alive and face whatever fortune sends."

76

They edged their way northwards, Thrax guiding them through a myriad of islands, negotiating treacherous channels and battling against the sea, which grew increasingly rough as wind and waves swept in from the west.

Pulcher vomited up his food, as did several of the Usipi. Oars snagged, the ship veered from side to side as the steersman battled to hold a straight course in defiance of the waves and the irregular pull of the oars. Twice, they almost collided with one of the other galleys, whose crews were struggling just as badly.

Sometimes, they managed to hoist their sails, using an increasingly blustery wind to drive them on, but more men fell victim to sea-sickness, hanging over the rails to empty their stomachs.

Thrax, who was immune to seasickness, laughed at their wretchedness.

"This is as calm as it's going to get," he informed them cheerfully.

The relative reprieve from rough weather lasted less than a day. Before long, Thrax warned Fullofaudes to lower the sail.

"Why?" the big Usipi demanded suspiciously. "It saves us rowing."

"Because we're in for some real weather," said Thrax, pointing to the west with his chin.

Facilis looked to the far horizon, where a thin band of grey hovered just above the sea. Within less than an hour, it had crept across the sky, bringing another wild burst of wind and rain. Fullofaudes shouted desperate orders to furl the sail, bellowing commands to the other galleys to do likewise.

"Row, you ugly bastards!" he roared at the oarsmen.

The Usipi rowed, but the waves grew higher, some of them sending torrents of salty water sloshing across the deck. Rain fell, hammering down and soaking everything.

Somehow, the ships survived. Even more amazingly, they managed to keep sight of one another, although Necrautis' galley was blown well off course and fell far behind. Eventually, Thrax told Fullofaudes where they could find shelter in the lee of an uninhabited islet. The men strained at the oars, the steersman heaved on the great steerboard, and the galley ploughed its way to calmer waters.

They ran ashore on a gravel beach, a deserted place that was protected from the worst of the waves but open to the sky. Rain continued to pelt down, making fires impossible.

The other two galleys limped in to join them and the crews huddled on the shore, wet and miserable.

Under the onslaught of the rain, there was no way of cooking the small quantity of food that remained. They drank some beer, but Fullofaudes rationed the amount because there was only enough for another two days.

Pulcher complained miserably, but neither Facilis nor Thrax paid much attention to his grumbling. They sat, shivering and wet, exposed to the rain while their guards huddled under a makeshift shelter of wooden poles, rope and woollen cloaks.

In response to Pulcher's continued complaints about the unfairness of their fate, Thrax commented, "I've been in worse scrapes than this. I've been sunk three times, and each time I thought I would drown or end up in a shark's belly, but I survived. Once, I clung on to a piece of driftwood for three days before I was picked up."

Pulcher was horrified.

"Sharks? Are there sharks in these waters?"

"Not that I've ever seen," shrugged Thrax. "The water's pretty cold up here, but you never know."

Pulcher lapsed into a frightened silence, which suited Facilis.

He said to the Captain, "It sounds like you've had an interesting life."

"I could tell you some stories," Thrax agreed. "But what about you? If you don't mind me saying so, you don't seem the type to be a Quaestor's assistant. What's your story?"

Facilis shrugged, "I was in the army before, about twenty years ago. I left after the revolt of the Iceni."

"The Boudican trouble?" Thrax asked, his eyes widening in surprise. "I heard that was pretty bad."

"It was," Facilis agreed. "I was wounded, so I managed to obtain a discharge."

He gave a rueful smile as he added, "I left the army and went home."

"Where is home?" asked Thrax.

The answer almost caught in Facilis' throat as the memories flooded back. Where was home now? But he did not need a long explanation. All he needed was a single word.

"Pompeii."

Chapter VII

The passing of twenty years had done nothing to diminish the memories. In the awful aftermath of the Boudican revolt, Facilis had found himself viewed almost as a pariah, tainted by his association with cowards. He had been charged with bringing the Second *Augusta* Legion to join the Governor's army but he had failed. The Legion had refused to leave its camp, terrified of being ambushed on the march by Calgacus and his horde of rebellious Britons who were rampaging around the south-west while Boudica's main army ravaged the south-east. Despite Facilis' pleas, the commander of the Second Legion had refused to leave the sanctuary of the fort.

There had been nothing Facilis could do. He had almost died delivering the Governor's message, having been caught by Calgacus' war band. Tumbling from his horse when it fell during his frantic bid to outrun his pursuers, he had expected to die. To his astonishment, Calgacus had let him go free, but Facilis' leg had been broken by his fall, and he had been unable to walk, let alone persuade the soldiers to march to the Governor's aid.

Instead of trying to help put down the revolt, the legionaries had cowered in their fort, terrified by the tales of the great rebellion that had seen an enormous British army destroy three towns, burning them to the ground in an orgy of destruction. Every day, they had expected to see that barbarian horde descend on them. Once Governor Paulinus' weakened army had been destroyed, there would be nothing to prevent the Britons wiping out the Second Legion.

But the British army had never arrived. Instead, messengers came with the news that Paulinus had destroyed the rebels. For some reason, Calgacus had vanished. Without his leadership, the Britons had fallen into their old habit of facing the Romans in open battle, and they had been slaughtered in their thousands. Boudica, the Queen of the Iceni, had died, and her army had been massacred.

It was only then that Facilis learned there had been no British army waiting to ambush the Second Legion. Calgacus had tricked him into believing that there had been two rebel armies when, in fact, there had only ever been one. That, he reflected bitterly, was why Calgacus had let him go free, allowing him to deliver his message. He may not have been responsible for the decision to remain in the fort, but he shared the soldiers' shame because he knew he had been duped.

With the revolt crushed, Governor Paulinus took awful revenge on the survivors of the rebellious tribes, but they were not the only casualties. Postumus, commander of the Second Legion, had committed suicide rather than face the disgrace of being the man who had refused to fight. Facilis soon found that he, too, was regarded as being in disgrace. During the long weeks of his recuperation, he was virtually ignored, left alone while Governor Paulinus wreaked revenge on the Iceni and their allies, killing and destroying with brutal savagery. Facilis knew that the Britons had been equally murderous during their rebellion, but he was disgusted by the bloody vengeance that Paulinus was intent on carrying out. The terrible slaughter during and after Boudica's rebellion had left him sick of war, appalled at how people could so easily descend into savagery.

It had not lasted long, of course. Paulinus' reprisals were so brutal that another Governor was soon sent to replace him, but the new man had made it plain that he had no need for Facilis either. Facilis realised that his association with the Second Legion's failure marked him as a man who was not reliable. It was the final insult. He had always done his duty, but he was too sick at heart to protest at the unfair treatment. Instead, he had asked to be discharged. The Governor had signed the papers without argument.

"You should go home," he had said coldly. "You have been in Britannia too long."

So Facilis had made the long journey home, relying on the few coins he had been given on his discharge to pay his way. Even on horseback it took a long time to travel across Gaul, down the length of Italy, stopping briefly in Rome to see the famous city again after so many years in Britannia. He would have liked to have stayed longer, but he was low on funds, so he had continued southwards, mile by sun-drenched mile, until he had eventually reached Pompeii towards the end of summer.

The place was the same as he remembered, yet also different. New shops, taverns, and eating houses had appeared. New statues lined the forum, and every face he saw was that of a stranger.

Facilis had been barely eighteen when he had left to join the army. Thanks to the influence and connections of his Uncle Firmus, he had found a post on the staff of Ostorius Scapula, Governor of Britannia, but he now marvelled at how immature and innocent he had been. He had grown into a man during his long years in Britannia, but he returned to Pompeii with no more wealth than he had possessed on the day he had departed.

A stranger opened the door to the house where he had expected to find his mother. The man who faced him was a slave who denied all knowledge of anyone named Sulpicia. When Facilis insisted on speaking to the master of the house, he was shown into a room off the atrium, a room he remembered so well, but which seemed so different. He found himself faced by a small, balding man who, after much clucking of his tongue and wracking of his brain, recalled that the lady who had once owned the house was now living near the Sea Gate.

"Ask at the fullery," the podgy man advised.

Facilis walked through the narrow, crowded streets, using the high stepping stones to cross from one pavement to the next. Below the elevated pavements, the street was a morass of animal droppings, human waste and rubbish that would eventually be washed away when it rained but which now filled the air with a stench that Facilis had forgotten.

He found the fuller's shop, an establishment with pungent smells of its own, mostly the heady stink of the urine that was used to clean and treat the clothes.

The owner, a thin man with a face marred by several warts, told him, "Sulpicia? She lives on the upper floor. You'll find the entrance round the side. Go up the stairs."

In a gloomy, narrow alley at the side of the building was a wooden stair that climbed the outer wall of the fullery. The steps creaked and sagged under his weight as he climbed them to a small door at the top. When he reached it, he stopped, uncertain of what to expect and nervous of the reception he might receive. Eventually, feeling foolish for standing outside the door, he knocked.

When the door swung open, he almost did not recognise his mother. She seemed to have shrunk, her hair had faded to a washed-out dull brown, and her eyes had lost their sparkle. She peered at him, frowning nervously.

"Hello, mother," he said. "It's me, Lucius."

He felt even more foolish for having to tell her who he was.

"Lucius?"

Then there was recognition and tears. There were hugs and kisses and more questions than he could answer. She tugged him into her tiny apartment and fussed over him, her eyes brimming with tears and her questions never ceasing.

He had questions of his own, but it took a long time for him to learn all the answers. His mother poured him some cheap wine, sent her slave, a skinny young girl with a pock-marked face, to the nearest tavern to bring back a meal, and insisted on hearing the story of Facilis' life since he had left home twelve years earlier.

"I cannot believe you are back," she repeated over and over, like a prayer.

Facilis kept his account as vague and short as he could. To most Romans, he knew, Britannia was a strange, dangerous island at the edge of the world, a place inhabited by giants and ferocious wild beasts. The recent stories of the brutal revolt by the Iceni had done nothing to diminish the awe with which most people regarded the Empire's newest and most distant province. Besides which, he reasoned that, for all her questions, his mother did not really want to know the details of what he had seen and lived through.

He was more concerned about what had happened to his mother. The few letters she had sent him over the years had made no mention of her reduced circumstances, and he wanted to know why she was living in a tiny, two-roomed apartment above a stinking fullery.

It was only after they had finished their meal of bean stew and drunk another cup of wine that Sulpicia eventually told her story.

"Things were very tight as regards money. Your father left a lot of debts, you know."

"I know. That's why I always sent you as much of my pay as I could afford."

His mother patted his arm as she gave him a grateful smile. "Yes, I cannot thank you enough for that. But still, your father's creditors were not happy. He had borrowed so much, and the interest was mounting faster than I could repay. So I went to see your Uncle Firmus."

"How is your brother?" Facilis asked.

"Oh, he is prospering," his mother replied with a fluttering hand. "He lives in Rome now. He's been admitted to equestrian rank."

Casting a jaundiced eye around the tiny living room, Facilis asked, "So what did Uncle Firmus do to help you?"

"He bought our old house. He paid a good price for it, too. Very fair. Then he paid off all the creditors and took over all the debts."

Facilis felt a sinking sensation in his stomach. "So now you owe him the money instead?"

"That's right," Sulpicia agreed, apparently contentedly. "He gave me enough to buy this place, and he sends me a portion of the rent from our old house, so I have enough to get by."

"And he keeps the rest of the rent to pay off the debts?"

"Yes. It's all too complicated for me, of course. But Firmus is my brother, so I trust him."

From what little Facilis remembered of his mother's brother, he would not have trusted Firmus any more than he would trust a wild wolf, but now was not the time to say so.

"Maybe I should go and talk to him," he suggested.

"But he's in Rome!" his mother protested. "You've only just got here."

Facilis did not argue, but it only took a few days for both of them to realise that, even with Firmus' alleged assistance, money was a problem. With Facilis having lost his army pay, he needed to find some means of earning a living. After a week, he told his mother that he was going to talk to Firmus.

"I'll be back as soon as I can," he promised.

Hiring an old, sway-backed nag, he rode to Rome, lodging in cheap, flea-ridden taverns along the way. When he reached the great city, he made his way to the lower slopes of the Esquiline Hill, where his uncle, Decimus Sulpicius Firmus, lived in a large, luxuriously elegant, two-storey house that filled an entire block.

Facilis remembered Firmus as a short, pudgy man with fussy habits and a shifty manner. His memory was not far wrong. Firmus had lost some of his hair, had put on even more weight, but his manner was just as Facilis recalled.

"Your father left considerable debts," he reminded Facilis unctuously. "I helped out as best I could, but, although your mother is my sister, I cannot afford to simply pay off what your father owed."

From the garish opulence of the house and the number of slaves in evidence, Facilis knew that was a lie, but he realised that accusing the man was not likely to achieve anything productive.

Facilis kept his face impassive as he asked, "How much do we owe you now?"

Firmus made a show of being uncertain, calling for one of his many slaves to bring him an accounts book, although Facilis suspected the man knew the amount of the debt down to the last sestertius.

Firmus studied the book, clucked his tongue, sighed, then said, "It now stands at ninety-two thousand, three hundred and sixteen sesterces."

Facilis could only gape in disbelief.

"Even after selling the house and me sending my pay?"

"Even then," Firmus confirmed. "As I say, your father was profligate."

His tone left Facilis in no doubt that Firmus believed his sister had entered into an ill-chosen marriage and deserved everything that resulted from her disastrous choice.

"Surely the rents from the house will reduce it considerably?" he queried.

"I'm afraid not," Firmus said smugly. "The rental market in Pompeii is not as good as that in Rome."

He shrugged as he added, "I really have done all that I can, you know. If it were not for the fact that your mother is my sister, I would not have done half as much."

Facilis wanted to ram the man's accounts book down his fleshy throat, but he took a deep breath and nodded his head, as if understanding his uncle's position. He decided to try a different approach.

"May I see the accounts?"

Firmus' face turned hard and pale as Grecian marble, and he closed the book firmly. Looking Facilis in the eye, he stated, "I will send you a copy of the recent transactions."

Facilis knew his uncle was cheating them, but a man who held the purse strings was not a person to fall out with.

He nodded, "Thank you," although he doubted whether he would ever see the promised copy. Even if he did, it would probably not match the book that was now firmly clenched in his uncle's hands.

Firmus gave him a stern look as he asked, "What are you going to do now that you are back?"

Facilis was forced to admit, "I don't know."

"Perhaps you should go into politics. A man like you, with your administrative abilities and military experience, could stand for public office. You could become a member of the town council, an aedile, perhaps."

"That costs money," Facilis pointed out.

"True. But I might be able to support you. I could lend you enough to finance a campaign."

Facilis could hardly believe his uncle's gall. He called on all his experience of concealing his feelings from senior officers to remain calm in the face of Firmus' suggestion.

"No thank you, Uncle. I don't think I am cut out for public office."

"You must do something," Firmus insisted.

"I'll find some work."

Firmus seemed genuinely astonished. "Work? You mean to become a labourer or a fisherman?"

"I'll find something," Facilis repeated.

He had left Firmus' house in a cold fury, determined that, whatever happened, he would pay off the debt his gambler father had left.

It was easier said than done. There were few jobs to be had in Pompeii. Slaves performed all the menial work, and other crafts like decorating, baking or construction required skills that Facilis did not possess. He was, at heart, a planner, an organiser, an administrator, yet he could not afford to stand for public office and would not demean himself by borrowing yet more money from his miserly uncle.

He also lacked connections. Patronage was how most people found employment, but Facilis had been away too long to know who to speak to. But without a patron, he would be lucky to find any decent work. Eventually, after several weeks of frustration, he heard someone in the forum mention the name of an old friend, a man who had attended the same tutor when they were boys. Desperate now, Facilis took a chance and called on his childhood acquaintance.

Decimus Quinctilius Sicilianus was tall, dark-haired and swarthy, with rugged good looks that Facilis had always envied. The boy Facilis had known had grown into a confident man with an apparently easy-going nature, a ready smile and a firm handshake. But Facilis knew that these outward displays concealed a quick mind and a ruthless business brain. Sicilianus had become wealthy through investing in a range of local enterprises, not all of which were strictly legal. He was not the sort of person Facilis had wanted to go to, but Sicilianus was one of the few people who remembered him and who was, more importantly, prepared to help.

"By the Gods, man, you look terrible," was Sicilianus' greeting. "What did they do to you in Britannia? I hear it's an awful place."

"It's not as bad as people say," Facilis replied with what he hoped was a modest smile. "In fact, it was easier than living in Pompeii without a means of earning a living."

Sicilianus returned his smile and gave a knowing nod. "You are looking for employment?"

Facilis was beyond pride. He admitted, "Yes. I was hoping you might be able to help me."

"Well, you survived Britannia, so you must have some talents I could use," grinned Sicilianus.

The next day, Facilis found himself visiting a local construction yard which lay outside the town, with a view of the great, looming mass of Mount Vesuvius in the distance. The place was run-down, with no evidence that anyone was doing any productive work.

Sicilianus had said, "The man who runs it for me is a lazy drunkard. His grandfather started the business but the grandson only owns a quarter of it. The rest belongs to me, but it's not making any money. I'd like you to go in and see what you can do. Kick a few backsides and sort things out if you can. If you can't, I'll cut my losses and shut the business down."

Facilis was no expert when it came to construction work, although he had learned a little from his days with the Legions. More importantly, though, he knew incompetent leadership when he saw it. The manager, a sour-faced, squint-eyed man by the name of Pedantius Secundus, was more than happy to allow Facilis to take over running the business.

"Sicilianus said he was sending someone," he grumbled. "But you're wasting your time. There's no money to be made in this line of work. We're too small to compete with the big firms and we don't have access to enough stone or marble."

Facilis replied, "I'll still take a look around it that's all right with you."

"Suit yourself," Secundus shrugged. "I'm going to Rennus' wineshop for a drink."

Facilis set to work. He quickly discovered that, in some respects, Secundus was correct, but the main problem was the man's indolence. He spent most of each day in Rennus' wineshop, and the rest of the day sleeping off his hangover. Facilis did not mind, because it left him with a free hand.

Chivvying the overseer and the slaves, visiting potential clients and suppliers, and spending time going over the accounts soon created a small improvement in business. It was hard work, requiring Facilis to spend most of the day either at the yard or talking to customers, but he threw himself into it, knowing that Sicilianus would reward him if he made a success of this ramshackle venture.

He made some progress, but what made the real difference was the earthquake.

It took Facilis more than a year to turn the business into a viable concern. For the first time in years, the firm made a small profit. Then, in the second summer, the ground shook and a dark, ominous cloud belched from the flat summit of Vesuvius. Some people said that lava had flowed down the slopes of the great volcano, but Facilis did not see that. What he saw was an opportunity. The tremors were so fierce that many buildings collapsed. Others developed great cracks in their walls, while yet more suffered from shattered roofs. Statues toppled, roads broke apart, and walls tilted alarmingly all over the town.

Fortunately, only a handful of people were killed, although many suffered minor injuries when walls and roofs tumbled around them. But, while the human price was mercifully low, everyone was stunned by how much damage the earth tremors had caused to the city.

During his years with the Legions, Facilis had seen more death and destruction than he cared for, but that experience allowed him to quickly overcome his initial shock, and he soon set his mind towards the task of rebuilding.

He spent the next three days agreeing contracts for repair work. There was no need to undercut any rivals because there was more than enough work to go round, but he trimmed his margins as much as he dared. He bought extra slaves and recruited masons, plasterers and carpenters from other firms, offering higher wages. By the end of the year, he had trebled the previous year's profit. The following year, he doubled it again.

"You're a bloody marvel," beamed Sicilianus when he came to visit. "You've worked a miracle here."

"No miracle," Facilis assured him. "Just common sense and hard work."

"Nevertheless, you deserve a reward. How do you fancy a quarter share of the ownership?"

"I can't afford to buy in to it," Facilis shrugged.

Sicilianus grinned, "No need. I've bought out Secundus. He's a waste of space. He'll probably drink himself to death with the money I paid him."

"So you own one hundred per cent now?"

"That's right. And, as a bonus for you in recognition of what you've achieved here, I'm giving a quarter to you."

"I don't know what to say," Facilis blinked.

"Then don't say anything. Just get to work and make us both some more money. And, for Jupiter's sake, find a better house to live in."

Facilis needed little encouragement to move house. He managed to obtain a modest town house at a very reasonable price because it had been badly damaged by the earthquake. The owners had decided to move away from Pompeii and were in a hurry to sell. Facilis took an advance on his share of the business profits, bought the house and made sure it was renovated to a high standard. When it was ready, he sold his mother's tiny apartment and they moved into the new home. Facilis even purchased a few more slaves to help run the place and, at last, he began to feel at home.

The next ten years were the best Facilis could ever remember. Not only did the business prosper, but he met Marcia.

She was the daughter of one of the town's leading bakers. Facilis had stopped at their shop every day on his way to the building yard. One day he fell into conversation with Marcia, a pretty, dark-haired, slim girl of around seventeen. Their conversations became longer each day and when Facilis learned that the baker needed some renovation work done on his extensive premises, Facilis made sure that his quote was the cheapest. He made a point of visiting every day, ostensibly to keep an eye on the work but really to speak to Marcia.

They were married three months later, with her large family shouting the traditional Roman marriage cry, "Talasio!" to celebrate the occasion. More than twenty years her senior, Facilis could not believe how fortunate he had been. The memory of Britannia, of the horrors of war and his personal disgrace, were forgotten. Some might view marriage to a baker's daughter as socially unsuitable for a former Tribune, but Facilis did not care. He was no longer a Tribune, and he had no real desire to climb the social ladder again.

Two years later, Marcia gave him a son, whom they named Lucius, and Facilis thought his life was complete.

Outside Pompeii, great events continued to take place, but few of them made much difference to daily life in the town. There was a great fire in Rome, for which the Emperor, Nero, blamed the Christians. Everyone else blamed the Emperor. Five years later, Nero was hounded to suicide, and there was the awful uncertainty of the Year of the Four Emperors, with civil war raging throughout the Empire. There was fear and alarm, rabble-rousing speeches in the forum, and talk of men being recruited into one or other Emperor's army. Facilis tried to remain aloof, hoping the danger would pass. His prayers were answered and, by the end of that turbulent year, Vespasian was in charge and things settled down again, with life resuming its previous normality.

Facilis was content. There was only one more thing he wanted, and he continued to work hard to achieve it. One day, he promised himself, he would pay off the debt that he and his mother owed to Sulpicius Firmus.

That day came when Facilis was fifty-one years old. He was now a respected businessman, a partner in several of

Sicilianus' enterprises, although Sicilianus never asked him to take a stake in any of his less than legal projects, knowing that Facilis would refuse. Even so, Facilis had, at last, saved enough money to clear the debts that had hung over him for so long.

He could still remember the day he had set off, kissing Marcia and his mother, embracing young Lucius, and mounting his horse. Behind him, a mule was laden with bags of silver, guarded by half a dozen burly slaves and a couple of ex-soldiers who were to act as his guards.

"I'll be back in a week or two," he told his family.

Marcia gave him a nervous smile as she said, "Hurry back. The mountain has been rumbling again, and it's been smoking for days now. It scares me."

"There's nothing to be afraid of," Facilis assured her. "If we are lucky, there will be another earthquake and we'll make another fortune to replace this one we're giving to fat Uncle Firmus."

Marcia had wanted to come with him, to let Lucius see the sights of Rome, but Facilis had asked her to stay, to care for his mother who was growing increasingly frail and whose mind was beginning to wander. Even when Marcia suggested they should all leave, he had told her there was nothing to be concerned about.

"Don't worry about Vesuvius. It's a big mountain, but even if the volcano does erupt, it's far enough away. No lava flow will reach the town."

"But some people have already left," she reminded him.

"We shall stay," he told her. "Our home is here."

How he regretted those words now. They haunted his dreams every night, reminding him of how wrong he had been, taunting him with the loss of everything he had gained.

But he had been happy that day, too intent on paying off the debt that had hung over him for most of his life, to think about anything else. He was even happier when he reached Rome and delivered the money to Firmus. The elderly money-lender had accepted it with poor grace, signing a paper to confirm that the debt had been repaid in full.

"You are a remarkable man, Facilis," he had said grudgingly.

Facilis resisted the temptation to tell his uncle exactly what he thought of him. Instead, he had wished him good day, taken his receipt, and set off for home.

He had seen the great cloud of dark, evil smoke long before he met the first refugees but, before long, the road was jammed with people, wailing and crying, shouting for help, or cursing the Gods.

"What has happened?" Facilis asked an exhausted-looking man who was pushing a hand cart that was piled high with an assortment of household goods.

"The mountain exploded," the man told him, his face bleak, his red-rimmed eyes filled with despair.

Facilis felt the blood drain from his face.

"Pompeii? What happened in the town?"

The man stared at him blankly. In a voice replete with doom and loss, he said, "There is no town any more."

Chapter VIII

Facilis sat on the sodden planking of the ship's deck, rain mingling with the tears that streaked his unshaven cheeks. Pulcher was staring at him incredulously, his own complaints momentarily stilled by the horror of Facilis' story.

Thrax looked stunned, sympathy competing with awe on his sun-browned face as he listened to the account of the death of Pompeii.

Facilis had never told anyone about that awful day and the equally terrible aftermath. Now, he could not stop. The words flowed like the tears of grief that even the torrential rain could not wash away.

"There was nothing left," he recalled. "It was as if Vulcan or some other God had smothered the town. The layer of ash and pumice was so deep that even the tallest buildings were buried."

Closing his eyes did nothing to remove the vision of what he had lost. He went on, "When the ash cooled, some people tried to dig tunnels down to the houses. A lot of them were after whatever they could loot, but some of us wanted to find our homes. And our families."

He shrugged, "It was useless, of course. There were no landmarks, nothing to tell us where to begin. Every tree, every hill, had been swept away. I sent some of my slaves down, but their tunnel collapsed and two of them were killed. After that, I gave up."

Bleakly, he added, "They are all gone. My wife, my son, my mother. I have no idea whether they stayed in the house or whether they tried to escape. I can hardly bear to think of how they died. But they are dead. Some people escaped, but many did not. Sicilianus is buried somewhere beneath the ruins. So are all of Marcia's family, all the men who worked for me. Even the drunk, Secundus, was killed by the volcano, not by the wine he consumed."

Gently, Thrax asked, "Is that why you rejoined the army?"

"I had nowhere else to go," Facilis sighed. "I would never accept anything from old Firmus, so the only other choice was to come back. Fortunately, I knew Julius Agricola. He had been on Paulinus' staff during the Boudican revolt. I know as much about Britannia as any man, so I came to see him. I don't think he really wanted me, but he found a position for me."

Facilis gave a sad smile as he added, "I think he felt sorry for me. The trouble is, even though Britannia is as far from home as it is possible to go, it's still not far enough to escape the memories."

Pulcher mumbled, "I never knew."

Facilis could not tell whether the Quaestor intended his remark as an apology. Not that it mattered. He did not want or need anyone's sympathy. What he needed was a miracle, because he wanted to forget and he could not. The events of those loss-filled days had been seared into his memory forever.

He took several deep breaths, calming himself after the effort of telling his story. Then he said, "Which is why, whatever happens to us now, I am prepared for it. I have nothing left to lose except my life."

"The Gods must have spared you for a reason," Thrax told him. "I don't believe it was just so that you could end your days as a captive of these thugs."

Facilis tried to smile, to thank the sailor for his words of comfort, but he had lived too long to put much faith in the Gods. They may have had some plan for him, but he suspected that, at best, they were simply playing some cruel game with his life for their own amusement.

Not wanting to spurn Thrax's kind words, he said, "I suppose we will find out soon enough."

The voyage continued, with the three battered ships slowly crawling northwards, sometimes powered by strong, blustery winds in their sails, but more often by the oars that splashed in ragged, uncoordinated strokes.

Thrax continued to guide them, picking a way through the maze of islands and jutting headlands, but even his advice could not transform the Usipi into competent sailors. The boats wallowed and splashed at a pace that Thrax constantly bemoaned, but Fullofaudes insisted that they must stay together, so they moved slowly, day after hungry day, clawing their way up the rugged coast like lost souls seeking a vanished refuge.

The lack of food was becoming serious. Men were growing thin and losing strength. Many were unable to man the oars for more than an hour before requiring a lengthy rest. Their faces grew gaunt and haggard, and their tempers grew short. There were arguments every night, with accusing fingers being pointed and angry voices being raised, especially that of Necrautis who constantly harangued the other men. None of the prisoners could understand what he was saying, although his dissatisfaction with Fullofaudes' leadership was evident.

The big German tried his best to alleviate their hunger, but there was little food to be had. The coast seemed deserted, a wilderness of rocks, heather and trees, with no sign of human habitation. Once or twice they spotted a small boat which Thrax identified as a fishing vessel, but they were never able to get close enough to catch the natives, who seemed to vanish into hidden inlets. On the few occasions when they saw signs of habitation, the Britons fled at the sight of the ships, leaving only empty houses behind. The Usipi, enraged, burned the houses before trudging back to their ships and continuing the nightmare journey.

Several times, Fullofaudes ordered an early halt, drawing the galleys onto a suitable beach long before dusk so that they could send hunting parties inland. Without exception, these forays failed to find anything more substantial than birds' eggs or a few edible plants such as nettles and dandelions. Thrax informed Fullofaudes that he had heard that some varieties of seaweed were edible, but the Captain was not able to positively identify which species could be eaten, and none of the Usipi dared risk poisoning themselves by consuming the wrong plants, although a few of them did resort to eating beetles if they were able to locate them while scrabbling for weeds to eat.

If they were able to find any birch trees, the Usipi cut the bark, allowing the sap to ooze out overnight. In the morning, they scraped the congealed sap from the tree and ate it raw. It provided some nourishment, but there was never enough for every man to be given a share.

Some men fashioned crude hooks from brooch pins and tried their luck at fishing but, without bait, their attempts were largely ineffective. A couple of fish were caught, but not nearly enough to feed everyone. Fights broke out as men argued over the meagre catches, and Fullofaudes had to use his fists to restore order. Determined to drive the Usipi on, he stalked the deck like an ogre, barking commands and overpowering the sullen mutterings of discontent by sheer force of his personality.

Facilis grew increasingly concerned. The rumbling from his stomach was a constant ache, but the gaunt, hollow-cheeked stares of the Usipi were more of a worry. He knew that look.

"They are growing desperate," he whispered to Thrax.

The Captain nodded grimly, "Aye, there's going to be trouble soon."

In an attempt to ease their plight, Facilis told Fullofaudes, "I speak the Briton's language. Perhaps I could negotiate with them. You have plenty of silver to buy food."

"They flee as soon as they see us coming," the German growled. "You can't speak to them if they run away."

"A few of us could try walking inland to find a village," Facilis suggested.

Fullofaudes shook his head.

"No, we must stick together. The barbarians would pick off a small group and will run from a large band."

"Then we will starve," Facilis argued.

"We will find food soon enough," Fullofaudes growled. "There must be some larger settlements somewhere around here."

His confident words proved groundless. The few villages they saw were tiny, no more than half a dozen roundhouses, and the inhabitants fled as soon as they caught sight of the galleys. The Usipi ransacked the abandoned homes but rarely found more than a few scraps of food.

Facilis lost count of the days. At some point, Thrax announced that they had reached the northern extremity of Britannia and could turn east.

"With luck, we'll have the wind in our favour for a while," he predicted.

They raised the sails, grateful for the respite from rowing, allowing the wind to push them along the shore that consisted of endless miles of rugged hills and long, sandy beaches.

That evening, they sighted the largest settlement they had seen, a collection of a dozen roundhouses clustered near the shore. Fullofaudes instantly issued orders to beach the ships and launch an attack on the village in an effort to find some food. Wearily, the Usipi hauled on the oars, urging the ships towards the land.

"Let me speak to them!" Facilis urged. "You don't need to fight them."

"We are Usipi," Fullofaudes replied. "We take what we want."

"Bloody fools!" muttered Thrax. "But let's hope they find something to eat."

Facilis sighed, "There won't be much. The people there have seen us already."

"Will they fight?" Pulcher asked anxiously.

"I doubt it. That's a small place. There won't be enough of them to oppose three ships full of fighting men. They can't know how weak we are from hunger, so I expect they'll run and hide, just like all the others."

Facilis' prediction was soon proved correct. The village had no stockade or defensive ditch, relying on its remote location for protection. At the sight of the three galleys, the inhabitants scrambled to gather up their belongings and ran into the wilderness beyond the village, driving their livestock ahead of them.

Fullofaudes cursed when he saw the Britons scurrying frantically out of the village, herding their sheep, goats and cattle into the hills and vanishing from sight.

"Pull, you lazy bastards!" he yelled. "They're getting away!"

Spurred on by the thought of catching the natives, the Usipi hauled on the oars, driving the ships onto the long, sandy beach with a bone-jarring crash. Fullofaudes immediately sent fifty men after the fleeing Britons, telling them to seize as much food as they could when they caught the villagers.

The rest of the Usipi scrambled ashore to ransack the village, seeking food. All semblance of order vanished as they ploughed through the roundhouses in a desperate search for something to eat. Fights broke out over scraps or crumbs, and one man was stabbed to death over a small hunk of bread that had been dropped in the villagers' haste to escape.

Fullofaudes yelled at his men, resorting to punching and pushing when his bellows of anger failed to stop the fighting. Eventually, he managed to restore some semblance of order and had them collect all the food together. There was not much. A few smoked fish, some bannocks, three scrawny chickens and half a dozen eggs.

"Not even enough for a mouthful each," Thrax grunted.

The men Fullofaudes had sent after the villagers returned just after dusk, empty-handed. Facilis could not understand what they said, but he grasped their meaning.

"They were too weak for a long chase, and it's too dark to find them now," he guessed.

"Another hungry night," groaned Pulcher, who had shed considerable weight over the past days.

There was water from a stream, so they could slake their thirst and re-fill the ships' water barrels, but there was not nearly enough food to go round. Some men chewed leaves from trees, or ripped up handfuls of grass which they tried to boil into a soup. Facilis refused to eat it, but Pulcher took a bowl and spent the rest of the night complaining of stomach cramps.

The Usipi huddled in the roundhouses, warming themselves by the hearth fires, while the three prisoners were left on the beach, crowded together under the spurious protection of a cloak stretched across four wooden poles that had been driven into the soft sand in the lee of the ships' hulls. It was a cold, miserable night, with only the sound of waves lapping on the shore to fill the empty silence of the dark world around them.

Facilis managed to snatch a whispered conversation with Thrax, wondering whether they might seize an opportunity to escape, but Fullofaudes posted a guard to watch them and had their legs tied together as well as checking the bonds around their wrists.

"Where would we go anyway?" Thrax asked. "Three of us can't row a galley, and the locals are just as savage as the Usipi. We'd be better waiting until we sail down the east coast. That way, we'll be a lot closer to friendly territory."

"If we don't starve to death before then," Facilis observed, although he knew the Captain was right. If they ran now, when they were as far north as it was possible to go, their chances of reaching safety were remote.

Reluctantly, they settled down for another hungry night, but when the morning burst over the rugged hills in a magnificent blaze of red and orange, there was more trouble in store.

Fullofaudes had another argument with Necrautis. Facilis could see the angry gestures and hear the coarse, furious tone of their voices. The other men of the Usipi began to slowly move behind one or the other of the two leaders, clearly showing their allegiance. Fullofaudes seemed to have more support, but Necrautis kept shouting, pointing and waving his arms in dramatic appeal.

Thrax grunted, "It looks like some of them want to turn back."

Facilis feared that the argument was about to become violent, with Fullofaudes wrapping his huge fist around the hilt of his sword, but a warning shout from one of their sentries prevented any further argument. All heads turned to the south, where they saw one of their men running towards the beach, pursued by a dozen natives who were brandishing spears, clubs, mattocks and axes. Even as they watched, the Usipi warrior, weakened by hunger, stumbled and fell. In an instant, the pursuing Britons pounced on him, hacking down at him with their brutal weapons, smashing bones and gouging his flesh to tattered ribbons.

Pulcher gasped, "Immortal Gods! There are hundreds of them!"

He may have been exaggerating, but not by much. The land that had seemed so empty suddenly burst into furious life, with armed men springing up from folds in the ground or leaping from the cover of bushes and heather. Dressed in animal hides and seal skins, long-haired and wild-eyed, they howled their fury, their wild yells demanding blood.

Fullofaudes bellowed his own command.

"To the boats!"

The Usipi ran down the beach, hauling themselves onto the ships, scrambling desperately into the rowing benches. Some men fell, sprawling on the sand, while others began to push the three vessels into the water, planting their shoulders against the hulls and heaving with all their strength. Other men splashed into the shallows, climbing aboard to join the men who had reached the oars and were frantically trying to row the ships back out to sea.

Fullofaudes organised a defence, shoving and pushing at fifty men who formed a ragged line to oppose the British assault. The sight of their swords made the natives skid to a halt, waiting for their full force to gather. Some hurled spears or threw stones at the Usipi who, without their chainmail and shields, which they had left on the ships, cowered down under the hail of missiles.

Slowly, the Usipi edged backwards. Fullofaudes stood behind them, shouting orders and constantly glancing over his shoulder to check on what was happening to the boats.

Facilis, still lying helplessly on the sand, caught the big German's eye and shouted to him.

"Get us aboard! For the Gods' sake!"

Fullofaudes grabbed three of his men and sent them running to the prisoners. They slashed at the ropes binding their legs, hauled them upright and dragged them into the cold, salt water until they reached the looming wooden walls of the nearest ship.

Facilis looked up at the deck bobbing above his head, while waves lapped at his thighs and fear clawed at his belly.

"Cut our hands free!" he barked at the guards. "We can't climb with our hands tied together."

Cursing foul oaths, the Usipi cut their ropes, then hoisted them upwards. Facilis grabbed at the rail with numbed fingers, pulling himself onto the deck before turning to snatch Pulcher's arm and drag the fat man upwards.

There was a roar from the beach. Still gasping for breath, Facilis turned in time to see a wave of long-haired Britons swarm down on the Usipi rearguard. Fullofaudes yelled a frantic command and the Germans turned to run. They surged into the waves, wading out after the ships which were now fifty feet from the shore, the oars still backing and pulling them further out to sea with each heaving, frantic stroke.

Men screamed and shouted, grabbing for ropes that were flung down from the prows of the three vessels. Behind the fleeing Usipi, some Britons charged into the water in pursuit, spears thrusting at exposed backs. Two Germans went down, their blood darkening the water. Others fell in their panic, spluttering back to their feet and splashing deeper into the water in search of sanctuary.

Fullofaudes turned to face two British warriors who had run after him. Facilis saw the huge German slash his sword in a clumsy arc that brought a line of blood welling from one man's arm. Then he stabbed at the second Briton, leaping awkwardly in the water, punching with his left hand and thrusting his sword in his right. The Briton's face contorted in agony as he staggered back and fell under the waves.

The majority of the Britons had remained on the beach, venturing no further than the shallows. They continued to throw javelins and stones, but most of them seemed content to have driven off the raiders.

Fullofaudes waded chest-deep into the water, pulling himself aboard, dripping and sloshing sea water all over the deck. He was the last man aboard. He turned to shout breathless defiance at the Britons who lined the shore, screeching hate. Then he sighed, turned his back and ordered the ships to sail eastwards.

Driven by strong, coastal winds, the three galleys used their sails to skirt along the northern coast. Despite their protests, Facilis and his two companions had their wrists tied again.

The attack from the villagers had badly shaken the Usipi. For the next few nights they doubled their guard and made sure that shields and armour were close at hand. This made them feel safer, but did nothing to assuage their hunger.

There were no more settlements, no sign of farmland or fishing villages. They foraged for food whenever they landed for the night, but there was little to be found until they came across a colony of nesting seabirds. A few of the Usipi braved the birds' fury to scale almost vertical cliffs and raid the nests for eggs. Using clubs, they also downed some of the birds, providing some meat for the evening's cooking pot, but one of the men fell from the cliff under the assault of the frenzied birds. His body was smashed when it struck the rocks at the foot of the cliff, but the rest of the Usipi were too hungry to care about his loss. They boiled the eggs and the scrawny birds, serving up a meal that was hardly a banquet, but was enough to sustain them a little longer.

The next night, Necrautis led a party of men inland, vowing to find some food. Fullofaudes let them go, but insisted that everyone else remain aboard ship. Necrautis and his gang returned in moonlit gloom, having gained nothing except a few cuts and bruises from blundering around in the dark. Necrautis exchanged more angry words with Fullofaudes, whose mocking replies could only mean, "I told you so."

The hungry voyage continued. They turned south-east, still able to rely mostly on their sails thanks to the prevailing westerly wind.

"Just as well," Thrax observed grimly. "Most of them are too weak to row for any length of time."

"Where are we now?" Facilis asked him.

"There's a great inlet here on the north-east. We can cut across it like a triangle rather than follow the coast."

Having hugged the land for so long, it was strange to be out on the deep ocean, with the coast a mere low, grey line on the horizon. The wind remained favourable, driving them through the deep swell, the ships rocked by the waves, rising and falling as they surged onwards. By dusk, they had reached the coast again and Thrax announced that, if the winds remained kind, they might reach Roman territory in two or three days.

"That's when the fun will start," he remarked. "They'll need to find a way past the fleet that's supporting the Governor's army."

"How?"

"By going out to sea and sailing directly for Germania."

The Captain shook his head morosely as he added, "We'll never survive that. They're in no condition to make a voyage like that."

"Then we need to make our escape soon," Facilis declared.

Thrax nodded, "I know, but I don't see how we are going to get away."

Facilis was too exhausted to argue. His hunger was like a burning fire within him. He was able to drink water, but he could not remember the last time food had passed his lips. He felt weak, dizzy, and unable to concentrate for any length of time. All he could do was lie on the deck, praying that the journey would soon be over.

Beside him, Pulcher had almost given up hope. The Quaestor barely spoke at all now. He lay on the deck, groaning softly from time to time, but rarely moving.

The Usipi were in little better condition. Some men continued to try their luck at fishing but few of them had any success. As if to mock them, a school of dolphins sported alongside the ships, darting and weaving to and fro between them. One man threw a spear, hoping to catch one of the playful mammals, but his throw only grazed the back of one dolphin. The blade brought a splash of blood from the creature which quickly dived beneath the waves. Moments later, the entire school had vanished into the depths, leaving the Usipi frustrated and angry.

Facilis knew that the men were on the verge of breaking. Hollow-cheeked and with sunken eyes, they could not last much longer without food.

As the next day drew to a close, the wind turned against them. The sails were hauled down and the oars shoved into place. There were fewer now, Facilis noted, because sickness had broken out, leaving some men unable to row. Those who manned the oars pulled with little enthusiasm and barely enough strength to keep the ships moving.

The sky was darkening, streaks of red and purple lining the western horizon, so Fullofaudes turned the ships towards the shore, seeking a safe place to spend the night. As the sun finally vanished beyond the hills, they beached on a narrow shelf of pebbles at the mouth of a small, tree-lined stream. It was a good harbour, but even here their luck did not hold. Necrautis' ship crunched on a jagged rock that lurked beneath the surface of the shallows. They all heard the smash of breaking timbers as the galley scraped across the rock. Sea water cascaded into the ship but Necrautis screamed at the rowers to pull hard and, with the aid of the incoming tide, they managed to land the stricken vessel on the beach.

Everyone gathered around the gaping hole in the side of the ship. Thrax was untied and taken to examine it. When he returned to slump down beside Facilis and Pulcher, who had been dumped by the edge of the stream, he grunted, "It isn't all that bad. Skilled men could repair it in a morning."

"Do they have skilled men?" Facilis asked him.

"They have some who claim to be carpenters," Thrax informed him, "and they have a few tools on board, but that's not really the problem. There's plenty of wood around here, but it won't be much use. The sap will be rising and it will take far too long to season the planks."

"What are they going to do?"

"They have no choice. They'll need to cut down a tree, saw planks and hope they can plug the gap enough to keep going without sinking."

"They could abandon that ship," Facilis suggested.

"There are too many men to crowd them all on to the two remaining ships," Thrax told him. "No. Fullofaudes is going to try to repair the damage, so I expect we'll be here for a couple of days."

"Where is here, exactly?" Facilis asked.

"I don't know exactly," Thrax admitted. "But we're somewhere north of the Tava."

Facilis tried to recall the maps he had seen. He said, "At least we are on the east coast, but we can't run yet. We are still too far north."

Thrax grunted his agreement. "Another couple of days' sailing ought to do it."

Facilis wondered how they would ever escape, even if an opportunity did present itself. He was so weak from hunger that he could not imagine walking a hundred paces, let alone running.

Thrax muttered, "Let's hope the locals leave us in peace long enough to repair the galley."

"Do you know which tribe lives around here?"

"They call themselves the Taexali, I think."

The name meant nothing to Facilis, although he could imagine the tribe's reaction if they discovered the Usipi. He tried to dismiss the gloomy thoughts from his mind, then sat up when he saw Necrautis and a gaggle of his men carrying another man into the light of the camp fires that lined the bank of the stream.

"What's going on?" he wondered.

They watched while the once-stocky but now starving Necrautis argued fiercely with Fullofaudes. Other men began shouting angrily, some spitting in disgust, others snarling vehement agreement with whatever Necrautis was suggesting.

Fullofaudes argued his case, but soon threw up his arms in a gesture of defeat. Grinning triumphantly, Necrautis barked some orders. Men hurried to the stream to collect water, while others dragged a large, heavy cooking pot from one of the ships. They set it on a circle of stones in which a fire blazed, filling the pot with water.

Only then did Facilis realise that the man who had been carried to the fire was dead. Whether he had died of hunger, or from sickness, or been killed when the ship struck the rock, he could not tell, but he saw the Usipi rip the clothes from the corpse.

Then he saw them brandishing their knives and his empty stomach lurched in revulsion.

Blinking uncertainly, Pulcher whispered, "What are they doing?"

Facilis could hardly bring himself to utter the words. "They're going to eat him."

Chapter IX

Calgacus twisted in his saddle, casting a frustrated look back down the long, straggling column of wagons, carts and wearily trudging people. Men, women and children snaked through the countryside, prodding their cattle, sheep, goats and pigs. Chickens squawked and fluttered in wooden cages, geese cackled and hissed, while a small army of dogs prowled up and down the length of the convoy.

"This is taking too long," Calgacus muttered darkly.

Beatha, sitting on a small pony, replied, "You can always go on ahead. You need to find Maelchon and get back to the war host."

"I'll see you safe first," he grumbled. "I just wish we could travel faster. It's going to take three or four days to get there at this rate."

"Everyone is going as fast as they can," Beatha assured him.

"They'd go a damn sight faster if the Romans were chasing us."

"But they are not."

"So far. We need to reach the hills before that treacherous bastard Venutius brings an army back to find us."

"Are you really so sure he will do that?" Beatha asked.

He could hear the strain in her voice, and knew what it had cost her to leave her home. He sighed, "I'm not prepared to take the chance that he won't."

He had made his decision as soon as he heard about the visit from the so-called Roman emissary. Venutius had crossed his path too many times in the past for him to take any risks with the safety of his family and friends. The stockade was strong, but with all the warriors away at the gathering of tribes, their home could not be defended. If the people were to remain safe, they must find a place of sanctuary.

Calgacus knew such a place. Over the years, Bridei had taken him on many hunting trips in search of boar, wolves or deer. There were steep, wild mountains to the north, the southern fringes of the great mountain range that dominated much of northern Britannia. Long, narrow valleys were home to scattered farmsteads, but also provided places that could not be approached easily. Far along one of these glens, high on a mountainside, was a large bowl that had been scraped from the hilltop, as if a giant had used a spoon to dig out a chunk of earth and rock. In this corrie there was a tiny upland loch, with enough space around it to build a small settlement. Screened by cliffs and sky above, and steep, forested slopes below, the corrie was visible only to the hawks and eagles that soared high above the hilltops.

Calgacus had noted this sanctuary years before and had often used it as a camp when on hunting expeditions. Over the years, he had ensured that several small houses were built and maintained. It had been a precaution that he had been unable to explain, but now it had proved worthwhile. With the Roman fleet patrolling the coast, there was a constant threat of raids. Now that Venutius knew where he lived, that threat was very real indeed.

"Runt and I need to go north anyway," he told Beatha. "We'll get you to the corrie, then we'll cross the hills and find Maelchon."

He scowled again, clucking his tongue impatiently before muttering, "I just wish we could go faster."

"We will get there soon enough," Beatha replied. "Don't take your bad temper out on anyone else. They have left their homes because you asked them to."

Calgacus inhaled deeply, calming the rage that burned inside him. He was angry because Venutius, who had haunted his steps for thirty years, had found him again. He was angry because he should be leading the war against Rome but was being compelled to travel north to confront Maelchon, and he was angry because he had been forced to abandon his home. Most of all, though, he was angry because some of the villagers had refused to leave their homes.

He corrected himself. The villagers had made their own choice, for their own reasons. What really irked him was that one of those who had elected to remain behind was his own son, Togodumnus.

"I am not coming with you," the young man had declared. "We have nothing to fear from Rome if we do not resist them. There is no reason why we should not offer them friendship instead of war."

"Rome has no friends," Calgacus retorted angrily. "Rome only has subjects."

It was an old argument; one they had had many times before. Togodumnus had never agreed with him and did not do so now.

"We are no threat to Rome," the boy insisted, gesturing at the dozen or so people who had decided not to leave.

"Will you turn your back on us, then?" Calgacus demanded. "Will you help the Romans against us? Against your own people?"

"It is not a question of that," Togodumnus declared. "Befriending Rome does not mean we must make enemies of anyone else."

"You don't know the Romans," Calgacus spat.

Beatha had stepped in, calming them. She had spoken earnestly to Togodumnus but the young man had refused to change his mind. With tears and embraces, Beatha had reluctantly left him and joined the convoy that was heading inland in search of sanctuary.

112

"He is old enough to make up his own mind," she told Calgacus in a voice that was thick with emotion. "I don't like it any more than you do, but we will only make things worse if we try to force him to come with us."

"Let's hope he doesn't live to regret his decision," Calgacus muttered. "Come on, we need to keep moving."

While Calgacus' column of refugees forged inland, five war galleys of the Imperial Roman Navy edged their way into the wide estuary of the Tava, oars rising and falling in unison, the decks crowded with heavily-armed soldiers.

Standing at the high stern of the leading vessel, Sdapezi surveyed the shore with an anxious eye.

"What do you see?" Venutius asked him.

"Nothing."

"They must have seen us by now," the Brigante observed nervously.

"What are you so worried about?" Sdapezi snapped. "This was your idea in the first place." He paused, his lips turning up in a sneer at Venutius' concern. "Don't tear your hair out. My orders are to keep you safe, so we'll stay well back and let the Marines go in first."

"Into a trap?" Venutius asked. "Calgacus may not be there, but his men can easily set off those landslides you saw."

Sdapezi gave a helpless shrug.

"Tell that to the Tribune," he sighed.

Aulus Atticus was near the prow, the very image of a Roman hero in his armour and red cloak, his plumed helmet gleaming in the afternoon sun. He was giving orders to the commander of the Marines, a burly veteran by the name of Publius Marius Quadratus. He was listening to the Tribune in gloomy silence, nodding his head occasionally, and looking as if he wanted to pick up the young officer and heave him into the sea.

Sdapezi could sympathise with Quadratus' sentiment. He had lost his own argument with the Tribune, who had ignored the Governor's injunction to heed Sdapezi's advice. Over-ruling both Sdapezi and Quadratus, Atticus had decided to make a frontal assault on Calgacus' homestead.

"Boldness is the key to victory," he told them earnestly, emphasising his decision by punching a fist into his open palm.

Sdapezi argued, "The hill is a death trap. There are rocks and fallen trees that can sweep us away if the barbarians let them loose. We should land further up the coast and approach the village from a different direction."

"Who is to say there are not equally formidable defences on the other approaches?" Atticus countered. "And landing further up the coast would mean a long march over unfamiliar territory."

Quadratus had tried to back Sdapezi, but the Tribune had been adamant.

"The forest will provide cover for us," he insisted. "If the Britons loose their rockslides, we can shelter behind the trees."

"It will also provide cover for the Britons," Sdapezi argued. "We should at least send scouts up the hill first."

"That would only give the enemy time to prepare," Atticus countered. "They will see our ships as it is. No, we must attack swiftly, with no hesitation. Our men are more than a match for a handful of barbarians. Remember that Calgacus has taken the bulk of the warriors away. We will be faced by old men and young boys."

Sdapezi was forced to concede that the Tribune had a point. What riled him was the man's haughty attitude, talking down to them as if he were an experienced general addressing raw recruits. He hoped the Tribune's assessment of the situation was correct because, if he were wrong, Quadratus' Marines would be walking into a deadly trap. For

114

his own part, Sdapezi was grateful that it would be Quadratus' men who would be leading the way.

Not that the prospect appeared to concern the Marines too much. Quadratus himself may have been displeased but his marines were keyed up by the chance to gain some plunder. They were also amused by Atticus' attempts to encourage them with a rousing speech. Standing on the open deck, he had harangued them at length, quoting examples of Roman victories from the past. His pompous words certainly raised the men's morale, but it was more because they were secretly laughing at him than because of his skill at oratory.

"The boy thinks he is Julius Caesar," Quadratus grumbled to Sdapezi. "Let's hope he's right about the place being poorly defended."

"He probably is," Sdapezi admitted, "but it could still be a tough nut to crack."

He looked up at the ridge on the northern bank of the wide river. A forest of trees barred their way, with the stockade virtually indistinguishable unless he looked carefully. It nestled on the skyline, blending in with the treetops. That was remarkable in itself, because most chieftains liked to have prominent homes that were visible from a great distance, showing off their power and influence. It was a reminder that Calgacus was no ordinary chieftain.

"Tell your lads to spread out when they climb the hill," Sdapezi advised Quadratus.

The Marine pulled a face. "That won't please the Tribune. He wants us to advance in close order."

"Through a forest?"

Quadratus chuckled, "He's in for a bit of a shock. Don't worry. We know what we're doing. The lads are looking forward to a fight."

Venutius butted in, "Just make sure they know not to harm any of the women. We need to take Calgacus' wife back with us. Once I've identified her, you can kill all the others."

115

"There's no profit in killing," Quadratus growled, irritated by the Briton's intervention. "Better to take slaves."

"These are Calgacus' people," Venutius stated. "It would be better to kill them all. But not Calgacus' wife. We need her alive."

"I know that," snapped Quadratus.

"We all know what to do," Sdapezi said, trying to pacify the Marine commander.

He shot Venutius a dark look as he added, "You just stick close to me and let Quadratus and his lads do their duty."

Venutius gave a surly nod, then there was no more time to argue because Atticus was calling for Quadratus to ready the men. The Centurion bustled away, barking commands at his Marines, who braced themselves for the landing.

The galleys headed for the beach directly below the stockade that was perched high above them. Driven on by the oarsmen, the bronze-capped rams dug into the sand, bringing the ships to a jarring halt.

Sdapezi clung to the deck rail to prevent himself falling. He turned to the dozen troopers he had brought with him.

"Wait until the Marines are ashore," he told them.

Quadratus' men were already leaping down from the deck, splashing through the shallows, scrambling onto the narrow strip of sand and clambering up onto the grass foreshore. Quadratus bellowed orders, the men spread into a long, ragged line, abandoning their usual close order, and ran across the grass towards the foot of the forested slope.

Aulus Atticus had wanted to lead the way, but he stumbled as he landed on the beach, and the Marines swept past him, leaving him to hurry after them as best he could.

Gripping Venutius' arm, Sdapezi ushered the Briton to the prow.

116

"Time for us to go," he said. "This was your idea, so you can see it through."

Chapter X

Togodumnus watched the ships with growing trepidation. All his life he had been convinced that his father was wrong about the Romans. Now, as he watched the soldiers pour ashore and begin the steep climb to the stockade, he felt doubt gnawing at his insides.

The stockade was eerily quiet. Usually full of noise and bustle, only a handful of people had remained behind, and Togodumnus felt strangely alone. He had always felt apart, for he had never been good at the warcraft the other boys enjoyed, but he had never been alone. There had always been people around him.

He had made up his mind to remain here, knowing it was the right decision for him, but knowing, too, how much it had cost his mother to leave him. She had begged him to join the others in their mountain retreat, but he had been convinced it was time to make a stand.

It was not the first time that he had defied his father. Calgacus had tried to teach him the art of war, had given him a sword and spear when he was fourteen years old, and encouraged him to learn how to use them.

"You are descended from Kings and War Leaders," his father had informed him gravely. "One day, you will be a chieftain and you must learn how to fight."

Togodumnus had tried, because it was not easy to oppose his father's will, but he had quickly discovered that he possessed no aptitude for weaponry. His attempts to wield a sword only served to make him look awkward and foolish.

"Using a sword is like any skill," his father had explained. "Watch any man who is an expert at what he does, whether he is a fisherman, a potter or a blacksmith, and you will see that his actions are made with confidence. The same applies in war. Don't wave your sword around hoping to do some damage. Hope is not enough. You must believe that every stroke is going to kill your opponent."

"How can I become confident?" Togodumnus had asked anxiously, eyeing his small sword as if it might bite him.

"Through practice. That is the only way. But be careful. You must find the balance between confidence and arrogance. Over-confidence is as bad as no confidence at all."

Togodumnus did his best but, try as he might, he could not master the skills required to wield a sword effectively. Had it not been for the fact that he was Calgacus' son, some of the bruises and cuts he received from the other boys during their practice bouts would have been far worse, but most of the boys were careful not to hurt him too badly. As it was, he often had to fight back tears of frustration and humiliation when he was bested by even the most hapless of the would-be warriors. Worse, he knew that his father was disappointed in him. For a man like Calgacus, who was huge, powerful and fast, it was impossible to understand how his son could be so inept at fighting.

His lack of skill was a burden. Among the Pritani, especially the fierce northern tribes, martial prowess was the measure of a man. The tribes were ruled by the strongest, for a weak chieftain would not be able to protect his land or people. Weak leaders were soon deposed or killed by stronger men. Togodumnus knew this, but knowing it could not turn him into something he was not. At his core, he knew he was no warrior, and that knowledge was the catalyst for his growing differences of opinion with his father.

Despite his failings, he had inherited some strength, although it was perhaps the inner strength that his mother possessed, rather than the raw willpower of his father. He had

119

eventually summoned the courage to confront Calgacus and tell him that he no longer wished to learn the art of war.

"What do you want to do then?" Calgacus had asked, his eyes unable to conceal his disappointment.

Togodumnus had expected anger, for his father was famed for a short temper. Somehow, though, Calgacus' disappointment was worse. Nervous but undeterred, Togodumnus steeled himself and recited his rehearsed speech.

"I want to learn how to speak Latin. I want to learn how to read. I want to study the world, to learn about caring for our livestock, how to grow the best crops. I want to learn how to work metal, how to carve wood, and how to build things. I want to know how to make life better for everyone, not just the tribal leaders."

"That is quite a list," Calgacus had observed reflectively.

"It is no less than a chieftain should know," the fourteen-year-old Togodumnus had replied as confidently as he could. "My uncle, whom you named me after, would have approved."

That was the argument that always defeated Calgacus. The man he admired above all others was his long-dead older brother, Togodumnus, one-time King of the two tribes of the Catuvellauni and Trinovantes. The older Togodumnus had been more interested in trade and farming than in fighting, and he had made the two tribes wealthy.

"Your namesake was also prepared to fight when the need arose," Calgacus had replied.

"But only when all else had failed," Beatha had put in, supporting her son. "It would do no harm for Togodumnus to learn these things. They are noble aims."

To Togodumnus' delight, his father had agreed, although with the proviso that he still spend one day each week practising with sword and spear.

120

So Togodumnus had become a scholar. He already had a smattering of Latin, because his mother was fluent, having spent many years living among the Romans. Now, she tutored him. She also knew how to read, and he quickly grasped the concept. The main problem was the lack of material to read, until Beatha somehow managed to persuade one of the infrequent traders who occasionally sailed into the Tava, to bring a box of scrolls from the south. When Togodumnus opened the box, he was astonished to find that the scrolls were copies of a famous Roman book.

"The Aeneid!" he exclaimed, his eyes wide with delight.

And so he learned of the glory of Rome, and his mind was filled with the desire to meet these wonderful people who had achieved so much. He was always first to the beach whenever a trading ship arrived. He would pester the merchants for news of what was happening far to the south, and would spend hours talking to them, practising his Latin and learning all he could. His father never spoke to these visitors, preferring not to reveal his identity, so Togodumnus soon adopted the role of spokesman for the village, pretending to the outside world that, despite his youth, he was the chieftain.

That was why he had been pleased to speak to the Emissary, the man who introduced himself as Venutius. Togodumnus recognised the name, of course. He could not fail to know it from the stories his father had told over the years, but he found the version his father had presented difficult to reconcile with the well-spoken, urbane man who promised friendship and wealth to any who would befriend Rome.

He had not been unaware of the barely suppressed anger of his mother and old Garco, but Togodumnus had decided that the stories he had heard must have been exaggerated. The Venutius who had sat opposite him, drinking beer and sharing bread, chatting openly, conversing in Brythonic and Latin with equal ease, was a clever, refined, and persuasive man.

He could see that man again now, climbing the hill, surrounded by Roman soldiers. He recognised the Centurion who had accompanied Venutius only two days earlier, but he also recognised that, this time, they had come with more deadly intent than on their previous visit, because they were preceded by a host of grim-faced soldiers who swarmed up the wooded slope towards the stockade.

Togodumnus had ordered the gates to be opened. He stood, alone, in the entranceway, while the few people who remained in the settlement cowered inside or hurried down the far slope to the main village, unwilling to face the hard-eyed Roman soldiers.

Togodumnus had assured them that his father was wrong, that Rome was no threat to those who offered no resistance. Now, seeing the swords and shields, the brutal toughness of the men who were climbing the hill, those assurances sounded naive and hollow.

"There is nothing to fear," he told himself as he spread his arms wide to show that he was unarmed.

The Roman soldiers advanced through the trees, edging cautiously into the open space on the slope immediately below the stockade. They were cruel-eyed, brutish men, not at all like the Romans Togodumnus had encountered before. Sweating from the exertion of the steep climb, these men held their shields high, gripped their short swords, and scanned the palisade for signs of a trap. They were keyed up, expecting a fight, and more than ready for violence.

"Welcome!" Togodumnus called, his voice sounding shrill and frightened as it echoed through the trees. "There is no need for your swords. There are no enemies here."

A young officer stepped into view, resplendent in plumed helmet and red cloak, a glistening sword in his right hand. His face was flushed with exertion from the steep climb, but his manner was harsh as he signalled to the soldiers to remain where they stood.

"Who are you?" he demanded, pointing his sword at Togodumnus.

"My name is Togodumnus."

"Come here."

The command was insolent and peremptory, but Togodumnus knew he had no choice. Slowly, he walked to meet the Roman. As soon as he was within a few paces, the Tribune waved his sword, gesturing to the soldiers.

"Search the place! Bring everyone out here. Kill any who resist."

"What are you doing?" Togodumnus gasped in alarm. "We are your friends!"

"This is the home of Calgacus, is it not?" the Tribune retorted. "He is no friend of ours."

"He is not here!" protested Togodumnus.

He whirled to seek Venutius, who had just emerged from the trees, his eyes wary.

"Venutius! Tell him I am your friend!" Togodumnus shouted.

To his dismay, the Brigante regarded him coldly.

"Your father is a known renegade," he spat. "He is no friend of mine. Did you really think we would leave you here unmolested while your father leads the rebellion?"

"But you said Rome did not desire war!" Togodumnus insisted, feeling his face flush as he realised how badly he had misjudged the Brigante Emissary.

"Rome desires peace," Venutius replied, "but on Roman terms. Your father has always refused those terms."

Cries of terror and anguish made Togodumnus turn. He saw soldiers shoving frightened men and women out through the gates.

A burly, mean-looking Centurion informed the Tribune, "The place is almost empty. There's a village down the slope, but it looks abandoned, too."

"Send a patrol to make sure," the Tribune commanded. "If there are any people, bring them here."

"Sir!" the Centurion acknowledged, turning away to bellow commands to the Marines.

"What are you going to do with us?" Togodumnus demanded, appalled by the Tribune's orders.

The officer answered, "Our instructions are to take your mother back with us. Where is she?"

"She has gone. Nearly everyone has gone."

"Gone where?"

"Into the hills."

Togodumnus regarded the Roman with a weary sigh of resignation as he explained, "My father guessed you would come, so he took everyone away to a safe place. I did not believe him, so I stayed. It seems I was wrong."

Venutius gave a harsh, mocking laugh.

"A fatal error of judgement," he grinned. Turning to the Tribune, he said, "You should kill them all. That will show everyone that Calgacus cannot defend his own home. His position as War Leader will be undermined at a stroke."

Togodumnus felt the shock of the Brigante's words like a blow to his stomach. He shouted, "No! You cannot do that. These people have done nothing to you. They stayed when the others left because they believed you would not harm them."

"I have my orders," the Tribune shrugged.

"You should make an example of him," Venutius suggested. "Crucify him. That will send a strong message to the barbarians."

Togodumnus felt his knees tremble, and his stomach lurch. He gaped at Venutius, unable to articulate his horror at the callous suggestion the Brigante had made so casually.

Then the other Centurion, the older one with the weary face and slightly battered armour, took a step forwards, catching the Tribune's attention.

"Sir, does the Governor not want Calgacus' family taken back unharmed?"

The Tribune frowned uncertainly, but Venutius interrupted, "He wants Calgacus' wife. Not this whelp."

The Centurion persisted, "But she is not here. Perhaps Calgacus' son could be of use to us instead. He would make a good hostage."

The Tribune continued to vacillate, frowning uncertainly, his eyes darting from one man to the other.

The Centurion pressed, "It would also be better to leave these others alive, Sir. Killing or enslaving them only creates more resistance from other barbarians. Better to let them go. That way, they can spread the news that we have destroyed Calgacus' home and they will also be more hungry mouths for the Britons to feed."

Venutius spat his scorn.

"You are growing soft, Sdapezi," he grunted sourly.

The Tribune said doubtfully, "The Governor ordered me to kill everyone."

"That was when he thought there would be an entire village," Sdapezi argued. "The situation has changed."

Togodumnus, desperate to save the lives of his people, blurted, "Spare them and I will come with you freely."

"You'll come with us anyway," mocked Venutius. "Unless Tribune Atticus sees sense and has you executed as an example to your fellow barbarians."

"I was not speaking to you," Togodumnus rasped. "You are not a true Roman, and your words are driven by hatred of my father. You can see no further than your own petty desire for blood and vengeance."

Venutius' face contorted in a grimace of fury, but Sdapezi hastily agreed, "Since when did our hostages make our decisions for us? We came to find Calgacus' wife but she is not here. We should burn the place and take this lad back with us. Let the others go to spread the news. We gain

125

nothing by killing a few unarmed men and women, and the more of them we leave alive, the quicker the word will spread that Calgacus' home has been destroyed."

Togodumnus added, "I have always opposed my father's resistance to Rome. I want to be a friend of the Empire. These people were prepared to befriend you. If you kill them, all you are doing is proving that my father is right about Rome. Is that really how you treat your friends?"

The boy is right," Sdapezi urged. "Why should we do Calgacus' work for him? I don't mind killing fighting men, but murdering helpless villagers like these only adds weight to what Calgacus tells his warriors."

Venutius snorted, "Do as you please. I really don't care."

At last, Tribune Atticus made his decision. He waved a hand to the commander of the Marines.

"Centurion Quadratus!"

"Sir?"

"Let these people go."

"As you command," Quadratus frowned, clearly annoyed at the loss of some potential slaves whose sale could provide some additional income.

"Tell your men to bring out anything of value from the houses, then to burn the settlement. Return to the ships as soon as possible."

Atticus said to Togodumnus, "Come. I will take you to see the Governor. He can decide what to do with you."

Togodumnus turned to the bewildered villagers.

"They are letting you go free," he told them, "but they are taking me as a hostage. Find my father and tell him what has happened."

There was no more time. Two of Sdapezi's soldiers moved behind him and ushered him down the path towards the beach. Indignantly brushing them off, he glared at Venutius as he passed him.

"I will not forget this," he rasped.

126

Venutius replied coldly, "You are a bigger fool than your father. It's not you I want dead, boy. It's him. You are nothing to me."

Atticus interrupted, "That's enough. Centurion Sdapezi, take them both back to the ship. And keep them apart."

Togodumnus had no more protests. Only his anger at himself for believing Venutius' lies allowed him to hold his head high as he was led down the winding path. When he boarded the galley, he looked back to the hilltop and saw the plumes of smoke already rising into the clear sky, destroying the last of his dreams.

Chapter XI

Facilis could not eat the broth that the Usipi served up. Thrax, more accustomed to desperation, had no such scruples and supped at the small portion they were served.

"When you've been shipwrecked as often as I have," he declared, "you can get used to anything. I've seen men drink their own urine before now."

Antonius Pulcher, Quaestor of Rome, also put aside his disgust and accepted a bowl of human broth.

"It tastes a bit like pork," he announced gloomily.

Facilis felt his empty stomach lurch at the thought, but restricted himself to drinking water from the nearby stream and chewing on a couple of bitter-tasting dandelion leaves which the Usipi had gathered from the woods that surrounded their campsite.

The Usipi may have resorted to eating one of their own, but there was still not enough food to provide more than a few mouthfuls of broth for each man. The big German, Fullofaudes, sent men inland to hunt for other sources of food. These men returned with a couple of scrawny chickens which they had caught at a village they found a short distance upstream, but their prize was obtained at a cost. Two of the men were wounded, one of them seriously, his arm having been almost severed by a British sword.

"He'll be next for the cooking pot," Thrax predicted with morbid humour.

The Captain's prediction was soon proved correct. The man died during the night and the Usipi instantly set about butchering him to cook another meal.

Yet the men were still hungry, in need of far more sustenance. The long days of rowing with scarcely anything to eat had taken their toll. Facilis thought the Usipi resembled walking skeletons. They were thin, their eyes sunk in cadaverous skulls, and although Fullofaudes pushed them as hard as he dared, they were too weak for anything except the lightest work.

As a consequence of their weak state, the repairs to the damaged galley took four days, far longer than they should have. Even then, Thrax was disparaging about the quality of the work.

"They may be able to fell trees, but they are hopeless at sawing planks," he muttered. "That patchwork won't hold up in a strong sea."

"At least we can get going again in the morning," Facilis said when the work was at last completed just as the sun was setting on the fourth day of their enforced stop.

"If the Britons let us live that long," Thrax grunted grimly. "I can't see them leaving us in peace much longer, not after those stupid buggers went and killed some of the locals for a couple of chickens."

"I think the Britons are the least of our problems," said Facilis, nodding to the centre of the camp where another furious argument was raging among the Usipi. Once again it was Necrautis and Fullofaudes who were doing the shouting.

"I don't like the look of this," Facilis whispered. "They are pointing at us far too often."

"What are they saying?" Pulcher hissed in a terrified voice.

Facilis could make little sense of the harsh, guttural snarls of the Germanic language, but he did not need to understand the words to know what was being said.

"At a guess, I'd say some of them want us as their next meal."

Pulcher's sallow face paled and his eyes bulged in horror.

"They cannot do that!" he protested. "We are Roman citizens."

"We are a long way from Rome," Facilis replied despondently.

He felt light-headed from hunger, as if he were detached from his surroundings. He knew this voyage of horror was real, yet a part of him insisted that he was a mere spectator, that events would not touch him. He was jerked back to reality when Fullofaudes stalked over to stand in front of where the three prisoners huddled on the ground near the stream.

"What is happening?" Thrax asked the Usipi chieftain.

Fullofaudes' face was pale and drawn. A stubbly beard covered his chin and cheeks, and his eyes held a haunted look, as if he were beset by demons. He stooped to check their bonds, then slowly eased himself up again, moving with the slowness of a man three times his age.

He told them, "I will set trusted men to watch over you tonight."

"Can you trust any of them?" Facilis countered. "They are starving and desperate."

"We will be leaving as soon as it is light," Fullofaudes replied evasively. His eyes refused to meet Facilis' gaze as he spoke, and he glanced furtively around the firelit clearing, as if expecting to be attacked at any moment.

Facilis could see the hungry desperation in the expressions of the Usipi who clustered round the fires. There was fear there, too, he realised. Two men had been butchered to provide food for the rest, but there is not much meat on a man, not enough to feed all the Usipi.

Facilis looked up at Fullofaudes.

"Are we going to be next?" he asked.

Fullofaudes gave a curt shake of his head.

"I told them that we need Thrax to pilot us home and we need the Quaestor as a hostage in case we run across the Roman fleet."

"What about me?" Facilis asked, astonished at how calm he felt.

"Two hostages are better than one," the German replied weakly. "You know the Governor and you speak the British tongue. You may prove useful."

"Look at your men," Facilis told him. "They have already taken the first step. Eating human flesh is easy for them now, but they are all wondering who will be next. Can't you see how terrified they are of falling sick? Any man who is ill or injured is likely to be killed now. But we are not Usipi, so they will want to kill us first, whatever you say."

"I told them to draw lots if they really want to eat each other," Fullofaudes informed him, showing a flash of his former confidence. "That shut them up for a while."

Once again, he scanned the firelit clearing. Men looked away when his eyes fell on them, guilt and shame momentarily overcoming their hunger.

Facilis went on, "You should sail south and surrender as soon as we reach the army. I will speak up for you."

Fullofaudes gave a snort.

"You know Roman justice. They will crucify us."

"Perhaps not. I could speak to the Governor. They might content themselves with making an example of only a few men."

"Including me," Fullofaudes retorted. "You are doing a poor job of convincing me."

"Would it be any worse than what you are suffering now?" Facilis challenged.

"I am still alive. I am still in command here. Our ships are repaired. We can still escape."

"What about us?"

"I will keep you alive as long as I can," Fullofaudes replied without conviction.

Facilis gave a slight nod, although he did not feel comforted by the German's assurances. Fullofaudes was only one man, and the Usipi were beyond desperation now. He tried to think of something else to say, anything that would help preserve his life, but the only thought that occurred to him was that there was more meat on Pulcher than on him and Thrax combined. Facilis winced at the unworthy thought, telling himself that his own hunger and fear had brought it to his mind. But if he could contemplate such horrors, what were the savage Usipi thinking?

"We are more valuable alive than dead," he told Fullofaudes again.

"I know that," the German grunted. "But ..."

His voice trailed off into the night, and he turned away from them with a resigned shrug.

"Jupiter, Best and Greatest," begged Pulcher. "Save us from these barbarians!"

Facilis whispered agreement to the Quaestor's prayer. The Gods had rarely done anything to help him, but still he prayed. There was nothing else he could do.

Men were looking at Fullofaudes as he returned to the nearest fire. Some of them hissed angry responses to his words, others looked away and stared into the flames in front of them, while many cast furtive, covetous glances at the three prisoners.

"Oh, shit," murmured Thrax as Necrautis pushed himself to his feet and began arguing again, his hand pointing at the three captives.

Facilis watched in horror as other men rose unsteadily to their feet, their hands drawing daggers from their belts. He felt sick with hunger and fear, knowing that he could not escape. Tied hand and foot, he was helpless.

Pulcher closed his eyes and muttered fervent prayers.

Fullofaudes was roaring at the Usipi, shoving some of them back, waving his arms furiously. But he could not confront all of them. To Facilis' horror, the dark-featured

132

Necrautis drew his sword and began walking towards the three prisoners.

Pulcher wailed aloud, his cry of alarm warning Fullofaudes. The big German whirled, cursed, and ran after Necrautis, shouting angrily.

Facilis watched in mesmerised horror as Necrautis spun round, swinging his sword to fend off Fullofaudes. It was a clumsy blow, weakened by hunger, and Fullofaudes dodged aside, allowing the blade to sweep past his belly. Then his hand lashed out, his fist crashing into the side of Necrautis' head. Necrautis staggered but did not fall. He tried to hack at Fullofaudes again, but this time Fullofaudes had his own sword ready. He blocked the cut, then stabbed forwards, driving his blade into Necrautis' chest, shouting with rage as he thrust the sword home.

Barely five paces from where Facilis lay helpless, Necrautis crumpled to the ground, his sword falling from lifeless fingers, his chest a mass of blood and gore.

Pulcher gasped as the Usipi stood still, turned to stone by the sudden, violent death.

Fullofaudes turned to face them, shouting a contemptuous stream of harsh words which Facilis interpreted as, "Now, you can eat him!"

A shocked silence fell over the camp. For a long, dreadful moment, nobody moved.

Then a man screamed somewhere in the night.

Chapter XII

The Usipi camp exploded in uproar as ferocious yells echoed through the darkness. Men leaped up, grabbing for their weapons as their sentries came stumbling back into the firelight, calling frantic warnings.

"We are under attack!"

Fullofaudes' stentorian bellows brought some semblance of order as men rushed to face the unexpected assault, their weakness temporarily forgotten as they formed a ragged line, peering fearfully into the darkness beyond the camp from where a storm of war cries was sending a howling promise of death.

Facilis could hear the sounds of fighting from beyond the blazing fires, but he could make out nothing except the dark shapes of the Usipi as they scrambled to form a defensive line. Fullofaudes and his men had reacted quickly, but most of them had left their shields and armour on the ships, and they were debilitated by hunger and exhaustion. Facilis had no idea how many Britons were attacking them, but he reckoned the Usipi would have no option other than to fall back to the galleys and try to escape.

He nudged Thrax.

"This is our chance," he hissed. Nodding towards the fallen corpse of Necrautis, he said, "He's got a sword. Let's cut our ropes."

Thrax needed no second invitation. The Usipi had forgotten about them, and they were facing away from the stream, battling against what seemed to be hundreds of howling, bloodthirsty barbarians.

Pulcher was praying again, but Facilis and Thrax wriggled and squirmed across the ground to where Necrautis had fallen. They found his sword lying beside his body. Fumbling awkwardly, hampered because his hands were tied behind his back, Thrax managed to pick up the sword. He wedged it against the ground while Facilis, sitting back to back with him, felt for the blade.

His fingers were numbed by the bonds that fastened his wrists, but he had no time to worry about anything other than cutting himself free. Risking slicing into a vital artery, he began to rub the ropes against the sharp blade.

"Hurry!" urged Thrax.

Facilis sawed his arms, feeling the ropes suddenly sag. He jerked away, thrashing his hands free. In an instant, he turned, took the sword and sliced at the ropes binding his ankles, then he cut Thrax's bonds. He could feel warm, sticky blood trickling from a cut on his arm, but he did not care. Driven by desperation, he sawed Thrax free.

"Take the sword," he told the Captain. "Free Pulcher."

Thrax scramble to obey. Facilis moved to the body of Necrautis, feeling for the man's dagger. He drew it from the belt, then scurried to join the others.

"The Usipi are falling back," Thrax said in alarm. "Which way do we go?"

"Across the stream!" Facilis hissed. "Get into the trees."

Behind them, the battle raged, but it was clear that the Usipi were suffering. Fullofaudes' booming voice could still be heard, but men were already running for the galleys, preparing to shove them off the beach. Briefly, Facilis wondered whether the tide would allow them to refloat the ships. If the tide had gone out, the galleys would be stranded and the Usipi would have no escape.

But that did not matter. What mattered was that they were free.

The three fugitives splashed across the shallow stream and plunged into the dense thicket on the far side.

Branches and thorns clawed at them, but Thrax used the short sword to hack a path into the darkness of the woods.

"What do we do if there are more Britons in here?" Pulcher wailed.

"Pray that there aren't," Facilis told him. "Now, shut up and keep moving."

From behind them, they heard the sounds of battle, but it was more distant now, muted by the woods that lay between them and the camp.

"Keep going!" Facilis urged, as Thrax continued to blaze a trail through the stygian gloom of the forest.

Facilis had no idea how long or how far they walked. It was slow going, feeling around in the inky blackness, tripping over roots, bumping into trees, and all the time listening for any sounds of pursuit. There were none, and soon even the sounds of the Usipi shouting to one another faded into the distance.

Pulcher fell to the ground, gasping with exhaustion.

"I can't go any further," he complained, his voice weak and barely audible.

"Maybe we've come far enough," Facilis agreed. "Let's rest here until morning."

They lay down in the darkness, seeking the most comfortable spots. As soon as they stopped, Facilis felt himself shivering. The effort of making their escape had tired him more than he had realised and now that the euphoria of nervous energy had worn off, he wanted nothing more than to fall asleep, but his exhausted body was cold, and he had no cloak to keep off the chill of the night. He burrowed down under a low bush, closed his eyes and tried to rest.

Despite the cold, he must have slept because the next thing he knew, warm sunlight was filtering through the green branches of the forest, and birds were singing and chirping in the trees. Groaning, he pushed himself up on his elbows and looked around.

Their resting place was indistinguishable from any other part of the forest, just a small space between the crowding trees, surrounded by undergrowth that was so dense he could not see more than twenty paces in any direction.

Thrax was already awake. Walking on painfully thin legs, he came to stand over Facilis.

"I found some food," he said, holding out his hand to reveal a clutch of stringy fronds with pale flowers at the tips.

Facilis eyed the offering dubiously.

"Are they safe to eat?"

"I think it's cow parsley," Thrax shrugged.

"You think? What if it's not?"

Thrax gave another shrug.

"Does it really matter? But I had some a while ago and I'm still alive."

Facilis tentatively accepted the plants and nibbled at them, grimacing at the sharp taste. His stomach gurgled but did not protest too much, so he continued to chew and swallow the meagre breakfast.

While Facilis was eating, Thrax poked Pulcher with his foot until the Quaestor woke up.

"I'm hungry," Pulcher complained sleepily.

"Have some parsley," offered Thrax.

Pulcher's expression showed his disgust at the offering, but he accepted the plants without question and gratefully bit into the fronds.

"Is there anything to drink?" he asked.

"Not unless you want to drink your own piss," Thrax grinned.

Pulcher declined the suggestion.

"Come on," Facilis told them. "Let's get moving."

"Where are we going?" Pulcher wanted to know.

"South. That's where the army is."

"But we have no food, and it could take days to reach them."

"Stay here if you like," Facilis shrugged. "I'm going to try."

He set off, following the easiest route through the wood, trying to steer towards the sun as best he could. He heard the sounds of movement behind him and knew that the others were following.

"You're a survivor, right enough," Thrax grinned as he drew alongside. "The Gods must have some purpose for you."

"We are not safe yet," Facilis replied. "We have a long way to go, and the barbarians will probably kill us if they catch us."

"We should stay near the coast," Thrax suggested. "Maybe we could steal a boat and row home."

"Good idea," Facilis nodded. "But let's get further away from the camp site before we think about that. Now that it's light, the Britons will be able to see the trail we left."

That reminder gave them strength, and they pushed on, full of determination.

The ground ahead of them began to rise. Staggering and stumbling, they clawed their way up a low hill. From its wooded summit, they could see the smooth, brilliant mirror of the sea barely half a mile away, stretching to the distant horizon.

"Neptune save us!" breathed Thrax. "There are the bloody Usipi."

For a horrible moment, Facilis thought that their erstwhile captors had found them, but Thrax was pointing out to sea. When Facilis shaded his eyes against the reflective sparkle of the morning sun, he made out three ships inching slowly down the coast, their oars moving in tired, ragged sweeps.

"It looks as if they've decided to keep going," he observed. "I wonder whether they'll make it all the way home?"

"I doubt it," grunted Thrax. "Personally, I hope they sink and drown."

"At least they aren't looking for us," Facilis said with a tired smile.

"I suppose they'll have some food now," Thrax observed grimly. "I reckon a few of them must have been killed last night."

Facilis did not want to be reminded of the Usipi's feeding habits. He turned his back on the sea.

"Let's keep moving," he told the others.

Their progress was painfully slow. All three of them were weak from hunger, and Pulcher was unaccustomed to walking under any circumstances. Facilis had to walk behind the Quaestor to make sure he kept moving, leaving Thrax to lead the way.

They eventually emerged from the woodland, crossed a grassy plain, climbed another hill, then descended into another huge stretch of forest. Oak, elm, birch, larch, hazel and rowan seemed to cover most of this part of Britannia, but Facilis did not mind. The trees provided cover and they were able to gather dandelions on the way. The plant tasted bitter, but they knew by now that it was edible. They also found some birds' eggs which they ate raw. Whenever they found a stream, they lay down and drank as much as their shrunken stomachs could bear.

By mid-afternoon, the trees had thinned. They plodded on, resting frequently, but with Facilis constantly urging them to keep going for as long as they could.

"I've been in worse scrapes," Thrax repeated several times, using the words as a mantra to encourage himself to keep walking.

Then, from somewhere in the distance behind them, they heard the sound of baying dogs.

Somehow, the three Romans forced themselves into a shambling run. Pulcher was weeping, his sunken cheeks streaked by tears, his eyes blurred and full of terror.

"We can't outrun dogs!" he wailed.

"If we find another river, we can escape," Facilis gasped in reply, knowing it was a vain hope, but unwilling to give in to despair.

Thrax was up ahead, leaving them behind, still clutching the sword in his right hand. He reached another long line of trees, staggering and swaying, exhausted by the effort of running. Then he stopped, jerking to a sudden halt, raising his sword as if to ward off some unseen assailant.

Facilis heard the Captain's anguished shout, then he gaped in horror as Thrax staggered backwards and crashed to the ground, the shaft of a long spear protruding from his chest.

Even as Facilis' numbed mind struggled to comprehend what had happened, the woods came alive. Only a moment before, he had been desperate to reach the inviting stretch of trees which seemed to offer sanctuary from their pursuers, but now, almost without transition, the woods had become threatening as a menacing horde of armed men emerged from cover and rose to their feet.

Facilis watched in horror as figures leaped out from the trees, long-haired, savage warriors who brandished spears as they spread out to encircle the two surviving Romans.

The Quaestor slumped to his knees, groaning, begging for mercy.

Facilis felt unutterably weary, barely able to comprehend what was happening. Thrax was dead, killed in an instant, all his grim determination counting for nothing. One of the Britons was already crouching over his corpse, using a long knife to hack off his head as a trophy.

Mesmerised by the awful sight, Facilis could do nothing except stare in horror at the glinting spearpoints as the Britons closed in around them.

Chapter XIII

The journey across the mountains into the lands of the Taexali was uneventful. Calgacus and his war band had left the refugees from their village in the high, hidden corrie before continuing northwards across the rugged, trackless wilderness of the high country.

"They'll be fine," Runt assured him. "There's good grazing in the valley, and there are deer in the high pastures, so they won't go hungry. They've got fresh water, and there's plenty of wood to build houses."

"The soil's not so good for planting barley and oats, though," Calgacus frowned. "Next year could be a hungry one."

Runt grinned, "I'll be happy if we live long enough to see next year. In fact, I'll be happy if we survive until tomorrow. Bridei was right, you know. Maelchon could be planning to hand you over to the Romans."

"That's a chance we must take," shrugged Calgacus. "But from what I remember of Maelchon, he's no friend of Rome. The Taexali have always been proud of their independence."

"I suppose that's true. But how are you going to persuade him to join us?"

"I haven't decided yet."

"Maybe you could try appealing to his better nature."

"You are assuming he has one."

"Good point," Runt conceded with a laugh. "Do you think Broichan was right about him? To me, it sounds like Maelchon is crazy."

"Broichan said he was eccentric and irrational. That's not the same as crazy."

"That's rich, coming from a druid. Maelchon is a King. I don't know any Kings who are entirely rational."

"I'm a King," Calgacus reminded his friend.

Runt laughed, "That proves my point, doesn't it?"

"You're not helping," Calgacus grunted through a reluctant grin. "How about some suggestions as to how we deal with Maelchon?"

Runt shrugged, "I suppose there is always the direct approach. Remember that mad bastard, Fiacha Cassan? He just marched into his enemy's hall and hacked his head off."

"I am not likely to forget," Calgacus replied. "He almost got us killed."

"The important word is *almost*."

Calgacus regarded his friend curiously.

"Are you seriously suggesting we walk into Maelchon's house and kill him?"

"Why not? The Taexali are a large tribe. There are bound to be quite a few men who dislike Maelchon and would be happy to take over. After all, he's reputed to be a nasty piece of work. According to Broichan, he spent years plotting against his own brother. He'll have made enemies."

Calgacus shook his head.

"You're the one who says I come up with crazy plans. That's just about the worst idea I've ever heard."

Runt smiled, "Are you telling me that you weren't considering it?"

"I suppose it may have briefly crossed my mind," Calgacus admitted with a grin.

"I thought so. I also thought you might forget to mention it, which is why I brought it up first, just so you'd realised how crazy it is."

"You've been around Broichan too much," Calgacus accused. "You're beginning to think like a druid."

"Maybe you should start thinking like one, too," Runt suggested. "You're going to have to come up with something clever to persuade Maelchon to join us. Whether he's mad or not, he wants to show everyone that he can make you crawl to him. If you do that, it will destroy your authority. He'll have won, and everyone will know it."

"I know," Calgacus grunted sourly.

"So, what are you going to do?"

"I'll think of something."

"You'd better think quickly, then. We're nearly there."

Maelchon's home was a large settlement, set on a ridge of high ground in a landscape of gently rolling hills and fertile lowlands. Fields, meadows and woodlands stretched out in every direction, roundhouses dotted the countryside, streams meandered across the fields, and the King's homestead dominated everything. Protected by a triple bank of deep ditches, with a high, earth wall that was topped by a tall palisade of thick timbers, the settlement was as large as any Calgacus had ever seen, containing dozens of roundhouses, stores and workshops. There were two wide entrances, each dominated by huge gates, and guarded by half a dozen spearmen.

The gates were closed, and the guards had obviously seen them approaching. Thirty armed men made a considerable force, and no village would take chances when so many potential enemies drew near. Calgacus could see men peering over the ramparts, spears in hand.

"Wait here," he commanded, holding up a hand to halt the war band. He turned to Adelligus. "Your father and I will go in. If this is a trap, it's better that only two of us walk into it. Wait until dusk. If we don't come out by then, go back and tell Broichan that Maelchon has betrayed us. Whatever you do, don't try to get us out. The war against Rome is more important than our safety."

Adelligus frowned, but he knew better than to argue.

"It will be as you say," he acknowledged.

"Then let's get this over with," Calgacus said to Runt.

Leaving the war band, the two of them rode up to the gates. Several men leaned over the ramparts to peer down at them. Calgacus recognised one of the men as Algarix, the shield-bearer with the squashed nose who had delivered Maelchon's message.

"The King said you would come," Algarix called down insolently.

"Yes, I have come. Now, open the bloody gates and let me speak to Maelchon."

Runt whispered, "You never were much of a diplomat, Cal. Getting angry won't make this easier."

"It will make me feel better," Calgacus growled. "And we need to let them know we are not afraid of them."

"Aren't we?"

"Of course not."

"That's good to know," Runt smiled. "I forgot that for a moment. Do you have a plan yet?"

"I'm working on it."

The gates swung open, revealing the stocky figure of Algarix, who stood in the wide entranceway, grinning at them. Four other warriors waited behind him.

"Leave your horses here," the shield-bearer told them. "Then follow me."

Calgacus and Runt dismounted, handing their horses into the care of the guards. Algarix gave a curt nod before turning and stalking into the village.

"Friendly chap," Runt observed quietly.

Calgacus nodded gravely. If Algarix's welcome was anything to go by, this meeting with Maelchon was going to prove every bit as difficult as he had feared. That sentiment was reinforced when the four swordsmen who accompanied Algarix took up position behind him and Runt, acting more like wardens than an honour guard

Calgacus concentrated on keeping his face expressionless as he followed the broad-shouldered shield-bearer through the settlement, ignoring the gawking looks, the whispers, the yapping of dogs, and the shouts of the excited children who darted alongside them.

The sounds, sights and smells of the village were the same as any settlement Calgacus had ever seen, but he noticed that there was an air of prosperity about the place. The women wore finely-made dresses and sported jewellery of gold, silver and bronze. The men looked fit and healthy, sharing the women's fondness for displaying wealth. They wore arm rings and finger rings, and their cloaks were fastened by large, ornate brooches. Most of the people looked well-fed, confirmation that this was a prosperous town.

The animals who shared the village, pigs and goats as well as dogs and cats, looked plump , which was a testament to the amount of feed the villagers had been able to store over the long, cold winter months.

The houses, too, were large and well-maintained, the thatched roofs in good condition and walls of daub scrubbed smooth and clean.

"Nice place," observed Runt in a low whisper. "Maelchon lives well."

He blew a kiss to a pretty young woman who was sitting in the open doorway of one of the houses, kneading dough on a large, flat stone. She returned a broad, teasing smile as they passed her.

"Very nice place," Runt murmured approvingly.

Calgacus grunted, "Let's hope Maelchon is as friendly."

"Just remember that killing him would not be a good idea," Runt warned. "I'd like to get out of here in one piece."

"Don't worry, I'll be careful."

"That will be a first," Runt grinned.

Algarix led them into a wide, open area in front of a large roundhouse, an imposing structure tall enough to accommodate two storeys, and with a circumference that dwarfed the dwellings that surrounded it. This was obviously the home of the King, but they did not need to enter the house because Maelchon was sitting outside, the focus of attention for a huge crowd of people who had gathered in the open space.

Calgacus took in the scene at a glance. Maelchon was seated on a large, high-backed chair that was carved with ornate, intricate designs. A small table sat in front of him, bearing a silver mixing bowl and a large, pewter mug. Standing on either side of the King, in the place of honour, were around forty armed men, dressed in fine clothes, bedecked with gold and silver jewellery, each of them wearing a sword. These, Calgacus knew, were the warriors of Maelchon's personal guard, tough men who knew how to use their swords.

With the rest of the villagers looking on, a handful of people waited in line to address their King. This, Calgacus realised, was a public meeting to witness the King of the Taexali dispensing justice. Claimants and petitioners would present their cases for judgement, and the King would pronounce his decisions for everyone to see.

"Wait your turn," Algarix instructed, gesturing for them to join the end of the queue before swaggering to take his place at the King's side.

"The arrogant bastard is making us wait," breathed Runt angrily.

"He's showing off," Calgacus agreed. His own temper was rising, but he tried not to show it. Under his breath, he told his friend, "We will wait. Everyone deserves a hearing. If we insist on jumping the queue, we'll only turn the crowd against us."

"Does that matter? It's Maelchon we need to convince."

"He's making this a public affair," said Calgacus. "Let's use that to help us."

While they waited, Calgacus studied Maelchon. The King of the Taexali was dark-haired, swarthy, with deep-set eyes that glinted in a face which had once been hard and

147

mocking but which now held a cruel edge. Maelchon was in his thirties now, and had gained weight since Calgacus had last seen him twelve years earlier. His face was podgy, with a double chin and fleshy jowls, his belly round and fat. The only resemblance to the lean, angry young man Calgacus had known was the spark in those hard, watchful eyes. What he did recognise was that Maelchon's stiff, upright stance and brooding expression radiated contempt for the petitioners who stood before him.

It was also apparent that, like many chieftains, Maelchon was eager to display his wealth. He wore a tunic with a diamond pattern of red, blue and yellow. A large, golden torc clung around his fleshy neck, and he wore a golden chain with a large amulet hanging on his chest. The seat of his chair was covered by a bearskin, and a jewelled dagger hung from a jewelled belt which encircled his broad waist.

He had obviously seen Calgacus and Runt, but he did not acknowledge them. Instead, he made a show of listening to the petitioners who came before him. He also turned his decisions into a performance, although Calgacus quickly realised that the judgements were unnecessarily harsh.

Two men who were in dispute over a flock of sheep were dismissed, with Maelchon confiscating the sheep for his own flocks. Then a man who had not settled a debt was sentenced to slavery, while another, accused of theft, was dragged away to have his hand cut off, despite his vociferous protestations of innocence.

"This doesn't look good," Runt whispered.

"We're not the only ones who don't like it," Calgacus replied softly. "Some of his warriors look uncomfortable about it."

The men who flanked Maelchon's chair were his war band, the elite warriors among the Taexali. Each would be an important man in his own right. Some, Calgacus knew, would revel in their status, would have no sympathy with the peasants who sought justice from the King, but others looked on with distaste because tribal law was generally more concerned with fines and recompense than with vengeful physical punishment. Maelchon's harsh rulings did not sit well with the more thoughtful warriors, and that gave Calgacus some hope. Still, they were Maelchon's sworn men, and Calgacus was a stranger, so every member of the war band was casting suspicious looks at him, clearly wondering what he intended to do when he addressed the King.

And then it was his turn.

Algarix beckoned him forwards.

"You may approach," he called in a condescending voice.

Maelchon flicked a hand to signal that Algarix should stand aside. As he did so, Calgacus caught sight of another item of ornate jewellery, one that he recognised instantly. On Maelchon's finger was a golden ring. Calgacus recognised it because it had once belonged to him. He had given it to Maelchon as part of the compensation he had paid when his daughter, Fulvia, had run off with another man on the evening before she was supposed to marry Maelchon. The ring, so some people believed, had magical powers, bringing good luck to the wearer. It certainly had not done Maelchon any harm, to judge from the opulence with which he surrounded himself.

The other thing the ring told Calgacus was that his first impression of Maelchon was correct. The ring, a band of gold with arcane symbols etched around its plain edge, was large enough to be worn on Calgacus' third finger, yet Maelchon's hand had grown so pudgy that it now adorned the little finger of his right hand.

Maelchon toyed with that ring now, twisting it slowly around his finger while his eyes studied Calgacus, who stood patiently, aware that a hushed silence had fallen over the watchful crowd.

149

After a long, deliberate pause, Maelchon drawled, "I knew you would come. I told my men that you needed us."

The warriors murmured in satisfaction, some of them grinning malevolently. Calgacus noted those men, knowing they would support the King in whatever he did. He also took notice of the men who appeared neutral, knowing he needed to impress them, to bring them round to his side.

I have come," he agreed. "Now, tell me what it is you want."

He heard a low murmur from the crowd, surprise at his insolent response.

The King's gaze flickered towards Runt, who had taken up position slightly behind Calgacus on his left side.

Maelchon scoffed, "I see you still have your dwarf with you. Where are the rest of your men?"

"Waiting outside," Calgacus replied defiantly. "They do not trust your hospitality."

He heard gasps of shock and surprise, saw some angry expressions on the faces of the warriors, but still he kept his gaze fixed on Maelchon.

The King barked, "Hospitality is given to welcome guests, Calgacus. You are not welcome."

"Then why did you insist that I come here when I should be with the war host that is preparing to protect you from the Romans, preparing to die to preserve our freedom while you sit here enjoying the sunshine?"

Maelchon's face darkened, the crowd murmured angrily, and Algarix rounded on Calgacus.

"Mind your tongue when you address our King!" the shield-bearer warned, taking a pace forwards and pointing an accusing finger at Calgacus. "You will pay for that insult."

Calgacus eyed the young man coldly as he replied, "I was not speaking to you, boy. I want to know why your King insisted I come here when we should all be fighting the invaders who are threatening every tribe."

150

Algarix glanced to Maelchon, but the King was staring at Calgacus, his eyes bulging furiously as he barked, "You know why! You wronged me, and I have not forgotten."

"I did not wrong you," Calgacus shot back. "And I paid you well for any insult my daughter offered."

"I want more!" Maelchon snapped. "You shamed me. Now you want me to help you fight the Romans, and you expect me to come running when you call, as if the Taexali are yours to command."

He leaned forwards, his eyes glinting furiously, his hands gripping the arms of his ornate chair so tightly that the knuckles were white.

He went on, "If you want my help, you will beg for it. You will crawl on your knees and plead with me."

Calgacus realised that Broichan had, if anything, understated Maelchon's state of mind. The King may not have been insane, but there was a hint of madness lurking in his baleful eyes. In some ways, that was a relief, because it meant that Bridei's fears about Maelchon plotting with the Romans were probably unfounded, but it also meant that Maelchon would be dangerously unpredictable.

Cautiously, Calgacus ventured, "I thought we had resolved our differences over my daughter, but if you still feel aggrieved, then I am prepared to make a public apology."

He paused before continuing, "But I will not beg you to join the alliance. Every tribe was invited, but none were compelled, except by the knowledge of the danger we face."

Maelchon's feral grin was transformed into a disbelieving stare. The entire village fell silent as if every man, woman and child were holding their breath, waiting to see how their King would respond.

For a long, tense moment, Maelchon continued to stare at Calgacus, then he sat back in his chair and waved a hand as if dismissing him as being of no consequence.

"You are an arrogant, stubborn man, Calgacus. But I know your tricks and your lies. If you are not prepared to beg for our aid, we will not help you. See how you get on without us."

A ripple of laughter ran round the spectators. It contained some scorn, but it also held more than a hint of relief, as if everyone had expected a more violent reaction from the King.

Calgacus did not care what the crowd thought. His long wait to speak to Maelchon had convinced him that meeting in public gave him the opportunity he required. Maelchon's desire to humiliate him in public meant that there were scores of other people Calgacus could influence.

The King, Calgacus thought, was like a petulant child, demanding recompense for a perceived slight. Years of brooding resentment had twisted Maelchon's character, and he realised that using rational argument to change the man's mind was unlikely to succeed, while using threats would only enrage him. But the relationship between a chieftain and his warriors was a complex one. These men would support Maelchon, would die for him if necessary, but he ruled them by consent, not through any divine right of leadership. That, Calgacus knew, was his best hope.

Speaking loudly and confidently, he declared, "I will not grovel, Maelchon. A War Leader does not behave like a slave. But I will ask again that you reconsider. It is true that we need your warriors, but it is also true that you need to join us for your own sakes."

The spectators fell silent again, and Maelchon's eyes narrowed suspiciously.

"What do you mean?" he demanded.

"I mean that the other tribes already view the Taexali with suspicion. They distrust your motives for not joining us."

"I care nothing for the other tribes," Maelchon snorted. "They are sheep."

"They are brave men who have vowed to oppose the invaders," Calgacus countered. "Whether you come with us or not, the other tribes will fight. Tell me, how will you feel if we defeat the Romans? What will the songs say of the Taexali if they are the only tribe who refused to fight? What glory will you gain by sitting at home while others shed their blood to defend you?"

His words had silenced the crowd, but Algarix stepped forwards to confront him again, seething with anger.

"You may not speak to our King like that!" he snapped.

Calgacus glared at the shield-bearer. He retorted, "I am a King, too, boy. I was a King when you were nothing but a spark in your father's eye. I have fought the Romans for longer than you have lived, so I think I have the right to speak to any man who would rather sit safely at home, gorging on meat and ale while others do the fighting."

Algarix snarled, "No man insults our King like that."

Maelchon's face was livid with rage as he shouted, "You are a King without a tribe, a King in exile. You dare to come to my home and accuse me of cowardice?"

"Your bravery is not in doubt," Calgacus stated. "It is your judgement I question. You have a chance to show the world how the Taexali can fight, yet you prefer to sit at home while the other tribes, whom you call sheep, have answered the call."

Algarix let out a low, warning growl, but Maelchon hesitated, his expression less severe, because some of the crowd, especially the warriors, were unsettled by Calgacus' harsh words. Calgacus sensed the shift in their mood and decided to press home his point.

"What shall I tell the other Kings?" he demanded, swivelling to look at the King's war band, making eye contact with as many of them as possible in order to force them to heed him.

He went on, "But then, perhaps it does not matter what I say because, if you do not come, everyone will believe the Taexali are afraid."

Angry voices were raised, men clutched at their swords or shook their fists, shouting that they were not afraid of anyone. In the tumult, Algarix grabbed Calgacus' arm.

"You will take back those words!" the shield-bearer rasped.

Calgacus stared into the burly young man's eyes, but his next words were addressed to Maelchon.

"Tell your lackey to let go of my arm," he said coldly. "Before I teach him a lesson."

Maelchon gave a wicked grin as he smirked, "I doubt whether you could teach Algarix anything, but feel free to try."

Algarix sneered as he tightened his grip on Calgacus' arm.

He declared, "Now, you will take back your insults. And you should know that I have killed nine men in single combat."

Calgacus stared at him coldly. He said, "I long ago lost count of the men I have killed. Release your grip now."

"Or what?" grinned Algarix. "Will you challenge me to a duel?"

Instead of answering, Calgacus jerked forwards, delivering a massive head butt to Algarix's face. The sound of the impact was loud and sickening, the blow so powerful that Algarix fell backwards without making a sound, blood spraying from his shattered nose. He sprawled on the ground at Calgacus' feet, unmoving and snoring blood.

Calgacus wiped a hand across his face before saying to Maelchon, "I think you should get yourself a new shield-bearer. This one is not much use."

Someone in the crowd laughed, and others gave soft cheers. Calgacus saw some of the warriors grinning, clearly not unhappy at Algarix's humbling.

Runt breathed, "By Toutatis, Cal. If that's your idea of diplomacy, we're in big trouble. A little bit of grovelling wouldn't go amiss."

"I don't grovel," Calgacus replied.

He turned to Maelchon, whose face was contorting as he tried to control his fury, recognising that the mood of his people had changed. The King looked down at the groaning figure of Algarix, then up at Calgacus.

He rasped, "You have not changed, Calgacus. Your arrogance is as breath-taking as ever. But you will pay for that insult."

"No insult was intended," Calgacus stated. "I gave him fair warning. Besides, there are far more important things at stake here. Swapping threats serves no purpose. If you wish to take some revenge on me for something that was not of my doing, then I think you should consider the consequences."

"Now you are the one making threats!" Maelchon barked, trying to regain some authority over the onlookers.

"It is no threat," Calgacus assured him. "I want you to join the fight against Rome, but that is your decision. You can let the songs record their opinion of you. Believe me, people prefer the stories they hear in song to the truth. What will the songs say about the Taexali? Will they say that you betrayed a War Leader who came to you for help, or will they say that you shared in the glory of defeating the Legions?"

"You say you will not beg," Maelchon retorted, "but it is plain that you need us. Why else did you come here?"

"Yes, we need your help," Calgacus agreed. "But even if you refuse to join us, I will fight the invaders anyway, because I am a warrior, and that is what warriors do. We are privileged among our people because we are sworn to defend them. We do not till the fields or work with our hands. We eat the best cuts of meat, we drink the best beer, we bed the best women. But there is a price for those privileges, and it is

155

a price paid in blood. I ask you and your war host to pay that price now. We have a chance to drive the enemy back, but only if we unite. Tell me, what will happen to the Taexali if the other tribes are defeated? What will you do when the Legions arrive at your home and demand that you surrender your freedom to them? Can you win if you fight alone?"

"We need no help," Maelchon insisted. "We are the Taexali. We have already driven off a Roman raid on our shores."

Calgacus hid his surprise. The Roman fleet had been patrolling the coast for several weeks, but he had not heard of any raids. So far, they had confined themselves to delivering emissaries like Venutius. If they had begun raiding, he knew the war was imminent, that it might already have begun, while he was here, trying to persuade Maelchon to see sense.

He said, "A raid is nothing. There are thirty thousand Romans ready to invade our lands and to enslave our people. No tribe, not even the Taexali, can withstand them alone. Either we join together or we fall separately. So, Maelchon, King of the Taexali, what is your decision? What do your warriors say?"

Maelchon hesitated. His men were looking at one another now, questioning and shrugging. Calgacus had brought them into the argument because he had seen many of them nodding approval at his words. Now he hoped they would voice their support.

He was not disappointed. One of the warriors, a tall, thin-faced individual with a serious expression, declared, "My King, we are warriors. We train for battle every day. We can run from morning till night and fight a battle at the end. We take slaves and plunder from our enemies because we are stronger than they are. We claim to be the best, but surely we must prove ourselves against the Romans if we wish to uphold that boast. Calgacus is right. We cannot let other tribes take the glory."

Other men murmured their agreement, and Calgacus saw that Maelchon realised he had miscalculated. He might still refuse, but he would be testing the loyalty of his people if he tried to enforce his will. Whatever his state of mind, he was intelligent enough to understand the mood among the villagers.

Calgacus continued, "You have said that you have already been attacked. Whether you wish it or not, you are at war with Rome. For all our sakes, do not face them alone. Join all the other tribes. Take part in the great alliance. Together, we can defeat them. I have said that we need the Taexali, and it would be an honour to fight alongside you, but I will not grovel, just as I would not expect you to grovel before the Romans."

Many of the warriors applauded his words, calling for Maelchon to agree.

The thin-faced man who had spoken in favour of Calgacus urged, "It is true, my King. Rome has made war on us. Since when did the Taexali sit back meekly when someone attacked us? We should strike back."

Maelchon regarded the tall man with a sour expression.

He said, "Your recent success has turned your head, Muradach."

"Perhaps it has," the man named Muradach shrugged. "But I still say we should not sit idly by while others have a chance for glory and plunder. The wealth of Rome is well known. Will we allow the other tribes to take those riches for themselves?"

This time, the roar of support was much louder. Whether it was Calgacus' impassioned speech, or Muradach's appeal to the warriors' innate desire for booty, the demand for war was almost unanimous.

Maelchon glowered angrily, but he knew he was beaten. With a grudging nod, he told Calgacus, "Very well, I will summon my war host."

157

Calgacus' thanks were drowned by the tumultuous cheer that greeted the King's promise. Men and women shouted their approval, and the warriors began boasting of what they would achieve.

The noise was so great that Algarix stirred, coming slowly back to consciousness.

Runt sighed, "It's a pity he didn't choke on his tongue."

Calgacus gave the serious-faced Muradach a nod of appreciation, which the tall warrior returned. The man saw Algarix struggling to sit up, and gave a faint smile.

"I wish I had done that to him," he said just loud enough for Calgacus to hear. "But watch your back around him."

"I hear you," Calgacus replied.

He did not really care about Algarix. He felt drained by the tension of the meeting, yet elated at the outcome.

Maelchon, though, was not finished. He called for silence, slamming his fist impatiently on the arm of his chair.

When the crowd at last settled down, he said, "There is one more thing we must attend to. Muradach led our attack on the raiders who landed a little way north of here. He killed a great number of them, and he also took two prisoners."

Calgacus was intrigued. "Prisoners?"

"One of them speaks our language," Muradach explained. "He claims to be an important man who knows the Roman Governor. That's why I let him live. I thought he might be valuable."

Maelchon butted in, "I was not sure what to do with him, but now I have decided. We will send his head back to the Romans, to show them how we deal with their raiders."

Muradach frowned, "They are half starved. They claim they were not part of the raiding party."

"I want their heads anyway!" Maelchon snapped. "They are Romans. If we are at war, let us strike a blow. Bring them!"

158

Algarix was sitting up now, dabbing at his crushed and bleeding nose, still dazed. Calgacus moved away from him, waiting while men went off to bring the prisoners. When they appeared, Calgacus was shocked by their appearance.

There were two of them, dressed in ragged, filthy tunics and Roman sandals. One was a large man, once fat, but now flabby and wasted. Both men looked drained and hollow-eyed, worn out and strained almost to breaking point. Their hair was unkempt and long by Roman standards, their chins covered by straggling beards. They were half-led, half-dragged into the village square and hauled in front of the King.

Calgacus said, "I would like to speak to them."

"And I want them dead," Maelchon retorted. "They are my prisoners, Calgacus, not yours."

The smaller of the two Romans raised his head when he heard the King speak. He turned, blinking in confusion and amazement when his gaze met Calgacus' eyes.

"Calgacus? Is that you?"

Calgacus looked at the man, frowning.

"Who are you?" he asked.

"Anderius Facilis. We met once before. A long time ago. I broke my leg and your friend there fixed it for me."

Runt beamed, "I remember you! That was during the Great Revolt. You were taking a message to the Second Legion."

Maelchon shouted impatiently, "Enough of this! Cut their heads off. We will send them to the Romans."

"Wait!" Calgacus barked. "I need to talk to these men. Will you give them to me?"

"Another favour?" Maelchon sneered. "You ask a great many favours. I think we have already agreed more than enough."

He signalled to his warriors.

"Do it!"

"Let me buy them from you!" Calgacus persisted, stepping in front of the two Romans to block the swordsmen who were drawing their blades to carry out the King's sentence.

Maelchon grinned, and Calgacus saw another snare closing around him.

"You wish to purchase them?" the King asked. "Very well, but the price is high."

"What do you want for them?" Calgacus asked.

He saw the spark in Maelchon's eyes as the King said, "Your sword."

Calgacus hesitated. Maelchon had demanded his sword once before, when Fulvia had run away from her marriage with him. Calgacus had refused to surrender it, and he knew Maelchon had not forgotten.

"The sword is an heirloom of my family," he said, stalling for time.

"That is my price," Maelchon shrugged. "Pay it now, or these men die."

"The sword will do you no good," Calgacus insisted. "It brings bad luck to anyone outside my family who tries to use it. The last person who took it was Cartimandua, Queen of the Brigantes. She lost her kingdom, and was forced to flee to Rome."

Maelchon frowned, but he could not withdraw his demand now. He had already conceded too much. He signalled to his guards.

"Kill the prisoners."

"No!"

Calgacus had won the major prize already, and he knew Maelchon would not back down over this second issue. The King needed to display his authority and was using the two Romans as a bargaining counter. Slowly, Calgacus looped the thick leather belt over his head, removing the great sword from his back. The fleece-lined scabbard, made of bronze and tin, gleamed like gold and silver in the afternoon sun. It was a glorious sight, a scabbard worthy of the songs that surrounded his sword.

There was magic in that blade, the stories insisted. Calgacus knew that was untrue, yet the sword was special. Iron blades are strong and sharp, but they can be brittle, or can bend with use. Yet, every so often, through some mystery of the blacksmith's art, or through the intervention of the Gods, or perhaps through mere chance, a blade will be produced that is not brittle, that does not warp or bend. Calgacus' sword was one such blade, and he knew that, in a sense, it was magical. Somehow, the lumps of ore that had been transformed into this long, heavy, killing blade, had become something more than a mere weapon.

Reluctantly, he passed it to Muradach, who handed it to Maelchon. The king's eyes glinted with pleasure as he laid it across his knees. He smiled triumphantly when he looked up.

"You may have your prisoners," he told Calgacus.

Chapter XIV

The two Romans were so weak that Calgacus and Runt
needed to support them as they walked to the gates. Once
there, they helped the men onto the horses, then led them out
to meet the waiting war band.

"Thank you," said Facilis weakly. "I know the value
of what you gave away for us."

"It was just a sword," Calgacus shrugged, although
the words almost caught in his throat.

"It was the sword of Caratacus, was it not?"

"It once belonged to him," Calgacus admitted. "And
others of my family before him."

"Then you have lost a great deal."

Calgacus told him, "I would rather have kept it, but it
was worth the exchange."

"To save two starving enemies?"

"No. For myself."

Facilis shot him an inquisitive look.

"For yourself?"

Calgacus explained, "Yes. I once knew a wise old
man who told me that you lose nothing when you lose
wealth, but you lose everything when you lose character. I
would not have it said that I stood by and watched men
executed just to spite me when I had the power to save
them."

"I do not know how I will be able to repay you,"
Facilis sighed.

"I'll think of something," Calgacus grinned.
"Personally, I am just as glad to get out of there as you are."

Adelligus shared that sentiment. His young face
showed his relief when he saw them.

"We didn't know what to think when we heard the shouting," he explained. "What happened?"

"I'll tell you all about it on the way home," Calgacus informed him. "Don't listen to your father's version. He'll exaggerate. Now, let's get out of here."

Two of the warriors doubled up on ponies to allow Calgacus and Runt to ride. They were unable to travel quickly because the two Romans were so weak they could barely remain upright, but Adelligus provided water and some hard-baked bannocks which served to revive them.

"I also need a bath," Facilis smiled as he gratefully chewed on the food.

"Yes, you do," agreed Calgacus, wrinkling his nose. "But it will wait. We have a long way to go. And I want to talk to you."

Pulcher, whose flabby flesh hung on him like an oversized coat, was too lost in self pity and terror to speak to anyone. The ordeal he had been through, culminating in Thrax's violent death, had left him shocked to the core. Surrounded by Calgacus' warriors, he rode in silence, his jaw slack, his eyes frightened as a hunted deer.

Facilis, in contrast, was only too happy to talk. He rode alongside Calgacus, reminiscing over their previous encounters.

"It seems our paths are destined to cross," he remarked.

"We have only really met once," Calgacus smiled.

"Twice," Facilis corrected. "You were in the *Cohors Auxilia Britannorum,* posing as a recruited soldier, when I was an aide to the Governor, Veranius Nepos. You must remember him. As I recall, you smashed his head with a stone."

"That's true," Calgacus grinned. "Although I don't think we actually met one another at the time."

"True enough," sighed Facilis. "I was too busy covering up your murder because I didn't want to alarm

163

anyone. Of course, I didn't know who you were at the time, although I heard later how you revealed your identity and marched out of camp, taking a hundred men with you."

"There were only around forty who came with me," Calgacus corrected.

"Stories often grow in the telling," Facilis shrugged. "Much like the tale you spun me when you captured me during the Great Revolt. You persuaded me that you had an army waiting to ambush the Second Legion if it left its fort."

He shot Calgacus an enquiring look as he asked, "How many men did you actually have?"

"A couple of hundred."

Facilis gave a regretful laugh.

"I thought as much. That episode ruined my career, you know."

"You don't sound all that bitter about it."

"As it turned out, it was a good thing. I went home and spent many happy years there."

Facilis' face took on an expression of deep sadness as he sighed, "But the Gods make us pay for any happiness we have, do they not?"

"So people say."

Facilis nodded, "It's true. I lost everything, which is why I returned to the army."

He gave a rueful grin as he added, "That hasn't turned out so well either."

"You are still alive," Calgacus pointed out, not sure why he felt sympathy for this man who was his enemy.

Facilis gave a weak smile.

"Yes, I am still alive. Thrax told me that the Gods must have some purpose in mind for me, which is why I have survived when so many others have not."

He gave another shrug as he confessed, "Although I must admit that I cannot conceive their purpose."

Calgacus told him, "In my experience, the Gods have no purpose except to play with the lives of men. That is why I pay as little attention to them as I can."

"They must have some plan in mind for the two of us," Facilis insisted. "Why else would we encounter one another again after so many years?"

Calgacus said, "Well, when you find out what their plan is, let me know. Personally, I am more interested in what your Governor's plans are. You are a friend of his, I believe?"

"I may have exaggerated that slightly," Facilis confessed. "But I would not tell you the Governor's plans even if I knew what they were. The truth is, though, that I have no idea what he intends to do. I am merely a lowly Assistant Quaestor these days."

"What about your fat friend? What does he know?"

"Less than I do, I suspect. He has few cares beyond where his next meal is coming from."

"Maybe I should torture him to find out the truth."

"That won't be necessary," Facilis smiled. "He is terrified of you. Just threaten him a little and he'll sing like a Greek actor."

Calgacus growled, "I could torture you as well."

"I don't think you will do that," Facilis replied calmly. "It would serve no purpose, and it would go against your character. I might lose my life but, as you said, you would lose everything."

"Don't read too much into that," Calgacus warned. "The future of my people is at stake. I would sacrifice you, or any man, if it meant saving them."

Growing more serious, Facilis said, "For what it is worth, I know there are three Legions poised to cross the river very soon. I also know that Julius Agricola is one of the best Generals in the Empire. The other thing I know is that you cannot hope to defeat him."

"I can try," Calgacus replied.

"You will fail," Facilis insisted. "You have opposed Rome from the beginning, but you have been pushed further and further north. Now the Legions have followed you. You have nowhere else to go. I have sailed all the way round Britannia. I know there is no land beyond your shores. You must surrender or die. Believe me, surrendering would be the sensible option."

"I never claimed to be sensible," Calgacus told him. "And there is another choice. We could win. I have beaten your vaunted Legions before."

"I have not forgotten that. I was with Ostorius Scapula when you led the Silures. But that was a long time ago, and Scapula was an impetuous commander. He took risks, and you tricked him into an ambush. You will not be able to do the same to Agricola. He is too clever for that."

"You seem very sure of his ability."

Facilis nodded, "I may not be a close friend of his, but I know him personally. He is a first-rate commander, and a very shrewd man. But he is also bold and energetic. When he comes against you, you will not be able to trick him as easily as you fooled Scapula all those years ago."

Calgacus rode in silence for a while, considering what Facilis had told him. Then he asked, "Do you think he would be prepared to negotiate?"

It was Facilis' turn to fall silent. After some thought, he said, "The only condition he will accept is total surrender."

Calgacus nodded, "That's what I thought. That is how Romans usually negotiate. It seems this Agricola of yours is not so very different to every other Governor you've sent here."

"He has been more successful than most," Facilis pointed out. "And he will not stop now. He needs to complete the conquest of this island quickly."

Frowning, Calgacus said, "That's what I don't understand about you Romans. What is there here that your

166

Governor wants? We have precious little gold, and few other resources. If he wants mountains, forests and wild beasts, he will have more than he could wish for, but there is not much else for him."

"There is glory," Facilis countered. "For a Roman General, victory is everything. And, as I said, Agricola needs it quickly."

"Why?"

"Because his term as Governor has already exceeded the normal five years. He could be recalled to Rome at any time, and then the glory of conquering Britannia will go to someone else."

"So we must fight because of one man's vanity?" Calgacus asked sourly.

"You must fight anyway," Facilis explained. "Rome will come north whoever commands. All I am saying is that I expect the Governor to press ahead as soon as he can. In fact, now that spring is here, I doubt whether he will delay much longer."

Calgacus gave the Roman a smile.

"It seems you do know a few things, after all."

"I have not told you anything that is a secret," Facilis replied. "I am only trying to convince you that you cannot win."

He gave Calgacus an earnest look as he went on, "I have seen too much death and destruction on both sides. Despite what you might think, I admire your people. I don't want to see more of them throw their lives away uselessly."

Calgacus nodded, "I believe you are sincere, Facilis, but I don't see any way of avoiding war. It is not in our nature to give in without a fight. This is our home, not yours, and we will defend it with our lives."

"Perhaps there is a way," Facilis countered. "If you like, I could go to the Governor on your behalf. If you wish to negotiate, I will act as intermediary. Perhaps that is my purpose here. The Gods have sent me to you to help you."

"I thought you said the only term the Governor would accept is total surrender?"

"Yes, but he might be generous to those who agree not to wage war."

Facilis' eyes were bright with eagerness as he urged, "Let me speak to him for you. I am sure that, if you submit to him, he would agree to grant you the status of a client King. You could become a Roman ally."

Calgacus shook his head.

"I appreciate your offer, but I have no interest in becoming a client King. It is just another word for a vassal. I have seen for myself how Rome treats its so-called allies. My sister, whom you call Boudica, was a Roman ally before you turned on her."

Facilis could not argue against that point. He knew how the Empire had treated Boudica and the Iceni, the actions of greedy officials and brutal soldiers combining to rouse the entire tribe into a bloody revolt that had cost thousands of lives.

He asked, "What about the other tribes? Do they all feel as you do?"

"Yes. They are accustomed to fighting, you see. They live by raiding their neighbours, so warfare is a way of life. That is why they will not surrender, no matter what you say. And, this time, they will fight together, not separately. Your Governor has never faced a united group of tribes. That is why we will win this time."

Facilis frowned, his eyes regarding Calgacus thoughtfully.

He asked, "Are you trying to trick me again? The tribes of Britain have not joined together since the days of your brother, Caratacus, and that still ended in defeat for you."

"It will be different this time. And this is no trick. I think you are too smart for me to get away with that again. No, the tribes have united, and they will oppose your army.

168

There will be no negotiations. I don't think I'll be sending you to speak to your Governor."

Facilis sighed, "I wish you would reconsider. From what little I saw of the Taexali, your allies are as much a danger to you as they are to Rome."

Maelchon sat in his roundhouse, casting a jaundiced eye over four young women who stood in front of him. They were slaves, specially selected for him by Algarix, who stood nearby, his face a mass of dark, swollen bruises.

"You," Maelchon decided, pointing at a slim, dark-haired girl. "Go up the ladder and wait for me. The rest of you get out of here."

The girl he had chosen gave a frightened nod, then clambered up the ladder that led to the upper floor, while the others hurried to escape his presence.

When they had gone, he said to Algarix, "Calgacus has bested me again. He turned my own war band against me, especially Muradach."

"Do you want me to kill him?" Algarix asked, his voice muffled by the injury to his bruised and swollen nose.

"Yes, but you will need to be careful."

"I always am. Nobody suspects your brother did not die naturally."

"Calgacus is not an easy man to kill," Maelchon growled, preferring to ignore the reminder of the sudden death that had allowed him to become King.

Algarix blinked, "I thought you meant Muradach. Do you not want him dead?"

Maelchon frowned, considering the question. He rubbed his chin, deep in thought. After a few moments, he looked up, a gleam of excitement in his eyes.

"No, I do not want Muradach killed just yet. I have a better idea, one that will see all my enemies removed. I will have my revenge on all of them."

169

Algarix gave a fierce grin as he asked, "What will you do?"

Thinking aloud, Maelchon explained, "Muradach and Calgacus wish us to join the opposition to Rome. Very well, I will give them what they want. Tomorrow, you will summon the local chieftains and their war bands. We will ride south in two days' time."

"We cannot gather the entire force of our tribe in so short a time," Algarix protested.

"No, but we do not need to. We can raise several hundred warriors. That will be enough. The Romans may launch their invasion at any time. Better to arrive quickly with a few hundred men than to arrive late with a few thousand."

"But what then?" Algarix queried uncertainly.

"Then, we make sure the alliance fails. I can easily disrupt the truce Calgacus and his pet druid have imposed. The tribes are always ready to fight one another. All I need to do is provoke a few arguments."

"But that will aid the Romans," Algarix frowned.

"No, the Romans will aid me," Maelchon told him. "With any luck, they will kill Muradach for me. That would be a pleasant bonus, although it is not essential. More importantly, joining the other tribes will give you an opportunity to kill Calgacus."

"That would be a pleasure," Algarix grinned. "But it will be difficult to do it in secret. He travels with a war band, which is why we were unable to ambush him on his way here."

"There is no need to do it secretly," Maelchon replied. "You have every reason to hate the man for the underhand way he tricked you. I am sure that you can easily find a pretext to challenge him to a duel. In a fair fight, you could beat him."

"That is something I am already looking forward to," agreed Algarix.

Another thought struck Maelchon. He reached for the great longsword he had extorted from Calgacus earlier. After admiring it for a long moment, he handed it to Algarix.

"You should wear this. The sight will antagonise him, and will help give you cause to challenge him. It would be fitting if he were to die by his own sword."

Algarix eyed the sword warily.

"He said it was cursed."

"A lie. Cartimandua lost her kingdom long after Calgacus recovered the sword from her. There is no curse."

Doubtfully, Algarix accepted the gift, but he still had concerns over his King's plans.

"What about the Romans?" he asked. "Calgacus is an arrogant man, but he has a point. If we fight them, we may be defeated."

Waving a hand in dismissal of the protest, Maelchon explained, "It is quite simple. Once Calgacus is dead, his alliance will crumble. I will ensure that the Kings squabble over the leadership. As a result, each tribe will go its own way, and we will be forced to return home. Even if Muradach is still alive by then, he will be compelled to agree that we cannot continue the struggle with only a few hundred men at our disposal."

"But the Romans will still attack," Algarix ventured.

"Of course they will, but they will be pitted against the Venicones and the Boresti before they reach us. I will allow those tribes to waste their strength against the Legions. While they are doing that, we will ensure that Muradach is dealt with. Then I will make peace with Rome, and lead our war host to aid them."

"You will submit to Rome?" Algarix asked.

"Let us say that I will befriend the Empire. Rome rewards its friends. There is an opportunity here, provided I am careful. I see no reason why I should not take control of the lands of the Boresti to the south, and the Vacomagi to the north. I will rule the largest territory that any King of the Taexali has ever controlled."

Algarix's grin matched that of his King as he grasped the extent of Maelchon's vision of the future.

Maelchon continued, "Best of all, my enemies will be destroyed. Calgacus, Muradach, even that squat excuse for a King, Bridei. I think submitting to Rome would be worth that."

His eyes took on a faraway, dreamy look as he went on, "After that, with the power of Rome to back me, who knows what I might not achieve? That she-wolf, Fulvia, Calgacus' slut of a daughter, is hiding somewhere in the west. I could find her and drag her back here."

"You could make her your wife," Algarix prompted.

"I would make her a slave," Maelchon retorted forcefully. "And I would make her watch while I had her faithless husband butchered to death. That would teach her the folly of refusing me."

"Everyone will fear you," Algarix assured him enthusiastically. "Which is how it should be. It is a great plan, worthy of a great King."

Maelchon smiled at the compliment, but he raised a cautionary hand.

"We must take it one step at a time," he warned. "I want to let the Romans work for me in this, but to achieve anything, Calgacus must die. To accomplish that, we must join his alliance. So, in the morning, summon the war bands. We will take the first steps on the path to my ultimate triumph and the ruin of everyone who has ever opposed me."

Smiling through his hurt and battered face, Algarix nodded, "It will be as you say."

Maelchon waved a chubby hand, saying, "Now, leave me. I have had a difficult day."

When Algarix had departed, Maelchon pushed himself to his feet and headed for the ladder that led up to his sleeping quarters. It had indeed been a difficult day, and he felt the need to inflict some pain. That would help ease his soul until his plans for revenge bore fruit. The girl who cowered in his bed would not thwart him as Calgacus had done. She was, after all, only a slave, and he would make her scream, just as he imagined hearing Calgacus scream when Algarix cut him to pieces with his own sword.

It took Calgacus and his war band three days to reach the hidden corrie, their journey slowed by the fatigue of the two Roman captives. It was almost dark by the time they rode into the high, hidden crater where a new settlement was being created. Already, trees had been felled, new houses were being constructed, and hearths created. The bowl of the crater came alive as everyone hurried to meet the riders when they climbed the steep slope and entered the new village.

Facilis and Pulcher had been blindfolded for the latter part of the day to prevent them knowing the precise location of the hidden settlement. When the cloth was removed from their eyes, they gaped in wonder at this hidden sanctuary. In turn, their ragged clothing and unkempt beards created a stir among the women and children who clustered around them, jabbering and pointing.

Pulcher recoiled in horror, but Facilis called out a greeting in the local language, smiling at the confusion his words generated.

While the crowd gaped at the two prisoners, Calgacus dismounted, swinging down from his saddle to meet Beatha, who had hurried to greet him. As soon as he saw her face, he knew that something was wrong.

"What has happened?" he demanded anxiously.

Beatha ran to him, hugging him tightly.

"Oh, Cal. It's Togodumnus. The Romans have taken him."

Chapter XV

Togodumnus had done his best to remain angry throughout the voyage south. He had been ignored by the Tribune, Aulus Atticus, and had refused to have anything to do with Venutius. The Brigante had made an attempt to talk to him, but Togodumnus had rebuffed the man, turning his back on him. Venutius had merely laughed, which helped fuel Togodumnus' anger.

His resentment at the way he had been treated allowed him to remain indignant, but other emotions soon took hold. The galleys had rowed south, following the coast until they entered the wide estuary of the Bodotria. That was when Togodumnus' anger had begun to turn to awe.

The wide, majestic river was alive with Roman boats. Dozens of transport ships brought a constant stream of supplies from the south, while war galleys patrolled the river, watching for signs of any British boats. They need not have bothered, Togodumnus thought bitterly. The Britons used the rivers and sea as much as anyone, but their lightweight vessels were tiny in comparison to the multi-oared Roman ships. Rome, he realised, had already conquered the sea. With their large fleet, they could strike, unopposed, at any point along the coast. Togodumnus had seen single ships before, had marvelled at their size, but he had never imagined how many galleys the Romans possessed. He counted more than thirty warships and twice as many transport vessels. It was an awe-inspiring sight that swamped his feelings of injustice.

That was only the beginning of the revelations. When they landed, Sdapezi and his troopers provided him with a horse and, led by Atticus, they left the bustling riverside dock and rode inland towards the vast camp where Julius Agricola had made his headquarters.

The sights he saw on that short journey stunned Togodumnus. Where there had been only open countryside the year before, there were now forts and watchtowers, ditches and palisades. Hordes of cavalry exercised their horses, the troopers armed with long lances and heavy swords, thundering up and down the fields in neat, precise formations. Elsewhere, artillery batteries practised loading and firing their ballistas and catapults, winding the horsehair ropes so tightly that the boulders and spiked missiles were hurled hundreds of paces.

Then there were the foot soldiers, the main power of Rome. He saw groups of archers and slingers practising with their missiles which would precede any assault by the heavily armoured legionaries, and he saw those armoured men as well. They were marching and exercising, locking shields, or running in mock attacks with their swords glinting in the sun. There were, Togodumnus realised, thousands of them, more than he could have imagined.

"This is only one part of the army," a voice informed him.

He turned to see Venutius riding alongside him. He hurriedly turned away again, but the Brigante continued to talk to him.

"Don't be a fool like your father," Venutius advised. "You can see the power of Rome. There are two other Legions further upriver, plus thousands of auxiliary troops. Rome will conquer, and any sensible man will join with them."

Togodumnus felt his anger rising again. He snapped, "You want me to be like you? You told them to kill me."

"Don't take it personally," Venutius replied smoothly. "I have nothing against you. My intention was to cause problems for your father, but, on reflection, perhaps it will be

175

even worse for him if you become a Roman ally. You said that is what you wanted. Now you have a chance to prove it."

"That was before they burned my home and took me prisoner," Togodumnus retorted.

Venutius regarded him with a patient smile.

"You are still taking it too personally. We were after your father, not you. You are an intelligent young man. I suggest you use that intelligence. Why not be part of the Empire?"

"Become a Roman slave like you?"

Venutius' hazel eyes grew hard for a moment, but then he relaxed and shook his head ruefully.

"I was a King once," he explained. "I have fought against Rome, but I soon learned that it is better to befriend the Empire than to oppose it. If you are sensible, you will do the same. Whatever has happened in the past, you are here now, and you should make the best of it."

"I don't need any advice from you," Togodumnus spat.

"Then think on this," Venutius continued airily. "Look at the people who have opposed Rome. Your namesake, Togodumnus of the Catuvellauni, the so-called Great King, Caratacus, Boudica of the Iceni, Brennus of the Ordovices, the druids of Ynis Mon. Where are they all now?"

"I know what happened to them," Togodumnus said grimly.

"All gone," Venutius nodded emphatically. "But I am still here. If you want to survive, you must learn to bend with the wind. If you try to stand up to it, you will be swept away by the storm, just like all those others. Don't be a fool, boy."

With that, Venutius tapped his heels to his horse and pulled ahead.

"You know I'm right, boy," he called over his shoulder, his smile triumphant.

Togodumnus stared at the Brigante's back. He loathed the man, but he could not deny the truth of what he had said. It was useless to oppose Rome. Everywhere he looked, all he could see were armed men who would soon cross the river and crush anyone who opposed them.

His spirits sank even further when they reached the Legionary fortress. Protected by a triple bank of ditches, it had a wooden palisade atop a high, earth wall, with wooden towers at each corner, and a massive gateway. It was an awe-inspiring sight which told anyone who saw it that the men who had built this fortress could accomplish whatever they set their minds to.

When the troop trotted through the gates, Togodumnus was astonished to see that, instead of the rows of tents he had expected, the Romans had constructed rows of long, low buildings, complete with red roof tiles.

He noticed the Centurion, Sdapezi, looking at him.

"How was all this built so quickly?" he asked.

Sdapezi laughed, "That's what the Legions do, lad. They build things. When we arrived here last year, there was nothing, but when you've got thousands of men available, it doesn't take long to put up a few buildings. The men would rather work at that than spend a freezing winter in their tents."

They left the horses at a large paddock, then Atticus led them through the vast camp to the Principia, the Headquarters building from where the Governor oversaw his campaign.

Feeling numb, Togodumnus followed the others into the building. Everything around him was strange and overwhelming. The sights and sounds bombarded his senses, giving him no time to gather his thoughts. The lime-washed buildings with their red rooftops, the teeming soldiers, the standards and banners planted in the ground outside the Principia, and the precise regularity of the camp's layout, all combined to reinforce his feelings of helplessness.

Once inside, Atticus went to see the Governor, leaving the others in an antechamber. Togodumnus sat on a low bench, bowing his head so that he would not make eye contact with anyone. He knew that the scribes and officers gathered in the tiny room were giving him curious looks, but he tried to ignore them. He needed to think, needed to decide what to do, but he was confused, beset by conflicting emotions.

He had been abducted against his will, had been threatened with death, had seen his home burned to the ground. All of these things told him that his father's dire predictions had been correct. But Sdapezi had spoken up for him, and the Tribune, Atticus, despite his pompous, superior attitude, had agreed to let him live when he could easily have ordered his death.

Now he had witnessed the awesome strength of the Roman army, and he knew that nobody could prevent them taking control of the north. His father would try, he knew that, but he was bound to fail. There were simply too many soldiers, thousands of them, each one better trained and equipped than all but a handful of warriors among the Pritani. Venutius was right, which was galling, because Togodumnus loathed the man and did not want to agree with him.

He sat there, lost in thought, dreading what might happen next. Occasionally, he glanced at the thick, wooden door that led into the Governor's office. Once he stepped through that doorway, his fate would be decided. The thought made his insides squirm. What was Atticus telling the Governor? What would Venutius tell him?

Before long, Venutius was called in to see the Governor. Finally, after a short wait, the door opened again and Atticus called for Togodumnus. He stood, took a deep breath, and walked into the office with his head held high.

Sdapezi followed, taking up a position near the door. Venutius and Atticus stood to either side, and Togodumnus faced Julius Agricola and Licinius Spurius across a wide table. He felt like a condemned man, but the atmosphere in the room was affable, almost relaxed. That only served to

178

confuse him further. He blinked nervously, forcing himself to appear calm.

After brief introductions, Agricola fixed his eyes on Togodumnus.

"I expect you harbour some resentment against us," the Governor began, his voice firm and self-assured but apparently friendly.

Togodumnus was close to panic. The Governor held the power of life and death over every person in Britannia. However friendly he might seem, his word was law, and he was facing Togodumnus, a twenty-one year old Briton who had never been further from his home than he was now. He swallowed anxiously, clasping his hands together behind his back to prevent them trembling.

Somehow, he managed to reply, "I do not like the way you treat people who want to be your friends."

"That was a misunderstanding," Agricola stated reassuringly. "Venutius was over-zealous in interpreting my orders. Fortunately, Tribune Atticus made the right decision. I can understand your reaction but, in the circumstances, he had no alternative."

Togodumnus wanted to argue, but Agricola's forceful manner held his tongue captive. He wanted to protest that it had been Sdapezi, not Atticus, who had kept him alive, but he could not contradict the Governor's forceful assertions.

Agricola went on, "I understand you are an educated young man. You speak our language very well."

"My mother taught me," Togodumnus managed to reply.

Agricola smiled benevolently.

"She also taught you to read and write, did she not?"

Togodumnus could hear the condescending tone in Agricola's voice, as if it was remarkable that any barbarian could learn such simple things as reading and writing.

For a brief moment, he wondered how his father would react to the Governor's question, and it was all he could do to nod, "Yes."

"Then you could be the very man we are looking for," Agricola declared genially. "Don't you think so, Spurius?"

Licinius Spurius, Commander of the Ninth Legion, smiled as he confirmed, "I believe so, Sir."

Togodumnus stared at the Governor in confusion.

"I don't understand," he stammered.

"What I mean," the Governor explained, "is that, once the northern part of Britannia has been pacified, we will need men who can govern it for us. Local men who know the people, but who also understand the benefits of being part of the Empire."

Togodumnus' mind reeled at the enormity of the Governor's suggestion.

"You want me to govern this region?" he gasped in disbelief.

"Not on your own, of course. There will be others, but yes, you are, I think, ideally suited to be a local magistrate. You speak Latin, and you are the son of a powerful chieftain."

Togodumnus shook his head in protest.

"The tribes would never accept me!"

The Governor laughed softly, "They would have no choice. You would be backed by Rome, with our troops stationed here."

Togodumnus could hardly believe that the proposal was serious, but the Governor's expression confirmed that he was in earnest.

"I'm not sure," Togodumnus stuttered. His face flushed, flustered by the unexpected turn of events. He had expected to be executed as the son of a famous rebel, yet here he was being offered a chance to become one of Rome's leading men in Britannia. It was too much to take in, and he did not know what to say. He did not even know whether he wanted this. Was it just another bribe, as his father had warned him, or did it present an opportunity to make a difference to the lives of his people? He could not decide, and his bewilderment was evident in his reaction.

"Think about it," Agricola advised with an avuncular smile. "There is plenty of time. After all, we have not yet brought the entire island under control."

He continued to smile as he added, "In the meantime, you are welcome among us. Centurion Sdapezi and his men will take care of you. Now, if you will excuse me, I have a great deal of work to get through."

Togodumnus felt as if he were in a dream as he was ushered out of the office, with Atticus, Venutius and Sdapezi close behind him. As soon as they emerged, a bevy of scribes crowded in to see the Governor. Once the ante-chamber had cleared, Togodumnus saw that two of Sdapezi's troopers were waiting for them.

"Am I a prisoner?" he asked, uncertain of his status.

"A guest," Atticus informed him, although Venutius' mocking snort of laughter suggested that he was a guest who would not be permitted to leave.

Just then, another soldier hurried into the room, his face relieved when he saw Sdapezi.

"Sir! There's a barbarian at the gate, asking to see Venutius. It's the same one who's been here before."

Tribune Atticus frowned, "In daylight this time? It must be serious."

Gesturing to Venutius, he said, "You'd better find out what he wants."

In response, Venutius treated the Tribune to a sarcastic sneer.

"Thank you. I would never have thought of that."

Atticus flushed, "Just find out what the message is and come back and tell the Governor as soon as you can."

Venutius gave a mocking bow before turning to Sdapezi.

"He will want to see the girl. Have her brought to my room."

Sdapezi gave a curt nod. Then he placed a hand on Togodumnus' arm.

"Come on. I'll show you to your quarters. You can settle in while I'm dealing with this other matter." To the soldier, he said, "Take the messenger to Venutius' quarters." The soldier gave a hasty salute before hurrying off.

Sdapezi took Togodumnus out of the Principia, walking briskly. Togodumnus barely paid attention to where they were going. His mind was racing, filled with questions.

"What's going on?" he asked Sdapezi as the Centurion bustled him through the fort.

"Nothing to concern you," Sdapezi answered, his manner unusually brusque.

Togodumnus allowed himself to be bundled along, but he could not ignore the sudden sense of anticipation that had gripped his companions. Sdapezi was on edge, keen to get Togodumnus safely aside, while Venutius was striding ahead, as if eager to meet this strange messenger.

A barbarian messenger, Togodumnus recalled. It could have been someone from Venutius' former home of Brigantia but somehow he doubted that. Atticus had expressed surprise at the man's arrival in daylight. That suggested the Briton usually made clandestine visits. Who was he? And who was the girl they had referred to? Why would the barbarian messenger want to see her?

He did not know the answers, but he could guess, and what he guessed left him feeling sick at heart. If he was right, this could only mean that Venutius was in contact with someone from the north.

There was a spy in the British camp.

Chapter XVI

Tucked near the centre of the vast camp, surrounded by barrack blocks that housed the legionaries, were two long, low buildings. They faced each other across a narrow strip of hard-packed earth that might once have been covered by grass but was now scoured clear by the tramping of hob-nailed military sandals. Each building had half a dozen low doorways, regularly spaced in the whitewashed walls, with small, shuttered windows set just above head height.

Flicking a hand towards the block closest to the headquarters building, Sdapezi said, "My men and I stay in there. This other one is for the Governor's guests. You're lucky, there's one room left, so you get it all to yourself."

If Togodumnus had any illusions about the status of the Governor's guests, they were dispelled by the sight of five of Sdapezi's troopers, each of them standing outside one of the doors. He saw Venutius stride to the closest door, the one nearest the Principia. The Brigante swept inside, presumably to prepare to meet the barbarian messenger.

Sdapezi ushered Togodumnus along the front of the building to the only door that was not guarded, the second last. Sdapezi threw the door open and gestured for him to enter.

"Wait in here. I'll send one of my lads over in a moment."

He made to shut the door, then realised that would leave the room in virtual darkness. Frowning, he stepped inside and reached for the shutters on the front window. While he was engaged in freeing the bolts, which had jammed in place through weeks of disuse, Togodumnus heard voices and the sound of heavy footsteps from outside. Someone was coming out of the end room, with at least two

183

soldiers acting as escort. Curious, he glanced to the open door and saw a girl walk past.

He caught only a brief glimpse, because she was past the doorway in an instant, with two burly troopers close behind her, but what he saw intrigued him. She was young, perhaps sixteen at the most, with long tresses of brown hair. From the fine linen of the ankle-length dress that she wore, she might have been a Roman, but her sad expression and the fact that she was guarded, suggested otherwise.

Sdapezi freed the shutters at last. Scowling, he hurried to the door.

"Who is she?" Togodumnus asked.

"Don't ask," Sdapezi shot back. "Wait here."

The Centurion pulled the door shut and hurried after the girl and her two guards, leaving Togodumnus more bewildered than ever.

He wondered whether he should try stepping outside. He knew that, if his father had been here, that is what Calgacus would have done, but Togodumnus was not his father. The doors were guarded for a reason, and it was unlikely to be for the safety of the rooms' occupants. Deciding to obey the Centurion's injunction, he examined his surroundings.

It did not take long. The room was spacious, perhaps five paces square, but it was sparsely furnished and the walls were bare. The floor was hard-packed earth, and the ceiling a thin layer of wooden planks. The light that scattered in through the lattice-frame of the window showed him that there were two beds, mere ledges of wood, one against each of the side walls. There were no blankets or rugs. A stool and a tiny, square table sat against the far wall, between the beds, and a small, iron brazier stood in one corner. Its cold emptiness reminded him that the room was chilly and damp, presumably because it had been unoccupied all winter.

That made him wonder who the other prisoners were. Prisoners or guests, depending on whose point of view he took. Venutius was one, obviously, and the mysterious girl another, but there were three other rooms that had sentries stationed outside.

He sighed. The more he thought, the more questions he came up with. It was, he reflected, a strange way for the Romans to treat someone they expected to be their ally, but he was beginning to realise that the Romans were a strange people. For all that he had read about them, and for all the talking to travelling merchants, he clearly had a great deal to learn about his hosts.

Or were they his captors? He still could not decide.

He was still standing in the middle of the room when the door burst open and a burly soldier barged in, carrying a bundle of blankets and giving him a cheery smile.

"Welcome," he said in bluff, coarse Latin, as if the universal language were not his mother tongue. "My name is Daszdius. The Centurion has appointed me as your principal bodyguard."

Togodumnus had seen this man several times. He had been with the party that had brought him here. Daszdius was broad-shouldered, short, and had legs that bowed outwards so much Togodumnus thought he could have driven a cart through them. He was in his forties, Togodumnus guessed, with a gnarled, weather-beaten complexion and cynical eyes set in a flat, snub-nosed face.

"Bodyguard?" Togodumnus queried.

Daszdius grinned, revealing a mouth of crooked teeth.

"Call me what you like," he replied. "We're going to be seeing a lot of each other."

He held up the bundle of blankets. Tossing them onto one of the narrow ledges, he said, "Your bedding. You can make the bloody bed yourself, because I'm no slave."

Togodumnus instinctively liked the trooper. He was a rough, coarse man, but he seemed friendly enough. He also appeared to be willing to talk.

"Can I ask some questions?" Togodumnus ventured.

"Sure. What do you want to know?"

Togodumnus decided to begin carefully. He asked, "What exactly is the arrangement here? The Governor said I was a guest, but I see armed guards everywhere."

"It's a Legionary fort," Daszdius grinned. "There are armed men all over the place."

"That's not what I meant."

"I know. Just kidding, lad. All right, here's how it is. Our troop is responsible for your safety. That means we go where you go. There are three of us allocated to you. One of us will always be around. We'll bring you your food, and we'll escort you to the latrines when you want to take a piss. If you want anything else, you ask us."

"Am I free to go for a walk, or take a ride?"

"If the Centurion says so."

"Does he ever say so?"

Daszdius smiled broadly as he admitted, "Not very often."

"I thought not. Well, that seems clear enough. How about some charcoal for the brazier?"

"I'll see to that," the trooper agreed.

"Thanks, but I have some more questions first."

"Fire away."

"Who are the other prisoners?"

Daszdius did not bother correcting his description. He said, "There's Venutius, of course. Next, there's a young princeling from Hibernia, but you won't see much of him. He's ill and hardly ever leaves his room. Then there are the two old duffers. A couple of potential trouble-makers among their tribes, so we were told, but they don't cause any bother for us."

"And the girl?"

"You saw her? Pretty little thing, isn't she?"

Togodumnus nodded, "Yes. Who is she?"

"None of us know. She's a captive Briton, that's all we were told. Venutius knows who she is, but he won't say.

186

He's a secretive bastard, isn't he? She's not allowed to talk to us. Not that any of us can understand her anyway. She doesn't speak anything other than your native lingo."

"When was she captured?" Togodumnus asked, hunting for clues that would help him build a picture of the girl's identity.

"No idea. Venutius found her among a batch of slaves last year, but she could have been taken any time in the past couple of years." Daszdius shrugged, "We've been told not to ask questions, so we don't."

"All right, I won't ask either. Tell me about Venutius. I get the impression you don't like him."

"He's a slimy, back-stabbing son of a sow," Daszdius growled, his voice suddenly full of venom. "I'd happily cut his lying tongue out, which is why the Centurion won't let me near him. Not that Sdapezi is fond of him. We both know what Venutius is like."

"Go on," Togodumnus invited. "Tell me what you know about him."

After a moment's thought, the legionary shrugged as if deciding there would be no harm in giving his opinion.

He explained, "A couple of years ago, we were part of a troop sent to hunt down your father and a rebel named Brennus. It was just after the Governor had put down Brennus' rebellion, and he was on the run, with your father helping him. We tracked them deep into Brigantia, where Venutius had set himself up as King. Our damn fool of a Centurion joined forces with him to hunt your father down."

"Sdapezi, you mean?"

"No, he was second in command back then. The Centurion was called Casca."

"Oh, yes, I remember my father talking about that," Togodumnus agreed. "He said you caught him in a trap."

"He caught us, more like," Daszdius said. "We thought we had him, but he turned the tables on us. We had him where we wanted, but he charged at us, him and half a

187

dozen against damn near fifty of us. I never saw anything like it."

Togodumnus was surprised to find that he felt proud of his father. Calgacus had never spoken of the actual fight, but Togodumnus had heard most of the details from others who had been there. Yet hearing the awe in Daszdius' words brought home to him just how famous his father really was.

"What happened?" he asked, wanting Daszdius to continue.

"Like I say, he charged at us. He killed Casca, plus a few others of our lads. But it was Venutius who really decided the outcome of the fight. The stinking coward was so afraid, he ran away, taking his warriors with him."

"He abandoned you and your comrades?"

The soldier nodded, "There were only three of us left alive. Me, Sdapezi and young Hortensius, but he was badly wounded. I thought your father would kill us, but he let us go. He said there had been enough killing."

"I didn't know that," Togodumnus frowned. "He didn't talk about that fight very often. All he ever told me was that he and the others had been lucky to get away."

"We were the lucky ones," Daszdius sighed. "Me and Sdapezi marched for days in the middle of winter to get Hortensius back safe. I still don't know how we managed it."

"But you did, and Sdapezi is a Centurion now."

"Yeah, and when we got back, we discovered that bastard Venutius had come grovelling to the Governor, spinning a pack of lies about how he'd escaped when all of us had been killed. Now, somehow, he's licked Agricola's arse so much he's back in favour and we have to traipse around after him, following his orders."

"So he's not a prisoner?"

"Special status, I suppose you would call it," Daszdius shrugged. "He's a prisoner, but he has privileges because the Governor finds him useful."

Togodumnus observed, "If you hate him so much, I'm surprised you didn't kill him when you were out on one of your visits to the north."

"I thought about it," Daszdius admitted freely. "But Sdapezi said word would get out. Most of the lads don't know Venutius the way we do, and someone would blab. Then there were the sailors who took us up and down the coast. We couldn't have hidden it from them."

"If you ever change your mind, I'll help you," Togodumnus said, surprised at how strongly he felt about the renegade Brigante.

Daszdius seemed amused. He grinned, "You don't look the type, lad. Your father, now, he would do it. I know that. But you don't have the eyes of a man who could kill easily."

"I might make an exception for Venutius," Togodumnus offered.

"I'll bear that in mind," Daszdius chuckled. Then, growing more serious, he asked, "But, while we're talking about your father, can I ask you something?"

"Of course."

Daszdius hesitated, lowering his eyes as he explained, "There are stories doing the rounds, you know."

"Stories?"

"About your father."

He paused again, then blurted, "I just wondered whether they were true."

"Which ones in particular?" Togodumnus asked, smiling to himself at the effect his father's reputation was having on the veteran soldier.

Daszdius glanced around as if to ensure they were alone in the room. Then he dropped his voice to a hoarse whisper as he confided, "Some of the lads in this Legion were in Hibernia. They say your father died and was brought back to life."

Togodumnus almost laughed aloud. He had heard that tale from Runt, and knew that a sorceress named Scota had performed a trick, using the innards of a dead mule to fool the Romans into thinking she had spilled Calgacus' guts before casting a spell to bring him back to life. It had been a ploy to terrify the legionaries and, judging by Daszdius' reaction, it had worked better than Calgacus could have hoped.

"I wasn't there," he replied cautiously, doing his best to portray a serious expression. "But my father told me it really did happen."

Daszdius' face stiffened, his eyes widening as his fears were confirmed. Togodumnus almost felt sorry for deceiving the legionary, but something told him it would be best not to reveal the truth of Scota's trick.

"Well, I'll be damned!" Daszdius breathed. "I thought they were talking bollocks. But it's true?"

"As far as I know, yes," Togodumnus nodded, trying to sound sincere.

Daszdius was obviously disconcerted by this news, but it did not diminish his appetite for gossip and rumour.

He whispered, "So he can't be killed?"

Togodumnus gave a soft smile as he said, "You Romans have been trying to kill him for years. You have failed every time."

"But the magic!" Daszdius persisted. "He was dead, but now he isn't. Is he a ghost?"

"He always seemed real enough to me," Togodumnus assured him, not wanting to mislead the poor man too much. "But I have no idea what effect the magic has had on him."

Daszdius frowned, but was prevented from asking any further questions by the sound of footsteps outside.

The door opened to admit Sdapezi. He regarded the two of them knowingly, as if suspecting something of what had been said.

"Is everything all right here?" he asked.

190

"I was just telling the lad how things work around here," Daszdius replied with an air of exaggerated innocence.

"You talk too much, Daszdius," Sdapezi rasped.

"Yes, Sir!" the trooper agreed. He had recovered some of his earlier poise and managed to give Togodumnus a conspiratorial wink.

"Just mind your tongue," the Centurion warned. Then he looked at Togodumnus. "Come on, the Governor wants to see you again."

This time, Agricola's office was crowded. Tribunes and Centurions stood shoulder to shoulder, jostling one another for space. Venutius was there, a smug smile on his lips, but every other man apart from Togodumnus was an army officer. Togodumnus felt like some performing animal as he was ushered into the centre to face the Governor and Licinius Spurius. Was this to be his fate, he wondered? Locked in a bare room until he was called for to play the part of a pet Briton for the Governor and his retinue?

Not only were his senses reeling from the ordeal of the past days, he was tired and felt badly in need of a wash. His clothes were crumpled and travel-worn, dull and shabby in the midst of so much polished armour and so many bright cloaks. The Tribunes, most of them not much older than Togodumnus, strutted like peacocks, while the Centurions, mostly older men, veterans of warfare, proudly displayed their medals of honour which hung on coloured ribbons around their necks.

The Governor, still in his purple-striped tunic, seemed less ostentatious than anyone, yet still contrived to dominate the room.

"Gentlemen," he announced, "for those of you who do not know, this is Togodumnus, the son of our famous enemy, Calgacus."

There was a stir among the officers that made Togodumnus' spirits wilt. He had heard of the Roman amphitheatres, where criminals were thrown into an arena to be killed by wild beasts. Aware of the cold, hard eyes of the assembled soldiers, he felt as if he were in the arena now, helpless and waiting to be savaged. The Governor may have referred to him as a guest, but there could be no doubt that his life hung on the whim of these men.

Agricola continued, "Unlike his father, Togodumnus wishes to be our friend. He has agreed to help us."

Once again, Togodumnus wanted to protest. He had given no commitments that he could recall. Yet the Governor pressed on as if his consent had already been given, and the truth was that he did not dare contradict Agricola now. Not if he wanted to remain alive.

The Governor turned to him and explained, "It seems your father is having difficulty bringing all the tribes together. We have learned that he has been forced to travel north to talk to one of the reluctant Kings."

His eyes bore into Togodumnus as he asked, "Were you aware of this?"

Togodumnus could not resist the pressure of the Governor's insistent gaze.

He nodded weakly, "Yes. I knew he had gone north."

"Did he say how long he expected to be away?"

"A few days," Togodumnus answered vaguely. "He does not confide in me about such things. He knows I do not agree with him about this war."

"Not to worry," Agricola smiled. "Thank you for confirming the information we received."

Venutius put in, "I told you my informant was reliable. Calgacus has gone north, leaving his assembled war host without a leader. Now is the time to attack."

Agricola gave the Brigante a cool nod.

"We will advance when we are ready. There is no rush."

Venutius argued, "Destroy them now, while they are leaderless."

192

"No," Agricola insisted. "I want Calgacus to lead them. If we defeat the barbarians while he is not with them, he will be able to continue causing trouble, and will become a rallying point for the barbarians. No, I want him to face us, and lose. That way, even if he escapes us, his reputation will be destroyed."

Venutius regarded the Governor with a sour expression, but backed down in the face of Agricola's assertive stare.

Togodumnus felt strangely detached from the men around him. The individual they were discussing was his father, yet they spoke of him as if he were some mystical, powerful being. Togodumnus knew Calgacus as a demanding, grim-faced disciplinarian who favoured his daughters and had little time for a son who refused to wield a sword. It was difficult for him to equate the man he knew, the father who was constantly preaching about the evils of Rome, with this awe-inspiring warrior who was famous enough to cause even the Romans some concern. On a certain level, Togodumnus knew his father was skilled in warfare, knew that he had often fought and usually won, but he had never witnessed these things, and it was oddly disturbing to hear other men speak of Calgacus the way Daszdius had done.

The discussion around him only served to increase his confusion, and he was forced to concentrate in order to take in what the Governor was saying.

Agricola explained, "Now, gentlemen, this is what we are going to do. It has been a hard winter, but the men are ready, and the grass is beginning to grow again, so there will soon be plenty of grazing for our horses and mules. In addition, our fleet has been bringing supplies north since the weather improved. They will be able to support our advance if we remain near the coast. That is the problem, and here is how we will overcome it."

He tapped the map on the table in front of him, the officers crowding in to get a better view.

The Governor explained, "There is only one route northwards, and it is a narrow one. The two rivers, the Clota and the Bodotria, almost cut the land in half. The gap between them is mostly marshland, with only a narrow section that is passable to our Legions. If we advance through that gap, we will be vulnerable. It is a bottleneck through which our supplies must come until we secure the coast."

"In eight days' time, the Twentieth Legion will advance through that gap. Our information is that, although the enemy has men watching, they have no large force that will oppose us. However, I wish to avoid having our advance blocked in a narrow pass. I have therefore ordered a bridge of boats to be constructed where the Bodotria narrows, several miles downstream from where the Twentieth will be advancing. The Second Legion will cross that bridge, thus outflanking any barbarians who try to block the advance of the twentieth."

Moving his finger on the map, Agricola continued, "To further confuse the enemy, our fleet will land Marines at various points along the eastern coast. They will carry out raids against several villages that Venutius' informant has identified for us. With luck, that will draw some of the barbarians away from our main advance.

"The Ninth Legion will follow once the other Legions and all auxiliary troops have crossed the river. Then we will move forwards in a body, ensuring that our right flank is always in contact with the fleet, so that we can be supplied and any wounded men can be evacuated."

Agricola looked up, searching the faces of his officers.

"Any questions?"

Aulus Atticus asked, "Will you leave any men to guard that bottleneck, sir?"

"Yes, a cohort of auxiliaries will be stationed there. Combined with our fleet, that will secure our lines of supply and communications."

He treated the gathering to a knowing smile as he added, "As you know, clever tactics and bravery in combat are all very well, but it is ensuring the logistics of a campaign which generally proves decisive."

Another officer asked, "Do we know how many barbarians face us, Sir?"

"We know there are several tribes who have joined Calgacus," Agricola replied evenly. "Numbers are difficult to ascertain."

Venutius put in, "There are not more than fifteen thousand. Even if Calgacus persuades the Taexali to join him, they will not add more than five thousand."

"But there could be twice as many," the Governor stated. "I am not convinced by these reports you have obtained. That is why we will advance methodically."

"That will be too slow," Venutius argued. "Calgacus' war bands can move quickly. You will not be able to catch them, and he will not face you in open battle with only twenty thousand warriors."

Agricola smiled, as if Venutius had presented him with an opportunity to reveal a master stroke.

He said, "That does not matter. However many men Calgacus has, it is a barbarian army. Most of them are farmers. They will be more concerned with returning to their homes to tend their fields than with remaining under arms. That is our big advantage, gentlemen. Time is the important factor. It is on our side. We all know these Britons. They are eager to fight, but they do not have the patience for a long campaign. That is why we will wait."

He glanced at Togodumnus, asking, "When is your spring festival?"

Togodumnus felt all eyes on him. Flustered, he blurted, "Beltane? In six days."

"Excellent," smiled Agricola. "We will allow our enemy their celebration. With a little luck, some of them may decide to return home for that festival. We shall allow them the opportunity to do that, then we will launch our attack. By that time, the enemy will have become restless and impatient. We already know there is some dissent among them, and that will grow the longer we wait. As you know, an impatient enemy makes mistakes."

His gaze swept the room as he added, "Having said that, I must emphasise that I want to complete the conquest of Britannia this year. We need to strike a balance. On the one hand, the longer we wait, the more rash and demoralised the enemy will become. There is also a good chance that disease will break out in their camps. We all know this is common when large groups gather together. On the other hand, I want to attack them before their alliance disintegrates under those pressures, because I want a military victory. We must bring them to battle and destroy them."

"How can we force them to fight?" Atticus asked.

"By depriving them of food. We will burn their fields as we advance. We will seize their grain stores and their livestock. We will not enslave their women and children, but will drive them ahead of us so that the enemy will need to feed them. They will be compelled to fight us or starve."

Licinius Spurius, Legate of the Ninth Legion, asked, "Does this mean we will advance up the east coast to remain in contact with the fleet?"

"That's right," Agricola confirmed. "The eastern side of the country has the best farmland. To the north and west, the terrain becomes more mountainous. The east offers the easiest route, and allows us to deprive the enemy of their most fertile land. It is also easier for the fleet to maintain contact with us as there are fewer islands and inlets to make navigation difficult."

Watching in helpless silence while the officers murmured their approval, Togodumnus felt a gnawing dread. The Governor spoke calmly and assertively, discussing death and destruction as if they were merely tactical requirements of his campaign. Togodumnus wanted to cry out; to tell the

Governor that there were real people living to the north, people with hopes and dreams of their own. He felt sick at heart, but he knew there was nothing he could do. Closing his eyes, he vainly tried to soothe his despair.

Agricola was still speaking, his voice drifting through Togodumnus' consciousness, fuelling his torment.

"There is one other thing I want to make clear," the Governor was saying. "Calgacus is famed for ambushing isolated units. He will strike at any small force that strays too far from our main body. He will also attempt to interrupt our supply lines. By keeping our army together, by using the fleet to support us, and by keeping the Ninth slightly behind the other two Legions to protect our supply column, we will defeat him."

Standing straight, jabbing a decisive finger at the map, the Governor announced, "That, gentlemen, is the broad plan. Over the next few days I will issue specific orders to each unit. Make sure your men are ready."

The officers murmured their assent, but Licinius Spurius asked, "What about the other matter Venutius' spy told us of? This barbarian raid that is supposed to take place soon."

Togodumnus opened his eyes. He turned his head to look at Venutius, but the man's self-satisfied expression gave no clues as to what lay behind this revelation. Togodumnus wondered what the mysterious messenger had told the Brigante. There was to be a raid, but who was behind it? His father was away in the north. Had someone else taken command of the war host? Where did they intend to strike, and what did they hope to achieve?

Togodumnus turned his attention to the Governor, hoping to glean some answers, but Agricola's confident reply to the Legate's enquiry gave little away.

"That will not be a problem. I have despatched Julius Macrinus and his cohorts to deal with it. Any barbarians who cross the river will receive a nasty shock."

Chapter XVII

Gabrain gave the order to launch the boats.

"Quietly, lads!" he hissed into the dark night as the shadows moved from the cover of the shoreland grasses and made their way down to the river. Gabrain followed, carrying his scabbarded sword in his left hand to prevent becoming tangled with it when he clambered aboard the tiny curragh.

This was his chance to show what he could do. He was King of the Venicones, a man trained for war, unaccustomed to idleness. He had spent too many days kicking his heels in bored frustration while the tribes had gathered their forces. His own men were ready to fight, and Gabrain had convinced himself that he needed to demonstrate that he was capable of striking a blow against the Romans. He was well aware that word of his embarrassing defeat by Calgacus had spread throughout the camp, and he suspected every man of whispering about him behind his back. He needed to show them that he could fight and win.

Not only that, sitting around for day after day, waiting for Calgacus to return, was not his idea of how a war should be fought.

"Are we warriors or women?" he protested loudly to anyone who would listen. "Calgacus has been away too long. We must do something."

The old druid, Broichan, had advocated waiting, insisting that they should do nothing until Calgacus returned from his mission to Maelchon of the Taexali, but Gabrain was impatient for action.

He had tried to speak to the other Kings, demanding that they support him, but that had proved fruitless.

Bridei, as Gabrain had known he would, had flatly refused. He had gone so far as to tell Gabrain not to be foolish.

"Wait for Calgacus," the squat-faced King had growled.

"Just what I would expect to hear from a Boresti," Gabrain sneered, storming off before Bridei could offer any more arguments.

Drust of the Caledones had refused to even see him. Instead, it was the dark-eyed Bran who met him.

"Many of our men would be glad to join you," Bran had said smoothly. "But our King is indisposed, and Broichan has a great deal of influence. Personally, I agree with you, but I am afraid we cannot help."

Gabrain had tramped away, muttering to himself.

"Drust is Indisposed? Drunk, more like."

Old Ebrauc, whose Damnonii warriors had been beaten by the Romans too often, also declined to involve himself in Gabrain's venture.

Gabrain despised them all, cursing their timidity.

"All the more glory for us," he spat as he told his warriors that they would be making the raid alone.

As he soon discovered, the lack of support made no difference, because he could only muster enough small curraghs and coracles to ferry three hundred men across the river, so he was forced to revise his plan.

He decided to limit his raiding party to three hundred of his best men, and to restrict his attack to a small, pinpoint raid. Some men volunteered to swim the river, using inflated pigs' bladders to help them across the wide water, which would add another hundred to the numbers. Gabrain knew that such a small force was not enough to carry out anything more than a pinprick raid. Even that, though, was better than doing nothing.

Old Ebrauc had shaken his head and observed, "The water is still very cold. They won't be much use in a fight if their limbs are numb from cold."

"They are Venicones," Gabrain had insisted. "They are tough enough to cope with a soaking in a little cold water."

Ebrauc had simply shaken his head and shrugged his shoulders.

Broichan was more forthright in his objections.

"This is madness!" the druid protested. "The Romans have ships patrolling the river all the way up to Giudi."

"Not at night," Gabrain shot back.

Bridei of the Boresti also advised him to abandon his plan, which only made him more determined to carry it out.

"You are not the War Leader," he told Bridei. "I agreed to follow Calgacus, but I will never do as a Boresti says. I will do as I see fit."

"You're a bloody fool, boy," Bridei muttered. "Go ahead and try if you must, but don't come bleating if things go wrong."

"Nothing will go wrong," Gabrain declared confidently.

He had won this small victory over the other Kings, had shown them that he was a true warrior, capable of making decisions for himself. Now he would lead his men across the dark waters of the upper reaches of the Bodotria to show the Romans that they should fear the Venicones.

Dark clouds concealed the stars and the waning moon. The Roman patrols would not see them coming, but Gabrain quickly discovered that the darkness held problems for his own plans. As the men plunged their paddles into the water, they cursed and swore at other boats who blundered blindly into their path. Harsh whispers were exchanged as men fended off neighbouring curraghs that came too close, paddles clashed together and boats collided, almost spilling their occupants into the river.

Gabrain swore with the rest of them, telling the men who paddled his curragh to press on regardless. He had chosen a spot where the river was barely three hundred paces wide, with easy landing on the southern shore. All they needed to do was keep moving.

"Faster, you whoresons!" he hissed.

His curragh was one of the larger boats, holding eight men plus himself. They dug their paddles deep, strained their muscles, and pushed the lightweight boat across the water, battling against the strong current. All around him, he could hear the sounds of splashing, as scores of tiny vessels crawled across the great river, while dozens of men clung to inflated bladders and kicked their legs to propel themselves in the boats' wakes.

It seemed to take an age before they reached the south bank, the boat grinding onto the pebbles. As soon as he felt the impact, Gabrain leaped out onto the shore, drawing his sword and looping the scabbard over his shoulder.

He whirled, trying to see how many others had reached the shore, but it was too dark to make out any detail. The river stretched away to the east, its inky surface only slightly lighter than the blackness of the land. Against this backdrop, he could discern a horde of dim, jostling shadows, but was forced to rely on his ears for guidance. He heard boats grounding on the shore, heard the splashes as men jumped into the shallows, and the dripping footsteps as they scrambled ashore.

"To me!" he called in a hoarse whisper. "To me!"

He could sense men gathering around him, although he had no idea how many. It could have been hundreds, or a few dozen. More boats crunched ashore, more men hurried onto the river bank, and Gabrain could hear the rasping sound of swords being drawn.

"Follow me!" he ordered as he turned inland. "Find the road!"

There was a roadway here, he knew, a route the Romans had built running parallel to the river, a supply road along which they could send troops or wagons. And just beyond the road was a small supply depot, home to no more than twenty soldiers who guarded stores of food and equipment. That was Gabrain's target.

Except that he could not see where it was. The night was so dark that the low wooden fence surrounding the camp was invisible, lost against the impenetrable blackness.

"We will be like ghosts," Gabrain had assured his men when he had explained his plan, but now they were more like lost souls, blundering in the dark.

Gabrain cursed the night. He tried to hurry, but every footstep jarred as he trudged, unseeing, across uneven ground, stumbling several times when he lost his footing.

"Where is the damned road?" he asked aloud.

Nobody had the answer.

He could hear men following him, the sound of their feet and breathing filling his senses, but he was still blind. He pressed on, pushing aside his growing doubts, telling himself that he must soon find the paved roadway. After that, it would be easy.

Then he saw a light. It appeared suddenly, a bright surge of flame as if someone had pulled aside a curtain to reveal a fire. He stopped abruptly, causing the man behind him to collide with him. In the instant it took Gabrain to recover his balance, the fire had spawned a dozen smaller flames.

"What is that?" a man blurted, an edge of panic in his voice.

"Demons!" breathed another.

Gabrain hissed at them to remain quiet.

"It's a fire," he told them.

What he could not fathom was who had lit the blaze, but its presence alarmed him. It should not have been here, and he knew in that instant that his plan had gone wrong.

Dark shapes moved by the fire. Gabrain's eyes were adjusting now, and he guessed it was barely sixty paces away. He had scarcely registered this, when the smaller fires rose in the air, steadied for an instant, then shot skywards with stunning speed before looping down towards the Venicones.

"Fire arrows!" came a startled shout.

Then another voice was bellowing orders from somewhere near the original fire. More shadows moved as a solid line of men rose from where they had lain hidden in the darkness.

Gabrain heard the grunts of effort, then javelins were thudding home amongst his men, some burying their iron tips deep into the earth, others striking flesh. Men screamed and more fire arrows fell among them, creating havoc and illuminating them against the black curtain of the night. Yet more arrows struck, and another volley of javelins thudded into the panicking Venicones.

Gabrain roared his anger, but other men were already shouting in terror.

"Run!"

"Back to the boats!"

Gabrain yelled at his men to stand, to rally around him, but few obeyed. With sickening realisation, he knew that he had already lost, that his war band was fleeing. And in pursuit, the dark line of men was advancing towards them, moving with grim steadiness, using the sputtering flames of the fire arrows to seek out targets.

"We must go, Lord!" one of his warriors shouted, tugging at Gabrain's sleeve.

The King shook him off, growling his defiance, but then he heard the sounds of fighting from his left, the clash of weapons and the yells of war and death.

"Lord!" the man yelled. "They are all around us! We must go back. Now!"

Gabrain hesitated, but the Roman soldiers gave a shout and broke into a lumbering run towards him. Even in the confused darkness he could tell that there were hundreds of them. He was a warrior, a man who despised cowardice, but he knew he would die if he remained where he was. It might be a brave death, but it would be a pointless one, serving no purpose except to prove his stupidity for walking into a trap.

Yelling a savage curse, he turned and ran for the boats.

The retreat was a rout. Men fought one another to board the curraghs. Grabbing paddles or plunging their arms into the water, they propelled the hide-covered vessels away from the shore, some of them half empty, as men abandoned their comrades in their panic to escape, while the Romans closed in on all sides.

There was fighting, but it was confused and chaotic, more of a slaughter than a battle, with the Romans hunting down the fleeing Britons. Only the confusion of the night prevented it from becoming a massacre

As he neared the boats, Gabrain heard someone running close behind him. He turned and caught a glimpse of a dark shape, a helmet reflecting orange light from the flickering fire arrows that dotted the ground. He swung his sword, jarring his arm with the impact as it gouged into a shield. He felt a stab of pain as a blade lashed across his forearm, but his opponent was just as blind as he was, and he managed to dodge clear, dragging his sword free and swinging it wildly to crash against his opponent's helmet. The man fell with a yelp.

"Lord! This way!"

Gabrain staggered as he ran for a boat. It was a small vessel, already nearly full of frantic, scrambling warriors, but he yelled at them to wait for him. The sounds of fighting were close on all sides now, and he had only one chance of escaping. He plunged into the shallows, water drenching his boots, then hands pulled him into the boat which lurched alarmingly as he half fell onto the wooden benches. His sword clattered into the boat's depths, and he grabbed for it, but could not find it.

"Go!" someone shouted, and the boat splashed away from the bank, its course ragged and uneven. Gabrain struggled to sit upright while men grunted and gasped with the effort of paddling the boat across the broad river.

"Give me a paddle!" he shouted.

Someone thrust a wooden paddle into his hands. He plunged it over the side, feeling it bite into the water, and he strained his arms and shoulders as he heaved.

More arrows whistled nearby. One struck a man in a boat which was no more than three paces to Gabrain's right. The victim arched his back, then toppled slowly into the water, the movement causing the boat to dip sideways. Water gushed over the side and the curragh was instantly waterlogged, the rest of the occupants yelling in alarm as they plunged into the cold water.

"Keep going!" Gabrain called to the warriors in his boat. There was nothing they could do to help the men who had been flung into the river. They would swim or they would drown, but anyone who tried to help them would only become targets for the archers on the shore.

"Keep going!" Gabrain repeated as arrows flew past their ears. At every moment, he expected to feel one of the sharp points bury itself in his exposed back, but now the night protected him because the archers could find no easy targets in the darkness.

Sweating and breathing hard, they pushed the boat back to safety. Gabrain did not stop paddling until the curragh crashed onto the northern shore with a jarring crunch. Wearily, he dropped the paddle and searched for his sword. It was lying in dank water at the foot of the boat. Taking some comfort from the familiar feel of its weight, he hauled it out and stepped ashore.

The survivors stood bemused, many of them ashamed at their flight, all of them grateful that they had escaped. Some were nursing wounds, others staring silently at the southern shore, where torches moved along the river bank as the Romans hunted for any survivors who had not managed to reach the boats.

Splashing and gasping breaths announced the arrival of men who had swum the river. They staggered ashore, exhausted and shivering, but at least they were alive.

Gabrain felt the bitter taste of defeat. He had led his men into a trap, and now the other Kings would mock him. He had ignored the warnings, dismissed the objections, and now he had failed. He was not used to failure, and the feeling hurt worse than the still bleeding cut on his forearm.

"How many got away?" he asked.

Nobody could tell him.

Gabrain swore softly, but he was glad of the utter darkness, for it meant he could not see the extent of the disaster.

Chapter XVIII

Anderius Facilis woke to a calm, peaceful morning. On the other side of the tiny shelter, Antonius Pulcher was snoring softly, buried beneath a pile of furs and blankets, his breathing slow and rhythmic. From outside, Facilis could hear the sounds of people moving around and talking. A woman laughed, a happy, carefree laugh that made Facilis feel deeply content. He had never thought to hear such a sound again. Even the distant wailing protests of a squalling baby were somehow comforting, confirming that he had left the horrors of his voyage with the Usipi far behind.

Facilis pushed aside his bedcovers and pulled on the clothing he had been given to replace his tattered tunic. Long, tight-fitting trousers, a linen shirt and a leather jerkin felt strange and foreign, but they had the advantage of being new and clean. The stout leather shoes were soft and comfortable, but he decided against wearing the thick, hooded cloak he had been presented with. The bright flashes of sunlight that were filtering through the tiny gaps in the crude, wooden shelter told him that it was another fine morning.

Pulcher snuffled and stirred, blinking in the dim light. He groaned, as if he had been dreaming of a more civilised bed and was disappointed by the reality of his surroundings.

"Good morning. Are you feeling better?" Facilis enquired.

Pulcher sighed, "I think so. I have a foul taste in my mouth, though."

"It serves you right," Facilis grinned. "If you hadn't eaten so much, you wouldn't have had that bellyache, and their medicine woman wouldn't have given you a purgative."

"There is no need for a lecture," Pulcher grumbled. "It was not the quantity of the food, it was its strangeness. My stomach is used to more refined meals."

"Your stomach, just like mine, hasn't been used to any meals recently. Unless you count Usipi broth."

Pulcher scowled at the reminder of the human flesh he had consumed. He pushed himself up on one elbow, squinting at the door.

"What time is it?"

"I don't know. Mid-morning, I would guess. Our hosts have allowed us to sleep in again."

Pulcher snorted, "They are a careless lot. They don't even bother to guard our door." He lowered his voice to a conspiratorial whisper as he added, "We should try to escape."

"How?"

"I don't know," Pulcher rasped. "You are the soldier, or so you claimed. But there are hardly any men in this place, and the few that Calgacus has left are either too young or too old to fight. We could steal horses and get away."

Facilis nodded thoughtfully. Calgacus had ridden away two days previously, taking his war band with him, but he had left the two Romans here to recover their strength. Clean clothes, a dip in the icy waters of the upland lake, and abundant food had worked a small miracle on their bodies and spirits, but Facilis had given no thought to trying to leave.

He said, "The women have spears, you know, and they know how to use them. I doubt that we would get far."

Pulcher's mouth twisted in a grimace that was almost comical.

"The women fight?" he spat. "They are savages, Facilis. We must get away. They could do anything to us."

"They have," Facilis replied. "They have fed us, clothed us, allowed us to wash and shave. They have given

208

us this shelter when many of their own people are sleeping in tents."

"Tents they stole from our army," Pulcher retorted, unwilling to concede that the Britons were remotely civilised.

"That is not the point," Facilis told the Quaestor. "The point is that they have treated us well."

"So far. But what do they intend to do to us? They might keep us as slaves."

"Yes, they might."

"Which makes it imperative that we escape while their menfolk are away."

"The men are away fighting against our army. They will lose, and will be forced to surrender. When that happens, they may let us go."

"Or they may murder us," Pulcher argued. "They have druids who delight in sacrificing captives."

"Well, let us take a few more days to look around. There may be an opportunity to escape, but if we try and fail, they will surely guard us more closely, so it would be best to devise a plan that is certain of success. As things stand, I don't even know where we are."

"We are in a filthy, rat-infested hovel, surrounded by barbarians," Pulcher asserted.

"I haven't seen any rats," Facilis said innocently.

Pulcher shot him a disapproving look.

"You like it here, don't you?" he accused.

"It is infinitely better than our time with the Usipi," Facilis replied, attempting to sound non-committal.

"That's not what I meant. I saw you talking to some of the women and children yesterday. You were enjoying yourself."

Facilis could not deny the accusation. He shrugged, "It was nice to talk to people who didn't want to kill us."

"You don't know that they won't turn on us," Pulcher insisted. "You cannot trust barbarians, Facilis."

Facilis could not be bothered arguing. Pulcher's dire predictions were spoiling his day, which had barely begun. He said, "Perhaps you are right. We should not take any chances. I suggest you remain here while I go and see if I can find us some breakfast. Are you hungry?"

"I could manage something," Pulcher agreed with feigned disinterest.

"I'll be back soon," Facilis told him. "Try not to insult anyone who comes to talk to you."

"They are savages, Facilis. I have no desire to talk to any of them, and I couldn't understand them even if I did."

"Some of them speak Latin," Facilis reminded him, taking a perverse delight from the Quaestor's sour expression. "Just wait here. I won't be long."

Leaving Pulcher to fret over what the Britons might do to him, Facilis opened the door and stepped outside, straightening up after ducking through the low doorway.

It was, as he had guessed, a fine spring morning, with gentle sunshine to warm him and a soft mountain breeze to caress his skin. He stood still, looking all around, taking in his surroundings.

The village was bustling with people, everyone busy, but nobody seeming to hurry. Houses were being constructed, wooden pillars, wattle and daub walls, and thatched roofs, but the task of building was being carried out as if there were no rush to complete these new homes. The workers, old men or teenage children, laughed and joked while they worked.

The new houses were being placed in what seemed to Facilis to be a haphazard fashion. There were no recognisable streets in the settlement, just a random scattering of roundhouses, stolen Roman army tents, and a variety of other shelters made from rock, wood and turf. Facilis supposed that, to Pulcher's eyes, it appeared chaotic, yet to him it felt oddly homely and welcoming.

Animals wandered the settlement; dogs, cats, pigs, and goats. There were chickens and geese, even some ducks paddling at the edges of the upland lake. Facilis had been told that the cattle were down in the valley where the grazing was better. He had also been assured that the Britons had fields of barley, oats and rye.

What they did not have were many men. As Pulcher had observed, the settlement was full of women and children, but only a handful of men, mostly grey-haired individuals who were too old to fight.

One of those men approached him now. There may have been no guard outside the door of their tiny shelter, but this man had obviously been watching from a distance. Now he stalked towards Facilis with a grim expression on his features. He was tall, grey-haired and walked with a pronounced limp, but he held himself erect and he wore a sword at his left hip.

"You are awake at last," he grunted in crude Latin. "Come with me. The lady wants to talk to you."

Facilis replied with a smile. "Good morning to you, too. Could I have some breakfast first?"

The man shot him a hostile look, and Facilis realised that, despite the limp and the prematurely grey hair, the Briton was not as old as he first appeared. He was probably around the same age as Facilis.

The Briton said, "I will send someone with food for your friend. You can eat with the lady. She is waiting."

With that, he turned abruptly and stomped away, clearly expecting Facilis to follow him. With a shrug, the Roman hurried to catch up.

His limping guide led him to a large roundhouse where a group of women were sitting on the ground outside the open doorway, chatting while they spun wool on hand-held spindles. One of them, Facilis noticed, was the fair-haired woman who had been introduced to him as Beatha,

Calgacus' wife. She smiled and rose to her feet when she saw him approach.

"Good morning," she greeted in Latin. "You have slept late."

"He wants some breakfast," the sullen guard rumbled.

"Thank you, Garco," said Beatha. "I will make sure he is fed."

Garco nodded before clumping away again.

"Forgive him," Beatha said to Facilis. "He was a recruit in your Auxiliaries once, and he has bad memories of the time."

Facilis was not sure what to say. He knew the other women were regarding him with curious eyes, their wool temporarily forgotten, their ears ready to pounce on any inadvertently inappropriate word. Not only that, Beatha was standing in front of him, fair and radiant as a goddess, and he did not know how to respond.

He was rescued by Beatha herself, who made her excuses to the gawking women and led him away from the roundhouse.

"Let us go for a walk," she told him, giving him no opportunity to protest.

She led him towards the loch that filled the deepest part of the hilltop crater. Near the side of the water were several fires where large cooking pots and clay ovens provided the settlements communal meals. Beatha spoke to one of the young women who oversaw the cooking, obtaining a wooden bowl filled with gruel.

"Not the most appetising meal," she said as she passed it to Facilis. "But we all have the same."

"It is fine," he assured her as he gratefully spooned the porridge to his mouth.

"You are looking a lot better than when you first arrived," she smiled.

"I feel a great deal better," he agreed.

"What about your friend? How is he this morning?"

"Pulcher? He's not really my friend. Circumstances threw us together, that's all. But he seems better."

"That is good," Beatha murmured, her tone suggesting there were some reason behind her enquiry that was more than mere politeness.

Facilis studied her while he ate, taking surreptitious glances, hoping she would not notice how much he admired her. With Calgacus gone, Beatha had assumed the role of host, taking a solicitous interest in the two Romans. She had not intruded, had left them to rest and recover from their long ordeal, but she had taken time to talk to them, to make sure they were being properly cared for. Facilis had taken an instant liking to her, a liking that was, he realised, already becoming something more.

She had admitted to being forty-six years old, but Facilis thought she could easily pass for a woman ten years younger. She was undeniably good-looking, even beautiful, with fair skin, blue eyes and golden hair. But her beauty was more than mere physical attractiveness. There was an air of calm, almost serene determination about her that he found fascinating.

He had felt a sense of loss when Calgacus had departed, because the giant warrior had been a link to Facilis' own past, but now he was pleased that Calgacus had gone, because it meant he could speak to Beatha alone. That thought sent a shiver of unaccustomed excitement through his bones.

Masking his thoughts, he asked, "What was it you wanted to talk about?"

Beatha hesitated, as if trying to make up her mind about some problem.

She said, "Come, let us go over to the side of the corrie. We can talk privately."

Facilis passed his now empty bowl back to the young cook, a pretty brunette with a spark of mischief in her eyes. She gave him a flirtatious smile as their hands briefly made contact, her touch lingering longer than it needed to. Slightly flustered, he turned hurriedly away to follow Beatha to the rim of the crater. Behind him, he heard laughter from the women who tended the cooking pots, and knew they were talking about him.

When they crested the edge of the corrie, Beatha sat down on a large rock that was spacious enough for both of them.

"Sit down," she invited.

Facilis sat beside her, trying to quell his growing sense of anticipation. They were still within sight of the village but out of earshot, and the seat she had chosen provided a panoramic view of majestic hills and a long, narrow, tree-filled valley that stretched away southwards. Directly in front of their rocky bench, the side of the hill fell away steeply, the slope covered by a dense forest.

"It is beautiful here," Beatha remarked.

"Its beauty is enhanced by your presence," Facilis said, not sure why he had spoken aloud, and almost regretting his words, but he found her so entrancing that he could not help himself.

"Thank you for the compliment," she smiled. "Calgacus warned me you had a silver tongue."

"I meant no offence," he assured her, feeling clumsy.

"And none was taken. But we have more important things to discuss."

Facilis did not want to discuss anything else. The morning was warm, he was here with a beautiful woman and he would have been happy to sit there with her all day. He recognised the feeling of attraction he felt, wondering how she could have such an effect on him when he had only met her two days ago.

He knew she was upset about the news of her son being taken prisoner by a Roman raiding party. This morning, though, she was calm, her fears under control, which, for Facilis, only served to make her more desirable.

214

Facilis frowned. He told himself his reaction to being near her was simply because he had not been this close to a woman for more months than he could remember, but there were other women in the village, some of them young and pretty, some, like the cook with the teasing smile, probably available if he wished to take advantage, yet he had barely paid any attention to them. They did not stir the same response in him. In contrast, there was something about Beatha that held him entranced and made him want to reach out to hold her. Every word she spoke, every tiny movement she made, captivated him.

He shook his head. If any man knew the answer as to why a particular woman could snare a man's emotions, that man would be the wisest person in the world.

"Are you all right?" she asked, tilting her head slightly to look at him.

"It feels a little strange, being here," he explained weakly. "The place, the clothes, the people. It's all very different."

"Yet Calgacus tells me you have spent many years in Britannia. You must know our people well to have learned our language."

"I have a knack for languages," he replied. "And, as you say, I was here for a long time. But I was never a part of it."

"Of course not," she smiled. "You are a Roman. All Romans want everyone to be like them. Rome will not change, so her neighbours must."

Facilis shrugged, "I suppose that is true. But it is because Rome is the greatest place in the whole world."

Beatha smiled, sweeping out a graceful arm to encompass the view below them.

"Some would say this is the greatest place in the world."

"I suppose it depends on your point of view," he conceded.

"I suppose it does," she agreed. "For a Roman, this place does not hold the same meaning as it does for us."

"What meaning does it hold?" he asked.

She frowned slightly, gathering her thoughts before telling him, "It is difficult to explain. Here, we are close to all the things that make up the world around us. The trees, the rocks, the rivers and hills, they all have spirits of their own, and here, we are close to them." She paused before adding, "And here, we are far from Rome."

He nodded, pursing his lips.

"Rome will be here soon enough," he ventured cautiously.

"Perhaps," she shrugged, as if she did not really believe him. "Rome certainly seems intent on seizing this land from us. Calgacus says that is because you Romans are afraid of anything different. You must conquer your neighbours because you fear them."

"Rome does not fear anyone," he said, the response almost automatic.

"Not even the Germans, who destroyed three Legions? Not the Parthians, who slew Crassus and slaughtered his army?"

"Those things happened a long time ago," he countered.

Beatha continued, "I think you even fear the Greeks, who excel in science and have a love of enquiry. Romans do not ask questions, do they? You simply follow orders. You keep things the same and you stamp out anyone or anything that defies your view of the world."

Facilis was astonished at both the passion in her voice and the extent of her knowledge. To hear any woman expressing these views was surprising enough, but to find a barbarian woman saying such things was beyond his experience.

She must have seen his incredulity, because she laughed, "It would probably shock your large friend, but I

216

was a Roman matron once. I gave it all up to come here. Well, not here exactly, but away from Rome."

Facilis nodded, "Pulcher finds many things about your culture shocking."

"But you don't?"

"Sometimes I find them mystifying," he admitted, "but I am trying to understand."

"I know. That is one reason I trust you."

He regarded her quizzically.

"I'm not sure I follow you."

"It is difficult for any of us to trust Romans," Beatha explained. "We know all about you, and we enjoy many of the things your Empire can provide, but we do not share your view of the world, and we know how Rome has treated other Britons."

"But you trust me?"

"Yes, I do."

"May I ask why? I am as much a Roman as any citizen."

"Before I answer that, I would like to hear your story. Calgacus tells me you have been through a great deal, but I would like to hear it from you."

Warily, Facilis asked, "What do you want to know?"

"As much as you are willing to tell me."

Facilis hesitated, wondering where to begin. Then he decided to tell her everything. The words came tumbling out, the memories fuelling his story. He told her of his first encounters with Calgacus, of leaving the army, of Pompeii and his lost family, and of his return to Britannia and the fateful voyage with the mutinous Usipi. He told his tale and, for the first time since fate had destroyed his home and family, he was able to tell it without tears.

When he was done, Beatha laid a gentle hand on his arm.

"I am so sorry," she said. "We heard about the volcano, but we could not imagine how dreadful it must have been."

They sat in silence for a long, peaceful moment, until Beatha seemed to become aware that her hand was still resting on his arm. She removed it, giving him another sympathetic smile.

"Despite the differences in our cultures, people are the same in many respects, wherever you go."

"Yes," he agreed.

He wished she would touch him again, or that he dared to reach out to hold her hand, but she sat very still, and he did not want to end their time together by taking too bold a step. Now that he had shared the story of his life with her, he felt closer to her, and he did not want the moment to end.

Feeling a compulsion to keep talking, he said, "People are essentially the same, which is why I think you should try to persuade Calgacus not to fight. He cannot hope to win, and Rome is not as bad a master as you make out."

"We wish to be our own masters," she stated firmly. "As I have told you, we know how much we would lose if Rome takes control. One thing you can be certain of is that Calgacus will never give in."

"Would you really lose so much?" he argued. "Your people have rulers already. They will pay tithes or taxes as it is. What difference would it make to pay those taxes to Rome? You would receive many benefits from being part of the Empire. It would also save many lives that will be thrown away if you fight."

Beatha remained calm as she replied, "I told you, I was a Roman once. I know how the Empire treats women. We would become property, little better than the cattle and other livestock. We would have no rights at all. Among our people, women are free to do as they please. They are not chattels. We can own land, make contracts, decide who we

218

marry and can divorce a man who mistreats us or is unfaithful. Can Roman women do these things?"

Facilis shook his head.

"You know they cannot," he admitted.

"And the men would lose the right to carry weapons. You cannot know how much of a blow that would be for them. Whatever you say, they would be subject to Roman law, backed by Roman force. That is too much to ask. We value freedom too much to surrender."

"Nobody is truly free," Facilis asserted. "Everyone has their place, and I know you have your own laws. You say women are free, but once they are married, surely they lose their independence?"

"Not in law, although there are always some who allow themselves to be subservient. However, our marriages are partnerships, which either may dissolve if they are mistreated, or discover their spouse has been unfaithful."

"You recognise adultery, then?"

She laughed, "You are thinking of young Anhareth, who served you your breakfast?"

He was thinking of someone else, someone sitting beside him, but he could not tell her that, so he gave a shy smile.

"Is she married?"

"Oh, yes, but her husband is away, like most of the men. I'm sure she wouldn't mind getting to know you better if that is what you want."

"I was just curious about your customs," Facilis insisted. "Besides, what would happen if her husband found out? I don't want an angry swordsman coming after me."

"You are probably right. Anhareth's husband can be a bit jealous. But I was trying to explain our laws. Let us say, for example, that he did learn that she had been unfaithful. He would then have three days to decide whether to divorce her. The same applies if a woman learns of her husband's infidelity; she has three days to decide what to do."

Beatha smiled as she continued, "And during those three days, the offended party can punish the offender without fear of retribution."

"Punish?"

"Within reason. One woman I know once emptied a slops bucket over her husband's head while he was sitting with his friends. Then she told him she wanted a divorce and he would need to clean his clothes for himself. That was seen as a good way of dispensing justice. Far better than the Roman way which sees a man fined, but a woman banished or imprisoned."

Facilis observed, "You make your way of life sound idyllic."

"It is far from that," Beatha admitted. "Life is hard for many. There are mean, spiteful people, there are men who beat their wives and children, there are warlords who take what they can because they are strong enough. But there are checks against such crimes."

"What sort of checks?" he asked, genuinely interested.

"For one thing, the Kings tend to keep order in their own territories, and they also keep a check on one another. If any King seems likely to become too powerful, the others will often unite against him."

She gave a teasing smile as she added, "I say 'Kings' but there are often Queens as well. Women are permitted to rule, you see."

"Yes, I remember that."

"There are also the druids," Beatha continued. "They have the power to judge Kings, although the Kings do not always abide by their decisions these days."

"The druids?" Facilis protested. "They are evil. They offer human sacrifices."

Beatha shrugged off the accusation with another smile.

220

She asked, "Is that so unlike Rome, where prisoners are thrown into the arena to be devoured by wild beasts? What is that if not human sacrifice? I would say it is worse, because it is done for pure entertainment. The druids at least have the excuse of religious ceremony."

"Calgacus does not like the druids," Facilis objected, feeling the need to offer some argument against Beatha's opposition to Rome.

"No, he does not. But there are few of them left anyway."

"For which you blame Rome, I suppose?"

"It was your army that destroyed them," Beatha agreed. "As it intends to destroy all of us."

"Not if you agree peace terms," Facilis urged. "I have already told Calgacus I will speak to the Governor if he wants to make peace."

"I know. But Calgacus wants peace on our terms, not on Roman ones. The tribes are united in that."

"At least let me try," he persisted.

Beatha shook her head emphatically.

"There is no point," she told him. "Rome has betrayed too many people who thought they were her allies."

"Then what is it you want from me?" he asked. "I do not think you invited me here just to argue about our respective cultures."

She treated him to another smile as she said, "You are quite correct. As I said earlier, I trust you. That is why I felt safe enough to come here alone with you."

"You have nothing to fear from me," he assured her.

"I know that. You are not the sort of man who would abandon a comrade, not even one as worthless as your large friend, Antonius Pulcher. Nor would you take advantage of a woman to make an escape."

"You seem very sure of that," he said, returning her smile.

221

"I am. Although I probably should have told you that you could not escape anyway." She swept her arm out, indicating the valley. "That is the only way out of here. There is nothing except mountains in every other direction. And the valley is guarded. Even if you could have overpowered me and stolen a horse, you could not get away."

For an instant, Facilis wondered whether she had overheard his conversation with Pulcher, but he realised she had merely anticipated his thoughts.

He said, "At the moment, all I want to do is recover my strength. I have already told Pulcher that we will be freed sooner or later, when our army comes north."

"You seem very sure of that," she remarked, mirroring his earlier comment.

"I am. Calgacus is not the sort of man who would kill prisoners unnecessarily."

"No, he is not, although there are others here who would gladly dispose of a couple of Romans."

"Your sullen friend, Garco?" he guessed.

"Among others. But, as you say, Calgacus would not allow it."

"He is an honourable man," Facilis nodded.

Beatha laughed, "Yes, he is. He is also our greatest hope against your Governor. If anyone can defeat your Legions, it is Calgacus. He is quite formidable, you know."

"He still cannot win. You must try to make him see that."

To his surprise, Beatha gave a soft laugh as she replied, "He will not change his mind. However formidable he might be, he is just a man, with flaws like any other man. And one of those flaws is that he is very stubborn."

She paused before adding, "He is also bad tempered and hard on everyone around him."

"Yet everyone follows him?" Facilis challenged.

"There are always those who will challenge him, because that is our way, but yes, most of us follow him

222

because we believe in him. You see, for all his faults, he is harder on himself than on anyone else. He leads by example, and our people admire that. They wish to remain free, and they know that he will not rest until he has driven your army back."

She grew suddenly serious as she continued, "That is why I need you to help me."

Facilis blinked in surprise.

"What do you want me to do?" he asked.

Beatha sighed, "My son has been taken from me. I am afraid that he will be used as a hostage against Calgacus. I am terrified that your Governor will threaten to kill Togodumnus unless Calgacus surrenders himself."

Facilis nodded his understanding. It would not be the first time a Roman captive had been used that way.

But he wanted to offer some reassurance, so he said, "Your son is more likely to be sent to Rome."

"Where he will probably be executed. Your new Emperor, Domitian, is said to be fond of executing prisoners."

Facilis could not argue with her about that. Domitian had been on the purple throne for little more than a year, but his reputation was already dark with savage deeds. Some said he had been responsible for the death of his older brother and predecessor, Titus, who had died of a mysterious illness in the prime of his life.

Beatha went on, "Calgacus will never surrender to save anyone, not even his son. There is too much at stake for all our people for him to do that. So, even if we win this war, I lose because my son will be dead. And if we are defeated, I will probably lose Calgacus, because he will die fighting Rome. Do you see my problem?"

"I understand. But what can I do?"

"You can speak to your Governor. Not about peace terms, but about my son. Tell him that Togodumnus' death will achieve nothing. Ask him to let my son go. In exchange,

I will let you go free. You and your fellow Roman, Pulcher. That is a fair exchange, I think."

Facilis was not sure how to respond. He asked, "Does Calgacus know what you intend to do?"

"Not yet. But he will not refuse me in this."

She looked into his eyes, her expression pleading for his help as she asked, "What about you, Anderius Facilis? Will you refuse me?"

His reply was immediate, because he could not refuse her anything.

"I will do as you ask."

Beatha stood up, brushing the back of her dress as she did so. She looked down at him, her eyes damp with emotion. "Thank you. We will leave tomorrow morning."

Chapter XIX

Under a sky of drab clouds the colour of damp clay, Calgacus stood in the now familiar enclosure of Cingel's tomb, on the broad summit of the sacred hill. It was as he remembered it, as if he had not been away for the better part of ten days.

In front of him, the Kings sat with their chieftains and advisers clustered around them, their banners and totems proudly on display.

It was the same, but some things had changed. When the Kings had last assembled, their mood had been one of mutual suspicion, but now it was one of gloom, defeat, and almost open hostility. The shift matched the change in the weather, Calgacus thought bitterly. The gusting wind seemed to fan the complaints, and the faint spots of rain fuelled the sense of doom that hung over the meeting. He felt his frustration growing as he listened to their grievances and accusations.

Broichan was doing his best to cajole the gathering into some sort of unanimity, but even the old druid's skills as an orator could not overcome the knowledge that Gabrain's raid across the river had ended in complete failure. That defeat had sparked fears and re-awakened doubts over the tribes' ability to withstand the Legions.

Gabrain himself sat to one side, his face flushed and full of rage, challenging anyone who dared mention his failure. There had already been some whispered comments, with Broichan needing to intervene to prevent scuffles breaking out.

"We were betrayed!" Gabrain insisted. "The Romans were waiting for us. But at least the Venicones have tried to do something, while the rest of you sit around on your backsides, talking and boasting, but doing nothing."

Bridei snorted, "If you'd boasted less about what you were going to do, word of your plan might not have got out."

That brought another round of mutual abuse which Calgacus only quelled by shouting louder than anyone else.

"All of you sit down and be quiet! We are chieftains and Kings, not squabbling children!"

Bridei looked chastened, but Gabrain refused to be silenced. He complained, "Two of my villages have been raided. The Romans are landing men on the shore, then withdrawing after they have destroyed our homes and fields. They seem to know exactly where to go."

Ebrauc, the aged King of the Damnonii, put in, "And their scouts are venturing further and further north. Their army will come any day now. They are building a bridge of boats to cross the river."

"And we are running low on food," Gabrain grumbled.

Calgacus had begun to think things could not get much worse when the arrival of Maelchon proved him wrong. The Taexali King had ridden south with seven hundred mounted warriors, the pick of his war host.

"The rest of my men will be here in a few days," he announced as he swaggered into the meeting place with his chieftains and bodyguards surrounding him.

One of those men was Algarix. His face was still swollen and bruised, but he strutted proudly beside his King, wearing the shining scabbard of Calgacus' sword on his back, letting everyone see it. He made a show of stopping in front of Calgacus, his lips curling in a wicked grin.

"This is a fine blade," he declared loudly. "I will make good use of it."

Calgacus had told the Kings that he had given the sword as a gift, telling them that the alliance was more important than a mere sword. He had tried to sound nonchalant about it, but it took all his resolve not to show how much he hated seeing Algarix wearing the famous blade.

Restraining his anger, he replied, "I hope you do."

With a mocking sneer, Algarix said, "I see you have found a replacement sword. I doubt whether it is as good as this one, though."

"It will be good enough to kill some Romans," Calgacus stated coldly.

In truth, the longsword he now carried on his back was heavy and cumbersome compared to the Sword of Caratacus, but he refused to give Algarix the satisfaction of hearing him admit that.

Algarix swaggered away to join the rest of Maelchon's bodyguard, grinning happily. Calgacus watched him, struggling to keep his temper in check.

Broichan proclaimed a formal welcome, but the atmosphere remained tense. The other Kings, who had insisted Calgacus persuade Maelchon to join them, were soon regretting their decision.

The first butt of Maelchon's scorn was Drust of the Caledones who, as usual, had been drinking for most of the day.

"Perhaps there is no need for us to fight the Romans," Maelchon declared loudly, grinning at Drust. "You could knock them out by just breathing on them."

Drust's warriors shouted angry protests, shaking their fists, but Drust himself merely lowered his eyes and wrapped his arms around his chest, hugging himself as if he could protect himself from Maelchon's scorn by ignoring it.

Maelchon turned a mocking eye on Gabrain, saying, "You need not fear now that the Taexali are here. We will show you how to fight properly."

Gabrain surged to his feet, snarling furiously, forcing Broichan to step between him and Maelchon, arms and voice raised as he demanded order.

Calgacus' temper boiled over.

"That is enough!" he roared, drowning out the residual murmurs of discontent. "We are here to fight alongside one another. We cannot beat the Romans if we fall out among ourselves."

The warriors grudgingly settled down, but Bran, again acting as spokesman for the Caledones, asked, "Can we win at all? The Romans seem to know what we are doing."

Gabrain growled his agreement. "We walked into a trap. It was as if they knew we were coming."

"Perhaps there is a spy in our camp," Maelchon suggested with malicious glee. "I wonder who it could be?"

He cast around, looking at each King in turn, raising more muttered protests with his unspoken accusations.

Gabrain, his young face flushed, leaped to his feet again, bellowing, "Do not hurl false allegations at me. I lost many good men!"

Maelchon grinned manically, while Calgacus clapped his hands together, demanding silence.

Angrily, he declared, "There is no reason to believe anyone has betrayed us deliberately. There could be several explanations as to how the Romans learned of our plans. It is clear that they had warning of Gabrain's raid, but I want you all to know that I think he did the right thing. Had it not been for word of his plan leaking out, he would most likely have succeeded in his aim."

Gabrain seemed surprised at the unexpected praise. He gave Calgacus a grudging nod before sitting down.

Ebrauc frowned nervously, "What explanation could there be?"

"The Romans have scouts," Calgacus replied patiently. "They also know how to interrogate prisoners or deserters."

"None of my men have deserted," Maelchon asserted loudly.

Despite his impatience with Maelchon's disruptive behaviour, Calgacus almost smiled when he heard Bridei mutter, "Only because they haven't had time."

His smile faded when he noticed Algarix lean close to Maelchon to whisper something in the Taexali King's ear. Maelchon gave a savage nod of delight before smirking at Calgacus and announcing, "There may be a simple solution to this mystery. Is it not true that your own son has joined the Romans?"

Calgacus cursed silently. He had not told anyone of the raid on his home but, somehow, Maelchon had discovered it. Not that it had been a secret, but he had hoped that the other Kings would not learn of it. Now, though, the word was out, and Maelchon was smiling his cruel smile, demanding a response.

Calgacus said coldly, "My son was taken against his will. Even so, he knows nothing of our plans, and could not have revealed any information."

Bran, quick as ever to pounce on problems, declared, "It is well known that your son is an admirer of the Romans."

"It makes no difference," Calgacus asserted, feeling his temper rise. "He cannot tell them anything because he does not know what our plans are."

Old Ebrauc asked, "What will you do if the Romans use him as a hostage against you? They may threaten to kill him unless you surrender."

Calgacus could feel the eyes of every man studying him closely, waiting for his answer.

Speaking firmly, he told them, "I will not betray our alliance for the sake of any man, not even my son. If the Romans kill him, I will take revenge in my own way."

Ebrauc gave him a studied look, as if recognising how much the admission had cost, and the aged King of the Damnonii gave a regretful nod.

Maelchon persisted, "If it was not your son who betrayed us, then who was it?"

Calgacus wanted to lash out at the Taexali King. Maelchon was speaking as if he had been personally betrayed, playing the part of an aggrieved victim.

229

Calgacus insisted, "It does not matter how they heard of Gabrain's raid. What matters is that we learn from it. There are many reasons why a man might tell the Romans of our plans. Some might be tortured, others could be threatened, or they might even be rewarded. What we need to do is keep our plans as secret as we can."

"That won't be difficult," spat Gabrain. "You haven't told us what your plan is."

"Maybe he doesn't trust us," Maelchon sneered.

Calgacus ignored the comment. He said to the Kings, "I will tell you my plan now, but keep it to yourselves. You have raised some problems, and I want to address as many as I can. So, to alleviate the food situation, we will disperse our forces into three camps. The Caledones and the Boresti will remain here, but the Venicones will move east, towards the coast, while the Damnonii and the Taexali will go west. That means we will not all be scouring the same area for food. But make sure you send foraging parties out every day."

He saw Gabrain give a satisfied nod.

The Venicones King said, "We will also be able to counter their raids if we are closer to the coast."

"Yes, but the raids are not the main problem. Ebrauc is correct; the Romans will come north soon. They will cross their bridge of boats, or come past the marshes at Giudi, or perhaps both. They may also use their ships to ferry men across the river in a third location."

Ebrauc observed, "We cannot stop them if we are separated."

"I don't want to stop them," Calgacus replied. "I want them to advance. Our main force will draw them on until they leave the river behind."

Now, Gabrain's face displayed alarm.

"You will abandon our homes to the invaders?"

Raising a placatory hand, Calgacus told him, "Only until they are far enough from their supply bases."

Gabrain challenged, "What if they stay near the coast where their ships can keep them supplied?"

"They won't. They need to destroy our war host, and they need to do it soon, so we will draw them inland. Do not attempt to fight them. I don't want them to know where our two flanking war bands are. They must have all their attention on what they believe is our only army."

Ebrauc frowned, "How do you know what they are going to do?"

Calgacus smiled, "I have my own sources of information. The Governor needs a victory this year. He will also want to kill or capture me, so we will use those two factors to lead him away from his ships. As I said, our main force will draw them inland. We can move much more quickly than they can, so we will let them know where we are, but will not let them catch us until we are ready."

Ebrauc remarked, "The Governor is no fool. He will suspect a trap."

"Perhaps. But he will have no choice except to follow us. By making small raids, then withdrawing, we will keep his eyes fixed on the main force. That is what he expects us to do, so we will not disappoint him. Then, when we have lured his army far enough, the other two forces will sweep in behind them."

He held his hands apart, then closed them, demonstrating how the Romans would be encircled.

"Can we beat them even if we surround them?" Bran enquired cautiously.

"We don't need to beat them," Calgacus replied. "If we get the opportunity, we will attack them, but only if we hold all the advantages. Our main aim, though, is to force them to dig in, to remain in their marching camps. We will cut them off from their supplies until hunger forces them to withdraw. Then we will fall on them while they are retreating."

"They might not retreat," Bridei pointed out. "They might keep coming."

"Then we will continue to deprive them of food. We will attack their foraging parties, ambush their supply columns, and leave nothing for them."

Inevitably, it was Maelchon who scoffed, "Do you really think we can defeat them by not fighting?"

Calgacus shot back, "If you have a better plan, I'd like to hear it. We are outnumbered, and we cannot face armoured men in a pitched battle. Raiding and ambushing small units will not defeat their army. Hunger will. Believe me, I have done this before. This is how we forced the Romans out of Eriu."

Some of the Caledones who had crossed the sea to Eriu with Calgacus chorused their agreement, and Broichan chimed, "This is true. Calgacus knows how to defeat the enemy. We all know that the Romans have beaten anyone who stands against them in the old way. This time, we must do something different."

The mood of the meeting was slowly changing. Calgacus could feel the shift as men began to murmur support for his plan. He sensed that he had persuaded most of the assembled chieftains, but there were still some who were not convinced.

"What do we do if this plan doesn't work?" Ebrauc asked.

"We must make it work," Calgacus told him.

Bran said, "It is not easy to encircle thirty thousand men. I think it would be better to draw them north, into the hills. We would have more chance of trapping them there."

Calgacus shook his head.

He replied, "We agreed to help Gabrain and the Venicones protect their homes as much as we can."

Old Ebrauc grunted, "Some of us have already been driven from our homes."

"That does not mean we should allow the same to happen to others," Calgacus insisted. "We cannot allow the Romans to simply march in here unopposed. We will do our best to defeat them before they reach the Tava. Remember, the longer we can keep them chasing us, or can pin them in their forts, the better."

He had their acceptance now, grudging as it might be. He told them, "That is the plan. We can do this."

Broichan put in, "Tonight, we must light the Beltane fires. We must make proper sacrifices."

Calgacus nodded, "Let the men enjoy Beltane. But tomorrow, we must begin. The Romans could cross the river at any time. We must be ready, so, in the morning, I want our forces to disperse into three camps. I also want to double the number of scouts who are watching for the enemy's advance."

Pausing for effect, he added, "This is the final confrontation. We cannot afford to lose. Only by working together can we win, so make sure all your warriors understand that. Go now, and tell them to be ready."

As the Kings and their followers slowly filed out of the hilltop sanctuary, Calgacus saw Broichan sidle over to him. From the frown on the druid's face, he knew what the old man was going to ask him.

"Can we really win this way?" Broichan enquired in a dubious voice. "I did not wish to disagree with you in front of the others, but I fear Maelchon could be right. I cannot see how we can prevent the Romans going wherever they want."

Calgacus sighed, "The truth is that I don't know. What I do know is that if we don't do something now, Gabrain and the Venicones might break away and fight separately, or they might even go over to the enemy. If either of those things happen, we are beaten. The alliance will fall apart."

Broichan gave a pensive nod.

"Then we must pray that you can do what you say you can. Let us hope the Gods grant us their favour."

"I'll leave the Gods to you," Calgacus told him. "But there is something else I need you to do for me."

"What is that?"

"Speak to each King individually. Remind them of what is at stake. You saw the mood they were in. They need some encouragement."

"I will do that," Broichan agreed.

"It wouldn't hurt if you could tell them that you have seen some favourable omens," Calgacus added.

Stiffly, Broichan replied, "I will make sacrifices tonight at the Beltane feast. The omens will be what they will be."

It was never wise to argue with a druid, but Calgacus had grown up with greybeards who were more fanatical than Broichan, and he had often challenged their view of life.

Speaking firmly, he said, "I think you should make sure the omens are favourable. We need the men to believe we are going to win. You can make them believe."

Coldly, Broichan replied, "I see why you were often in dispute with the druids of Ynis Mon."

"Only about some things," Calgacus told him. "On one matter we were always agreed. The Romans must be opposed. You know this. We must both do whatever is necessary to achieve a victory. I went to Maelchon and I gave away my sword, the most precious thing I owned. Now, you can do your part. We need favourable omens."

Broichan glared at him, but eventually gave a curt nod.

"I will make the sacrifices," he agreed. "I am sure the Gods will smile on you, even though you mock them."

Calgacus shrugged, "As I said, you deal with the Gods. I will deal with the Romans."

Radiating disapproval, Broichan rasped, "So be it."

Scowling, the druid stalked off to summon his acolytes and make the arrangements for the sacrifices.

Heaving a sigh of relief, Calgacus turned to head down through the forest of wooden pillars that surrounded the hilltop sanctuary. As he did so, he saw Runt waiting for him, a worried frown creasing his brow.

"What is it now?" Calgacus asked his friend. "Has Maelchon started another argument?"

"No, it's nothing like that."

"Thank the Gods. I seem to spend more time fighting our own people than fighting the Romans. So, if it's not Maelchon, what is bothering you?"

"You're not going to like it," Runt informed him.

"Just bloody tell me!"

Runt shrugged, "Beatha is here."

Chapter XX

Beatha rode into the vast camp like a figure from legend. Dressed in close-fitting trousers, a sleeveless leather tunic, with thick, golden rings around her upper arms, and a torc adorning her neck, with her blonde hair tied back, and a bright cloak of blue, yellow and green falling back from her shoulders to drape across the rump of her pony, she resembled a Goddess of War as she led a small troop of riders between the scattered fires and shelters of the assembled tribes.

Behind her rode Facilis and Pulcher, the latter looking uncomfortable and slightly comical with his bulk dwarfing the small horse beneath him. His discomfort was increased by the six warriors who rode behind him, because they were all women, dressed in wild-looking costumes, and with blue, painted designs etched on their faces. Bare-armed and bare-legged, they stared straight ahead, paying no heed to the crowds of men who stood and stared to watch them pass.

At their head, Beatha adopted the same, stern attitude. She ignored the lewd comments and licentious invitations that were called out as she and her small escort picked their way through the vast, sprawling camp. Staring fixedly ahead, she steeled herself to become something other than her usual self. She knew that she needed to be hard, to do whatever it took to set her son free.

She did not know where Calgacus was, but she soon spotted the boar standard of the Boresti, planted on the side of a low, wooded hill some distance from the sacred enclosure of Cingel's tomb. Nudging her pony with her knee, she guided it towards the Boresti camp.

Adelligus met her as she dismounted, his young face bearing a mixture of delight and concern. Beatha understood his mood, and quickly forestalled his inevitable question about his pregnant wife.

"Fallar is fine," she assured him. "She wanted to come, but I would not let her."

Adelligus nodded, "This is no place for her."

Beatha smiled back, understanding the mild reproof that this was no place for her either. Gesturing towards the two Romans she had brought with her, she said, "Make sure these two are guarded at all times. Keep them safe. Now, I need to talk to Calgacus. Where is he?"

Adelligus jerked his chin to indicate a spot behind her.

"Here he comes now. He doesn't look very happy."

Beatha turned, seeing a grim-faced Calgacus striding towards her from the direction of Cingel's tomb, accompanied by Runt and a grinning Bridei.

"What are you doing here?" Calgacus demanded as he drew near.

"I missed you, too," Beatha shot back, her tone sharp. "Is that any welcome to give your wife?"

Calgacus hesitated, knowing that they were the centre of attention. Realising that he could not show any outward sign of annoyance at her arrival, he reached for her, placing his hands on her shoulders as he leaned down to kiss her.

"That's better," she said reprovingly as he released her from his embrace.

"Come on," he said, "Let's find somewhere we can talk."

"You are angry with me," she accused as he turned abruptly and led the way among the trees, ignoring the inquisitive looks of the Boresti warriors.

"I've had a bad day," he replied. "I wasn't expecting you to turn up here."

Beatha said, "I am sorry to disappoint you. Have I spoiled your plans for Beltane?"

"Of course not."

Undeterred, she persisted, "So you don't have another woman lined up for this evening?"

Before Calgacus could utter a denial, Runt put in, "Actually, he's got three or four to choose from."

"They'll be disappointed then," Beatha affirmed, sharing a silent laugh with Runt.

The little man grinned, "All the more for the rest of us."

"Just make sure I don't see you," Beatha warned. "That way, I won't be forced to lie to your wife when I see her."

Runt laughed, as did Bridei.

The Boresti King smiled, "At least you brought a few more with you. There aren't nearly enough women here to make it a proper Beltane."

"We are here to fight," Calgacus retorted, "not to celebrate."

"Speak for yourself," grinned Bridei irrepressibly.

Calgacus gave a weary sigh, knowing that the three of them were ganging up on him. Beatha, as she so often did, had quickly gained allies to counter his bad temper, and he knew he would gain nothing by arguing with her.

Attempting to retain some authority in the face of his friends' amusement, he gestured at the two Roman prisoners behind them.

"Why did you bring them?"

"I'll tell you once you have calmed down a little," Beatha replied evenly.

"I am calm," he insisted, a statement that brought another bout of laughter from the others.

He scowled, wanting to snap at them, but Beatha laid a hand on his arm, giving him a gentle squeeze.

"A little calmer would be even better," she advised him.

"All right," he conceded with little grace. "Let's sit down and talk. It seems we have a lot to discuss."

The woodland had been converted to a camp. Small shelters of interlocked branches and turf clung to the trunks of the trees and filled almost every space beneath the spreading boughs. Fires crackled and smoked in rings of stones, cooking pots bubbled, and warriors laughed and chatted with one another.

The six women who had accompanied Beatha were met by welcoming shouts of delight. At an approving signal from Beatha, they hurried off to find their menfolk.

"I notice you brought the good-looking ones," Calgacus observed.

"Why not? They make quite an impression, don't they? And they wanted to come. Their husbands are all here."

She paused before adding in a teasing tone, "I think they wanted to be sure their men spent Beltane with them and not with any of the other women you've got here."

Calgacus declined to begin another argument he knew he would lose. War, like every other aspect of life among the Pritani, was often a shared activity. The war bands had gathered here in response to Calgacus' summons and, inevitably, many women had followed.

Some women were happy to share the hardships of a campaign, but going to war was not something that Beatha had ever done, so Calgacus understood that she must have a compelling reason for travelling all the way from the mountain sanctuary.

Near the centre of the woodland, they came to a large clearing ringed by massive oaks, birch, and chestnut trees, and dotted with tiny shelters. Calgacus led his companions to a small fire set in a crude hearth of stones beneath the overhanging branches of an ancient oak. He gestured for Beatha to seat herself.

"This is home," he explained.

"Nice," she commented drily.

Bridei, still smiling broadly, declared, "I'll have some food and drink brought."

The two Romans, Facilis and Pulcher, were taken to a separate fire on the far side of the clearing. Two of Adelligus' spearmen stood over them, although Calgacus suspected that was an unnecessary precaution.

"The fat one is too scared to try anything," he observed. "And Facilis is too smart."

"Best to keep them under guard," Beatha told him. "I need them."

In response to his questioning look, she explained her plan to exchange them for Togodumnus. Calgacus listened patiently, then gave a resigned shrug.

"I doubt it will work, but it's worth a try. I don't know what else to do with them in any case."

He frowned, not wanting to discuss their son while others could overhear. Beatha had made it public by her arrival, but he wanted to talk to her in private because his public reaction to Togodumnus' abduction must be harsher than she would want to hear.

He was rescued from continuing the discussion when a plump, elderly woman brought a batch of bannocks, liberally smeared with creamy butter, while a younger woman delivered a welcome pitcher of beer. As the five of them helped themselves, Calgacus seized the opportunity to change the subject.

He said, "I think everyone is beginning to wish Maelchon hadn't come here. He's done nothing but cause trouble."

Bridei put in, "You should put him in his place. Start by taking your sword back from that arrogant bastard, Algarix. He's taunting you, and Maelchon is enjoying every moment of it."

"I won't do that," Calgacus replied. "Much as I'd like to, I will not start another fight among the tribes. I'm more worried that Maelchon has only brought a few hundred men. We need the rest of his warriors to arrive soon."

"Never mind that," Bridei grunted, "What do you think about his claim there is a spy? It would explain how the Romans knew about Gabrain's raid."

Calgacus shrugged, "I suppose it is possible someone is sending information to the enemy, but I don't want rumours to start, so keep your thoughts to yourself."

Runt put in, "I expect Maelchon will start rumours anyway. He seems to enjoy upsetting people. I can't think of any other reason why he'd act that way."

Bridei spat, "He's a sneaky son of a bitch. Maybe he's the spy, and he's accusing everyone else to turn attention away from himself."

Adelligus shook his head.

"No, he wasn't here when Gabrain made his raid, so he couldn't have told anyone about it."

Calgacus cut in, "I don't like all this talk of spies. All the Kings have motives for doing a deal with the enemy. As Maelchon so kindly pointed out, even I could be under suspicion. My son has been captured."

"We trust you," Bridei protested. "And you know I would never betray our people either."

"I know that," Calgacus agreed. "But the other Kings might not believe you. Every man has his price, and if suspicion spreads, you'd soon find plenty of people willing to believe accusations against you."

Adelligus asked, "So, what do we do? If there is a spy, it could be any one of the Kings, or any of their chieftains. That's around fifty suspects."

Beatha put in, "You could easily discount some of them. For example, Gabrain was the one who walked into the trap."

"And walked back out again," Calgacus countered. "If he was secretly working with the Romans, what better way to conceal the fact?"

"I can't believe he'd do that!" Beatha exclaimed.

241

"Neither do I," Calgacus agreed. "I'm just trying to show you that we can't discount anyone. There's the simple greed factor, where someone might accept a bribe of gold and silver, but there are other factors, too."

Counting on his fingers, he explained, "I want to get Togodumnus back. That is a strong motive. Gabrain wants to protect his villages, which will be the first to suffer when the Romans cross the river. Drust just wants a peaceful life with plenty of beer, and he's got Bran looking for a chance to take over from him. That gives both of them an incentive to do a deal with Rome. Even old Ebrauc might be tempted to help the enemy to regain all the land he's lost."

He looked each of them in the eye as he went on, "I'm not saying any of these things are true, but if we allow rumours to start, all these accusations could be made, and that would destroy our alliance. So, keep it to yourselves, and don't let anyone mention spies or traitors."

The men nodded their acceptance, but Beatha persisted, "That's all very well, Cal, and I understand the need to prevent rumours spreading, but what will you do if there really is a spy? The Romans will soon learn all about your plan."

Adelligus suggested, "Can you not ask Broichan to cast some spell or brew a magic potion that will reveal who it is?"

Calgacus smiled at the young man's innocence.

"I doubt it very much," he said. "In my experience, such things only happen in the stories druids tell to enhance their own reputations. I've never actually seen one of them do any real magic."

Runt's face crumpled in a concerned frown. He said softly, "Beatha is right, though. If there is a spy, we have a big problem. You've just told them your plan. The Romans are likely to learn all about it in a day or two."

Calgacus nodded sombrely, his eyes fixed on the writhing flames in the tiny fire. Then he looked up, his face smiling broadly.

"I hope they do," he said. "In fact, I am counting on it."

Chapter XXI

As darkness fell, people began to gather for the Beltane ceremonies. Each tribe kept to itself, setting aside a portion of ground where they stacked two great pyramids of wood. These portals were traditionally set on high ground, but there were so many people assembled in the area around Cingel's tomb that any piece of open ground was used.

Calgacus and Beatha watched as the Boresti gathered in an open meadow near their woodland camp. Many of the warriors had been drinking since dusk, all of them were expectant and excited. Jokes were told, songs were sung, and then Bridei appeared, carrying a flaming torch. He walked to the two stacks of piled wood, each one taller than he was, and put his torch to them, letting the flames take hold.

A great cheer went up, a cry that was echoed by distant shouts of acclamation from the other tribes who were observing the same ritual.

A druid, one of Broichan's young acolytes, moved to stand between the two fires as the flames raged higher and higher. He held up his hands, calling prayers to the Gods to bless this occasion, reminding them of the trials the people had been through during the winter, and asking for their favour as a new year of growth arrived at last.

Calgacus murmured, "He'd be better asking for help killing the bloody Romans."

Squeezing his arm, Beatha said, "I know you don't enjoy these things, Cal, but Beltane is important. You can't expect people to forget it just because you have a war to fight."

"We all have a war to fight," he muttered. "But you're right. I'd be as well commanding the grass to stop growing as order this lot to forget about Beltane."

Runt appeared in the darkness, presenting them with wooden cups of beer.

"Drink up and enjoy yourselves," he encouraged before wandering away, a little unsteady on his feet.

"Liscus always enjoys himself," Beatha remarked with a laugh.

They sipped at the dark, heady brew, watching as the Boresti brought a score of war ponies towards the fire, prodding the beasts with the butt end of their spears.

"Horses?" Beatha enquired.

"We don't have many cattle left," Calgacus explained.

This was the main point of the ceremony, the herd of terrified beasts being driven between the two enormous bonfires, symbolising a transition through a gateway as the year moved from winter to spring and the promise of summer.

To the wild accompaniment of drums, flutes, horns and raucous singing, the horses were driven towards the fiery portal. Some men danced into the path of the charging horses, twisting and turning as they demonstrated their bravery by risking being trampled, dodging aside at the last moment. One, forgetting in his befuddled state that horses could gallop faster than cattle, was too slow and was fortunate to only be clipped by the shoulder of a panicking pony. He was tossed aside, ending up in a sprawling, drunken heap on the ground, much to the amusement of his fellows.

The horses were slowed once they had cleared the fires, hundreds of men waiting to block them and force them to turn. As the beasts' panic diminished, they were caught, calmed, and led away to rejoin the lines of ponies that were tethered beyond the hill. Their part was over, but three young bulls had been gathered and now these were prodded, lowing and protesting, through the flaming gateway. On the other side, they too were met by waiting men and slowly led back round the fires to where Bridei waited with the young druid.

Calgacus watched while the first bullock was led forwards. At a signal from the young druid, a man wielding a heavy club stunned the beast with a crushing blow to its skull. As it sagged, its legs buckling, the druid cut its throat with his bronze knife, watching dispassionately as the life slowly ebbed from the victim. Once the bull had fallen to the ground, the druid slit open its belly, squatting down to peer at the vital organs.

Calgacus waited, holding his breath.

At last, the druid stood up and declared, "The Gods favour us. This will be a good year. We shall have victory over our foes!"

A great cheer rose from the throats of the tribesmen, and Calgacus smiled as he turned to Beatha and whispered, "Broichan has done his work."

He looked away, not interested in seeing the other cattle slaughtered and butchered to provide meat for the Beltane feast. Not that it would be much of a feast, for the cattle were thin and scrawny, and there were more than two thousand warriors waiting to be fed.

Calgacus tried to concentrate on the music, the thumping of drums, the frenetic dancing of the flutes and the wild blasts of the horns, but he had never been able to appreciate the joy that others seemed to find in such sounds. Frowning, he drained his cup, wondering why he was unable to enter into the spirit of the evening.

Beatha, sensing his mood, finished her own drink, tossed her cup aside and squeezed his arm again.

"Come on," she told him. "Let's find somewhere we can be alone."

Calgacus looked at her in surprise, but saw her inviting smile.

He grinned, "We could go back to the camp."

"Everyone will be going there soon," she reminded him.

"Then let's go to the far side of this hill. There are bushes that will give us some privacy."

Leaving the rhythmic thumping of the music and the wild chanting of the dancers, they slipped away, circling the wooded hill by moonlight. All around, they could hear the noise of celebration as each tribe sang, danced and drank the night away. In every direction, the night echoed to the sounds of revelry, while fires blazed, marking the beginning of the new season.

"There will be some sore heads in the morning," Beatha observed.

"They'll still need to go to war," Calgacus growled.

"Not until I try to get our son back," she reminded him. "You must give me time to do that."

Calgacus frowned. The expectations aroused by Beatha's suggestion that they find somewhere private were doused by the reminder of why she had come here in the first place. He had not wanted to discuss their family concerns in front of others, but now he had no choice. There was still a promise in the way she held on to him, but he knew her well enough to realise that it was a promise she would keep only after they had resolved the issue of what to do about Togodumnus.

Cautiously, he ventured, "I am worried about him, too."

Beatha said, "I know what you are thinking, Cal. Togodumnus is a man, and he made his choice. He could have come with us, but he decided to stay, to offer no resistance to Rome."

"Yes, he did. But that does not mean I want to leave him to suffer the consequences of a bad decision. What worries me is why they took him at all. The only thing I can think of is that Venutius wants to use him against me in some way."

"That was my thought as well," Beatha agreed with a worried frown.

247

There was a quiet tension between them, neither of them wanting to articulate their fear. They both knew that, if Venutius had his way, Togodumnus might already be dead. But if he lived, he could still be used against them.

Cautiously, Calgacus said, "The strange thing is that they have made no demands of any sort. They have not asked for a ransom, nor for my surrender."

To his relief, Beatha responded emphatically, "I know you cannot surrender, not even for our son. The tribes need you, and I would not trust the Romans anyway. They might kill both of you. I could not bear that."

Calgacus put his arm around her shoulder, drawing her close as they walked slowly round the foot of the wooded hill.

"I am sorry," he said softly. "I am glad you understand. I want to know that Togodumnus is safe, but the fate of all the free tribes is more important than the fate of one man, no matter who he is."

"I understand," Beatha whispered.

"I know you do. But that doesn't make this any easier. Sometimes I wonder whether I am fooling myself by insisting that I am the only one who can lead our people to victory. You know what I think of anyone who boasts about their achievements. Usually, the ones who crow the loudest about how strong or how clever they are, only say those things in order to convince themselves. They are like those drums we can hear. Loud and insistent, but hollow, good for nothing except making a loud noise."

"You are not like that," she assured him. "You really are the only one who can save us from being conquered. You have proved it many times."

"So you don't think I should offer to surrender in order to free Togodumnus?"

"No. That would mean we would all lose. My head knows this, but my heart tells me I am a mother, and I need to know my son is safe. Not knowing what has happened to

248

him is so hard to bear. That is why I want to exchange Facilis and Pulcher for him."

Calgacus warned, "Don't put too much faith in Facilis. I like him, but if Venutius has Togodumnus, he won't let him go just because we release a couple of Roman prisoners."

"Venutius is not the Governor," Beatha argued. "Facilis says he knows Agricola personally. I trust him to do his best."

"I believe he will," Calgacus smiled. "I saw the way he looked at you. I think he would do anything you asked of him."

"Are you jealous?" she asked, her smile matching his own.

"No. You are very beautiful, so it is only natural that men will look at you."

"Now you are trying to flatter me," she laughed.

"I am serious," he insisted. "But you have certainly made a conquest of your own where Facilis is concerned."

"Then we can trust him to do his best for us, and for Togodumnus. I will take him and Pulcher south tomorrow and hope that they can persuade the Governor to free our son."

Calgacus nodded, "It's worth a try. And if it doesn't work, I suppose I'll just need to fight my way into the Roman camp and drag him out."

"Don't joke about such things," Beatha chided. "I don't want you doing anything stupid just because Venutius is involved."

"Don't worry," he sighed. "But, one day, I'll kill that treacherous bastard."

"One day, but not today. Not tonight."

She leaned close, holding his arm tightly as she went on, "This is the last night we have together for some time, so where is this private place you mentioned?"

He had known her for most of his life, yet she still retained the ability to amaze him with her inner strength. She was deeply worried about their son, but she knew that Calgacus also needed her. He understood just how much effort it was costing her to push her fears over Togodumnus to the back of her mind. He also knew that, when death was an imminent prospect, people always tried to reaffirm life. Beatha had lost her son to the Romans and might soon lose him as well. For her own sake as much as his, she needed to share this night with him.

They had reached the northern side of the hill, where the land opened into a wide, shallow valley that was bathed in pale moonlight. The horse lines were to their right, in a lush meadow of open ground, but to their left was a great expanse of bushes, long grass, dips and hollows. He pointed towards this patch of overgrown wilderness.

"Over there, but I don't think we're the only ones with this idea. I'm sure I saw another couple going in there."

Beatha smiled, "I think that was Anhareth. She must have found her husband. Or maybe someone else's husband."

"Let's go further on," Calgacus suggested impatiently.

"There are fires down that way," Beatha pointed out, looking ahead to where another pair of Beltane fires had been lit on the far side of the broad plain.

"They're on the other side of a stream that runs down there," Calgacus replied. "Don't worry, we'll keep well away from them. They won't disturb us."

They moved into the bushes, picking a cautious way in the dark, until they found a small, secluded dip in the ground.

"This ought to do," Calgacus said expectantly.

Beatha laughed softly, "It's been years since we did anything like this. It reminds me of our first time. Do you remember that?"

"I'll never forget it. It wasn't that long ago."

"Yes it was. We were young then, not like now."

"You're not old," Calgacus assured her, taking her in his arms and kissing her to emphasise his words.

"Liar."

"It's me who's growing old," he murmured as he continued to kiss her softly. "Every time one of these young hotheads challenges me, it gets tougher to beat them."

"But you still win," she murmured softly. "You always win. Even if you are an old man now."

"Come here and I'll show you how old I am," he growled playfully.

"Spread a cloak on the ground," she laughed. "It's chilly out here with no fire."

"I'll soon warm you up," he promised.

In the darkness, they removed their clothes, spreading one cloak on the grass and pulling the other over their naked bodies as they clung together, kissing and touching, revelling in the familiar feel of each other's skin.

Calgacus forgot the war, forgot Togodumnus, forgot the cool of the night. All he knew was Beatha, lying beneath him, her arms wrapped around him, her soft whispers of encouragement urging him to love her.

All the worries and tensions of the day were banished by their urgent need for one another. Beatha moaned her pleasure as she drew him inside her, and he abandoned himself to the joy of her body. He lost all sense of time, knew nothing except Beatha, until his release came and he sagged against her, both of them gasping with exhausted relief.

"Just like our first time," Beatha whispered contentedly.

"Every time is just like the first time with you," he told her.

She laughed at that, then she asked, "Would you like to try for a second time?"

"You'll need to give me a little while. I told you, I'm not as young as I used to be."

"That's no excuse," she teased. "Perhaps I should go and find another man if you are not up to it."

He grabbed for her, pulling her close and kissing her fiercely.

"That's better," she giggled when he at last pulled his lips away from hers. "I didn't really want to go looking for anyone else. I'm not as young as I used to be, either."

"You're still very beautiful," he assured her. "I told you, I saw the way that Roman was looking at you."

Beatha wriggled herself on top of him, planting her hands beside his shoulders and looking down at him, her blonde curls tumbling around her face.

"I knew you were jealous!" she teased.

"No, I'm not. You are here with me. That is all I need to know."

"Yes, I am here, but what are you going to do about it?"

There was only one thing he could do, so he did. Their second time was slower, less desperate, but just as passionate. It seemed to last forever, and when they were done at last, they were both exhausted and bathed in sweat.

"If you want a third time, you'll need to fetch your Roman lover," Calgacus groaned.

Beatha, still lying on top of him, whispered contentedly, "You are the only man I need."

He held her close, feeling the soft contours of her body against him, his only thought that he wanted to be with her forever.

Then he offered a silent prayer to Camulos that forever would not end in a few days' time.

Chapter XXII

They awoke as the first, tentative glimmerings of dawn were creeping over the eastern horizon. Huddled together under the thick wool of the cloak, they were still cold, reluctant to move, and unwilling to let go of each other.

"We should get up," Beatha said. "I want to have a wash."

"It will take a while to warm some water," Calgacus observed.

"Didn't you say there was a stream down the hill? That will do."

"It'll be cold," he warned.

"I'm cold now. It will be invigorating. Come on, everyone else will be asleep. We'll have the place to ourselves."

She pushed at him, forcing him to move. Reluctantly, shivering in the grey light of the early dawn, he stood up. Then he bent to grab at his cloak, which Beatha had wrapped over her body. He pulled it away, making her shriek in mock outrage as she tried to snatch the cover back.

"You're horrible!" she accused, laughing.

"It was your idea to get up," he retorted. "Now, put your cloak on and grab your things. If you really want to bathe in the river, there's no point in getting dressed here."

He fastened his own cloak around his naked body, rummaging around the clearing to find his clothes, boots and sword. He bundled them together, checked that Beatha had gathered her own belongings, then the two of them picked a cautious way out of the bushes and down the gentle gradient towards the shallow stream that meandered slowly along the valley floor.

The world was coming to life. Birds were chirping to welcome the day, the grey twilight gradually turning to full daylight. There were few other people moving around, only a handful of figures visible on the far side of the stream, moving quietly among the debris of the previous night's festivities.

"Whose camp is that?" Beatha asked, nodding her head to indicate the random scattering of tents and shelters on the far side of the stream.

"That's Maelchon and the Taexali," he replied sourly. "Most of them will still be sleeping, but let's move downstream a bit. I'd rather give them a wide berth."

"You don't expect trouble from Maelchon, do you?"

"I always expect trouble from that mad bugger. But not the sort you mean. No, I just don't want to have the bother of meeting him."

"He'll be sleeping off his hangover," Beatha stated. "Come on, here's a good spot."

She carefully placed her clothes on the grass beside the gently burbling water, unfastened her cloak and folded it neatly, placing it on top of her other belongings.

"You look incredible," Calgacus told her admiringly.

She smiled at the compliment.

"You are seeing me through misty eyes," she replied.

Delicately, she stepped into the shallow stream, making a shivering noise, then squatting down to splash water over herself.

Calgacus decided he may as well take the plunge. He walked a little way down the bank then, casually dropping his cloak, he stepped into the stream, catching his breath as the chill water rose around his lower legs.

"It's bloody freezing!" he protested.

Beatha laughed, "I thought you were supposed to be tough."

The stream was only four paces wide at this point, and barely deep enough to reach his knees. The bottom was sand and gravel, fairly smooth, with no rocks or pebbles. Taking a deep breath, he lowered himself into the icy water, dropping to his knees, then plunging his head under the surface. He held his breath as long as he could, letting the water wash away the grime of the past days. With no soap, he used his fingers to scrub at his skin.

After a few moments, he felt warmer, his body having adjusted to the chill of the water. Feeling relaxed and refreshed, he lay on his front, holding his head above the surface, allowing the stream to wash over him. Looking around, he noticed that there were several Taexali warriors a little way upriver, some filling buckets, while others were leading horses down to drink.

"Time to go," he said to Beatha.

Pushing himself up, he waded to the bank, the cool air on his wet skin making him shiver. He splashed onto the grass, retrieved his cloak and began to towel himself with it. He took a few, pleasant moments to watch Beatha dry herself, then shoved his head under the hood of his cloak and rubbed his long hair in an attempt to dry it.

He had turned his back on the stream, and his head was buried deep in the thick wool of his cloak, so he did not see or hear the man approaching. Only when Beatha called out an urgent, frightened warning did he turn, holding his cloak in front of his naked body.

He froze, appalled at what he saw.

Algarix was there, his squat, battered nose dominating his angry face, his eyes blazing hatred, and his left arm clamped around Beatha's waist. In his right hand he held a sharp dagger which he was holding to her throat.

Calgacus cursed himself. He had been careless, too engrossed in watching Beatha and in enjoying their early morning bath. He had paid little attention to the Taexali camp and had not noticed Algarix, who had appeared as if from nowhere. The shield-bearer's trousers were dripping wet from having waded across the stream, and his cheeks were unshaven, covered by a dark shadow of stubble, but his eyes were wild with anticipation, and the knife in his hand did not waver.

Beatha stood very still, her eyes radiating fear. She was still naked beneath her cloak, and she trembled, her face contorting in a grimace of helpless outrage as Algarix's left hand delved inside the covering to claw at her belly and breasts.

"Leave her alone," Calgacus warned menacingly.

Algarix grinned at him, an expression of pure hatred.

"Come and stop me," he challenged.

Calgacus' eyes flicked towards his sword, lying beside his piled clothing, three paces away, closer to Algarix than to himself. He dared not try to reach it, for the tip of the Taexali shield-bearer's dagger was pricking Beatha's neck. She would be dead before he covered the distance to his sword. He twisted his head, looking across the river, but there were only a handful of men and they were clearly not prepared to become involved. They stood, motionless, watching the confrontation.

Algarix chuckled, "I didn't think you'd make it this easy for me, but you are an arrogant fool, aren't you?"

"What do you want?" Calgacus demanded, his heart pounding with fear for Beatha.

"I want you dead," Algarix replied. "You tricked me, and humiliated me in front of my tribe. You must die for that."

Calgacus said, "I'll fight you if that is what you want, but let her go."

"I can't do that," Algarix sneered. "I'll tell everyone you attacked me to try to get your sword back. I only killed you in self defence. That will be believed because everyone knows you want your sword. But I can't let her tell the truth, can I?"

Calgacus saw the appeal in Beatha's eyes, but he still dared not move.

Algarix went on, "I'll deal with her afterwards, though. It's a while since I've had a woman, and she'll do very nicely, even though she is a bit old for my taste."

"Let her go and we can settle it between us," Calgacus said, desperately seeking a way to get the man away from Beatha. "If it's a fair fight, nobody can blame you."

Algarix did not move. His eyes flashed red with rage, and his voice shook with fierce anger as he blurted, "You did not allow me a fair fight last time! Why should I allow you one now?"

Dread filled Calgacus' heart, but he could not let the Taexali shield-bearer see his fear.

He rasped, "Then stop hiding behind a woman and come and kill me. I don't think you've got the guts to even try."

"All right."

Without warning, Algarix smacked a fist into the side of Beatha's head, stunning her, then he shoved her aside, sending her sprawling on the grass. He thrust his dagger into his belt, then reached back over his shoulder to draw his sword.

Calgacus' sword.

The great blade slid free of the shining, fleece-lined scabbard, its sharp edges glinting in the early sunlight. Gripping the long, leather-corded hilt in both hands, Algarix moved forwards, blocking Calgacus from reaching his own sword.

Calgacus stepped backwards, gripping his cloak, bunching a thick wad of material in his right fist, ready to use the cloak like a net.

Algarix laughed, "I see you shivering, old man. Fear does that."

The sun was behind him, dazzlingly bright. Calgacus placed his left hand on his brow, trying to shade his eyes, trying to judge when and how Algarix would attack. He had hoped the Taexali would rush at him, allowing his anger to take control, but Algarix was too good a swordsman to make such a basic error. He advanced slowly, holding the sword in a two-handed grip, the blade raised in front of him, one edge facing Calgacus.

With only his cloak to protect himself, Calgacus knew he needed to provoke Algarix into giving him an opening of some sort. Shouting a challenge, he lashed out with his cloak, casting it at the sword, hoping to entangle the blade in the wool.

Calgacus had always relied on his speed in combat, but Algarix was equally fast, dodging aside to let the cumbersome garment flap helplessly past him. The heavy wool fell to the ground and, before Calgacus could whip it back, Algarix stamped one foot heavily down, trapping the cloak. As he did so, he launched a vicious counter-attack, swinging the huge sword at Calgacus' head.

Calgacus leaped backwards, just managing to release his grip on the cloak in time to avoid the sweeping blow of the great blade. The tip whistled past his head, missing him by a finger's breadth. Moving backwards as quickly as he could, he stumbled slightly, slipped, then regained his balance just as Algarix advanced again.

Calgacus felt panic rising in his chest. Unarmed and naked, he knew he had little chance against an experienced warrior like Algarix. His only hope was to get past the deadly blade so that he could use his superior height and reach to knock Algarix down. But Algarix was too good to allow him any opportunity to get close. As it was, he was being forced to retreat one step at a time, the sword driving him inexorably backwards.

Calgacus' heart was hammering in his chest. He could not block the sword, he could not reach Algarix, and he plainly could not talk the man out of his rage-filled thirst for vengeance. There was nothing he could do except keep moving and hope to avoid Algarix's attacks. But how long could he keep that up?

Another ferocious sweep of the sword forced him to jump back. Then he stopped, because he had run out of room. He felt the sharp prickles of a large bush behind him, twigs scraping and scoring his back, buttocks and legs. Wildly, he thrust out his arms, trying to find a way round the obstacle while keeping his eyes on Algarix, but he could find no gap through which he could escape

The Taexali grinned triumphantly, barking an incoherent shout of joy as he raised the sword over his right shoulder, ready to deliver the final, killing blow.

Then Beatha smashed into him.

Appearing out of the bright sunlight like a wraith, she threw herself at him, slamming her shoulder into his back. Gasping with effort, she hurled herself at him with all her strength, trying to knock him over. She almost succeeded but, even caught by surprise, Algarix was strong and fast. He did not fall, but he staggered under the impact, losing his balance and stumbling forwards as he tried to retain his footing.

Calgacus reacted instantly, knowing he would not have another chance. He leaped forwards, driving his left fist into Algarix's belly, lashing his right into the side of the man's head like a hammer. The blows would have felled most men instantly, but Algarix somehow managed to remain upright. He tried to swing the sword, to hack Calgacus down, but Calgacus was inside his reach now, and swept up his left arm to smash Algarix's forearm. Then he drove his knee into Algarix's groin.

The Taexali yelled in agony, dropping the sword. This time, he went down, but Calgacus grabbed at his tunic, hauled him up and delivered a crushing head-butt to the man's already battered nose. When he released his hold, Algarix collapsed on the ground, groaning and spilling blood, his knees raised and body hunched over in agony.

Calgacus scooped up his fallen sword. As he stood over the downed Taexali, he heard Beatha call to him.

"Do it! Kill him!"

He glanced at her. She was on her hands and knees, her breath coming in great gasps, her eyes wide but a fierce, vengeful expression on her normally tranquil face. Naked under her cloak, she seemed like some savage goddess come to claim the soul of the defeated.

"Do it!" she repeated, her cry echoing in the still air.

Calgacus saw the men on the far side of the stream, all of them watching him closely, but none of them prepared to intervene.

He hefted his sword, slowly swinging the blade until the edge nicked the writhing man's neck, drawing a faint skein of blood. Then he stepped away.

In a loud, clear voice, he declared, "We are here to fight the Romans. I will not kill a man of the Pritani, not even a worthless piece of shit like this."

He slammed the tip of his sword into the grass, leaving the quivering weapon standing upright, then he bent down, roughly grabbing at Algarix until he had hauled the scabbard and thick, leather swordbelt over the man's unprotesting body.

"I'm taking my sword back," he rasped at the still groaning shield-bearer. Then he walked to where Beatha was slowly rising to her feet. Without a word, he held out a hand to help her up, then he led her away.

Chapter XXIII

Facilis and Pulcher had watched the Beltane festival with very different outlooks. Facilis had been fascinated by the rituals, and mesmerised by the sight of a druid sacrificing the bulls, even if the druid in question had been a relatively young man, his beard and partly-shaved head a lustrous brown rather than the grey Facilis had always associated with the demonic priests who, so Roman dogma insisted, were bloodthirsty savages who revelled in dismembering humans. As far as Facilis could see from where he and Pulcher had been dumped at the edge of the wood, the sacrifices were little different to those carried out by Roman priests, even though there was no temple and no statue of a god or goddess. The Britons did not seem to mind such things, and he recalled Beatha telling him that their gods and goddesses inhabited the natural world around them.

"What was the cheer for?" Pulcher asked anxiously after the first victim had been sacrificed.

"Their priest has prophesied victory," Facilis told him. "He claims the omens are in their favour."

Pulcher spat, "Superstitious nonsense. They are savages."

Facilis did not argue. He suspected Roman priests would be forecasting favourable omens for the Governor's campaign in a very similar manner to the ritual he had just witnessed. Yet he knew that the Gods could not favour both sides. Cynically, he wondered which of them were the superstitious savages and which were the believers in the true Gods.

He noticed other differences in the customs observed by the Britons. The huge bonfires, for one thing, and the ritual of driving the animals between them. There was also

261

the barbarians' insistence on drinking themselves senseless, something Facilis found quite alarming as well as alien.

Yet the night held him enthralled. The wild music and the chaotic dancing filled the people with a joyful abandon that called to him, making him want to take part.

He could not do that, of course. Two guards still watched him, although they, too, had consumed vast quantities of beer and their attention was more on the festivities than on their prisoners.

Pulcher nudged him, hissing, "We could escape now. They are drunk, and they have not bothered to tie us up."

"There is no need to escape," Facilis replied. "They are going to send us back anyway."

"Do you really think we can trust them?" Pulcher scoffed. "Treachery is a way of life among barbarians."

"I trust Beatha," Facilis stated.

Pulcher gave him a sharp look.

"That's because you want to bed her."

Facilis shook his head, denying the accusation, but a flutter in his heart told him the Quaestor's shot had hit close to the mark. Despite himself, Facilis knew that Beatha held him in thrall every bit as much as the spectacle of the Beltane feast. He had looked for her, but had been unable to see her, and her absence had left an aching void in his heart. The realisation of how much he wanted to be close to her had shocked him, but he could not help himself. He kept searching the crowded darkness, trying to locate her, but unable to see her anywhere among the milling mob. He eventually realised that she must be with Calgacus.

Thinking of the giant War Leader confused him. He instinctively liked and admired Calgacus, yet his feelings for Beatha, his desire to be with her, aroused his jealousy. He was reminded of his bitter thoughts, the dark, secret thoughts he would never reveal, when the Usipi had threatened to kill and eat him. He had silently prayed that they would kill Pulcher first. The memory of that selfish thought made him feel tainted, just as his latest dreams made him wish he could unthink them.

That was impossible, of course. The dreams rose again now, taunting him. He closed his eyes, his mind wandering, envisaging Calgacus' death in the coming war. Was that so unlikely? Far from it, Facilis told himself. And if Calgacus were to die, Beatha would be alone. Facilis saw himself with her, imagined himself taking her back to civilisation.

That was where his dream faltered, because, in his mind's eye, the place he took her to was Pompeii, and Pompeii no longer existed.

The whole thing was impossible, he told himself. Not only that, the thoughts were unworthy of a Roman. Calgacus had done him no harm. In fact, he had saved Facilis and Pulcher. To wish for his death for selfish, carnal reasons was morally wrong, and Facilis knew himself to be a moral person. Why, then, was the thought so powerful? Had his physical desire for Beatha affected him so much?

He sighed softly. His thoughts were in turmoil, as chaotic as the dancing of the barbarians, as wild as the thumping drums that filled the air with their booming thunder and seemed to make the earth tremble beneath him. He was an outsider here, an onlooker, yet he felt, somehow, a part of it. That, too, he knew, must be a symptom of Beatha's influence on him. He was a Roman, and could never be anything else. To become non-Roman was unimaginable, an act so heinous as to be a deadly sin. And yet ...

And yet he would stay here, he knew, if it meant he could be with Beatha. That realisation shocked him as much as the private, selfish thoughts of Calgacus' death.

With an effort of will, he forced himself to examine his situation rationally. Beatha had brought him here only because she wanted him to plead for her son's life. He was nothing to her, he knew. Yet he also knew that he would do as she had asked him. What else could he do? He would overcome his secret desire and do as his personal honour demanded. He was a Roman, and would follow the stoic tradition of Rome.

Not daring to meet Pulcher's eye, he insisted, "They will let us go. All we need to do is wait."

Pulcher sniffed, "I hope you are right. I do not know how much longer I can put up with being among them. This place is disgusting. Do they never wash? The whole camp smells of horses, sweat and filth. And the food is awful."

"It's no worse than army rations," Facilis corrected, knowing the Quaestor's professed dislike of the British diet had not prevented him devouring every morsel that had been handed to him. Pulcher had lost a great deal of his former weight, but he was still fatter than anyone Facilis had seen among the Britons.

He did the same when that evening's food was brought to them. Their guards plied them with beer and shared the small portions of meat from the Beltane sacrifices. Facilis had no great liking for the dark, gritty beer, but he drank it and soon began to feel its potent effects. He pretended to enjoy the brew because he knew it would annoy Pulcher.

The Quaestor whispered, "The Governor should have attacked tonight. He could wipe out the whole lot of them. They are too drunk to fight back."

Again, Pulcher's words reminded Facilis of where his true loyalties should lie. The people around him were his enemies, if not personally, then certainly politically. They had treated him well, but they were at war with Rome and Facilis knew there could only be one outcome to their resistance. However much he owed Calgacus, however much he desired Beatha, they would be on the losing side, and there was nothing he could do to prevent that. He had tried to persuade them of the folly of resistance, but they had both made it clear that they would not submit to Rome.

264

Facilis ruefully conceded that he had allowed himself to become too wrapped up in his personal feelings while Pulcher, despite his constant pessimism, had not lost sight of the true situation. The Quaestor was correct; an attack now would end the war at a stroke. Which raised a major question in Facilis' mind.

Focusing his thoughts, Facilis nodded, "Yes, it would be an easy victory, but I don't think they would have held this celebration if our army had crossed the river. The Legions must still be in their camps."

"What are they waiting for?" Pulcher complained.

"I don't know," Facilis admitted. "But the Governor must have his reasons. He needs to complete the conquest of Britannia soon."

He gave the Quaestor a weak smile as he added, "We can always ask him when we see him."

"If we ever see him," Pulcher grunted sourly. "You may trust these savages, but I do not."

"Don't worry. They want us to speak to the Governor. We will be back among our own people very soon."

Pulcher sighed, "Not soon enough for me."

Facilis could not help smiling at the fat man's pessimism, but Pulcher's gloomy outlook on their future had given Facilis a new resolve. He would return to the stability and safety of Rome, he would speak to the Governor, and he would do his best to help Beatha regain her son. He would do all these things, but he would not forget that he was a Roman.

It was a long night but, when the festivities slowly began to fade, their guards led them back to the clearing where they huddled under a crude shelter of interlocking branches, wrapping themselves in their cloaks against the cool night air. Facilis had not thought that he would be able to sleep, because his mind was racing, but he pretended to be sleepy because Pulcher was still grumbling.

265

He must have been more tired than he realised, because the next thing he noticed was that it was morning, a bright sunny dawn scattering light through the leafy canopy of the woodland camp. Dust motes danced in the rays of warm sunlight, and the rough framework of the shelter cast freckled shadows across his face.

He was not sure why, but he sensed that something unusual had happened. The Britons were slowly coming to life, many of them nursing sore heads, but it was not their quiet movements that had roused him from his deep sleep. Curious, he crept out of the shelter, nudging the snoring Pulcher awake as he squirmed past him.

"What is it?" Pulcher asked sleepily.

"I'm not sure," Facilis told him.

The two haggard-looking guards who sat by the fire looked at him with bleary eyes. When he questioned them, he received only a vague shrug.

"Some trouble," one of them grunted. "A fight of some sort, I think."

Looking around, Facilis saw Calgacus striding back into the clearing, his face radiating righteous anger. Beside him, Beatha looked worn and tired, and the cluster of warriors who crowded around them were clearly anxious about something.

Calgacus soon restored order, barking commands, gesturing emphatically with his hands. Then he stalked away, taking most of his warriors with him. As he left, Facilis noticed the sword on his back, the glittering gold and silver scabbard of the famous Sword of Caratacus.

"Something important has happened," he informed Pulcher.

The Quaestor gave a worried frown.

"Will it affect us?"

"I don't know, but I think we will soon find out. Beatha is coming this way."

Facilis watched as Beatha walked across the clearing towards them. She was wearing the figure-hugging outfit of tunic and trousers that would have sent Roman matrons into a faint, but which seemed to suit her new identity of War Queen. Yet her face was pale, her blonde hair was untidy, and her demeanour showed that she was on edge.

Facilis stood to meet her, but she waved him down.

"May I sit with you for a while?" she asked, clearly making an effort to control her emotions.

"Of course."

Beatha signalled to the guards to move away. Obediently, they shambled to the far side of the clearing where a cooking pot was being manned by a plump, cheerful woman who was doling out bowls of porridge.

Beatha sat, cross-legged, on the ground beside the small fire, her face a mask of worry. Facilis was forced to remind himself that she was his enemy. Yet she was also the means of his escape. They had an understanding, each requiring something from the other and, despite his resolve to do his duty, Facilis felt that they shared a personal attachment. Why else had she come here?

"What is wrong?" he asked her, speaking in Latin so that Pulcher would be able to follow the conversation.

She shook her head, forcing a smile.

"Have you ever wondered who you really are?" she asked.

Facilis frowned, "I'm not sure what you mean."

With a sigh, she explained, "I have never been a violent person. I have never really hated anyone. I once hit someone who was holding me captive, but that was the only time in my life that I've ever been really angry. Until today."

She paused, looking upwards as if seeking inspiration or consolation. Then she continued, "Today I was so filled with hate that I could have killed someone. I wanted to see him suffer."

267

"Who was it?" Facilis asked gently. "Was it King Maelchon? I noticed Calgacus has his sword back."

Beatha regarded him with a nod of respect. "You are observant as well as clever," she said. "No, it was not Maelchon. It was his shield-bearer. He tried to kill Calgacus."

"Tried, and obviously failed," Facilis observed. "I assume he is dead?"

"No, and that is what disturbs me. I wanted Calgacus to kill him. I wanted to see him die, to watch his agony. But Calgacus let him live, and now I feel as if I am no longer the person I thought I was. I have never felt such hatred for anyone, and it scares me that I should feel this way."

"Anger and hatred are normal emotions," Facilis told her. "We all feel them. Perhaps you have been lucky that you have not experienced them before now."

"Perhaps," she acknowledged with a sigh, clasping her hands together as if to prevent them trembling.

"What will happen now?" Facilis asked. "Will there be war with Maelchon?"

"I don't think so. The fight was a personal grudge. Then again, nobody can be sure how Maelchon will react."

"Is Calgacus going to confront him?"

"No. He is going to ask the druid to speak to Maelchon first."

"That is sensible," Facilis agreed.

"Yes. Calgacus is angry, but he usually manages to see the right way to deal with problems. It will be better if the druid makes the first approach. In any case, Calgacus has a lot of other things to attend to."

She sighed again, adding, "I suppose he is used to people trying to kill him. It's just that I don't often see it happen."

"Your husband is a remarkable man," Facilis observed.

Beatha's wan expression brightened slightly as she agreed, "I know."

Facilis instinctively knew that Calgacus' fight could have far-reaching consequences for the British alliance. The tribes were accustomed to using violence to settle disputes, and even if the attempt on Calgacus' life had been due to a personal feud, it could easily escalate into open warfare.

He also recognised that he had an opportunity to obtain information that might prove invaluable to the Governor. Yet he hesitated because it would mean taking advantage of Beatha's obvious distraction and distress. He did not want to do that, did not want to betray her trust in him. Part of him wanted to reach out, to take her in his arms and comfort her, but he suppressed those feelings, reminding himself of who he was and why Beatha had brought him here. Whatever their feelings for one another might have been, any friendship between them was doomed because they were on opposite sides of the war. Beatha had known this all along, he realised. She had brought him here because she wished to use him to free her son. Very well, he decided, he would do that for her because he had given his word, but he would also use her to gain information, however much the deception cost him. He did not like what he must do, but he knew where his duty lay.

Hating himself for asking the question, he said, "Where has Calgacus gone?"

Beatha's own emotions were so jagged that she was oblivious to his internal conflict. She said, "He's gone to speak to the other Kings. He wants to make sure they hear his side of the story first."

Facilis nodded sympathetically. He needed to be cautious, he knew, to probe without her realising what he was doing. He loathed himself for tricking her, but he told himself he had no alternative. Soon, he and Pulcher would be back among their own people, and all of this would be behind them. Facilis was pragmatic enough to know that he needed some leverage if he were to gain the Governor's favour, so he squashed his concerns and gently tried to tease information from the unwitting Beatha.

He said, "I suppose he is right, but I suspect it will take him a long time to talk to all of them. There certainly seem to be a lot of tribes gathered here."

She nodded, seeming to pull herself together. She said, "Yes, there are a lot of tribes here. More than have ever faced Rome before. That is why Calgacus believes he can win this war."

"That's what he told me, too," Facilis agreed, "but I'm afraid he will need more men than he has here."

Beatha replied, "Oh, there are a lot more of us than you saw here. There are two other gatherings like this one. Calgacus is going to visit them today as well."

Facilis sensed Pulcher's interest, so he feigned disappointment as he said to Beatha, "Will I get a chance to speak to him before he goes?"

"I doubt it," she answered. "I will be taking you two south very soon. That's what I came to tell you. As soon as you have eaten, we must set off. Calgacus believes your army will cross the river any day now, so we need to hurry."

"We will be ready," Facilis assured her.

"Thank you," she said, although her smile could not hide the strain she was under. "I will have everything arranged."

When she had left, Facilis turned to Pulcher, who was fidgeting with excitement.

"We must tell the Governor about this!" the Quaestor blurted. "There are far more barbarians than we thought."

"We will."

"Do you think he will reward us?"

"I suppose he might."

"You did well," Pulcher told him. "She likes you, so she told you more than she should have."

Facilis nodded glumly. He had done well, the Quaestor had said. So why, he wondered, did he feel so sick at heart?

Calgacus was waiting for Beatha near the horse lines, where her six female warriors were preparing the mounts for her journey south.

"Well?" he asked. "Did he believe you?"

Beatha nodded, "I think so. But I feel awful, trying to trick him like that."

"It was better coming from you. He wouldn't believe me, because of how I tricked him all those years ago. But he fancies you, so he'll want to believe you."

"I dislike using people," she frowned.

"Sometimes it is necessary. In war, we must do whatever we can."

"I still don't understand," she told him. "Why do you want the Romans to know you are splitting your army into three parts?"

"I want them to think they are facing a lot more of us than we really have," he told her.

"I can see that," she said, "but I am still confused. I know I don't understand war, but is it really wise to let them know you have divided your army?"

"If it makes them think we outnumber them and can surround them, it will make them cautious," he explained.

She regarded him closely for a moment before saying, "there is something you are not telling me, isn't there?"

His only answer was a faint smile, and she knew she had guessed correctly, but she knew better than to press him for an explanation.

He gave her a gentle kiss on the lips before saying, "I think you should go now. Take your two Romans and make sure they deliver their message. With any luck, it will help them convince the Governor to release Togodumnus. That's what is important."

Chapter XXIV

The days seemed to drag past. Togodumnus had soon found that, although the soldiers continued to insist that his official status was that of a guest, he was a virtual prisoner in the Legion's camp. With preparations for the invasion of the north well under way, nobody wanted a civilian wandering the camp and getting in everyone's way.

He was permitted to take a horse and ride around the neighbouring countryside, but only if Sdapezi's troopers accompanied him, and only if he avoided the areas where the Roman cavalry and artillery were practising their drills for the imminent campaign. This did not leave him much scope, and he was not a great horseman in any event, so he only ventured out twice. Both times, he soon returned to the camp, feeling depressed by what he had witnessed.

Those short excursions only served to reinforce his belief that his father's gathering of tribes could not hope to withstand the Roman army. There were too many men, too much raw power for any Pritani war host to have any hope. He knew that the only sensible option was to acknowledge the superiority of the Empire, to bend with the wind instead of opposing it. The Governor had offered him a place among the leading citizens of the north, and that, he tried to convince himself, was the best way to ensure the survival of his people, of his friends and of his family.

Yet that was the path that Venutius had chosen, as the renegade Brigante never failed to remind him whenever they encountered one another in the camp.

"Your father is doomed, boy," Venutius would gloat. "Have you ever seen an army like this? And this is only one Legion. There are two more, plus the navy, and the auxiliaries, not to mention archers, war dogs, and cavalry. You have made the right choice."

Togodumnus knew he had made the rational decision, yet when he heard Venutius talk of the necessity of submitting to Rome, he could not help doubting himself. Instinctively, he distrusted anything Venutius said, and hated himself for agreeing with the man.

Yet what choice did he have? If he announced that he did not wish to participate in Agricola's vision of the future, his prospects would be bleak. His meetings with the other hostages soon confirmed this.

There were three of them. One was a young man, barely sixteen years old, a prince from Eriu who had been deposed during the recent civil war that had engulfed that island. Togodumnus only spoke to him once, because the boy rarely ventured out of his room, claiming illness. Their conversation was brief, barely more than a few passing words, because the young man made it plain he did not want anything to do with Togodumnus. Perplexed by the rebuff, Togodumnus asked Daszdius about his fellow hostage.

The guard explained, "He came to us looking for help to recover his kingdom after he'd been chased out by some other warlord. The Governor agreed to send some troops to install him as one of our client Kings, but your father helped kick our expedition out of Hibernia, so he's not exactly pleased to learn you are here."

"My father has made a lot of enemies," Togodumnus grumbled, "and they all seem to blame me."

His attempts to engage the two other hostages in conversation fared no better. They were older men, both from the south, chieftains whose tribes had been less than enthusiastic about becoming Roman. As leaders of the opposition to the Empire, both men had been dragged from their homes and brought with the Legions so that the Governor could keep an eye on them. Their families knew that the men's lives would be forfeit if there was any hint of rebellion while the Governor was subduing the north. In turn, the two hostages had lost all influence with their people because they were not permitted to send or receive messages. They were, naturally, unwilling to befriend anyone who supported Rome, and they regarded Togodumnus with suspicion. In view of his pro-Roman stance, he supposed he could hardly blame them, but their hostility left him in a strange, lonely limbo, caught somewhere between the unwilling hostages and the privileged status that Venutius enjoyed.

Togodumnus was intelligent enough to realise that he had not yet earned the Governor's full trust and, until he did, his situation was unlikely to change. In this bizarre menagerie of hostages, he was alone.

There was, though, another hostage who shared his plight. The girl's room was next to his own, only a thin wall of wattle and daub separating them. Sometimes, if he lay very still and quiet at night, he thought he could hear her moving around, but there was no way to communicate with her, because both of them were guarded at all times and she was rarely permitted to leave her room. When she did, she was surrounded by Sdapezi's troopers and nobody was allowed to speak to her. Togodumnus saw her only twice, catching brief glimpses of her sad, downcast face as she was bustled past him. He tried to call to her, but she did not acknowledge him, keeping her eyes lowered. The only reaction came from the guards who chased him away with gruff warnings to mind his own business.

In effect, Sdapezi's troopers were the only people Togodumnus could talk to. Daszdius was chatty, but he was a simple man, a soldier who knew all there was to know about horses, fighting, drinking, gambling and whoring, preferably in that order, but who had little interest in anything else. Most of the other troopers were the same, even the young Briton named Hortensius who claimed to have joined up to avoid starving to death in his home village.

To Togodumnus' surprise, his main companion in conversation was the dour Centurion, Sdapezi. He often stopped by to check on all the hostages but spent more time chatting to Togodumnus than to all the others combined. Twice, he turned up in the evening, bringing a jug of wine which he insisted they drink together.

Initially, Togodumnus suspected this was part of the Governor's ploy to test his loyalty, but he soon decided that there was another, far more mundane explanation.

Sdapezi was lonely.

"We're a cavalry unit," the Centurion explained on their second evening, when the wine jug was almost empty. "But we're in a Legionary fort. Cavalry and infantry don't get on at all, you know. They usually keep us separate. Not only that, we're Auxiliaries, not citizens, so the bastard Legionaries look down their imperial Roman noses at us. That's why it's a pleasant change to have someone sensible to talk to."

"What about your men? You can talk to them, can't you?"

Sdapezi gave a snorting laugh.

"I said sensible. But no, I can't get too close to them. I'm an officer. They expect me to stay apart. Discipline would go to pieces if I was too friendly with them."

He gave a wistful shrug as he went on, "That's one thing I discovered after I got this job. I used to think my old Centurion, Casca, was a snooty bugger, but I soon learned he had it right. Not that he got much else right."

"He was the one who joined up with Venutius to hunt my father down, wasn't he?"

"That's right. And got himself killed for his trouble. He made two big mistakes, you see. He under-estimated your father and he trusted Venutius."

"I take it you won't do either of those things," Togodumnus smiled.

"No chance. Not that we're likely to come up against your father. Our job is to keep you and the other guests out of trouble, so we won't be going near any fighting if I can help it. As for Venutius, though, he's as shifty as they come, always looking for ways to advance himself and put others down. Take my advice, lad, and stay away from him if you can."

"I won't have much chance to avoid him once we march north, will I?"

"True enough. But don't let him rile you. I think he sees you as an easy target for taking out his hatred of your father."

"I'll do my best to ignore him," Togodumnus promised.

"Good. Don't worry, I'll watch out for you. I owe your father that much."

Togodumnus could tell that the Centurion meant well, although he doubted whether Sdapezi would think twice about helping him if the Governor changed his mind and decided to order Togodumnus' execution. Sdapezi was a soldier, his jailer, and he could not allow himself to forget that.

What was abundantly clear, however, was that the Centurion detested Venutius. Togodumnus tried to exploit this shared sentiment, hoping the wine might have loosened Sdapezi's tongue.

"What about the girl in the next room? She's obviously important, and Venutius seems to be in charge of her."

"The Governor is in charge," Sdapezi shot back. "But his orders are that we do as Venutius says regarding her."

The Centurion's eyes narrowed in warning as he added, "One of the things he says is that she is not to speak to anyone, so don't bother asking any questions about her, because I know as much as you do."

"I think you know a bit more," Togodumnus persisted. "Venutius is using her to extort information from someone in my father's camp, isn't he?"

Sdapezi gave a curt nod.

"It doesn't take a seer to work that out, lad, but that's as far as my knowledge goes. Why are you so interested anyway?"

"I am only interested in the girl," Togodumnus replied casually. "She seems very sad and lonely. I suppose I don't like the thought of her being in Venutius' power."

"He won't do anything to her as long as she's valuable to him, and my lads have been warned off touching her. All we need to do is make sure she is kept away from everyone else."

"That's what I don't understand," Togodumnus frowned. "Why is she not allowed to talk to the rest of us?"

Sdapezi gave another of his habitual shrugs as he answered, "I expect it's because Venutius enjoys having some control. I told you, he's got a hunger for power. He likes manipulating people. And, if he's the only one who knows who the spy is, it gives him a lot of influence with the Governor."

"I suppose that must be it," Togodumnus sighed. "But can you at least tell me her name?"

Sdapezi shook his head.

"No, because I don't know it. Now, we'd better drop this subject. If you want a woman, there are some whores in the civilian camp. I can have one brought in, although I can't guarantee you won't end up with a dose of something unpleasant."

"I'll give that a miss for the time being," Togodumnus replied with a shy smile.

"Suit yourself. Now, I'd better be going. We'll be moving out in a couple of days, so tomorrow is likely to be busy."

For Togodumnus, the following day was far busier than he could ever have expected. It began routinely enough, with a wash and shave, followed by a breakfast and a few jokes shared with Daszdius, then several hours with nothing to do except stare at the plain walls. Late in the morning, though, Sdapezi came to his room with a summons.

"The Governor wants to see you," the Centurion announced.

They made the now familiar walk to the Principia, which was as busy as ever, with scribes and messengers fretting impatiently as they waited their turn to see the Governor.

They were forced to wait a little longer because the Tribune, Aulus Atticus, admitted Togodumnus as soon as he arrived.

On entering the Governor's office, Togodumnus saw that there was a stranger sitting on a low stool in front of the desk, facing the Governor and Legate Licinius Spurius.

The man wore British-style trousers and tunic, but his hair, although long and untidy, had a Roman look to it. When he stood and turned round, Togodumnus saw a serious-faced man of around fifty, with brown eyes that resembled deep pools of melancholy.

Agricola said, "Togodumnus, I would like you to meet Lucius Anderius Facilis. He has a rather intriguing tale to tell. I'd like you to hear it."

Facilis offered his hand, which Togodumnus took in greeting.

"You have your mother's look about you," Facilis remarked with a weary smile.

"You know her?" Togodumnus blinked in astonishment.

"She is the reason I am here," Facilis replied. "Take a seat and I'll explain everything."

Togodumnus sat on a stool, listening while Facilis recounted his adventure, beginning with his capture by the

278

mutinous Usipi, taking him through all its horrors, then detailing how Facilis and his companion had been rescued by Calgacus before being brought south by Beatha.

"My mother is here?" Togodumnus asked, unable to conceal his eagerness.

Facilis shook his head.

"No. She brought me to the bridge of boats. Once there, I persuaded the sailors to put me on one of their small boats and bring me here. Your mother is waiting on the far side of the river."

"Waiting? For what?"

Facilis said, "For you."

The Governor interrupted, "It seems your mother wishes to offer us two captives in exchange for you. The other prisoner is still being held until Facilis returns with your answer."

A ghost of a smile flickered around the edges of Facilis' mouth as he said, "Poor Pulcher is terrified. Your mother has six of the wildest female warriors I've ever seen. They've plastered their hair with lime, painted themselves all over with strange symbols, and they're half naked."

Legate Spurius commented drily, "That must be a sight to amaze our soldiers."

"It's a sight that terrifies them," Facilis informed him. "It's as if the Amazons have appeared out of legend."

Agricola snapped, "Never mind that. The question is, what answer do we send back?"

Once again, Togodumnus found himself under the Governor's intimidating gaze, the steely eyes demanding the truth.

The unexpectedness of the situation confused him. He sat back, exhaling softly, raising his eyes to the ceiling as he sought a suitable response.

Thoughts flashed through his mind, scenarios played themselves out, and he knew what he must do. He had a chance to go back to his family, to resume his former life, but how long would that life be? He was no warrior, nor did he have any desire to fight. He had always wanted peace with Rome. Yet he knew now that Rome did not desire peace except on its own terms.

Bend with the wind, Venutius had advised him.

But he was not Venutius. Much as he detested the thought of war, he could not bear to see his people destroyed. There was, he knew, only one way he could help them, but it was a dangerous path to walk, and he was afraid that the Governor would see through any attempt to mask his true intentions.

Then he recalled the lessons his father had tried to give him all those years earlier, when he had attempted to show him how to wield a sword.

"It is like any skill," Calgacus had told him. "Don't wave your sword around hoping to do some damage. Hope is not enough. You must believe that every stroke is going to kill."

Togodumnus did not have a sword, had never mastered the skill, but he had other talents. Now he must use those, and use them with absolute confidence. He could not simply lie, hoping to deceive the Governor; he must be certain that his words would be believed.

He took a deep breath, then held Agricola's stare, speaking firmly and convincingly. He could do this, he knew, because there was a great deal of truth in what he must say. That truth must disguise the lie.

He told the Governor, "I have said that I wish to be a friend to Rome. That has not changed. I wish to remain here so that I can help my people once the war is over. My father is wrong to oppose you, but I am not him. As for my mother, it is obvious that she has made this offer out of concern for my safety. As far as she knows, I am merely a prisoner, taken against my will."

Facilis confirmed, "She is worried about you."

"She need not worry," Togodumnus shrugged.

"So you will not go back?" Agricola asked. "Even if it means the death of our Quaestor?"

The days he had spent among the Romans had taught Togodumnus a great deal about how they viewed the world. He used that knowledge as he replied, "From what Anderius Facilis has said, I believe you had probably already given him and Quaestor Pulcher up for dead. Facilis is free now, but if Pulcher dies, you still have the better of the bargain."

Agricola gave a soft chuckle. "Did you overhear my earlier conversation with Licinius Spurius? That is exactly what I told him. Is that not so, Spurius?"

"It is indeed," the Legate agreed with an unctuous smile.

Togodumnus inclined his head, acknowledging the compliment. Then he continued, "However, I have a suggestion that might see your Quaestor freed."

Agricola's eyebrows rose.

"Go on," he invited.

"If Facilis gives my answer, or if you give no answer at all, my mother will continue to believe you are holding me against my will. Can I suggest that I go to talk to her myself? I will tell her that I have decided to stay. I will try to persuade her to release the Quaestor. She is not a cruel person, and I have always been able to persuade her to my side of any argument."

He watched Agricola closely, surprising himself by seeming to be able to read the man's thoughts. The Governor was weighing up the probability that Togodumnus might try to escape, or might say or do something that would aid the Britons. He quickly came to the conclusion that there was nothing Togodumnus could say that would hinder the invasion, and that it would be no great loss if he ran away.

"Very well," Agricola decided. "You may go back with Facilis and give this message in person. Perhaps it will help your father see sense."

Smiling confidently, Togodumnus replied, "I doubt that very much, Sir. But it will harm his reputation when the tribes learn I have joined you. That can only help shorten the war."

Agricola rewarded him with a friendly smile and Togodumnus knew he had succeeded in the first part of his hastily devised plan.

Now all he needed to do was warn his mother that there was a spy in the British camp, and do it without letting the Romans know.

Chapter XXV

The short voyage upriver did not take long. Aided by an incoming tide, the rowers drove the small supply boat against the current with practised ease.

Togodumnus found the experience vaguely unsettling. On his left, the southern side of the Bodotria was Roman territory, alive with soldiers, traders and thousands of camp followers. Forts and watchtowers were visible, cavalry units patrolled the shore, and he could make out the banners and flags of the infantry units who were gathering for the invasion.

Other ships plied their way up and down the mighty river, carrying supplies, messages, and hard-eyed marines who were ever ready to pounce on any Britons who might be foolish enough to attempt to cross the river. The sight of these rough men reminded Togodumnus of his own capture, and he turned away, studying the northern shore.

Here, it was so different. The countryside looked the same; green, lush, forested, with marshes and hills but, although the land appeared devoid of life, there was an indefinable brooding threat on the north bank. This was untamed territory, free of Rome, inhabited by wild tribes who would need to be conquered by force of arms.

Togodumnus could feel the watchful menace of the northern shore. Even though he was from the north himself, he could understand why the Romans viewed the wilderness as a land to be feared. He had seen and heard that fear in the faces and voices of the soldiers in the Ninth Legion's fort. It was not fear of the Britons, he knew; it was fear of the unknown. Even Daszdius, who had frequently journeyed north as part of Venutius' escort, had asked him whether it was true that there were giants in the north, or one-eyed

Cyclops, or werebeasts who hunted men at night. Laughing, Togodumnus had assured the trooper that all these stories were true. Daszdius had joined in the laughter, but his eyes had revealed his doubt.

From what Facilis had told him, Togodumnus guessed that his mother was helping stir the Romans' anxiety.

"Does she really have half-naked female warriors with her?" he asked the Roman as they stood beside one another on the wooden deck of the small galley.

"She certainly does. Very impressive they are, too."

Facilis seemed tired, torn between relief at returning to civilisation and a sense of loss, as if a part of him had been left behind in the north. Togodumnus guessed the man's sombre mood was a result of the harrowing voyage he had undertaken as a prisoner of the Usipi.

Not that Facilis' former captors were a concern any longer. The Governor had consulted a writing tablet, one of many that were stacked on his desk.

"Here it is," he had smiled as he scanned the report. "Yes, three ships were intercepted by our fleet. The Usipi, it seems, were still trying to sail across to Germania, but they were caught before they got there."

He gave a casual wave of his hand as he explained, "I have ordered the ringleaders to be crucified and the rest sold into slavery."

Togodumnus had expected Facilis to be pleased at the news, but the Roman had instead appeared rather withdrawn, as if he regretted the Usipi's fate.

"It's funny," he confided to Togodumnus, "I rather liked Fullofaudes. He reminded me of your father. For all his brutality, he was a man with a sense of honour."

It was an odd compliment, but Togodumnus quickly realised that Facilis was unusual for a Roman. For whatever reason, he did not display the almost unshakeable arrogance and self-belief that most Romans seemed to possess. He was

284

thoughtful, introspective, and clearly intelligent, but his eyes held a haunted look, as if there was an emptiness inside him.

Togodumnus sensed Facilis growing more uneasy as they neared the bridge of boats the Roman engineers and sailors had constructed at a point where the river narrowed to less than a hundred paces across. Chained and roped together, the galleys had their masts lowered and their rails dismantled. Long planks had been fastened to form a wide roadway over the decks, a temporary bridge that rose and fell with the river, but which would allow the Legions to march across to the northern bank. Earth had been strewn over the planking, and high sides were now being added so that animals could be walked across without the sight of the water terrifying them. It was, Togodumnus reflected, an impressive achievement.

"The war will start very soon," Facilis observed pensively.

Togodumnus knew he was correct. The bridge was almost complete, and the soldiers ready, only awaiting the Governor's command.

"I will let you deliver your message before we begin our march," Agricola had told him. "It will help unsettle your father's allies."

Togodumnus had smiled, concealing his secret thoughts.

Now it was time.

The galley edged to the northern shore, bumping against the gravel bank. The soldiers who guarded the northern end of the bridge had horses waiting for them, and Togodumnus, accompanied by Facilis, Sdapezi and Daszdius, was on his way northwards only a few moments after disembarking.

They had scarcely ridden fifty paces before mounted figures appeared on the crest of a low rise that overlooked the bridge. Togodumnus recognised his mother's blonde hair and the way she sat, tall and erect, in the saddle. Behind her, just as Facilis had described, were six women, their hair spiked and bleached white, the skin of their faces, arms and long legs decorated by swirling lines, vivid splotches, and jagged symbols. In their midst was the portly figure of Antonius Pulcher, his face as white as the lime-coated spikes of the women's hair.

"Amazons, right enough," murmured Sdapezi, not quite managing to conceal his nervousness.

The women stared belligerently at the four riders, who drew to a halt twenty paces from them. After a moment, Beatha nudged her pony and slowly came to meet them.

Togodumnus had never seen her dressed for war. He gaped at her leather tunic and close-fitting trousers, the long boots and the sharp knife at her waist. Her hair was tied back, and she wore a torc of gold around her throat. She sat with a regal bearing, but he could see the tension in her eyes. She was looking him up and down, searching for any signs that he had been mistreated, and he realised that, for all her warlike appearance, she was still his mother.

He found his throat constricted by emotion, preventing him from speaking to her. He knew that she had been hurt by his refusal to leave their home, and now he must hurt her again. The knowledge made him falter.

Beatha looked at him with evident concern.

"Togodumnus? Are you well?"

He swallowed, cleared his throat and nodded, "I am well."

"You are free now, Togodumnus," she told him.

He looked into her eyes, willing her to understand him, praying that she would listen properly to what he was about to tell her. He was ready now, in control of himself again, and it was time to deliver his message.

"You should not call me Togodumnus," he said, his voice firm and cold. "I have renounced that name."

He could see the shock in her eyes, the slackening of her jaw.

"What do you mean?" she gasped.

"I have decided to remain among the Romans," he told her. "It is the right thing for me to do. So, I am no longer Togodumnus. I have taken the name Cingel."

Beatha blinked uncertainly, her anxiety transmitting to her pony which skittered sideways, forcing her to tug on the reins to bring it closer to Togodumnus.

"Cingel?" she repeated, frowning uncertainly.

"Yes. You remember the story of Cingel, don't you? I have found my own magic cauldron, filled with inexhaustible wealth and opportunity. It is called Rome. Like Cingel, I have decided the best thing to do is to join them."

Beatha's face was pale, her cheeks quivering with emotion. She stretched out her hand, pleading with him.

"Why are you saying these things, Togodumnus?"

"I am Cingel," he reminded her, putting as much emphasis as he could into the name. "I have seen the power of Rome, Mother, and I know Father cannot win this war. You should tell him that. He should make peace, as I have done."

He saw his mother swallow anxiously, then she sat upright, remembering that she was a daughter of Kings, and wife of a War Leader.

"Is that your final word?" she asked.

He could see how much his rejection had hurt her. That was all to the good, because the Romans, especially Facilis who understood what they were saying, would believe that he was truly on their side. But if his mother did not listen to his hidden message, it would all be in vain.

He asked her, "Do you remember the story of the Great Bear of the Mountains? You used to tell it to me when I was a boy. You should tell it to Father. I think he would learn something from it. He believes he is as strong as a bear, but he will find the story instructive. Tell him that, if he wants to live, he should pay heed to the Great Bear's downfall. And tell him about Cingel. Make him understand

287

that I am doing what I believe to be the best thing for our people."

Beatha's expression clouded, then began to clear as understanding dawned.

Hastily, Togodumnus moved his horse, drawing alongside her so that their knees touched, forcing her to turn her head to look at him. He hoped that the movement would prevent the Romans from noticing the flash of comprehension in her expression.

Adding a rough tone to his voice, he went on, "I will not come with you. I believe I can serve our people better by being a friend to Rome. I am sorry, but that is my decision."

He saw her blink, saw the tears fill her eyes, but they were tears of pride, not hurt. She nodded, unable to speak.

He said, "I told the Governor you would release the other prisoner. He is no use to you now, and I know you would not kill him out of petty vengeance."

With a visible effort of will, Beatha drew herself together. She waved a hand to her warriors.

"Let him go!" she called, her words almost a sob.

Then she leaned towards Togodumnus, wrapping one arm around him to embrace him.

"I understand," she whispered. "I love you."

"I love you, too," he replied softly, feeling his own tears stinging his eyes. "Be strong."

As she broke away, Togodumnus raised his voice so that everyone could hear.

"I think you should go now. When this war is over, we will be reunited, but I cannot come with you. This is my choice."

Beatha's face grew stern as she regarded him coldly.

She said, "You are right. You are no longer Togodumnus. You are Cingel. It is as well your father is not here to see this day, but I will tell him what you said."

Tugging fiercely at the reins, she wheeled her pony, jabbing her heels to its flanks to urge it back up the hill, passing the startled Pulcher who was riding down towards the Romans, scarcely believing he was being allowed to go free. Togodumnus turned to ride alongside him.

"We will take you back now," he informed the quivering Quaestor.

Sdapezi shot Togodumnus an enquiring look.

"What did you say to her?"

Facilis interjected, "He told her that he was staying with us, that his father should give up the fight."

Sdapezi nodded, satisfied by the explanation, but Togodumnus saw a look of hurt and loss in Facilis' expression. For a moment, he wondered whether the Roman had detected his secret message, but then he noticed that Facilis' eyes were fixed on Beatha's retreating figure. When she and her escort had vanished over the crest of the hill, Facilis turned a bleak face towards him.

"That must have been difficult," the Roman observed.

"Yes, but she took it surprisingly well. I think she knows where my loyalties lie."

"She is a remarkable woman," Facilis agreed.

Then Pulcher was blabbering his thanks, and Sdapezi was urging them to return to the boat.

Togodumnus knew he had achieved what he had set out to do. He had passed on the warning, but there was still more to be done. The prospect filled him with trepidation, but he had made his choice and he knew he could not turn back. Now, he must truly emulate the legendary Cingel by defeating his enemies from within.

Chapter XXVI

After seeing off Beatha and her captives, Calgacus and Runt made their way around the low hill which bore the tomb of Cingel, and headed towards the eastern edge of the vast camp.

Old Ebrauc already had his small tribe preparing to leave. Men, women and children, many of them looking less than at peak fitness thanks to the excesses of the Beltane festival, were busy dismantling shelters, loading carts and herding livestock, the first wagons already trundling on their way to the west.

"It's nice to know we can rely on at least one person to follow orders," Runt observed.

Ebrauc, riding on an ornately decorated chariot, gave them a wave and called out a promise to have the new camp established within two days.

"Don't forget about us!" he smiled.

"Never!" Calgacus promised.

Satisfied that Ebrauc had matters well in hand, Calgacus and Runt continued their walk, seeking out Gabrain.

The Venicones, like the other tribes, had celebrated long into the night, but they were slowly coming awake, gathering up their things and preparing to depart. Gabrain, though, was unhappy, his mood deteriorating further when he heard about Algarix's attempt on Calgacus' life.

"Are the Taexali committed to this war?" he demanded.

"They have come as we asked," Calgacus replied evasively.

"Only a few of them. We need the rest of their war host."

"Maelchon has promised that they will be here soon," Calgacus assured him. "But your task is to set up a new camp further east, so get your men moving as soon as you can."

"Some of them believe you are sending us away so that you can abandon us," Gabrain growled, managing to convey the impression that he shared the sentiment.

"You know that is not true," Calgacus replied. "It is simply that we need to divide our forces before disease and hunger get a grip on us. I also need you to be in a position where you can circle behind the Romans once they cross the river."

Gabrain gave a curt nod, clearly not entirely convinced.

He said, "I will trust you for the moment. Let us hope this plan works."

"A lot will depend on what the Romans do," Calgacus replied. "Remember, if their scouts find you, drive them off, but don't get involved in a fight with the Legions. Fall back if necessary."

"You think they might come after us?" Gabrain asked.

"I cannot read the future," Calgacus replied. "But, whatever happens, we will face them together. I promise you that. Dividing our forces does not mean we will act independently. When the time for battle arrives, we must join forces again."

Gabrain gave a curt nod, turning away and calling for his horse, shouting for his warriors to break camp.

Calgacus sighed, "Well, that's two groups on the way. Let's hope the Taexali are also moving."

Runt frowned, "Do you think it's a good idea to walk into Maelchon's camp on our own? After what you did to Algarix, I don't expect we'll be given a very friendly reception."

Calgacus nodded, "I know. That's why we will stop off in Drust's camp first."

"If you are thinking of taking an escort," Runt said, "we'd be better with some of our own lads."

"We don't need warriors," Calgacus replied. "That would only cause more tension. What we need is a druid."

"Broichan?"

"He'll be with the Caledones."

Picking a winding route through the camp of the Venicones, they walked round the northern edge of Cingel's tomb, to where the Caledones were based.

As they headed into the vast, sprawling swarm of tents and shelters where Drust's tribe had set up their temporary homes, Calgacus saw the druid standing near the centre of the encampment. He was talking to Bran, who broke off their discussion and greeted Calgacus with a smooth smile which was in stark contrast to Broichan's dark scowl.

"If you have come to talk to our King," Bran said, "I was just explaining to Broichan that he is unwell."

Broichan snorted, "Unwell? The fool is still insensible from drinking too much."

He shook his head, his expression full of contempt as he rasped, "You will get no sense from him this morning."

"It doesn't matter," Calgacus shrugged. "There is something else I need to talk to you about."

Broichan sniffed, "Were the omens not to your liking?"

"The omens were perfect," Calgacus replied. "It is Maelchon who is the problem."

Broichan pulled a face at the mention of the Taexali King, but Bran grinned, "We heard about your trouble. I see you reclaimed your sword. Congratulations, although I suspect Maelchon will take offence."

Broichan interrupted, "You had better tell me your version of events. I take it you do not deny fighting Algarix?"

"Only in self defence. He attacked me while I was unarmed."

"And naked, so I hear," Bran put in.

"I was bathing."

"With your wife?"

Broichan gestured impatiently for Bran to be silent. Then he fixed his raptor stare on Calgacus and asked, "Why did you let him live?"

"Because we are here to fight the Romans, not one another."

The druid's face was set as hard as stone as he said, "And I suppose you now want me to sort out the mess you have created?"

Calgacus refused to rise to the bait. He merely shrugged, "I would appreciate your help in persuading Maelchon to put an end to this petty feud and play his part in this war."

Broichan snorted and shook his head, but it was a gesture of resignation, not a refusal.

"Very well," he sighed with an exasperated air.

Bran asked, "Would you like me to accompany you?"

Now it was Calgacus' turn to shake his head.

"Maelchon is my problem," he told the young chieftain. "You should try to get Drust sober."

"Will he be needed today?" Bran asked. "The Romans have not crossed the river, have they?"

"Not as far as I know, but they could do so at any time, so your warriors need to be ready."

"Oh, they are ready now," Bran assured him smoothly. "In fact, they are becoming bored with nothing to do. They came looking for plunder and battle."

"They'll get it soon enough," Calgacus informed the young chieftain. "Now, Broichan and I need to go and see Maelchon."

"I wish you luck," Bran grinned happily. "If he kills you, I will ensure the Caledones avenge you."

"That is not particularly comforting," Calgacus smiled, unable to resist the effect of Bran's good humour.

"Come!" snapped Broichan. "Let us get this over with."

He wagged an admonitory finger at Bran as he added darkly, "There will be no killing or avenging unless I say so."

Bran bobbed his head in a slight bow of acknowledgement, but his lips were still curved in a broad smile, and he gave Calgacus an encouraging wink as soon as Broichan's back was turned.

Calgacus returned a quick wave of farewell, then set off after the druid, who was setting a fast pace.

When Calgacus and Runt caught up with him, Broichan complained, "As if we did not have enough problems, Bran worries me."

Calgacus' eyebrows rose in question. He had expected Broichan to berate him further for becoming involved in a fight with the Taexali, but the druid had surprised him.

"Oh, why?"

"He is building a following for himself among the Caledones," Broichan replied. "He is no great fighter, but he is shrewd, cunning, and clever. I fear it is only a matter of time before he makes an attempt to remove Drust as King."

"How soon?" Calgacus asked, recognising that Broichan held far less sway over Bran than he did over Drust.

After a slight pause, the druid admitted, "I am not sure. He is ambitious, but he is also prudent. However, there are already some mutterings about a new King being chosen."

"Will the Caledones still fight if Bran leads them?"

Broichan scowled, "He leads them now in all but name and they are still here, but I cannot be certain of his intentions."

"He has not exactly been at the forefront of those clamouring for war," Calgacus pointed out.

Broichan nodded, "That is true. I have spoken to many of the other chieftains among the Caledones and reminded them that Drust was their chosen King, but I fear he is not helping matters. He spends his entire time drinking."

Runt put in, "I don't think we need to worry too much. Whoever leads them, the Caledones are eager for war. Take a look around you."

The camp they were passing through was a mess. The detritus of the previous evening's celebrations were everywhere. Discarded mugs, platters, and even items of clothing littered the ground, some shelters had collapsed, fires had burned down to ash and cinders, while dogs snarled at one another as they fought over scraps of discarded food.

Many of the warriors were still sleeping, while others sat or stood around listlessly, most of them looking the worse for wear. There were, though, always men who were prepared to engage in light-hearted banter. Seeing Calgacus looking at them, one group called out to him.

"When are we going to fight?" asked one. "My arse is getting sore from all this sitting around."

"We'll fight as soon as you are sober," Calgacus called back.

"We fight better when we're drunk," came the laughing response.

"How would you know?" Calgacus shot back. "You're never sober."

The Caledones laughed loudly at that, agreeing he was correct.

Runt grinned, "See what I mean? There's nothing wrong with these lads' spirits. They'll do."

"You're right," agreed Calgacus. "Let's hope the Taexali are just as keen."

"Their warriors are," Broichan put in. "It is Maelchon who is reluctant to fight."

"Then we must change his mind on that," Calgacus insisted.

The druid seemed uncharacteristically uncertain as he frowned, "That may not be easy. He has already rebuffed me once."

"What? When? How?"

Broichan cast a sidelong look at Calgacus but declined to face him. Looking straight ahead, he continued to march through the camp as he spoke.

"I heard about your fight earlier," he admitted with a deep sigh, "so I went to see Maelchon to learn more."

Calgacus pursed his lips. He supposed he should have known the druid would have heard about his confrontation with Algarix. But the revelation that Broichan had already been to see Maelchon was completely unexpected.

"What did he say to you?" he wanted to know.

Broichan frowned deeply as he admitted, "Nothing at all. He would not speak to me. His guards insisted that he was sleeping and was not to be disturbed."

Calgacus was surprised. Few men would deny a druid access to wherever he wanted to go.

He asked, "What happened?"

Broichan's voice was thick with suppressed outrage as he explained, "As I say, his guards refused me entry to his tent. It seems they fear him more than they fear me."

His brow furrowed in a deep frown at the memory as he continued, "However, it was not an entirely fruitless visit. I did manage to speak to several of his chieftains."

"And what did they say?"

Broichan recounted, "It seems your fight with Maelchon's shield-bearer has caused some consternation. Most of them believe you should have killed him. Algarix is clearly not popular."

With a cynical grin, Calgacus observed, "I suppose that the men who think I should have killed him also believe that they should be the King's new shield-bearer?"

Broichan grunted, "No doubt each of them would have put himself forward if Algarix had died. The position of

King's shield-bearer is a prestigious one, and jealousy is a great motivator. But the Taexali are unsettled. There has been some dissension among them."

"About what?"

Broichan sighed, "About Maelchon. It seems many of them do not approve of his behaviour."

"They think he ordered Algarix to kill me?"

Broichan shrugged, "Some of them do."

Runt asked, "What do we do if he tries again?"

"He won't attack us if we are under a druid's protection," Calgacus replied, giving Broichan a hopeful look.

"You will be safe enough," Broichan assured them confidently, "although I suspect wearing that sword is likely to inflame Maelchon's temper."

"I won it fairly," Calgacus returned. "I gave it to him once, and he gave it to Algarix, who tried to kill me with it. Now, it's mine again, by right."

"That is the law," Broichan agreed.

Runt growled, "Speaking of swords, there's one easy way to deal with Maelchon. A blade would solve the problem permanently."

"Don't tempt me," muttered Calgacus.

Flapping a hand as if to wave away the suggestion, Broichan warned, "Do not do anything hasty. The Taexali are a proud people. Killing their King will only turn then against you. We must try persuasion."

"I hope you have some good arguments lined up," Calgacus told him.

Broichan gave him an enigmatic smile but said nothing.

Runt murmured, "I can see this is going to be fun."

They were nearing the shallow stream now, approaching a series of stepping stones that had been placed in the water to allow easy crossing. The Taexali camp, a huddle of shelters and lines of war ponies, was on the far side, a little way to their left. After picking their way carefully across the river, they strode towards the camp.

Calgacus could tell that the Taexali were in a sullen, resentful mood, although he could not decide whether their resentment was aimed at him or at their own King. Men cautiously rose to their feet, summoning their neighbours when he led Broichan and Runt into the camp. By the time the three men had reached Maelchon's shelter, they had a crowd of curious warriors trailing behind them. The men's mood was not hostile, but it was not overly friendly either. There was an air of apprehension, as if the Taexali knew they were about to witness a confrontation and were not certain what outcome to hope for.

Calgacus walked grimly on, aware of Runt fingering the hilts of his twin swords. Broichan, though, seemed unperturbed. His earlier anger had been replaced by a stern determination, and he held his head high, striding confidently through the camp, gripping his staff firmly and looking neither to left nor right.

Several chieftains, including the thin-faced Muradach, were standing outside Maelchon's large shelter. The King's tent was a collection of leather sheets stretched over a wooden framework to resemble a roundhouse. Two enormous men stood guard at the entrance, each of them as big and brawny as Calgacus.

"You may not enter," one of them growled as he held up a hand to deny them admission. "The King is not to be disturbed."

Calgacus had no great desire to go into the tent, a move that would be akin to entering a bear's den. Like the last time he had confronted Maelchon, this meeting would be best held in front of many witnesses.

Speaking loudly to ensure that the onlookers could hear, he replied, "Then go and tell your King to come out here. I want to know why he is still sleeping when the rest of our army is preparing for war."

"The King may not be disturbed," the guard repeated doggedly.

Broichan took a pace forward. He rasped, "If you do not fetch him now, I will place a curse on you that will haunt you and all your descendants forever!"

The two huge warriors grew pale. They looked at one another uncertainly, wavering under Broichan's wrathful gaze.

The druid went on, "And I will curse your King for eternity. I say again, let him come forth to explain why he has not obeyed the commands of the War Leader."

One of the guards swallowed nervously, but before either of them could make up their mind, the leather flap of the entrance was thrust aside and Maelchon stormed out, his fleshy face contorted in indignant outrage.

He was dressed in fine, brightly coloured clothes, his golden torc around his neck and the ring he had obtained from Calgacus on his finger. His hair had been combed, his chin and cheeks recently shaved, but his eyes were bloodshot and puffy, showing that he had not fully recovered from the excesses of the Beltane feast.

He could not have failed to hear Broichan's threats, yet he adopted an aggressive stance as he stepped to confront his visitors.

"What have we here?" he sneered. "A group of petitioners, perhaps? Why are you disturbing me?"

Calgacus felt his temper rising. Ignoring the King's jibe, he snapped, "Why are you still here? You were supposed to accompany the Damnonii this morning."

Maelchon gave no indication that he had heard Calgacus' reproach. The King's eyes bulged and he pointed a fat finger as he barked, "You stole my sword! Now you walk in here, wearing it on your back like a prize. I demand that you return it to me."

Calgacus was determined not to betray any weakness in the face of Maelchon's furious expression or the harsh poison in his voice.

Forcefully, Calgacus repeated, "You were supposed to move west this morning. The other tribes are preparing for war, but you are sitting here on your backsides, doing nothing. I want to know when you are going to march."

"When you give me my sword back," Maelchon rasped, spreading his hands in a contrived gesture of openness.

"It is not your sword," Calgacus told him. "I gave it to you as a gift, but you gave it away. And the man you gave it to tried to kill me. He failed, and I took the sword from him. It is mine."

He looked around at the faces of the men who encircled them and asked, "Where is Algarix, anyway?"

"I sent him away," Maelchon replied casually. "What use is a shield-bearer who cannot even kill an unarmed man?"

Calgacus stared belligerently at Maelchon as he accused, "You sent him to kill me."

"If I had sent someone to kill you, you would be dead," Maelchon snorted dismissively. "I knew nothing about Algarix's intentions. I heard about it this morning from those who witnessed it."

He leered provocatively at Calgacus as he added, "You were saved by a woman, were you not? A fine feat to boast of. But the sword is mine. I merely lent it to Algarix. It was not his to lose."

"I warned you it would bring bad luck to whoever used it," Calgacus reminded him. "Do you really want to risk the curse yourself? Or will you give the sword to another of your warriors? That would hardly be a welcome gift, would it? The man you gave it to would know you have marked him."

Maelchon hesitated, knowing Calgacus was right, but not willing to relinquish his demand. Before he could offer any argument, Broichan intervened, stepping between the two men.

The druid's own fury was obvious, his frame shaking with rage, his face contorted and his cheeks spotted red by anger.

He rounded on Maelchon, barking, "Will you bandy words over a bauble while the fate of your tribe hangs in the balance? I will not listen to this foolishness. The sword clearly belongs to Calgacus by right of victory. That is my judgement, and I will hear no more about it. Now, Maelchon of the Taexali, will you obey the commands of the War Leader, or will you shame your entire tribe by skulking in your tent?"

Many of the watching warriors shrank back from Broichan's fury. The wrath of a druid was not something to be endured lightly, and anyone who crossed one of the greybeards was likely to find himself cursed.

Maelchon blinked, stunned into momentary silence. Then he threw up his arms, yelling at Broichan.

"You dare to accuse me? You are no druid. You are a puppet of Calgacus, a supporter of drunken idiots like Drust, of cravens like Bran, and doddering fools like Ebrauc. You may not judge me! I am Maelchon, King of the Taexali, and I do not recognise your judgement."

An awed silence fell over the camp. Calgacus found that he was holding his breath. In his time, he had frequently argued with druids, but he had never seen anyone openly insult one of them the way Maelchon had done.

The greybeards were few in number now, and had lost a great deal of their former prestige and influence, but Broichan radiated the power and authority of the druids of old, the men who had been trained on the now-destroyed sacred island of Ynis Mon.

In the tense stillness, he raised a liver-spotted hand and pointed a gnarled finger at Maelchon.

In a cold, iron-hard voice, he declared, "Now you have forced me to make another judgement, and you will heed this one. I say that you are not fit to be a King. The Taexali deserve better than you."

Maelchon's face grew suddenly pale, and his eye twitched as he stared at Broichan in disbelief. Then, with a visible effort of will, he recovered and jabbed his own finger at the druid's face.

"You cannot judge me!" he shouted. "I am King here! You are nothing!"

The old man spat his words like an incantation as he rasped, "I am a druid, trained in the lore, keeper of memories, upholder of the laws, custodian of the ancient customs, interpreter of dreams and sacrifices. I understand the ways of the animals, I intercede with the Gods, and I judge mortal men, even Kings. You have been judged, and you have been found wanting."

The power that resonated from Broichan's speech held everyone in shocked silence. Calgacus had rarely heard such a claim to omnipotence, not even from the druids of Ynis Mon. He had heard that, in generations past, druids could halt a war by simply walking onto the battlefield and demanding that the two sides lay down their weapons. Kings had trembled when a druid came to their home, because the druids of former times were beyond the rule of men.

But that had been long ago, when every village headman called himself a King, when a ruler's authority extended only as far as the reach of his arms. By the time Calgacus had been born, the world had changed. Kings ruled vast swathes of land, governed thousands of people, and commanded great war hosts. Those Kings, men like his father, the Great King, Cunobelinos, would heed the advice of druids, but they would not be dictated to. The druids could advise, could influence, could manipulate, but they could no longer command.

Yet Broichan had turned back time. He stood there, tall and fierce, his eyes flashing angrily as he confronted Maelchon and judged him.

To his surprise, Maelchon's mouth twisted in derision as he laughed, "You cannot judge me, Druid. Ynis Mon was burned by Rome. The Gods showed their displeasure at you and your kind by allowing the Romans to desecrate your sacred groves. If the Gods no longer pay attention to you, why should I? Now, take your pathetic War Leader and leave me in peace. The Taexali will take no part in your war."

Broichan did not waver in the face of Maelchon's denial of his authority.

He demanded, "So you refuse to fight alongside the other Pritani?"

"Why should we be commanded by a man who treats us with such contempt?" Maelchon replied haughtily. "Why should we fight for meddling fools like you who utter threats against us? I command the Taexali, and I will decide what we do."

The druid rasped, "What sort of King brings such shame on his people? I say again, you are not worthy of the Kingship."

He turned slowly, locking his eyes onto the watching men, holding their gazes, demanding an answer to his next question.

"Is there no man here who will denounce Maelchon as unfit to be King? Will you permit yourselves to be ruled by such a man? A man who openly scorns the Gods, who refuses to answer a call to arms because of a petty argument over a sword that does not belong to him? Will you happily live under the curse your cowardice will place on you?"

The Taexali shifted uncomfortably, many of them lowering their eyes so as not to meet the druid's questing gaze. Others, though, exchanged looks, raised eyebrows and muttered quiet agreement.

Maelchon whirled, his fists bunching.

He yelled, "I am your King! You will obey me!"

He pointed a furious finger at Broichan and Calgacus as he screamed, "I command that you throw these sorry excuses for men out of my camp!"

For a moment, nobody moved. Calgacus saw the two guards flex their muscles, preparing to follow the King's command, but Broichan held up a hand, glaring at them.

He barked, "The Gods will curse the first man who lays hands on any of us!"

The guards hesitated. They were big, crude men, accustomed to following orders, and they were clearly torn between their loyalty to Maelchon and their fear of the druid's curse.

Calgacus tensed, knowing that once one man had taken the fateful step to obey the King's command, others would follow. If he drew his sword, there would be bloodshed, but if he allowed himself to be ejected from the camp like a thief, he would lose everything.

Broichan stood like a statue, facing Maelchon, unbending in his certainty. Calgacus swore silently, knowing the druid had gone too far. He had pushed Maelchon into a position where only one of them could win. Instead of persuasion, he had used confrontation.

Then Muradach, tall, lean and grim-faced, stepped out of the crowd, men parting to let him pass.

"I say Maelchon is not our King," he declared, his voice steady, his eyes locked on Maelchon.

The King gaped at him. Then he sneered, "Muradach? Are you so keen to die? That is the price of betrayal, you know."

"It is you who betray us," Muradach countered. "You sent Algarix to kill Calgacus, hoping to destroy the alliance and give victory to Rome. You have not summoned the war host as you promised."

"You lie!" Maelchon roared, his face flushed red with rage.

"I do not lie," Muradach stated calmly. "I interrogated Algarix this morning, when I dragged him back after his fight with Calgacus. He admitted everything, including how your brother, our former King, died. You ordered his murder so that you might rule us. Again, I say you are no longer our King."

A ripple of outraged agreement ran round the assembled warriors, but Maelchon jabbed a finger at Muradach.

"Traitor! Kill him!"

Again, Calgacus saw the two warriors of the King's bodyguard prepare to obey, but then both stiffened, and he saw that other men had stepped beside Muradach, indicating their support for him.

Maelchon's jaw tightened. He glared at Muradach.

"What treachery is this? I will have your head."

Broichan said, "Stand aside, Maelchon. The Taexali will have a new King, not one who is a kinslayer."

Maelchon spun round, trying to face Broichan and Muradach at the same time, his eyes wide with alarm.

"Who will be King? You, Muradach? You are nothing more than my father's bastard."

"The people will choose their own King," Muradach replied evenly.

Maelchon gave a snort of mockery.

He shrugged, "It will not be you, anyway. I will make sure of that."

Even as he spoke, he whipped a knife from his belt and threw himself at Muradach, shrieking with rage. His attack was ferocious, his only aim to hack and slash at his former supporter, but it had been too many years since Maelchon had fought anyone, and he had gained too much

305

bulk and weight to move quickly. Muradach ducked aside, dodging the flailing knife, then smashed forwards, head lowered, to ram his shoulder into Maelchon's large belly.

Maelchon let out a loud gasp of pain as he fell. Muradach straightened, lashing out with his foot in an attempt to kick Maelchon's dagger from his hand, but the King slashed a wild sweep, forcing Muradach to leap back. Then Maelchon was pushing himself up, swearing and calling curses down on all traitors.

Calgacus took a pace forwards, reaching for his sword, but Muradach waved a hand at him.

"No! Keep out of this. It is a matter for the Taexali."

Calgacus stopped, but Maelchon turned to see who Muradach had spoken to and, as he did so, Muradach drew his own dagger. He sprang forwards, his body crouched, his left arm up to ward off Maelchon's knife hand, his own dagger held low, ready to strike upwards.

Maelchon turned, but he was too slow. He tried to move, to avoid the killing blow, but he was already out of breath and his bulk pinned him where he stood. He swung his right hand, but Muradach blocked the blow and drove his dagger into Maelchon's chest, just below the ribs, driving it upwards to seek out the King's heart.

Maelchon gasped. He stiffened, every muscle tensing, then he dropped his arms, the knife fell from his fingers, and he toppled slowly backwards, falling to the ground like a felled tree.

Muradach, holding his blood-drenched dagger in his fist, stood over the twitching body, his expression even more dour than usual. For a long moment, nobody spoke, then Muradach straightened and gave Calgacus a look of weary resignation.

"He was not always this way," he explained sadly. "Somewhere, somehow, he lost himself."

The Taexali looked on in grim silence, but Muradach swiftly took charge.

"Maelchon was King, and shall receive a proper funeral. We will burn him as befits a King. Prepare a pyre for him. Once he has been cremated, we will go west, as the War Leader commands."

He stepped away from the corpse, allowing the men to retrieve the body, and walked slowly over to Calgacus.

"Was that all true?" Calgacus asked him. "About Maelchon killing his own brother, I mean?"

"I'm afraid so," Muradach confirmed. "I intercepted Algarix when he staggered back after his fight with you. I persuaded him to tell me the truth."

"Persuaded?"

Muradach smiled, holding up his blood-stained dagger as he explained, "Let us say that the treatment I prescribed for his damaged manhood made him eager to speak before I carried it out."

Calgacus shot a dark look at Broichan.

"You knew about this?"

The druid's shoulders twitched in the faintest of shrugs.

"I spoke to Muradach this morning," he admitted.

"You might have told me!" Calgacus objected.

"No," Broichan replied sternly. "It was necessary that the truth was spoken by one of the Taexali."

Calgacus shook his head and sighed. There was little point in arguing with Broichan. The man was impervious to criticism. Besides, Calgacus reflected, much as he hated being duped, the druid was probably correct. The accusation had carried more weight because it had come from Muradach.

Dismissing Broichan's subterfuge, he turned back to Muradach.

"Where is Algarix now?"

Muradach's expression grew sour.

He said, "I'm afraid he escaped. My men did not think he was in much condition to go anywhere, but he managed to take a horse and he rode away. I sent men after him, but they lost him. Still, I doubt that we will see him again. Everyone in our tribe will know he is an outcast now."

"Good riddance," muttered Runt.

Calgacus asked, "But the Taexali war host? You said it was not coming."

"That is also true," Muradach admitted. "It seems Maelchon had no intentions of summoning the entire tribe. Those of us who are here will remain, but you can expect no more to join us before the Romans attack."

"Can you not summon them now?" Calgacus asked. "We need as many men as we can find."

Muradach gave a sad shake of his head.

"The chieftains who came here agreed to support me as War Leader, but I am not a King. If I sent word, there is no guarantee that anyone would heed it. Even if they did, it would be many days before they could reach us."

Calgacus wanted to scream his frustration, but he knew he could not afford to let the warriors see how much Muradach's news meant to him, so he simply nodded and said, "Then we shall win without them. It is enough that you are here."

Muradach gave a solemn nod.

"You need not worry about our loyalty," he said. "We will join Ebrauc as soon as we have observed the rites for our dead King."

"Burn him well," Calgacus said under his breath. "I don't want his shade haunting us."

"I will make sure of it," Muradach promised.

The Taexali chieftain held out his hand, and Calgacus gripped it firmly, bringing a cheer of acclamation from the warriors.

Calgacus signalled to Runt and Broichan that it was time to leave but, as they walked out of the camp, he vented his frustration.

308

"The bastard was laughing at us all the time. And now he's left us with a big problem."

"Then it is just as well that we have disposed of him," Broichan remarked with grim satisfaction. "He will not cause any more trouble."

"You had it all planned out, didn't you?" Calgacus accused.

An incongruous smile appeared on Broichan's normally stone-hard face as he replied, "I told you, I spoke to the Taexali chieftains this morning. In particular, I talked to Muradach at great length. He told me what he had learned from Algarix, and we discussed what needed to be done. Most of the chieftains were unhappy at Maelchon's deception, so it did not take much to persuade them to support Muradach, especially when they learned how Maelchon's predecessor had been murdered."

"I still say you could have warned us," Calgacus grumbled.

"I did not deem it necessary to burden you with the details," Broichan replied smugly.

"You," Calgacus told the druid, "are a devious old bastard."

"Coming from you," Broichan retorted with unexpected humour, "that is a compliment."

Chapter XXVII

Venutius was waiting for Togodumnus when he returned to the Ninth Legion's fort. The Brigante swaggered from his open doorway, a mocking sneer on his lips.

"Did you deliver your message, then?" he enquired.

"I did."

"It's a pity your father wasn't there to hear it. I'd have liked to have seen his face when he heard you wanted to become a Roman."

"If you had been there to see it," Togodumnus replied caustically, "he would have killed you, truce or no truce."

"That," Venutius grinned, "is why I did not accompany you. It occurred to me that it might be some elaborate trap to lure me into your father's clutches."

"You have an inflated opinion of your own worth," Togodumnus told him. "My father wasn't there. I am sure he will kill you if he ever gets the chance, but he will not go out of his way to hunt you down. He has more important things on his mind."

Venutius gave a scornful laugh. "You think so? Ah, well, he always did have trouble getting his priorities right. Then again, we all have other things on our minds, don't we?"

For a brief heart-stopping moment, Togodumnus wondered whether Venutius had somehow seen through him, but the Brigante had already turned away, laughing softly to himself as he returned to his room at the end of the block.

Sdapezi gave Togodumnus a gentle nudge.

"Ignore him, lad. Come on, get back to your room. Daszdius will bring you your supper."

Togodumnus nodded thoughtfully, but he kept his eyes on Venutius until the Brigante had gone indoors.

Something about the man's mood and mocking smile worried him. Yet there was no way Venutius could have guessed his intent.

He ate his supper, a platter of bread, figs and cheese, then told Daszdius that he was tired and wanted to go to bed early.

"It's still light," the soldier frowned. "But I suppose it's nearly always light up here. The days seem to last forever, and it will be an early start tomorrow."

"It will?"

Daszdius grinned, "Tomorrow, we are marching north. This is the start of it, lad. The final campaign, so everyone says."

"So they do," agreed Togodumnus. "Good night, Daszdius."

He could not lock the door, nor could he bar it, because that would arouse suspicions, so he lay quietly on his bed, staring at the ceiling, only closing his eyes when Sdapezi checked on him after dusk. He ignored the Centurion's soft enquiry, pretending to be asleep. Sdapezi closed the door, and Togodumnus knew he had until dawn to accomplish his next aim.

He waited, listening to the fading sounds of the outside camp, steeling himself to take the next, irrevocable step. He knew there were guards outside each door of the block, but all he could hear were the occasional thumps of footsteps and some low murmuring as the soldiers exchanged a few words and tried to fend off the boredom of their long, night-time vigil.

Lying on his bed, Togodumnus pressed an ear to the thin wall that separated his room from the end room, the apartment where the mysterious girl was kept.

He listened intently, convincing himself that she was lying on the bed just on the other side of the wall. He was sure he could hear faint movements when she turned.

He steeled himself, hoping she would not scream when he attempted to contact her.

Taking his knife, a thin-bladed eating utensil that had a suitably sharp point, he rolled onto his left side and began to gouge a hole in the plaster.

The Romans had built this fort quickly, using timber frameworks, and adopting the British method of using wattle and daub for interior walls. Between the main support pillars were interwoven twigs of hazel, with a lime-washed covering of mud and straw. The tip of his knife soon penetrated the daub, showering him with white, dusty fragments. He struck a thin wand of hazel, manoeuvred the blade upwards, then pressed it against the daub plaster which formed the outer layer of the far side of the wall.

The Romans were great builders, he knew, but in a fort designed to be used only for one winter, they had not spent a great deal of time or effort putting up substantial walls. Hazel was strong, but it was pliable, so he was able to insert his knife between the crudely interwoven strands and force it through to the thin covering of daub that formed the opposite wall. He was through it in no time, feeling the knife give as the pressure stopped. Quickly, he tugged the blade free and put his mouth to the narrow tunnel he had carved, giving a soft, whispered call.

"Are you there?"

His enquiry was met only by silence.

He called again, still eliciting no response.

"I know you are there," he whispered. "Talk to me. I am a friend."

This time there was movement, soft and cautious, the sound faintly audible through the gap he had created. He waited expectantly, his nerves tingling with anticipation.

At last, a quiet, frightened voice whispered back, "Go away. I cannot speak to you. They will kill me."

"No, they won't. Did Venutius tell you that? He is a liar. He needs you alive."

There was another long silence, but he could hear her breathing, and he knew her face must be close to the hole in the wall.

"They will know what you have done," she hissed, her terror plain. "They will see where the plaster has fallen away."

"Cover the hole with pillows and blankets," he told her. "Don't worry, we are leaving tomorrow."

"They will punish me if they discover it."

"I will tell them it was my doing," he assured her. "Please don't be afraid. I need to talk to you."

"Why?"

"I need to know who you are. What is your name?"

"You are trying to trick me," she breathed. "This is a test so that Venutius can punish me."

"No. My name is Togodumnus."

"I know who you are," she replied coldly. "They say you are one of our people who has joined with Rome. Just like Venutius."

He could hear the distrust in her disembodied voice. He needed to gain her confidence, but he did not know how to convince her.

He said, "I am not like Venutius. I can promise you that."

She did not answer, so he went on, "At least tell me your name. You can do that, can't you?"

"No. You are trying to trap me."

"That's not true. I want to help."

"The only way you can help is to get me out of this place. Can you do that?"

"No," he admitted, "I cannot do that."

"Then leave me alone."

He hesitated, dreading that her fear and distrust might cause her to call the guards. Speaking urgently, he whispered, "All right. Don't talk. Just listen. I will tell you my story."

313

Lying in the darkness, his voice a mere whisper, his lips pressed to the ragged hole he had gouged in the wall, he told her who he was, told her about his family, his home, and his dreams. He told her about Venutius, about being captured, and about the offer the Governor had made. Then, even though he had not intended to, he told her that he had passed a message to his mother, warning that there was a spy in the British camp.

He heard her sharp intake of breath, heard her alarm.

He said, "You need to help me. I know that whoever is sending messages to Venutius must be doing it because of you. But if we can warn my father, he can do something about it."

"What can he do?" she demanded. "Kill my ... kill the person sending the messages to Venutius?"

"He would not do that. He would find a way to trick the Romans."

"And how would he get me out of here? Venutius has promised that I will be released once the Romans have won."

"You cannot trust Venutius," he told her.

"I don't. I have seen the way he looks at me. He makes my skin crawl. But what choice do I have?"

"Help me. By working together, we could save a lot of lives."

"You want to help the Romans," she accused.

"I want peace. I want to help our people. I can do that best by working with Rome. You may think that is wrong, but your friends are helping Rome in a way that could see thousands of our people killed. Venutius does not care about that. He cares for nothing except himself. Surely you can see that my way is better?"

"Perhaps, but what can I do about it?" she sighed softly.

Sensing he had made a breakthrough, Togodumnus said, "Someone you know is bringing messages in. Can you get messages out?"

"No. Venutius does not allow me to speak to ... to the messenger."

Attempting to conceal his disappointment, he said, "Then we must think of something else. Between us, we can surely come up with a plan of some sort."

"You are a fool," she told him. "Even if you are telling me the truth, there is nothing either of us can do."

"There must be. If you warn your messenger that my father knows about him, he will stop bringing information to Venutius."

"And Venutius will kill me," she retorted. "Or give me to the soldiers for their fun. He is always threatening me with that."

"Venutius is not in command here," he assured her. "I can speak to the Governor. He trusts me now. I will tell him ..." His voice trailed away. What could he tell the Governor that would preserve the life of a hostage who had outlived her usefulness?

"What?" the unseen girl prompted. "What will you tell him?"

"I will tell him you are an important person. You must be, otherwise why would anyone betray our plans? I will tell him that, if he wants me to help him govern the north, he must keep you alive."

"Why would he do that for you?"

"I am sure I could convince him. You are obviously someone of rank and importance. I could tell him that you and I will work together to help govern the province."

"Women do not govern in the Empire," she shot back. "I know that much."

"But they do among the Pritani. The Governor understands that. I can convince him of your importance."

"You know nothing about me," she reminded him.

"I am not stupid," he told her. "Whoever is bringing messages to Venutius must be highly placed in our alliance, and you are obviously important to them. It follows that you are from a noble family."

"You said, 'our alliance'," she breathed. "Whose side are you on?"

"I am of the Pritani," he assured her, his words imbued with fierce pride. "I want the best for our people. That is all. You could help me. The tribes cannot win this war, even if my father learns who the spy is, but we can save a lot of lives. If we work together, you and I could help heal the wounds of war. The Governor is as much a politician as a general. He will not let Venutius harm either of us if he thinks we can be useful to him."

There was another long, pensive silence.

At last, she said, "What if you are wrong? They might kill us both."

"They can do that whenever they want," he agreed. "But we should not let fear control us."

"I cannot help it," she whispered. "I am afraid of Venutius. He has promised to do awful things to me if my ... friends do not do as he demands."

Togodumnus told her, "Venutius is a cruel, vindictive man who desires only power and influence for himself. He is using you for his own ends, but he will have no power over you if your friend stops bringing information to him. I will not let the Governor do anything to harm you. I promise."

He thought he could detect a hint of hope in her voice as she said, "Are you sure of that?"

"Yes," he told her fervently. "I am sure."

Warily, she said, "Even if I agreed to do as you ask, there is no way I can pass a message to ... my friend."

"We will think of something," he assured her. "Once we leave this place, we may find an opportunity to do something."

She gave a soft laugh, the first sound of any emotion other than fear and suspicion.

"You are mad," she declared.

"Perhaps I am. But will you help me anyway?"

"I am not sure. I don't know what I can do."

"You could start by telling me your name."

After a brief pause, she said, "Thenu. My name is Thenu."

"Thenu," he repeated, savouring the word. "That's a lovely name."

"It was my grandmother's name."

"Well, Thenu, are we at least friends now?"

"I think so."

"Good, because you know enough about me to have me executed. But I still know nothing about you other than your name. If we are to devise a plan, I need to know all about you and your friend who is passing information to Venutius."

She did not reply. He waited, allowing her time. Then, to his relief, she whispered, All right. I will tell you, although I still don't see what good it will do."

"Let us take one step at a time," he replied. "Don't be afraid. You can trust me."

He felt elated. He had convinced her to trust him, and soon he would know the truth of Venutius' blackmail and betrayal.

His dreams were suddenly shattered when he heard Thenu gasp in horror as the door to her room was flung open and soldiers burst in.

Togodumnus caught a glimpse of faint light through the hole in the wall, then it was blocked as Thenu hurriedly shoved a pillow or blanket against the opening on her side of the wall.

He heard a muffled voice say, "Wake up, girl. Venutius wants you."

Thenu's soft sob of terror struck at Togodumnus' heart. Close to panic, he rolled off his bed, fumbled in the darkness to find the covers and hastily shove them against the hole he had created. Without light, he could not tell whether

317

it would be enough to conceal his work, but there was no time to worry about that now. In four steps he was at the door, yanking it open.

The guard outside was not Daszdius, but one of the younger men, a big-boned lad who was pleasant enough but too simple-minded to do anything other than obey his orders. He spun round in surprise when the door opened, and held out his arms to block Togodumnus' path.

Togodumnus pushed past him, stepping outside into the night. To his left, he saw Sdapezi and two guards bustling Thenu out of her room. By the dim light of an oil lamp that one of the soldiers was holding aloft, he could see that her face was pale and frightened. She looked tiny and vulnerable, helpless in the hands of the large soldiers, her hair tousled and dishevelled, her eyes wide with terror. When she saw him, she flung him a silent appeal that made his chest tighten with anguish.

Summoning all his resolve, he faced the Centurion.

"What's going on?" he demanded.

"Get back in your room," Sdapezi ordered brusquely. "This is nothing to do with you."

Standing his ground, Togodumnus asked, "Where are you taking her?"

"Venutius needs to see her," Sdapezi replied. "A messenger has turned up. That's all. Now, get back indoors."

Togodumnus felt helpless. The young soldier behind him gripped his elbow, easing him round. As he turned, he saw and heard more men at the other end of the block. He caught a glimpse of a dark shape, but all he could make out was a pair of eyes in the night.

A surprised voice called in Brythonic, "Thenu? Is that you? Are you all right?"

"I am well, Dwyfel," she called back in a small, frightened voice.

Gruffly, Sdapezi commanded, "That's enough. Come on, Venutius wants to see you and he wants to hear this message."

He jabbed a finger at Togodumnus as he added, "And you get back in your room."

The Centurion's tone was harsh but not hostile. He was, Togodumnus realised, only doing his duty. Allowing himself to be eased back through the doorway, Togodumnus obeyed the command.

The soldier slammed the door shut behind him. He leaned against it, sighing with relief. His conversation with Thenu had not been discovered. She had been dragged from her room because the spy had come to speak to Venutius, to deliver another message.

And she had given him a name.

Dwyfel.

Togodumnus had no idea who Dwyfel was. The name meant nothing to him, but Thenu would return to her room soon, and he would learn everything.

He was so relieved that there was no immediate threat to Thenu that it took a few moments for the significance of Dwyfel's arrival to strike him. When it did, he broke out in a cold sweat. The spy was running a huge risk by crossing the river and visiting the Roman fort to deliver his latest message.

Which could only mean that something important had happened.

Chapter XXVIII

Facilis joined the other senior officers in the hastily convened meeting. They crowded into the Governor's office, many of them still rubbing sleep from their eyes, or unshaven because the summons had come so urgently.

Outside, it was still dark, two hours before dawn. The air was still, the night peaceful, but the mood among the officers was one of puzzled excitement mixed with nervous apprehension, all of them wondering why they had been summoned to another conference just as the campaign was about to begin.

As soon as he entered the small room, Facilis could sense the excitement. The Governor was dressed for war, wearing a gleaming breastplate and a kilt of studded leather strips. His red cloak was as bright as blood in the guttering light of several oil lamps and his plumed helmet lay on the desk in front of him, replacing the usual heaps of documents and writing tablets that had now been cleared away and packed into large chests.

Beside the Governor, Licinius Spurius, Legate of the Ninth Legion, was similarly attired, immaculate in his expensive armour and spotless cloak, although his dark, heavy eyes gave him the appearance of a man who needed a few more hours' sleep.

Facilis could sympathise with the Legate. His own sleep had been fitful and haunted by dreams of fleeing from wild barbarians and exploding mountains. Being woken to attend this meeting had been like being rescued again, but it had left him feeling tired and listless, and he watched the proceedings as if he were a mere spectator rather than a participant.

The two senior officers waited patiently while the Tribunes and Centurions filed into the room. Facilis, now wearing military uniform, felt strangely aloof from the others. The Centurions were older men who had risen through the ranks, but the Tribunes, the men whose rank he now shared, were all much younger than he was, privileged men appointed because of their noble birth and political connections. Once, he had been like them, but now he was an anachronism, neither one thing nor the other. He noticed some of the officers casting sidelong looks at him, their curiosity aroused by his presence, but he did his best to ignore them. They would hear all about him soon enough.

Venutius was also there, looking pleased with himself, taking a position of importance at the front of the crowded room. Facilis also noticed young Togodumnus, who looked even more tired than the Legate. The young man stifled a yawn as he stood near the back of the room, trying to remain inconspicuous. He exchanged a brief smile with Facilis, who was once again struck by how similar to his mother the young man was. He had Beatha's eyes and smile, the same gentle, soft-spoken nature. Facilis could understand why Beatha had tried so hard to get her son back, and how much it must have hurt her when Togodumnus told her that he wished to remain with the Governor.

He was snapped from his reverie by Agricola's welcome. A hushed silence fell over the room as the Governor said, "Good morning, Gentlemen. I apologise for the early call, but we have received some vital information that requires a slight change to our plan."

A brief buzz of interest flew around the room, but the Governor allowed no time for questions. He continued, "I am setting off at first light to visit the other Legions and give them the new orders in person. Then I will join the Second Legion who will be crossing the river by the bridge of boats."

He paused before adding, "I will ask Venutius to explain what we have learned of the enemy's intentions."

321

Proud as a peacock, Venutius took the floor. He smiled benignly as he recounted, "It seems that the Britons have decided to split their army into three separate forces. They intend to lure us into a trap where they can surround us."

The officers listened in intent silence while Venutius explained in great detail how the Britons proposed to draw the Legions onto their main force, then send the two flanking armies around to encircle the Romans and cut them off from their supplies. He went so far as to name the various tribes who would form the three divisions.

"Thank you, Venutius," said Agricola when the Brigante had finished his report. Then, to Facilis' embarrassment, the Governor gestured to him.

"Gentlemen, I wish to introduce Lucius Anderius Facilis, who was, until recently, a captive of the Britons. You will see that I have appointed him as a Tribune on my own staff. Facilis, can you tell the meeting what you know of the enemy's plans?"

Facilis had already given the Governor a full report, but he understood that Agricola was giving him an opportunity to introduce himself to the other officers.

Shaking off his feeling of detachment, he cleared his throat and said, "I can only confirm what I saw with my own eyes and heard for myself, Sir. But, yes, I was informed by a very reliable source that the enemy had three separate camps. I only saw one for myself, though."

"How many men would you estimate were in that camp?" Agricola prompted.

"That is difficult to say, Sir. I would guess there were at least fifteen thousand. Possibly a few more."

Agricola nodded, "Thank you, Facilis. That suggests that we face three times that number, perhaps more."

Venutius protested, "There are no more than twenty thousand in total! And now they have divided into smaller groups."

Calmly, the Governor declared, "I think it is wiser to err on the side of caution when it comes to numbers. But, however many barbarians there are, the threat posed by their plan is, I hope, clear to everyone."

He smiled confidently, adding, "And this is how we will counter it."

Facilis could not help but admire the Governor's style. Agricola dominated the room, stating his thoughts plainly and forcefully, over-riding Venutius' objection with calm authority. He held the men in his palm as he explained his new campaign plan.

"We, too, will divide our forces. As planned, the Second Legion will turn east as soon as it has crossed the river, and will follow the coastal route. However, the Twentieth will not join it. That Legion will simply march north from its present position. These two Legions will form a two-pronged attack, each of them driving back one of the enemy's flanking forces. The Ninth will follow behind, taking a central position between the other Legions, but will stay several miles further back, so that our advance will resemble an inverted triangle. This will mean that the enemy's main force will be caught between our two flanking Legions and will be unable to lure us into a position where we can be surrounded. Even if the enemy evade the Second and the Twentieth Legions, they will be unable to surround us because the Ninth will be following at a distance, and our forces will be too widely spread for them to surround us."

The Tribune, Aulus Atticus, asked, "I thought your intention was to bring the enemy to battle, Sir? How can we do that if our own army is divided?"

"That is simple," Agricola replied smoothly. "We will advance in three columns until we have driven the enemy back. Then we will join together and deliver the final blow. It goes without saying that we must remain in constant communication, because we will need to be flexible when it comes to the timing. Once the barbarians realise that their

323

plan has been foiled, we will need to strike quickly, before they simply disperse. We must drive their two flanking units back onto their main force, then join together and crush them."

As he spoke, the Governor held up his right hand, closing his fist to demonstrate how the barbarians would be destroyed. It was a gesture Facilis had seen before, made by a former Governor who had been confident of an easy victory. That Governor had died within a few weeks of declaring his intentions, and Facilis felt a shiver of foreboding run down his spine when he saw Agricola make the same promise.

The Governor concluded, "That is all, Gentlemen. Go and prepare your men. My own staff should be ready to leave at daybreak."

The meeting broke up, the men chatting excitedly to one another as they streamed out of the office. As he followed the crowd into the antechamber, Facilis found himself accosted by Aulus Atticus.

The younger Tribune stared at him with an unfriendly, arrogant expression.

"So, you were a prisoner of the Britons?" Atticus enquired sharply.

Facilis felt too weary to bandy words with a young patrician. He simply nodded, "That's right."

"And that qualifies you to become a Tribune?" Atticus asked scornfully.

Facilis became aware that other Tribunes had stopped to watch the confrontation. Atticus might be the ringleader, but they were all curious as to how he had suddenly attained their prestigious rank. Few men made the step from Assistant Quaestor to Tribune in one go, and it was evident that these young officers wanted to know what lay behind his promotion. Facilis was experienced enough to know that some of them would be merely curious, some jealous, while others, like Atticus, would be openly disparaging.

He had known this would happen at some point, and he also knew that there was only one way to deal with it. He needed to establish his right to be among them. Forgetting his tiredness, he gave the young Tribune a studied look.

"The Governor seems to think I am qualified," he stated firmly.

"The Governor seems to think a lot of you," Atticus retorted. "He believes your estimate of the barbarians' numbers over Venutius. Why is that?"

Facilis had come across men like Atticus before. He was ambitious, a man who intended to achieve high office and who wanted no rivals. If he had known Facilis better, he would have understood that the new Tribune's sudden elevation was no threat to him, but Atticus was clearly the sort who needed to throw his weight around. He was playing to his audience of fellow officers, enjoying himself in casting scorn on a man who, although older, was new to his rank. If Facilis did not stand up to him now, Atticus would never leave him alone.

With a sigh, Facilis said, "I would have thought it was obvious why the Governor prefers to believe that the barbarians outnumber us."

Atticus put on a mock frown of puzzlement.

"Obvious? It is not obvious to me, except that you are his favourite for some reason."

"It should be obvious to anyone with half a brain," Facilis stated loudly.

Atticus looked genuinely shocked. He demanded, "Are you insulting me? Do you know who I am?"

"I really don't care who you are," Facilis told him curtly. "But, as you clearly need things spelled out for you, I will tell you why the Governor insists that there are more barbarians than Venutius' spy tells us. It really is very simple, but I will use short words so that you can understand it. You see, there is more glory to be gained by defeating fifty thousand barbarians then by beating fifteen thousand."

"Are you saying the Governor is deliberately exaggerating the number of enemies we face?" Atticus rasped angrily.

"He wouldn't be the first," Facilis smiled.

Hearing the murmur of amusement from the other officers, he knew that he had scored a hit.

"How would you know?" Atticus challenged, attempting to regain some prestige. "You were only an Assistant Quaestor, were you not? That hardly qualifies you to make such accusations against your betters."

"It is true that I was an Assistant Quaestor," Facilis agreed, his tone harsh. "But, I was with the army in Britannia before that. I was a Tribune before you were born, boy. I served with Ostorius Scapula, Veranius Nepos, and with Suetonius Paulinus. I was here during the Boudican Revolt, which is how I know Julius Agricola. He was a Tribune back then as well. If all that is not enough for you, I speak the local language and I know Calgacus personally. So, I think I am well enough qualified to be on the Governor's staff, don't you?"

A burst of laughter and applause from the other Tribunes made Atticus flush furiously. He opened his mouth, seeking a retort of some sort, but the door to the Governor's office swung open again, and Agricola stepped out. His gaze swept the room, taking in the scene instantly.

"Making friends, Facilis?" he smiled.

"I was just telling young Atticus about my experiences in Britannia, Sir. He seemed interested."

Agricola reached out to pat Atticus' arm. He said, "You could learn a lot from Facilis, young man. See that you pay attention to what he says."

Atticus flushed again, but he gave a hasty nod.

"Yes, Sir."

"And you should all learn that it is unwise to keep a Governor waiting. We will be leaving within the hour. I suggest you all go and prepare for a long day on horseback."

Grinning, the officers scurried out of the antechamber, Atticus following them with as much dignity as he could muster.

When the younger Tribunes had left, Agricola turned to Facilis.

"Problems?" he asked.

"Nothing I can't handle, Sir."

"Good. I am glad you are on my staff, Facilis. These young officers are all very keen, but experience counts for a lot. Just make sure you can keep up with the rest of us."

"I'll do my best, Sir."

Facilis had obtained a few items of kit from the Quartermaster, but it did not take him long to pack them into a leather sack which he would hang from the pommel of his saddle. Weighing the bag in his hand, he reflected that it contained everything he owned in the world. It was a vaguely unsettling feeling, and he once again felt a detachment from reality, as if this were still part of his dreams.

"Get a grip of yourself, Facilis," he muttered, trying to shake off the black cloud that was smothering him. "What is wrong with you? You're still alive."

He recalled his confrontation with Aulus Atticus, and the satisfaction of putting the arrogant young Tribune in his place brought a faint smile to his lips. As a rule, Facilis avoided confrontation, and he had surprised himself at how much he had enjoyed humiliating the younger man.

"You are growing old and bitter," he told himself, making a silent promise to apologise to Atticus as soon as he could.

Pleased with himself for making that decision, he swung his small bag over his shoulder. It was almost time to go, but there was one more thing he needed to do.

He went to say farewell to Antonius Pulcher.

Sitting forlornly in an empty barracks room, the fat Quaestor was feeling sorry for himself. Even the extra rations he had been able to consume had failed to cheer him up.

"I'm being sent away," he complained. "You are given a Tribune's rank, but I'm being sent to some barbarian settlement to help establish a new colony in the middle of Brigantia."

"You may have got the better of the deal," Facilis informed him. "There is likely to be some hard fighting before this campaign is over. At least you'll be far away from that."

Pulcher nodded glumly. "I suppose so. And this place is said to be well away from the coast, so there is no chance of being taken on another ship. You heard about the Usipi?"

"Yes. The Governor told me."

"I hope they suffer," Pulcher spat venomously. "Slavery is too good for them, if you ask me. They should all have been crucified."

His face brightened as an idea struck him. He said, "I wonder if I could buy one of them? I'd show him what it means to be a slave."

Facilis was appalled at the vindictive expression on the Quaestor's face, but he was in no mood for an argument, so he merely said, "I expect most of them will end up in the arena anyway."

Pulcher grinned, "You're probably right. That's a show I'd like to see. Imagine those brutes chopping each other into little pieces."

"I'd rather forget all about them," said Facilis.

Pulcher asked, "Is something wrong? I thought you would be pleased at being promoted."

The way the Quaestor pronounced the word made *promotion* sound like an undeserved prize, but Facilis merely shrugged, "It feels a bit strange, being back on a Governor's staff after all these years. Still, it's a lot easier than civilian life."

"What do you mean?" Pulcher frowned.

Facilis explained, "Life's simpler in the army. There are rules, and you either keep to them or you are punished. Back there, in the world we are keeping safe, the Emperor makes laws, and someone always finds a way to exploit them. It doesn't matter what rules there are, somebody will always find a way round them. Things are more black and white here, I suppose."

"More dangerous, too," Pulcher remarked with unusual empathy. "You are welcome to it. Now, I must get ready myself, because I have a boat to catch."

He shivered at the thought, adding, "I hope it's the last one I see for a while."

"I wish you well," Facilis told him.

They clasped hands, an awkward, uncomfortable gesture because there was no real friendship between them and never could be. Yet they had shared an unforgettable experience and had come through it, while so many others had not. As Facilis left the Quaestor, he felt that another chapter of his life was ending. That meant a new one was beginning but, somehow, the prospect did not cheer him.

He made his way to the stables, where he had been assured that a horse would be ready for him. The first grey haze of pre-dawn was low on the eastern horizon as he trudged through the camp. Men were up and about now, bustling around, Centurions shouting orders, equipment being given final inspections, and Facilis knew that the final act in the conquest of Britannia was about to begin. He knew the outcome was inevitable, no matter how many warriors Calgacus had assembled, and no matter what tricks or traps he laid. Facilis had tried to warn him, but Calgacus had refused to listen, so now there would be war, death and destruction. In the end, though, the Empire would crush the barbarians, just as it had always done.

Why then, Facilis wondered, did he feel the weight of doom pressing down on him?

Chapter XXIX

Calgacus was sore, having spent two days in the saddle, patrolling the land and watching the Legions' ponderous advance, but he felt as if he had been punched in the stomach when Beatha eventually found him and told him that his own son had turned down the chance to be released, preferring to remain among the Romans.

"I can't believe he'd do that to us," he breathed hoarsely.

To his astonishment, Beatha smiled, "He is doing it for us, Cal. Don't you understand what he said?"

"All I heard was that he wants to be a Roman," Calgacus growled.

"Then pay attention," she scolded. "He is doing a very brave thing, and he is trying to help us."

"Help us? How?"

"Do you not know the story of Cingel?"

Calgacus frowned, "Broichan mentioned something about him. He's the person buried up on that hill back at the meeting place. He had a magic cauldron of some sort."

"Yes, but there is more to the story than that."

"You know I don't pay heed to stories," he grunted.

"Which is why you don't understand. Togodumnus could not say much because the Romans were listening, but by telling me he has taken the name of Cingel, he has told me why he is staying there. You see, Cingel joined his enemies so that he could defeat them."

Calgacus' eyebrows arched in surprise. "He intends to defeat the Romans from within? How, exactly?"

"Calm down," Beatha urged. "We must keep this secret, otherwise Togodumnus may be in danger, but you need to know the truth."

"So tell me."

Beatha said, "He mentioned the story of the Great Bear of the Mountains."

"Another bloody story?"

"Don't you know that one either?"

"Why should I?"

"Because I used to tell it to the children when they were little. Perhaps I should have told it to you."

"Tell me now," he sighed.

Patiently, she explained, "It is an old legend, about the downfall of the Father of all Bears, who ruled the hills and forests for countless lives of men."

"Give me the short version," Calgacus interrupted.

Ignoring him, Beatha continued, "The Bear ruled all the animals, but the wolves wished to overthrow him. Yet however much they tried, he was too strong and too clever for them. They despaired of ever killing him, but then they spoke to the Fox. He was a servant of the Great Bear, but he betrayed his master. He revealed the Bear's plans to the wolf pack. Whenever the Bear went to fish in the rivers, the wolves had beaten him to it. They had soiled the waters and driven the fish away. When the Bear went in search of fruits and berries, the wolves had dug up the plants and dragged them away."

"Is this the short version?" Calgacus demanded. "You're as bad as old Broichan. What is the point behind this?"

Beatha scolded, "That is the point, Cal. The Fox told the wolves everything the Bear was doing. Eventually, he lured the Bear into a trap. The wolves had dug a great pit and he fell into it. Then the wolves covered the pit with rocks and earth, burying the Bear forever. Which is why the earth sometimes shakes. It is the Bear trying to free himself from beneath the ground. It is also why wolves always flee from bears, because they fear the bears will take revenge for the downfall of the Father of their race."

"That sounds like a druid's tale, right enough," Calgacus grumbled.

Exasperated, Beatha demanded, "Don't you see? It was the Fox who was really responsible for the Bear's defeat."

Calgacus frowned, "Are you saying what I think you are saying?"

Beatha nodded. "You were right. There is a spy in our camp. That was Togodumnus' warning."

"Did he say who it was?"

She shook her head.

"No. Either he doesn't know, or he wasn't able to tell me. But it proves he is trying to help us."

Calgacus nodded, knowing Beatha needed to vindicate their son's desertion.

He said, "All right. Now we know for certain. Come on, let's get back. I'll need to tell Broichan."

"Be careful of Broichan," Beatha warned, laying a hand on his arm.

"What do you mean?"

"I mean you need to win this war, Cal. Look at what Broichan did to Maelchon. If you fail, the tribes will lose confidence in you and Broichan may turn against you. That would be dangerous."

"Druids are always dangerous," he agreed. "But so am I."

"What are you going to do?"

He grinned fiercely as he informed her, "I'm going to make the Romans wish they'd never come here."

Broichan was not pleased at hearing confirmation of their suspicions that someone was sending information to the Romans.

"How can we defeat them if our secrets are betrayed?" he demanded angrily.

"By using the knowledge to our own advantage," Calgacus told him.

"You wish to keep it a secret?" Broichan asked.

"That's right. Even if we discovered the identity of the spy, it would only make the Kings distrust one another even more than they do now."

"Then what do you propose to do?" Broichan snapped. "The Romans have crossed the river. They are marching north, and they have split into three columns. You cannot surround them now. Your plan has already failed, thanks to this betrayal."

Calgacus could hear the threat in the druid's voice, but he replied calmly, "I know exactly what the Romans are doing. I've been tracking them for the past two days. Don't worry. They are doing what I wanted. The spy has helped us, but now we must move quickly."

Broichan's habitual scowl deepened as he demanded, "Do you mean to tell me that you deliberately lied to the Kings? Your plan was false all along?"

Calgacus grinned, "Not entirely. If there had been no traitor passing information to the enemy, that plan would have worked."

"But you knew there was a spy?"

"We all suspected there might be," Calgacus admitted. "I merely made my plans to allow for that possibility."

"So, what will you do now?" the druid asked sharply.

"Now, I'm going to tell the Kings my new plan. And this one will work."

He gave the druid a brief outline of what he intended to do. When he had finished, the old man regarded him closely.

"You are taking a huge gamble," he observed.

"If we don't gamble, we lose anyway," Calgacus replied. "Now, I have five Kings to talk to, and a lot of distance to cover to reach them all."

Signalling to Runt, he said, "Come on, let's go and tell them the good news."

He began by collecting Bridei and taking him to find Drust of the Caledones. For once, Drust was almost sober. Even so, Bran insisted on joining them so that he could listen to what Calgacus had to say.

"The King values my advice," the young chieftain informed them.

Drust nodded his agreement, so Calgacus told the three men what he intended to do.

"We have only one choice now," he explained. "We must bring our forces together again and fall back to a position where we can face the Romans on ground of our choosing. I have found a hill where we will be able to make a stand and also have a chance to lure the Legions into broken ground where they will not be as effective as our own warriors."

The three men had differing reactions to his announcement.

Bridei, squat and pugnacious as ever, simply grinned fiercely and said, "Whatever you say."

Drust's eyes had been dull and heavy, his mood inattentive until Calgacus mentioned the prospect of battle. Only then did he show a spark of interest and mumble that his tribe would be ready.

The only objection came from Bran.

He frowned, "I thought you had always opposed fighting this way. I am puzzled by your change of mind."

"It is not through choice," Calgacus informed him. "The Romans have foiled my first plan. We must fight them soon, but to do so on open ground would be folly. So, we will retreat to a high, steep hill where we can ambush them as they advance. It will be the same plan, but carried out on a smaller scale on a battlefield."

"It sounds risky," Bran remarked cautiously.

"All war is risk," Calgacus replied. "But there is more. Their Governor is obviously concerned about maintaining contact with his fleet, because he is leading the Legion on their right flank, the one nearest the coast. I want to draw him inland, away from his ships."

Bran did not appear convinced, but he gave a reluctant nod.

"As my King says, our warriors are ready."

"Good," Calgacus said. "Now, I am going to speak to the other Kings. I want them to leave a small force in front of each of the two Roman Legions on the flanks, to screen our withdrawal. The rest of the tribes will gather here tomorrow, ready for a long, quick march. We will be gone before the Romans realise it. Tell your men to bring only their weapons and as much food and water as they can carry easily."

Leaving the three men to relay the plan to their warriors, Calgacus and Runt rode west, accompanied by Adelligus and a dozen mounted men. When they found Ebrauc and Muradach, he repeated his story. This time, the response was more unanimous.

Old Ebrauc grumbled, "We came all this way, and now you want us to march back again?"

"That's right. We need to bring the Romans together if we are to have any chance of surrounding them, so gather your men and rejoin the main force tomorrow. Leave only a few hundred to keep an eye on the Romans facing you. Their job will be to screen our withdrawal."

Ebrauc sighed, "I suppose we are not doing much good anyway. The Romans are moving slowly, protecting their supply columns. Our raids are costing us as many men as we are killing. Perhaps it would be better to make a stand. That would finish things one way or another."

In a slow drawl, Muradach commented, "It strikes me that this is an act of desperation. The Taexali will do as you ask, but I am not convinced we can win this way."

"Trust me. We need to give battle soon, because we must help the Venicones protect their land."

"Does Gabrain know you intend to withdraw?" Muradach asked.

Calgacus replied, "I am going to speak to him next."

"Good luck with that," grunted the Taexali War Chief.

Leaving the two chieftains unhappy at the prospect of a retreat, Calgacus and his companions climbed back into their saddles and set off on the long ride to the east. The warmth of the afternoon was turning to the cool of evening by the time they reached Gabrain and the Venicones.

As Calgacus had expected, this last meeting was the most difficult. Gabrain's face flushed red as the King made furious accusations of being deserted, and threatened to launch his own attacks on the Legions. It took all of Calgacus' powers of persuasion to convince the younger man that the retreat was necessary.

"This is your last chance," Gabrain eventually conceded. "We need a victory, and we need it soon. If this plan fails, I will fight this war my own way."

"We will have a victory," Calgacus assured him. "Just bring your men to join us tomorrow. Now, I need to get back before it grows dark."

Wearily, he and Runt led their tiny column of horsemen back to Cingel's tomb, squinting into the westering sun as it sank lower in a clear, cloudless sky.

"That was a long day," Runt observed with a tired sigh.

"But worth it."

"Yes, do you suppose they will all do as you asked?"

"I think so. And no doubt one of them will send word to the Romans."

"Which one?" Runt wondered aloud.

"It doesn't really matter. All we know is that one of the five tribes is harbouring a traitor. Agricola will soon know what we are doing."

Runt grinned, "In that case, I suppose it's just as well you didn't tell them the real plan.

Chapter XXX

Togodumnus' nerves were fraying. He was constantly on edge, worried that he might betray himself, more worried that he could not find a way to send another message to his father, and even more concerned for Thenu's safety.

He glanced again at Thenu, sitting on her pony, looking frail and lost, surrounded by Sdapezi's troopers. She was barely twenty paces away, but she might as well have been on the other side of the country for all the chance he had of speaking to her again. Ever since the Ninth Legion had crossed the river, she had been kept apart, always in the midst of half a dozen mounted men, with only Venutius permitted to talk to her.

That annoyed Togodumnus more than he would have believed possible. The Brigante treated Thenu like a prized possession, showing her off but never allowing anyone else to come close to her.

The only thing Togodumnus was grateful for was that their secret communication on that last night in the fort had not been discovered. When she had returned from her meeting with Venutius and the messenger, Dwyfel, she had been upset, but her tears had been spawned by anger rather than fear.

"I don't care what they do to me," she had declared furiously. "I will tell you everything."

And she had. In urgent whispers, she had given him the details of the information Dwyfel had brought, revealing Calgacus' plan to split his army into three divisions. How easily the Governor had countered that, Togodumnus thought miserably. He had not seen Agricola since that early morning conference, because the Governor was leading the Second Legion, more than twenty miles to the east, and some distance ahead of the Ninth Legion. To the west, the Twentieth was also forging ahead, driving back Calgacus' flanking forces, preventing the tribes from surrounding the Roman army.

"Be grateful we're with the Ninth," Sdapezi had told him. "They're under strength since your father chopped one of their cohorts to pieces in Hibernia, so the Governor is keeping them in reserve. If you ask me, he's also keeping Licinius Spurius away from any real fighting. The man's a stuck-up prig, and he's no experience of war."

Togodumnus was surprised to hear the Centurion discuss the Legate's shortcomings so openly, but Sdapezi grinned at his astonishment.

"Don't get me wrong," Sdapezi told him. "This is the place to be. Close enough to the war to claim part of the credit, but far enough away from any real fighting. The Governor wants all his guests to be kept safe, so you'll be well out of harm's way."

That, though, was part of Togodumnus' problem. Thenu had told him everything he wanted to know. She had told him about Dwyfel, and she had revealed the name of the person who was behind the betrayal of Calgacus' plans. The words had tumbled from her lips like a torrent, driven by her loneliness and her rage at Dwyfel's acquiescence to Venutius' demands. By the time she had finished her tale, Togodumnus knew who the traitor was, but he had no way of letting his father know.

He had considered trying to escape, somehow leaving the camp at night and riding north, but he discounted the idea almost immediately. His tent was guarded at night, and even if he could have evaded Sdapezi's guards, the camp was always protected by a ditch and earth rampart, with sentries patrolling the perimeter. There was no way of escaping at night, and the day was even worse. He was on horseback, but so were Sdapezi's soldiers. He might surprise them and gain a short head start, but they would run him down before long.

The other problem was Thenu.

He could not leave her. She had trusted him, and he knew that he could not desert her now, not when everyone else she had trusted had let her down.

"I was supposed to marry Dwyfel," she had explained in bitter whispers. "But I can hardly bear to look at him now. He says he is trying to help me, but he does not realise what he is doing."

She had paused for a long time before saying, "Venutius wants more and more from him. Do you know what he demanded this time?"

"I can hardly begin to guess," Togodumnus had replied.

"He wants Dwyfel to kill your father. He says I will be freed when Dwyfel brings him Calgacus' head."

Togodumnus had felt fear clawing at him. Scarcely able to breathe, he asked, "Did he agree?"

"Yes."

Her answer was so faint it was barely audible, but that solitary word made Togodumnus' position almost unbearable. He knew so much, yet he was trapped. He had told Thenu they would find a way to warn his father, but it had been four days since they had crossed the Bodotria, and still he could find no means of escape.

Late in the afternoon, the Legion stopped again. They were covering no more than a few miles each day, their progress hampered by the terrain of marshes and woodlands, as well as by the need to ensure their supply wagons were protected. Sdapezi said the other Legions had been attacked, raiders darting in to try to ravage the mules and wagons. The Ninth had been unmolested, but Licinius Spurius was taking no chances of having his supplies destroyed, so the Legion advanced at the pace of the slowest vehicle.

"That's the good thing about being the reserve," Sdapezi had chortled happily.

For Togodumnus, the ponderous advance was as frustrating as his inability to think of a plan that would warn his father of the danger he was in. The days dragged, each one a monotony of tramping feet, clopping hooves, and the rumble and creak of the wagons. Togodumnus could only sit on his horse and fret while the invading Romans trudged their way northwards.

Their advance was slow and methodical, inexorable and seemingly unstoppable. During the day, cavalry patrols scouted ahead and to either side, while the Legionaries formed a phalanx of armour and weapons, and auxiliary troops protected the long tail of the Legion's supply train. Even if the Britons had tried to launch an attack, the Ninth Legion would not be caught unprepared.

Togodumnus had heard so much about the Roman army's methods, but seeing them put into practice made him realise just how impossible it was for his father to defeat the Legions. Even at night, the Romans worked hard to ensure that they were safe. Three hours before dusk, the soldiers halted to dig their entrenchments and plant a stockade of wooden stakes that would form a vast marching camp. It was an extraordinary achievement to construct a fortified camp every night, but the Legionaries were accustomed to the work, digging with picks and shovels, and using wicker baskets to pile up the earth. The organisation and effort required was beyond anything Togodumnus had ever imagined.

"Nobody can break into a Roman fort," Daszdius had informed Togodumnus proudly when he had first watched, enthralled, as the Legionaries built a camp in an incredibly short time.

It was not breaking in that concerned Togodumnus. He wanted to break out but that, too, seemed impossible.

The men who were not involved in digging the perimeter wall were kept busy. Tents were being pitched, the horses fed and watered. Cooking fires were lit, jugs of wine unloaded from the supply wagons. The evening meal, porridge, bread, sausage meat, cheese and whatever else the Quartermasters had been able to locate, was the highlight of the day. After their meal, the soldiers who were not on sentry duty would relax, tell their coarse jokes, play dice, and regale one another with gruesome tales of what the barbarian Britons would do to them if they caught them. Togodumnus had even overheard some of the soldiers relate stories about Calgacus and how he could not die because he was already a ghost. Yet these were tough, hardened men who feared their own Centurions more than they feared their enemies, and even the threat of the supernatural could not halt their steady progress.

Eventually, the trumpets would call for men to bed down for the night, and the camp would fall silent until dawn heralded the beginning of another long day's march.

The early evening, though, when the camp was still being constructed, when men were busy setting up tents, tending the animals or trying to avoid the Centurions and catch a few precious moments of idleness among the bustle, was the time when Togodumnus had nothing to do.

Like the other hostages, he was told to stay out of the way while the tents were erected. With only a handful of guards, they stood in a group, each of them doing their best to ignore the others.

Togodumnus had long since given up trying to be friendly with the Governor's other prisoners. They avoided meeting his eye and refused to talk to him. That did not concern him too much. There was only one person he wanted to talk to and she was as close as she would ever be.

Thenu saw him looking at her, and she hurriedly turned away, guilt radiating from her every movement. Togodumnus cursed silently, praying that nobody would notice her reaction. He glanced around, checking on the others.

The few troopers who were guarding them were chatting idly to one another. The hostages were engrossed in watching the flight of a horde of swifts who were darting and swooping above their heads. The sky was alive with the sight and sound of dark brown shapes with sickle wings that reminded Togodumnus of barbed arrowheads. The birds filled the air with their noisy flight, zooming with a dexterity and speed that provided a distraction from the mundane events taking place below them.

Togodumnus decided to take advantage of that distraction. Casually, he sauntered over to where Thenu was standing, head bowed, beside one of her guards who was looking up at the spectacle of the swifts' aerial display.

She looked up as Togodumnus approached, her face pale, her eyes darting around in near panic.

Togodumnus smiled, trying to encourage her to relax. He glanced at the guard, but the man was still grinning at the sky, watching the flocking birds hunt insects in a whirling, mesmerising flight.

Togodumnus decided to take a risk. As far as he knew, only the young British trooper, Hortensius, spoke Brythonic. The chances were that this guard would not understand their conversation.

"Just look at those swifts," Togodumnus said to Thenu, pointing upwards.

Feigning an interest in the birds, still looking skywards, he went on, "Will Dwyfel come back soon, do you think?"

The question caught her off guard. She stiffened, taking a sharp breath, but she recovered quickly, imitating his stance and looking up, forcing a smile to her face.

"I don't know."

"If he does, tell him I let slip that my father knows there is a spy. That might scare him off."

"Do you think that will work?" she whispered.

343

"I don't know. But it is worth a try. Dwyfel will believe you, won't he?"

"Yes."

"You don't mind trying to trick him?"

"He deserves it. I cannot believe he agreed to murder your father."

She hesitated, a gasp of shock escaping her lips.

"What if he has already done that? What do I do if he brings your father's head to Venutius?"

"Pray for his sake that he does not try," Togodumnus told her. "My father is not easy to kill. Better men than Dwyfel have tried and failed."

He was searching for something else to say when a shout of anger interrupted them and ended their apparent engrossment in the swooping birds above their heads.

"What are you doing?" barked Venutius.

Togodumnus turned to face the Brigante. He did not know where Venutius had been, but the man was back, and his hazel eyes were blazing angrily. He berated the guard in Latin, heaping insults on him for being lazy and inattentive. The guard, annoyed at being found out, turned to give Togodumnus a warning shove in the chest, pushing him away from Thenu.

Thenu gave a squeal of alarm, but Togodumnus stood his ground.

Facing Venutius, he snapped, "We were just watching the birds! There is no need for you to be so angry."

"Nobody is to speak to her!" Venutius snarled, waving his arms furiously.

"Why not? She is frightened and lonely. What harm can it do to have a friendly conversation with someone who speaks the same language?"

Venutius' eyes narrowed. He took a step closer, thrusting his head towards Togodumnus and lowering his voice as he rasped, "She is my prisoner. You will keep away from her. Is that understood?"

"Or what?" Togodumnus challenged. "The last time I looked, Julius Agricola was in charge around here, not you. You cannot threaten me."

Venutius looked at him coldly.

"Oh, yes," he sneered, "I forgot you are the Governor's little favourite. You are to help him rule this province once it has been conquered. Isn't that right?"

"That is the Governor's intention," Togodumnus agreed, not caring about the scorn and hostility in Venutius' words as long as it diverted the man's ire away from Thenu.

He went on, "So, I suggest you mind what you say to me."

"The puppy thinks he has teeth!" Venutius smirked. "Are you trying to threaten me, boy?"

Togodumnus could feel his knees trembling as he faced the Brigante. He recalled the stories his father had told of the man's cruel and vindictive nature. Until now, he had thought those stories were exaggerated because Venutius, though often scornful and smug, had seemed like a noisy, yapping dog who would turn tail at the first signs of a larger foe. Now, for the first time, he saw the venom in Venutius' expression and he knew the truth of the man's character. He did not like what he recognised, but it was too late to back down now.

Venutius snarled, "Just stay away from my prisoner, boy. She is mine."

Summoning all his outrage, Togodumnus replied, "I will speak to the Governor about this. I know she must be someone of importance, otherwise you would not be using her. If you treated her as a friend instead of a slave, she might help us when this war is over."

"She is helping us," Venutius mocked. "And the Governor approves of her status, so go ahead and talk to him if you wish, but don't be surprised if he refuses to listen to you. You should learn the reality of the situation, boy. The

Governor wants to win quickly, so he will use her in any way he can."

The force of Venutius' argument made Togodumnus' heart quail. With a sickening realisation, he understood that the Brigante was right. For all his fine words and promises, the Governor would have no qualms about using Thenu in any way he could, just as he was trying to gain Togodumnus' allegiance by dangling the prospect of a favoured position once the war was won.

Weakly, he protested, "You should not treat her this way!"

Venutius laughed harshly, "I will treat her any way I like, boy. She is useful to me, as well as to the Governor. And when she has outlived her usefulness, I might just keep her as a slave. She's pretty enough, and it's been hard to resist the temptation of tasting her properly. But once the barbarians have been beaten, there will be no need to keep her virginity intact." He grinned maliciously as he added, "I might even let you have her after I've finished with her."

They were speaking in Latin, so Togodumnus knew that Thenu could not understand what they were saying. Switching to the native tongue, he said to Venutius, "I thought you had promised to release her once her friends have done what you want? Was that just another of your lies?"

Still speaking Latin, Venutius snapped, "What I do with her is my business, not yours. Don't have such concern for a slave girl and her idiot friends."

"I thought as much," Togodumnus retorted in Brythonic. "But let me warn you, I will speak to the Governor. You will not mistreat her this way."

Venutius laughed, "Do you think a Roman cares what happens to a slave? You are as much a fool as your father."

"I will make him care," stated Togodumnus.

"You would jeopardise your own position over a slave girl?" Venutius mocked. "You really are pathetic, boy. Or perhaps you think you are in love?"

Togodumnus felt his face flush. He snapped, "Just leave her alone!"

Venutius spat, "I have had enough of this." Turning to the guard, he barked, "Take her to my tent. And bring me a whip. I will show this puppy how a slave should be treated."

Togodumnus was consumed by rage. For the first time in his life, his temper snapped. He lashed out, swinging a wild punch at the Brigante, catching him on the mouth and knocking him backwards.

Thenu screamed, the guard yelled angrily, and Venutius staggered, blood spattering from his lips, his eyes burning with fury as he struggled to retain his balance.

Togodumnus felt strong arms grabbing him as the guard seized him.

Unable to move, he yelled, "You will not whip her!"

Venutius stood up, shaking his head and wiping blood from his mouth with the back of his hand. His eyes shot venom at Togodumnus, but before he could say anything, Sdapezi arrived, demanding to know what was going on.

"This hostage hit me. He was talking to my prisoner, in defiance of your instructions," Venutius complained in a loud, self-righteous voice, making sure all the spectators knew he was the aggrieved party.

Sdapezi looked at Togodumnus, who protested, "He said he was going to whip her. She has done nothing."

Sdapezi wasted no time listening to recriminations. He ordered the guard to release Togodumnus and to take Thenu to her tent. She went unprotesting, her head bowed, as the guard ushered her away.

Sdapezi turned to Venutius and Togodumnus.

"Both of you calm down," he told them. "There will be no whippings, and no more punches. Your tents are ready, so I suggest you both go and wait for your dinner. Separately."

To reinforce his suggestion, he signalled to his troopers to accompany them.

Dabbing at his swollen lip, and giving Togodumnus a malevolent glare, Venutius hissed, "You will pay for this, boy."

"That's enough, I said!" Sdapezi barked, waving the man away.

Angrily, Venutius allowed himself to be escorted to his tent.

With a sigh, the Centurion asked Togodumnus, "What did you do that for, lad? I warned you, he's a nasty piece of work."

"He was going to whip her," Togodumnus repeated.

"I'll do my best to see that doesn't happen," Sdapezi promised. "But you've made a real enemy of him now."

"I don't care," Togodumnus asserted. "It was worth it."

"I'm sure it was," the Centurion smiled. "I wouldn't mind giving him a smack in the mouth myself, but he'll create trouble for you over this, you know."

"The Governor won't let him do anything to me," Togodumnus insisted, although he had to force down his own doubts about that belief.

With a glum nod, Sdapezi sighed, "Maybe you're right, but Venutius still might take out his spite on the girl."

Togodumnus pleaded, "Don't let him hurt her!"

The Centurion frowned, "I might be able to prevent her being given a flogging, but there are other things he could do. She might be sent away, or sold."

"He can't do that, can he?" Togodumnus asked, his voice rising in near panic.

"She's a slave," the Centurion shrugged.

"Not Venutius' slave, though. She's technically an imperial slave."

"That's a fine point of law that would keep the Senate occupied for a few hours," Sdapezi replied. "Out here, on campaign, nobody will lose much sleep over one slave girl."

"He must not be allowed to punish her!" Togodumnus begged.

"I'll try to smooth things over," Sdapezi promised. "But you can help by staying away from her. We don't want Venutius finding out about your little secret, do we?"

Togodumnus felt a surge of panic when he heard that.

"What do you mean?" he managed to ask, his throat constricting in fear.

Sdapezi tapped a finger to the side of his nose.

"I checked all the rooms as we were leaving the fort," he explained with a grin. "I found your little communication funnel."

Togodumnus felt faint with the horror of discovery, but the Centurion was smiling at him.

"All I wanted was to talk to her," Togodumnus said weakly.

"You could hardly do anything else through that little hole," laughed Sdapezi. "It's all right, lad, I haven't told anyone. But, like I said, stay clear of her, and Venutius too, for that matter."

"He can't do anything to me," Togodumnus insisted.

He tried to sound confident, but his heart was pounding and he knew he had made a mistake by hitting Venutius. He had seen the malevolent spark in the Brigante's eyes, a look that told him Venutius would take any opportunity to exact some revenge.

"He can't do anything to me," he repeated softly, hoping that saying it often enough would make it true.

Chapter XXXI

The fine weather of the previous few days began to deteriorate as clouds scudded in from the west, driven by a stiff breeze that made the leather tents flap and flutter noisily. The clouds also delivered light spots of drizzly rain that pattered softly on the shelters and made the grass slick underfoot.

The sound of the rain kept Licinius Spurius awake. The Legate had found sleep difficult in any case, his mind unable to rest. By the flickering light of a small oil lamp, he sat on a stool, a goblet of wine in his hand, a pitcher on the small table beside him, while he mulled over his situation.

He had not wanted this posting. Britannia was a wild place, as far from the centre of the Empire as it was possible to be. He knew why he had been sent here, of course. The Emperor, Domitian, had taken a fancy to Spurius' wife and had ordered him to take command of this distant Legion to get him out of the way.

What irked Spurius was that his wife had shown no inclination to oppose the Emperor's decision. Not that opposing Domitian was a sensible idea, for most people who did that ended up being invited to open their wrists and quietly join their ancestors. But Spurius' wife had always been ambitious for herself. He suspected she had gone out of her way to bring herself to the Emperor's attention. She had certainly refused to come to Britannia, as most Legate's wives would have done. Instead, she had insisted on remaining in Rome, and had openly admitted that she would sleep with the Emperor if he asked her to.

"It will help your career," she had informed Spurius with no hint of embarrassment.

The memory of her matter-of-fact acceptance of the situation made him want to vomit, but he still did not know whose behaviour appalled him most. Domitian, corrupt and venal, was to blame, but Antonia had made it plain that she was looking forward to becoming one of the Emperor's many lovers. Worst of all, though, Spurius had accepted the situation and meekly packed himself off to Britannia. He loathed the place almost as much as he despised himself for his lack of moral courage. If he had been a real man, he would have opposed the Emperor, would have commanded his wife to accompany him here. Yet what would that have achieved? He knew Domitian's reputation. Anyone who denied the Emperor whatever he wanted would not live long.

Spurius had never thought of himself as a coward, yet now he knew that he was exactly that.

Bitterly, his thoughts turned to his wife. Spurius imagined her, flinging herself at Domitian, submitting to the Emperor's carnal desires. The Gods knew those desires were depraved, and the mental images that haunted Spurius accentuated his feelings of helpless rage. He needed to show everyone that he should not have been treated this way. He wanted desperately to return to Rome as a hero. Then he would publicly divorce his wife. The Emperor would have tired of her before long, because his appetites constantly demanded fresh female conquests, willing or not.

Spurius imagined his wife crawling to him on her knees, begging him to take her back. He would refuse, and she would be cast out of his house. Then his honour would be restored.

He sighed, knowing the reality would be very different. Antonia was not the sort of woman who would beg for anything. Yet that did not diminish Spurius' desire for military glory. He must become a hero. He must prove to everyone, not least to himself, that he was no coward.

That, he mused miserably, was unlikely to happen unless something changed dramatically. The Ninth Legion

351

was being kept in reserve, following in the rear while the other Legions forged ahead, driving the enemy before them. Spurius had another vision, one of military victory. He saw himself at the head of the Legion, bleeding from a slight wound but still bravely carrying out his duty, charging against a horde of Britons who had ambushed the other Legions. Spurius and the Ninth would save the day.

That was another dream, he told himself. Julius Agricola seemed determined to keep all the glory for himself. He had gone to join the Second Legion, putting himself in the forefront of the campaign where he could claim the credit for any success. The other Legates did not seem to mind, but the knowledge added to Spurius' feeling of injustice. It was not as if Agricola was a particularly able Governor. In his wine-induced gloom, Spurius imagined how he could have done the job every bit as well as Agricola.

He drained his goblet, refilled it from the pitcher, and drained it again. Bitter thoughts continued to assail him, thoughts of his wife cavorting with the Emperor while he was stuck out here in a barbarian wilderness with no opportunity to prove himself. He had been unjustly posted here, and was now being unjustly prevented from demonstrating his ability.

Part of the problem was that the Ninth was below strength and under a cloud. One of their cohorts had been on the disastrous expedition to Hibernia and had returned with barely a quarter of their number left alive. Those survivors had told stories of demonic warriors who could not be killed, and of witches and screeching banshees who lurked in the forests, waiting to pounce on anyone who dared venture into their domain. Above all, they spoke of Calgacus, an almost mythical warrior who could not be killed, a giant who wielded a magical sword, whose footprints burned the grass, whose voice was like booming thunder, and who could kill a man with one look from his gorgon eyes.

On the Governor's orders, Spurius had clamped down on those stories, threatening to flog any man heard repeating them. Yet the whispers continued, he knew. The dark, mist-shrouded forests and murky swamps of northern Britannia lent themselves to such tales, and the men's morale was low. Even the experienced Centurions were cautious, their eyes constantly scanning the landscape as the Legion marched slowly into the wild north.

Spurius was not immune to those whispers. He wanted a battle where he could see his enemy and use the superior power of the Legion to win a decisive victory. The Governor had promised just such a battle but, so far, the only reports Spurius had heard from the other Legions was of sudden raids, with painted savages appearing from nowhere to charge into unwary units, wreak havoc, then vanish into the swamps. What chance was there to gain glory against such an enemy?

A polite cough from the entrance to his tent dragged him from his reverie. He looked up to see one of his slaves.

"Master, the Brigante, Venutius, wishes to speak to you privately."

"At this hour?"

"He says it is important," the slave nodded.

"Very well. Show him in. And bring another goblet. And a fresh jug of wine."

The slave scuttled out, returning moments later with Venutius. The Brigante took an offered stool, accepted a cup of wine and waited until the slave had departed.

"You could not sleep either?" Venutius enquired.

"I do not require much sleep," Spurius lied.

Venutius smiled, "I am glad you are still awake. There is something I need to discuss with you."

"What is that?"

Venutius gently tapped a finger to the corner of his mouth, where his lips were slightly swollen.

He asked, "You heard about my argument with the boy, Togodumnus?"

"I heard he hit you."

353

"Yes, but he did more than that. Your guards were lax. They allowed him to talk to the girl. They must have spoken for some time, because the boy knows who she is."

"Does that matter?" Spurius asked in a bored tone. "I know you have kept her identity a secret, but I cannot see that it makes much difference."

"If word gets out of who she is, my spy in the British camp will be compromised," Venutius explained.

Spurius shrugged, "Are you sure she told Togodumnus who she is?"

"I am sure she has told him something. I questioned her a little while ago, and I could see guilt in her eyes."

"I see. Still, Togodumnus is on our side. What difference does it make?"

"He is Calgacus' son. I do not trust him. He has been snooping around the girl. Who knows what else he has been doing?"

"The Governor thinks he could be useful to us," Spurius reminded the Brigante.

Venutius took another sip of wine before saying, "That is what I wanted to discuss with you."

Spurius' goblet was empty again. He refilled it, spilling a little of the dark liquid as he did so.

He took another mouthful, then asked, "What, exactly, is it you want to talk about?"

"The Governor sees Togodumnus as an ideal person to help govern this province once the rebels have been eliminated. However, I believe that would be a mistake. The very fact that he hit me demonstrates that he is not suited to a position of responsibility."

"He is young," Spurius countered.

"He is impetuous and prone to violence. Just like his father who, I might add, is our most notorious enemy."

"I see. Go on."

With a smile that reminded Spurius of a Nile crocodile, Venutius said, "I think there are better choices for the task of governing the new province."

He sipped again, then added, "Me, for instance."

Spurius felt a sudden chill. The shadows on the sides of the tent seemed to grow darker as the light from his lamp sputtered. Venutius was staring at him intently, studying him to gauge his response, and the man's gaze made the Legate feel uncomfortable. There was a touch of menace lurking behind those cold eyes, an edge of steel to the softly spoken words.

Feigning disinterest, Spurius said, "It is not the greatest of ambitions."

Venutius smiled, "Oh, I think that, with the right help, I could make it a worthwhile position."

"With the right help?"

Waving an airy hand, Venutius explained, "There will need to be a military presence here in the north. The barbarians cannot be left unsupervised."

Spurius felt slightly offended at the Briton referring to the natives as barbarians. The man was barely civilised himself. Yet he sat there, facing an Imperial Legate and talking as if he were an equal. This was a side to Venutius that Spurius had not seen before, and it unsettled him more than he cared to acknowledge.

Wishing he had not drunk quite so much wine, Spurius agreed, "I suspect a permanent Legionary fort will be established in the north."

Venutius leaned forwards, placing his goblet on the table with a gesture of decisiveness.

Lowering his voice, he said, "I would suggest that you volunteer for that position. With you as military commander and me as civil magistrate, I am sure we could combine our talents to our mutual benefit."

Spurius took another gulp of wine. He could barely taste it now, and he knew he had drunk more than was good for him, but he felt a sudden need for it. Venutius' cold, calculating eyes reminded him of a snake, but Spurius felt his heart beating faster as his imagination tried to anticipate what the Brigante was going to say next.

He needed to be cautious, he told himself. Keeping his voice even, he replied, "I doubt that there would be much benefit for either of us. From what I have seen of this country, there is little of value here."

"It is not as rich as your famous eastern provinces," Venutius agreed. "But there are always opportunities for men who are prepared to seize them."

"Such as?"

"Slaves, for example. Taxes, for another. Wild beasts for the arena. There are bears and wolves up here. There are also many wildfowl, and the rivers teem with fish. The forests can provide an almost inexhaustible source of timber. If we were clever, we could create a demand for these products. Everyone likes to boast of possessing things that come from far-off places, and I am sure the wealthy citizens of Rome are no exception. We could control the export market. I believe there may also be gold in the hills. There is certainly coal and lead, as you know. Controlling them could make us rich."

Spurius wanted to hesitate, but the wine had loosened his tongue.

He blurted, "You are talking about embezzling funds that are due to the Emperor?"

"Would that bother you so much?" Venutius asked. "From what I hear, I would have thought you would be happy to take a chance of benefitting at the Emperor's expense."

Spurius snapped, "What do you mean by that?"

"It was merely an observation," Venutius smirked.

Spurius wondered how much the man knew. It was impossible to prevent rumours, of course, but he had hoped that the circumstances of his posting here would not have reached the ears of the common soldiers, and would certainly not be known to a mere barbarian.

But Venutius was talking again, planting ideas, providing justifications.

"Everyone knows this is a poor province," he explained. "The Emperor will be pleased with what we send to him. I am merely suggesting that we ensure that a healthy percentage is retained for our own use. After all, if we are not here to supervise the collection of taxes, the Emperor would receive nothing."

"A procurator will be appointed to collect the taxes." Spurius pointed out.

"I doubt that any procurator will come this far north. The dangers of the journey could perhaps be explained to him. And if he did come, then I am sure he could be persuaded that we are doing our best to raise the taxes."

Venutius shrugged as he added, "We might need to offer a small percentage as an inducement."

Spurius did not argue. Most Procurators accepted bribes to turn a blind eye to such things. But there was a greater obstacle looming in Spurius' mind.

"The Governor is no fool," he objected. "And he takes a dim view of any illegal activity. He has dismissed several officials for dishonesty."

"The Governor's term of office is almost up," Venutius countered. "His replacement may be more to our liking. In my experience, every man has his price. Once Britannia is conquered, there will be no prospect of gaining military renown, so financial reward is all that is left. The next Governor will be an administrator, not a soldier."

This time, Spurius did hesitate. He knew that it was not uncommon for Governors and other imperial magistrates to enrich themselves. As long as the imperial coffers were sent a reliable stream of income, nobody bothered too much about what the men who sent the money were up to. Nobody except the locals, of course, but they did not really count.

They might send representatives to Rome, to appeal to the Emperor, but if Spurius and Venutius were in charge in the north, they could easily prevent any such representatives setting out for Rome.

"You paint an intriguing picture," the Legate said thoughtfully.

"I hope it is one that interests you," Venutius smiled. "What do you say? Do we have an agreement?"

Spurius took another sip of wine. Every man has his price, Venutius had said, and he had judged Spurius correctly. This was an opportunity to hit back at the people who had treated him so badly. He might not return to Rome as a hero, but he could return as a wealthy man.

He nodded slowly.

"Let us say that we have an understanding," he agreed.

Venutius raised his goblet in a toast.

"Excellent. It is a plan for the future, of course. I appreciate that the natives have not yet been crushed, but that is only a matter of time, thanks to my spy. But there is one major obstacle."

"What is that?"

"Togodumnus. The Governor seems to prefer him as the local civil magistrate."

"Ah, that is true. I had forgotten about him. But no doubt you have a plan to deal with that problem?"

Venutius smile held no humour at all as he agreed, "There are a number of ways to handle him, but I think we need something simple and not too public. If we accuse him of treason, the Governor may wish to become involved. That could be awkward as we would need to fabricate some evidence or bribe some witnesses. No, I think a simple accident would be best."

"What sort of accident?" Spurius asked.

"Oh, a fatal one, of course."

It was well past midnight when Togodumnus pulled on his trousers and tunic, fastened his cloak and crept quietly out of his tent. As always, there was a guard. It was the burly veteran, Daszdius. He shot Togodumnus an enquiring look.

"Where are you going?" the soldier asked.

"I can't sleep."

"So stay under cover and keep dry," Daszdius grunted. "I wish I could."

Togodumnus grinned, "This isn't real rain. We usually get a lot worse than this."

"That's something I'll look forward to," Daszdius grumbled.

Togodumnus looked around. The camp was in darkness, the outlines of tents visible in the dim light of a crescent moon that occasionally flitted out from behind the scattered, ragged screen of clouds to cast a pale, ghostly light. He could make out the vague shapes of the guards who stood watch outside the tents of each of the hostages. Beyond them, the perimeter wall and fence of stakes was a dark line against a cloud-shrouded sky.

He told Daszdius, "I want to talk to the girl."

"You know you can't do that," the soldier growled.

"Then let me speak to the Centurion."

Daszdius grinned, "That's easy. He can't sleep either."

They found Sdapezi awake, sitting in his tent rolling dice by the light of a small oil lamp, playing a game against an imaginary opponent. Daszdius waited outside while Togodumnus went in and sat on the ground facing the tired-looking Centurion.

"I know what's bothering you," Sdapezi sighed. "But you can relax. He didn't hurt her. All he did was ask her a lot of questions and make some threats."

"Are you sure he didn't hurt her?"

"He scared her, that's all."

"Let me talk to her. She must be terrified."

359

"I can't do that," Sdapezi said grimly. "Anyway, you should worry more about yourself. Venutius has gone to talk to the Legate."

"About me?"

"I can't imagine it's about the weather," the Centurion shot back. "That's why I'm still up and about. I'm waiting for him to come back. Not that I expect the devious bugger to tell me what he's up to, but the Legate might have new orders for me."

"What sort of orders?"

"I'm no oracle, boy, but I doubt that they'll be pleasant."

"You don't need to obey them," Togodumnus insisted desperately. "You report directly to the Governor, not to Licinius Spurius."

Sdapezi shook his head.

"That's a thin straw you are clutching at, lad. I'm a soldier. I obey orders. That's the way it is. But don't panic yet. We don't know what the Legate is going to say."

Just then, the tent flap opened and Daszdius stuck his dripping head inside.

"There's good news and bad news," he announced cheerfully.

"Spit it out," Sdapezi snapped.

"The rain has stopped," Daszdius informed them. "And Venutius is coming back."

The two men hurried outside, in time to see Venutius, his head covered by his hood, strolling back to his tent, his two escorting guards maintaining a discreet distance behind him.

Sdapezi marched to meet the Brigante.

"What have you been up to this time?" he demanded.

In response, Venutius flashed a broad smile.

His eyes fixed on Togodumnus as he replied, "Oh, nothing at all. Just a friendly discussion, that's all. I wanted

360

to talk to the Legate about what would happen to me when this war is over."

They knew he was lying, but there was nothing they could do.

"All right," Sdapezi sighed. "It's late. I suggest we all try to get some sleep. The nights are short enough up here."

He turned to Togodumnus, holding out one hand in a signal for the younger man to return to his tent. Then he froze as a warning shout of alarm cut through the night. For an instant, everyone stood still, then the world exploded in a maelstrom of sound.

"What in Jupiter's name is that?" Daszdius asked, as a wave of ferocious, deafening noise echoed through the night.

Togodumnus knew what it was. The roar of ten thousand throats boomed through the night, battering at them like a wave of thunder.

"It's my father," he told the soldiers. "He's come to kill you all."

Chapter XXXII

Lucius Anderius Facilis felt out of place. As his old friend, Quinctilius Sicilianus, would have put it, he was like the only eunuch at an orgy, able to watch, but unable to take part. The memory of Sicilianus, buried beneath the thick layers of rock that now covered Pompeii, did nothing to soothe Facilis' mood. He had thought that returning to the army would ease his loss, but although he could perform his duties as well as anyone, he seemed to have lost whatever enthusiasm he had ever had for the task of civilising the Britons. His experiences among them, brief as they had been, had shown him that the natives seemed to manage perfectly well without Rome's civilising influence, and that knowledge made him question whether Calgacus might be right about Rome's motives for making war.

Facilis could not reveal his doubts, of course. To do so would be to invite scorn, perhaps even dismissal.

Not that there was anyone he wanted to discuss his private thoughts with. The Governor, although of a similar age to Facilis, would not understand, and the Tribunes were so young, so naive, so keen and unquestioning that Facilis felt they were almost like another race of men, strange beings who spoke his language but whose thought processes were entirely alien.

His altercation with Aulus Atticus had resolved one issue, but it had raised another problem. Facilis knew the other Tribunes spoke about him when they thought he could not hear them. He had noticed their surreptitious looks and the wary way they treated him. To the other Tribunes, he was a relic of Rome's early days in Britannia, a man who was out of touch with the new realities of the conquest. Not only that, he was the man who had been a prisoner of both the Usipi and the Britons. Those experiences set him apart more than the difference in age could ever do. These men could never understand what he had been through.

Unable and unwilling to make concessions, Facilis had vowed to lose himself in his duties, to keep himself occupied so that he had no time to question himself. That worked well enough during the day but now, in the dark watches of the night, when sleep eluded him, or nightmares assailed him and brought him awake in a cold sweat, he had too much time to think.

Listening to the intermittent spatter of light rain on the leather fabric of the tent, he stared, unseeing, into the darkness, trying to judge what time it was. Still some hours before dawn, he guessed.

There were few sounds audible from beyond the thin walls of his tent. Apart from the sentries, everyone would be snatching a few, precious hours of sleep.

Some, like the Governor, would be sleeping soundly, Facilis knew. Julius Agricola rarely lost sleep. He was one of those men who was supremely confident in his own ability, sure that he could bend the world to his way. How Facilis envied that sort of confidence.

Yet Agricola had every reason to be confident. The latest reports from the cavalry scouts had confirmed that the enemy were pulling back. Thousands of them had been seen withdrawing to the north-west. There were still some barbarians facing the Second Legion, for they had ambushed one patrol late that afternoon, but the Governor had been delighted at the news of the Britons' withdrawal.

"We have foiled the enemy's plan," he had declared. "Tomorrow, we will catch the few barbarians who still face us, then we will drive on in pursuit of their main force."

Facilis had tried to offer a word of caution, reminding the Governor that Calgacus rarely did what anyone expected, but Agricola was not concerned.

"There is nothing he can do," the Governor had insisted. "Soon, we will have him where we want him. Then we shall destroy his army."

Just as they had destroyed every settlement, every farm and shack they had come across so far, Facilis thought ruefully. The Second Legion was leaving a swathe of destruction in its wake, leaving nothing for the natives, driving the inhabitants before them, sending hundreds of refugees fleeing in search of safety.

Facilis recalled the small, hidden village high in the hills where Calgacus' people were making a new home for themselves. Would those homes suffer the same fate, he wondered? What had the people done to deserve that, except to be non-Romans?

That was the answer, he knew. The Britons must become Romans or die. Beatha had told him that not everyone wanted to be a Roman and now Facilis thought he could understand that sentiment. It was an understanding that made him question what he was doing as part of the military force that was intent on enforcing Rome's vision of civilisation.

He had told Pulcher that things in the army were black and white. He still believed that, but his own life was far from straightforward. He was assailed by self-doubt, by longings that could never be satisfied, and by ghosts from his past.

Yet what choice did he have? What else could he do? Where could he go?

He did not have an answer that satisfied him. What he did know was that he must conceal his doubts from everyone else. He would not allow anyone to see how much he hated what they were doing. He would be a model of efficiency, would blot out everything else, and would harden his heart to the consequences of the expansion of the Empire. He was, after all, only one man. What could he do to change things?

Even as he made the decision, he felt its wrongness, but he still could not find an alternative. He was determined not to sink into despair, for that would lead him down a dark, dangerous path. No, he would face whatever fate brought him, but he vowed that he would not allow it to affect him as the past had done. He had too many ghosts already.

The sound of hurrying footsteps on the grass made him look to the entrance of his tent. Someone untied the fastenings and stuck their helmeted head through the gap.

"Anderius Facilis?" the shadow enquired.

"Atticus? Is that you?"

"Yes," the young Tribune replied.

From his tone, Facilis knew that Aulus Atticus had not wanted to come to him.

"What is it?"

"There's a barbarian at the gates," Atticus replied. "He keeps repeating that he wants to talk to Venutius. He doesn't seem to know any other Latin."

"Venutius is still with the Ninth Legion, isn't he?"

"That's right."

Facilis could hear the grudging reluctance in Atticus' voice. He knew why the younger Tribune had come to him and how much pride it must have cost him.

Facilis asked, "You want me to speak to him?"

Atticus gave a curt nod. "I think that would be best. I wouldn't trust any of our British scouts to translate accurately. Their loyalty is questionable at best."

"I'll talk to him, then," Facilis agreed, throwing off his blanket. "Help me put my breastplate on, will you?"

Fumbling in the darkness, he pulled his tunic on over his head, fastened his kilt of leather strips, tugged on his thick-soled sandals, then held his breastplate in place while Atticus reluctantly fastened the ties. Finally, Facilis pinned his cloak in place, rammed his helmet on his head and buckled on his sword. Then he followed Atticus outside.

The rain was still falling in a light, almost half-hearted drizzle, filling the air with the smells of wet grass and damp leather. By the camp's entrance, a few, oil-soaked torches sputtered and hissed in defiance of the rain, casting eerie shadows. A handful of nervous soldiers stood watch, javelins held ready, their eyes peering out beyond the opening in the earth rampart.

"The picquets say he is still there, Sir," the Tesserarius in charge of sentries reported. "He's just sitting on his horse, waiting."

"Let me out," Facilis commanded. "I'll talk to him."

"On your own?" Atticus asked.

"Come along if you think you can contribute anything," Facilis invited.

He frowned, knowing he should not mock the young officer in front of the men. To cover his mistake, he said, "Perhaps it would be better if you stayed here in case it's a trap."

Stiffly, Atticus nodded, "I will do that."

Facilis suspected Atticus would not lose any sleep if he were to be killed. He said, "I doubt whether they would set a trap to catch just one man, but let's find out."

He walked to the gate. When the ditch and rampart had been dug, a gap had been left in the earth wall to allow access for the Legions' wagons. There were four such entrances to the marching camp, one on each side. These were the vulnerable points in the fort's defences, so each one was protected by a secondary wall, a short section of rampart and ditch that was dug some twenty paces beyond the main wall. This short barrier blocked the direct approach to the gateway, creating two narrow passageways to the left and right of the main entrance. The gateway itself was blocked by a barrier created by a felled sapling, stripped of its branches. The long trunk was laid on supports made from wooden stakes which were lashed together as an X shaped frame. The

366

gate would provide no great deterrent to a determined enemy, but it was always guarded by a detachment of soldiers.

Facilis signalled to them to move one end of the barrier to let him pass. Two legionaries grabbed one end of the sapling while two more held the supporting stakes. Acting in unison, they swung the end of the barrier outwards, allowing Facilis to pass. As soon as he had stepped beyond them, they heaved the barrier back into place.

Guided by a signal from the Tesserarius, Facilis turned left, passing the outer wall where he could make out the silhouettes of more sentries. One of them pointed, indicating that Facilis was going the right way.

"Over there, Sir!" the soldier called. "He seems to be on his own."

Facilis waved an acknowledgement. He skirted the outer wall, giving it a wide berth to avoid falling into the deep ditch that fronted it, and walked out into the darkness beyond the camp.

Thirty paces from the fort was a man on horseback. His stocky pony snorted, tossing its head. The rider leaned forwards, patting the animal's neck to reassure it.

Facilis could see the man's long hair, could make out his impressive bulk, could see, too, the hilt of a long sword on the man's back. This was a swordsman, a person of high rank. In the rain-filled night, Facilis could make out no details of his face, but when the Briton spoke, he had a young man's voice.

"I am a friend," he recited in stilted Latin. "I have come to speak to Venutius of the Brigantes, who is a guest of the Governor."

Replying in Brythonic, Facilis informed him, "Venutius is not here. He is in one of our other camps, with another Legion."

The Briton seemed disturbed by this news.

"I was told your Governor was in this camp," he ventured cautiously.

"He is. But Venutius did not accompany him. You may speak to me. I am Lucius Anderius Facilis. What is your name?"

The Briton hesitated before grudgingly admitting, "I am Dwyfel. I have visited your camp before, when you were south of the Bodotria. I brought messages to Venutius."

"I know about that," Facilis agreed. "So, Dwyfel, what news do you bring this time?"

"Venutius said we should only talk to him," the Briton said in a worried tone.

"Venutius is not here. If you have urgent information for the Governor, you must tell me. There is nobody else here who speaks your tongue."

The young British nobleman was in a quandary. He hesitated for a long time before asking, "Will you tell Venutius I had no choice? This news is urgent, and I cannot go to your other camp now."

"I will tell him," Facilis promised. "You can trust me."

"Then know this, Roman. Calgacus has tricked you. He has tricked everyone. You must tell your Governor to gather all his cavalry, all his fastest men and march now."

"March where?" Facilis asked warily.

"To the camp of the Ninth Legion. Calgacus is going to destroy it tonight. If you wish to save your comrades, you must go now."

Facilis' initial reaction was to wonder whether this might be another of Calgacus' ruses, a ploy to make the Second Legion abandon its camp so that he could ambush it on the march.

Cautiously, he said, "We cannot do that. The Governor will not leave his camp at night."

Snorting with impatience, Dwyfel snapped, "He must, or your friends will be slaughtered. Calgacus pretended that he wanted us to retreat, but he waited until the last moment, then led his entire war host south. By this time, he will have

368

passed between your two main forces and will be at the gates of the Ninth Legion's camp. He intends to destroy it. If you wish to save your comrades, you must go to their aid now, because there will be nothing left by dawn."

Roused from a deep sleep, Julius Agricola was alert enough to realise the implications of what Facilis was telling him.

"The entire enemy army is attacking the Ninth Legion?" he asked, his shock evident in the ashen pallor of his face.

"That is what the messenger, Dwyfel, told me, Sir," Facilis confirmed.

"Do you believe him?"

"I think so, Sir. He came a long way at considerable risk to himself. He seemed genuinely concerned that we should believe him. He was very anxious about the girl Venutius keeps prisoner. When he learned she was in the Ninth's camp, he was very upset. He thinks she will be in danger if the fort is sacked."

Aulus Atticus objected, "It is a trap. He wants us to leave here in the dark so that the enemy can ambush us."

Facilis informed the Governor, "I know all about Calgacus and his tricks, Sir. I agree this may be a ruse, but we cannot ignore the likelihood that the message is genuine. To be on the safe side, I have sent a small patrol out to check the surrounding area. If there is a trap, they will discover it soon enough."

Atticus continued to argue. He stated, "It does not matter. The Ninth Legion is entrenched in its marching camp. Nobody can storm one of our forts."

"Calgacus has done it before," Facilis reminded the Governor. "During the Governorship of Ostorius Scapula he destroyed a fort and wiped out an entire cohort."

"He cannot wipe out a Legion!" Atticus protested. "Besides, this is fanciful. The Britons do not fight at night."

369

"Not true," Facilis countered. "They made a night attack on the Usipi, which is how I escaped. Calgacus is capable of anything. I think we should take this news seriously."

He paused, then went on, "I believe Calgacus deliberately tricked us into dividing our forces into three so that he could attack them separately."

Both men turned to Agricola. He was still pale, but had overcome his initial shock. He returned their questioning looks with a decisive expression.

"It seems I have underestimated Calgacus after all," he admitted. "But perhaps we can turn this to our advantage. You are correct, Atticus, that the Ninth Legion will be safe enough in its fort, but if Venutius' spy is correct, and he has been reliable so far, this could be the chance we need."

He stood up, thrusting a finger to accentuate his orders.

"Summon all the cavalry and the auxiliary skirmishers. I want every man who can move quickly to be ready to march within the hour. The rest of the Legion can follow at daybreak."

Atticus frowned, "But why, Sir? Even if the report is true, the attack is bound to fail."

Agricola smiled as he explained, "Because we can trap Calgacus while he is attacking the fort. He will be caught between our two forces, one in the fort, the other outside. But we must hurry. There are only a few hours until dawn and we have more than twenty miles to cover. So, rouse the men now and let us finish this war. I want Calgacus dead or captive by daybreak."

Chapter XXXIII

Calgacus knew the dangers and difficulties of fighting at night, so he kept the plan simple.

The warriors had tramped back to rejoin the main force, their mood dispirited, many of them grumbling at yet another day without a blow being struck. Then Calgacus had told them his true intention and the mood had changed in an instant. With little urging, the war host streamed south, riding at a fast canter, heading between the widely spaced Roman Legions that were advancing on the flanks, aiming directly for the Ninth Legion's marching camp.

Calgacus led the way. Behind him came ten thousand horsemen, with other men on foot jogging in their wake, desperate to take part in the battle. Some horses bore two warriors, others had men clinging to the pommels of their saddles, running alongside the horses in great, leaping strides, so keen to join the attack that they were willing to risk the danger of falling and being trampled.

Old Ebrauc rode in his chariot, his face grim and determined, his tribesmen thundering behind him. Even Drust of the Caledones rode with an unflinching resolve as they hurried south.

Calgacus had sent Adelligus ahead to locate the fort and to leave guides to keep the war host on the right route when darkness fell. Guided by these warriors, they forged on under a rain-laden sky of dull clouds.

It was well after dark by the time Adelligus met them in a wide bowl of grassland.

"Leave the horses here," the young man advised. "The fort is over the next ridge."

"Let's take a look," Calgacus said as he swung himself out of his saddle.

Adelligus led him over a low hill, down the far slope, across a patch of boggy ground, and up another low slope. On the far side, he could make out the dark outline of the fort, its huge size revealed by the sparks of flickering torchlight and braziers at the gateways. It was impossible to see everything, but he could visualise the rows of tents, the neatly pegged horse lines, the standards planted in the earth. He knew the fort would be several hundred paces long on each side, roughly rectangular, with a gate on each side. The earth wall would be faced by turf to prevent it washing away in the rain, the ditch would be wide and deep, containing a scum of muddy water, excrement, and whatever other obstacles the Romans had found. On top of the earth wall would be a row of sharp stakes, lashed together to form a solid hedge. Sentries patrolled the walls, each man required to complete a circuit within an allotted time, reporting to the guard commander and handing in the token he had been given before setting out on his long trek around the camp's perimeter. Using the tokens, the guard commander could keep check on every man, ensuring that nobody was shirking. This system also meant that a silent approach to kill one sentry would soon be discovered, even if the attackers could accomplish the almost impossible feat of crossing the ditch and scaling the wall without being detected.

"It won't be easy," Runt observed, mirroring Calgacus' own thoughts.

"No, but we can do it," Calgacus replied confidently. "Let's get back and tell the others what they need to do."

The Kings and chieftains gathered round him as he explained the plan.

"We will attack on three sides, with a diversion on the fourth side," he told them. "The main thing is to be as quiet as possible. No war cries, horns or drums. Don't speak. Don't even fart. Once we are in position, walk towards the fort. Don't run. There is a lot of open ground to cover, but in the dark, it might take the sentries a while to realise what is happening. The rain will help mask our approach."

Bran, ever ready with an objection, asked, "What about the other Legions? We are in danger of being surrounded."

"They don't know we are here," Calgacus replied. "But we need to get away quickly. As soon as daybreak comes, everyone must break off the attack and return here to the horses. We can move much faster than the Legions, but we need to make sure we don't find ourselves trapped here, so get out as soon as it grows light. Understood?"

Bran gave a hesitant nod, and the other chieftains murmured their agreement.

Calgacus went on, "Bridei and I will take the Boresti to the left. Gabrain, you take your Venicones to the right. Send a small group of men right round to the other side of the camp. They are not to attack, but their task is to make a lot of noise once the real attack has begun. They will keep the legionaries on the south wall occupied. That will draw them away from the rest of us."

Gabrain nodded wickedly. "Very well."

Calgacus continued, "The rest of you, go for the north gate. But give us time to get in position before you move."

"How will we know when to start?" Muradach asked.

"Gabrain has the furthest distance to go, so he will begin the attack. Watch for the Venicones moving forwards. And remember, keep quiet until they spot you, then let them hear you."

He looked at each man in turn as he went on, "Go for the gates. Keep away from the ditches. They are wide and deep, probably with sharpened stakes or thorn bushes at the bottom. The soldiers also use them as their latrines, so it's not pleasant if you get stuck in there. And you will get stuck. Once you fall in, it's very difficult to climb back out, so go for the gates. You must be quick. As soon as they spot you, run as fast as you can and overwhelm the guards before the rest of the soldiers wake up."

Bran objected, "The gates will be too narrow for us all to get in."

"Not necessarily," Calgacus told him. "The Romans fight best in the open, where they can form up in regular ranks. They have wide entrances to their camps so that they can get out quickly. What we need to do is force our way in before they know they are under attack."

Bran gave a doubtful nod, but Gabrain was eager to set off. Calgacus held up a cautionary hand.

"Remember," he told them, "keep quiet, then run as if your lives depend on it, which they do. Get in, kill as many as you can, and get out as soon as the sun begins to rise."

It was not a subtle plan, he knew, but there was no way to trick the Romans with a stratagem. He was relying on surprise, sheer numbers, and the aggressiveness of the warriors to achieve the victory. It was a gamble, but he was confident it would work. The Romans always took precautions against a night attack, but they would not be expecting an assault by thousands of tribesmen who were supposed to be far to the north.

With the orders given, there was one more thing he needed to do. He found Beatha, looking small and vulnerable in her hooded cloak.

"Stay here," he told her. "If anything goes wrong, take a horse and ride north as fast as you can."

She nodded, "Anhareth will stay with me."

Old Ebrauc hobbled up, leaning on his stick.

"I am too old to go on this venture," he said. "I will remain here with you, too. I would appreciate your company."

Beatha smiled at the old man. "Of course."

Broichan offered a quiet prayer to the Gods, then he drew Calgacus aside, giving him a hard, uncompromising stare.

374

"You planned this all along," the druid accused. "You never had any intentions of taking on the entire Roman army."

Calgacus shrugged, "I had to consider the possibility that the Taexali might not join us. We do not have enough men to tackle the whole invasion force, but we do have enough to destroy one part of it."

"Which is why you wanted the enemy to divide his forces?" Broichan asked.

Calgacus nodded, "That's right."

Broichan gave another curt nod. He said, "You tricked everyone. Including me."

"It was necessary," Calgacus explained. "Now, we have a chance of victory."

"You must take that chance," the druid said insistently. "I pronounced the omens favourable. Now, it is up to you to ensure my prediction was correct."

Calgacus understood the implicit threat in the old greybeard's words. Broichan would lose prestige if his prediction of success was seen to be wrong. Knowing how jealous druids were of their reputations for infallibility, Calgacus understood that any failure would be attributed to him. Broichan would have no scruples about switching his support to someone else. Calgacus had this one chance to achieve success, and if he failed, he would be discredited and discarded, because a man who could not win when the omens were advantageous was clearly out of favour with the Gods.

He had staked everything on this surprise attack, and he could not afford to lose.

He forced a confident smile, assuring the druid, "Have no fear. We will win."

Broichan returned a stiff nod. "Then go and destroy our enemy. May the Gods be with you."

The warriors silently followed their chieftains as they went to take up their positions.

"Keep quiet," Calgacus reminded them. "We must be like ghosts. They must not suspect us until we are upon them."

Crouching low, their hoods covering their heads against the persistent drizzle, he led the Boresti in a wide circle to the left, keeping a long, thin stand of tall trees between them and the Roman fort. He was grateful for the pattering rain and the stiff breeze because, although the men obeyed his injunction to remain silent, it was not possible for so many of them to move without making some noise. Their legs brushed through long grass, their boots trampled damp twigs, and their combined footsteps sounded like thunder in his ears.

Yet the night remained calm and quiet. The Boresti hunched down in the shelter of the line of trees, gazing towards the fort, some three hundred paces away.

Bridei edged close to whisper, "What happens if the spy betrays us by making a noise?"

"The attack will still go ahead. If we are quick, we can reach the gates before the soldiers have time to wake up."

Runt observed, "This could all go horribly wrong, you know. The gates are designed to be bottlenecks. We could be trapped."

"Or we could break through," Calgacus replied. "When we do, I want to head straight for the commander's tent. If we can kill the Legate, that will give the Romans a shock."

"He'll be well protected," Runt pointed out.

Calgacus shrugged, "That's no reason not to try. We need to make this count. We need to give the Romans such a shock that they'll call off their invasion. The best way to do that is to destroy one of their Legions. You never know, we might be able to capture their Eagle standard."

Fingering the blade of his sword, Bridei grinned, "I think Liscus is correct. You are crazy. But I like your style."

The rain slowly petered out, but droplets of water continued to drip from the trees overhead. Still there were only the usual sounds of the night to disturb the silence. A fox barked somewhere in the distance, the leaves rustled in the breeze and still they waited.

Calgacus had put his iron helmet on his head. He drew his sword, forcing himself to remain calm. Some of the younger men, less experienced, fidgeted and fretted, whispering to one another. Others sat or crouched in the damp grass, their hoods still covering their heads, lost in private thoughts. The need for silence made rousing speeches impossible, but Calgacus moved among them, offering whispered words of encouragement. The men grinned savagely, assuring him they were eager to take Roman heads.

"How much longer?" Bridei hissed softly when Calgacus rejoined him. "It will be light before long."

Adelligus, peering between the trees, warned, "I think I see something moving."

Calgacus crept forwards, looking far to his right, seeking signs of the advancing tribesmen, but it was too dark for him to make anything out.

"Are you sure?" he asked the young man.

Adelligus frowned but before he could answer, they heard the roar from the northern side of the vast camp.

Calgacus did not hesitate.

"Go!" he hissed, pushing himself to his feet.

All around him, men surged up, running towards the fort. He was soon overtaken as younger men, most of them wearing no armour, forged ahead. Encumbered by his chainmail, his legs no longer as fast as they had once been, Calgacus charged after them.

"Get to the gates!" he called. "Quickly!"

He doubted whether anyone could hear him. They pounded across the uneven ground, risking tripping or stumbling in the dark, breathing hard and howling hatred.

He could see the vague shapes of the soldiers who manned the outer barrier, hurling their heavy javelins at the onrushing horde. Then they vanished down the far side of their short, isolated wall, clearly deciding that to remain beyond the camp's gates against such a vast horde would be fatal.

The Boresti were soon streaming past the outer barricade, running to left and right to charge into the narrow spaces beyond, where the sentries had mustered behind their secondary barrier, a felled tree resting on crossed stakes. Calgacus heard the clash of arms as the tribesmen reached the barricade.

The world was a riot of sound, of screams and yells, of swords and spears hammering against shields, of shouted commands, and pounding footsteps. Dark shapes jostled together as the tribesmen tried to force their way into the gateway. Soon, a heaving mass of shouting men was hemmed into the narrow gap, the outer defence work behind them, the main fort stretching to left and right.

Some men, pushed inexorably by the press, fell into the ditch that bordered the main wall. Most survived the fall, coming up spluttering and cursing, covered in mud and slime, but some broke bones, some were impaled on the sharp stakes that were embedded in the foot of the trench, while others were killed or wounded by javelins flung from the ramparts above them.

And still the main body shoved forwards, unable to stop because of the press of bodies crowding behind them.

Calgacus could barely move. Men were crowded so close together that he was penned in, unable to wield his sword, incapable of anything except being swept along by the torrent of warriors. He could not see what was happening ahead of him, but he could imagine the tribesmen jabbing their spears over the tree trunk that formed the gate.

378

"Shove it over!" he screamed, not knowing whether anyone could hear him over the tumult, but knowing that they must breach this barrier or die like rats in a trap.

He could hear the frantic calls of the Roman bugles summoning the soldiers to the gates. And he knew they must break through soon or the attack would fail.

He was jostled and pushed, shoved on, and he pushed the men in front of him, praying he would not fall. If he went down, he would not be able to get up again and would be trampled into the muddy ground by the hundreds of men behind him.

Panic threatened to grip him, wedged in as he was, unable to do anything except stumble in the crowded, seething darkness.

Then there was a loud, jubilant shout as the flood broke and he knew the sheer press of men had burst through the gateway, overwhelming the few Romans who manned the barrier.

The roar of triumph echoed through the night as the Boresti surged into the fort. Calgacus was swept along, tripping and stumbling over the bodies of dead and wounded warriors, leaping over the long trunk of wood that had formed the gate, dodging past fallen legionaries who lay, bloody and mangled, on the ground. Warriors were already hacking at the dead Romans, cutting off their heads to keep as trophies.

There was no semblance of order. The tribesmen yelled and screamed as they dashed into the camp. But they had only passed the first obstacle. Beyond the walls was an open space, some twenty-five paces wide, a killing ground they must cross before they could reach the Roman tents. In the dim light of a pale, half-concealed moon, Calgacus saw that legionaries were hurriedly forming up at the far side of that open space.

There was only one thing the Boresti could do.

379

"Charge!" he bellowed, pointing his sword. "Kill them!"

Bridei was there, rushing forwards, dozens of warriors with him. They launched themselves at the thin line of Romans, many of whom had not had time to don their armour but merely wore their tunics, sheltering behind their large, rectangular shields, short swords ready. The Boresti smashed into them but the Romans held, thrusting and stabbing, killing the unarmoured tribesmen and throwing the attack back.

Bridei, reeling back, his face streaming blood from a cut on his forehead, waved his sword, urging his men to use their superior numbers to outflank the legionaries, but more and more soldiers were rushing to join the defenders, many of them in full armour. The Centurions shoved them into place, forming two ranks that stood back to back so that the Boresti who streamed around their flank could not attack them from the rear.

Calgacus looked for Runt, for Adelligus, for the men of his own village, the men he had trained, the warriors who wore chainmail and fought together like legionaries. They had become separated in the mad, milling crush of the gateway, but he knew they must be close.

"Catuvellauni! To me!" he yelled, brandishing his sword high.

Some of them heard him and came in answer to his call. Runt was there, a sword in each hand, and Adelligus, with fifteen men from the village.

"We need to break that line!" Calgacus told them.

The men grinned, nodding that they were ready. With hundreds of other tribesmen streaming in through the gates behind them, they formed into a compact group, half a dozen of them with shields forming a short front rank. Calgacus joined the second rank.

"Forwards!" he shouted.

The tiny group of Catuvellauni formed an island of order in the chaos. Boresti charged around them, flinging themselves at the Roman line, unable to break it.

Calgacus' men walked steadily, conserving their strength. When they were only five paces from the Romans line, they broke into a run, keeping together so that they all smashed their shields into the defenders at the same time.

There were a few, desperate moments of heaving and stabbing. One villager went down, his throat gushing blood, a legionary staggered back, and swords splintered wood or gashed at leather-covered wicker shields.

"Now!" yelled Calgacus.

The men in front of him heaved with all their strength, pushing to left and right. Calgacus leaped between them, almost falling over the body of a dead tribesman, but aiming for a gap between two legionaries. A sword came for him, but one of his own warriors blocked it with his shield, then Calgacus' mighty sword flung the Romans aside and he was in the space between them.

Runt followed, his swords darting out, taking down one Roman and driving back another, then Adelligus was there, hacking at another soldier, and the line was broken, crumbling as more and more warriors charged into the ever-widening gap.

Yelling and hacking, the Boresti poured forwards, overwhelming the defenders, many of whom abandoned their doomed comrades and ran for the spurious safety of the tent lines.

"Kill them all!" Calgacus roared as Bridei, his face a mask of blood, led his warriors after the fleeing Romans.

Calgacus gasped for breath. They had done it. They were inside the camp and the way was open for them. He had no idea whether the attacks on the other gates had succeeded, but with the Boresti inside the camp, the Romans would be caught between the warriors inside and those still hammering at the other gateways

What he needed to do now was find the Legion's commander and kill him.

He must gather his own warriors together. He turned, seeking them in the frantic confusion of the night.

He was still looking around when the assassin struck.

Chapter XXXIV

Runt's warning shout was almost too late. Calgacus heard his friend's urgent yell over the tumult of the battle, and he spun, not looking, just knowing that he was in mortal danger.

From the corner of his eye, he caught a glimpse of a dark shadow, a hooded figure slashing at him with a long knife. The blade had been aimed at the back of his neck, where his flesh was exposed between the rim of his helmet and the top of his chainmail tunic. It almost found its target.

Calgacus' wild move had thrown the assailant off, but still he felt a burning cut sear the back of his neck, followed by a savage blow as the blade slammed into the top of his left shoulder. He kept moving, spinning to his right, swinging his sword in an arc as he felt himself falling. His long blade hammered into something, the impact jarring his arm, and a man screamed in agony.

Calgacus scrambled clear before turning. Runt was already there, kicking at a hooded figure that was writhing on the ground, groaning aloud. Calgacus saw that the man's right leg had been almost severed beneath the knee. Blood was pumping in a widening pool on the muddy earth, and bones and shreds of flesh were visible in the pale moonlight.

Savagely, Runt yanked the hood from the man's head. "Algarix!"

Calgacus looked down at the stricken face of the former Taexali shield-bearer.

"Algarix?"

The wounded man stared back, his eyes filled with hatred. Shock had dulled his pain, but left him gasping for breath.

Through gritted teeth, he hissed, "You will not escape vengeance. My King will kill you."

Breathing hard, Calgacus frowned, "Your King is dead. He was killed by his own foolishness."

Algarix tried to laugh, but the sound escaped his throat like a hoarse cackle.

"How little you know," he rasped.

"What do you mean?" Calgacus demanded.

Algarix did not answer. He merely continued to gasp his strangled, gurgling laughter.

"The pain has turned him mad," Runt said.

Algarix laughed again. Then his head slumped back as he looked up at the two men standing over him.

"Kill me now," he sighed.

Calgacus said, "No. I do not kill wounded men."

"Then give me my dagger so that I can end my life," the shield-bearer pleaded, his eyes closing to shut out his pain.

"No need," said Runt. Casually, he bent down, stabbing one of his swords into Algarix's throat, driving it deep.

He stood up, responding to Calgacus' reproving frown by saying, "That was kinder than letting him bleed to death. And safer for us, too."

Then he looked at Calgacus, his face etched with concern.

"Are you all right?"

Calgacus raised a hand to the back of his neck. His fingers came away sticky with blood.

"Just a nick, I think. But my shoulder hurts. It's as well I was wearing my chainmail, though."

"The treacherous bastard must have followed us down here, hiding among the Boresti."

Calgacus nodded, "I wonder what he meant when he said his King would kill me."

"His mind was wandering. That happens when men are near death."

"You're right," Calgacus agreed. "Forget him. We have work to do. Come on."

Around them, the fort was in utter disarray. Tents had collapsed, horses were running wild, stampeding and causing more chaos, men were brandishing torches, setting light to anything that might burn, although the rain had left everything so damp that the flames struggled to catch hold.

Small knots of legionaries had banded together, fending off attacks, trying to join into larger groups but hemmed in by the tribesmen who continued to hurl themselves at their hated enemy.

Warriors were running amok, yelling and fighting, wild-eyed and lost in an orgy of destruction. The noise was deafening, the sights scarcely believable. Wounded and dying men lay sprawled everywhere, their blood soaking the ground that was littered with discarded swords and shields. To add to the chaos, the rain-soaked ground, trampled by thousands of feet, was becoming a quagmire of mud and blood.

Calgacus could see little in the gloom, but he knew war, and he could sense what was happening by listening to the sounds of the battle.

"The Romans are trying to hold the other gates, but they've been pushed back," he decided. "They are surrounded, and some of them are panicking."

"So, what do we do now?" Runt asked.

Calgacus glanced around. More than a score of his own warriors had gathered beside him, their eyes sparkling with eagerness as they awaited his command. Making up his mind, he raised his sword and pointed along the dark avenue which, as in every Roman military camp, connected the eastern and western gates.

"Gabrain's men are over there somewhere. We'll go and help them. That will take us past the Legate's tent. With any luck, we'll find him close by. I have a hankering to capture a Roman Eagle."

His warriors shouted their approval, and Runt grinned with delight. Fuelled by the excitement of battle, they set off, heading into the depths of the camp.

Togodumnus was astonished at how calm he felt. The roar of the attacking tribesmen was stupefying in its power, in its threat and promise of death and destruction, yet he did not feel afraid. It was only when Sdapezi began shouting urgent commands that he felt the first stirrings of anxiety gnawing at his belly.

"Gather all the hostages together!" the Centurion yelled. "And rouse all the lads. Form up here!"

Men were already tumbling out of their tents, slipping and sliding in the mud, scrambling for armour, shields and swords, asking what was happening, and shouting at one another to hurry. Bugles were blaring their calls to arms, and the sound of fighting rolled across the camp like a growl of ferocious anger.

Togodumnus could see legionaries running frantically towards the gates, could hear the bellows of the Centurions urging them to hurry. Auxiliary troops, whose tents were nearer the centre of the camp, were also grabbing for their weapons, looking terrified and confused.

"What is happening?" Venutius demanded, his voice high-pitched with alarm.

"How in Jupiter's name should I know?" Sdapezi shot back testily. "Just stay here."

Nobody seemed to know exactly what was happening. The sounds of battle were raging all around, as if the camp were under attack from all sides. Only the training and discipline of the legionaries prevented complete panic. They ran to their allotted places as quickly as they could, many of them not bothering to take the time to fasten on their armour.

Sdapezi's own troopers were nervous, but they obeyed their Centurion. They dragged the terrified, sleep-befuddled hostages from their tents, shoving them into a group and forming a circle around them, locking their shields together.

"We wait here," Sdapezi shouted over the bedlam.

Daszdius asked, "Shouldn't we try to reach the horses? We could get out."

"How?" Sdapezi retorted. "The bloody barbarians are already inside the fort. They've seized at least one of the gates, and I'm not going to try to fight my way out past them. We stand here. Now, hold your line and keep your eyes peeled."

Togodumnus tried to edge close to Thenu. She was looking at him, her eyes desperate with fear. He wanted to reassure her, but he could find no words of comfort. The Pritani had come, and they both knew what that would mean for anyone caught within the fort. At best, Thenu might be spared, because the warriors were always keen to take female slaves, but she might just as easily be raped and murdered. For himself, death seemed the most likely outcome. Surrounded by Roman soldiers, he would never be able to persuade the battle-crazed warriors not to kill him. All he could do was hope that Sdapezi's men could withstand the inevitable attacks. Yet he could feel their fear and confusion as they huddled together, sheltering behind their shields, peering into the murderous night where screaming death wailed all around them.

He watched, too amazed to do anything other than follow Sdapezi's orders. He saw Licinius Spurius, accompanied by a group of legionaries, running towards the north gate, the Legate almost stumbling in his haste. One man held the Legion's Eagle standard, while others clustered around him, prepared to die to protect the symbol that embodied the Legion's soul. Spurius led his escort into the gloom of the camp, and they soon vanished from Togodumnus' sight.

387

Togodumnus knew the layout of the camp. Most of the soldiers were based to the north, the legionaries' tents near the perimeter, the auxiliaries closer to the centre. That was where the fiercest struggle was taking place. On the other side of the camp, near the Legate's tent, there were fewer soldiers because this was where the horses, baggage and artillery were based. The legionaries whose tents occupied the southern edge of the fort would have run to the south wall to protect it, and now they were cut off by the Britons who were surging into the fort through the other gates.

Sdapezi had recognised the danger of the situation. "They've broken in through the east gate," he growled. "Some of them will probably be coming this way."

Togodumnus soon saw that the Centurion was correct. Men appeared like spectres in the night, the first of them running for their lives. He saw a wounded legionary clutching at his belly, stagger between the ruined tents, then fall to the ground. Another man ran past, weapons discarded, ignoring his fallen comrade, too panicked to pay heed to his surroundings. He tripped on a tent rope, sprawling on the ground, then a wild-haired savage leaped on him, plunging down with a long spear to take the fallen man in the back.

"Jupiter, Juno and Minerva!" breathed Daszdius. "The barbarians are in the camp, right enough."

Sdapezi called out, "Stand steady, lads. They'll be after easy pickings. Stay together and they won't touch us."

Togodumnus doubted whether any of the troopers truly believed the Centurion's words, but they maintained their discipline and stood their ground, trusting to the strength of their circular wall of shields to keep them safe.

In moments, more long-haired, shrieking nightmares were darting through the tents, stabbing and slashing at anything that moved, howling in savage delight as they rampaged through the fort.

"Steady, lads," Sdapezi repeated. "They can't break us if we stick together."

"They've broken everyone else," came a muttered growl from Daszdius.

"Hold your tongue!" barked Sdapezi.

Even though he had never mastered the art of swordsmanship, Togodumnus had learned enough from his father to know that Sdapezi's troop were at a serious disadvantage. There were only thirty of them, a mere handful compared to the hundreds of Britons who must now be rampaging through the fort. Even if they were not seriously outnumbered, they were cavalry troops, armed with long, heavy swords that were designed to give a man longer reach when fighting on horseback, and which needed room to wield properly. Standing shield to shield in a defensive huddle, they would not be able to strike back at their enemies.

Togodumnus found himself wishing they would be ignored. There was a chance the Britons might pass them by, because the main fight was taking place on the far side of the fort, near the north and west gates. He could see men moving in that direction, legionaries falling back, savage tribesmen charging forwards.

But the Britons were everywhere, and prepared to attack any Roman they found. A handful of them, their blood roused by their success, saw Sdapezi's troop and charged at them, yelling wildly, hurling themselves at the cluster of shields with no thoughts other than to kill their enemy.

There was a furious crash as warriors flung themselves at the wall of shields. The troopers tried to fight back, but their long swords were virtually useless in the confined space. Daszdius solved the problem by swinging his sword overhand, high over his shield, smashing it down on the skull of one blue-painted Briton, killing the man instantly.

Other troopers quickly followed his example. The Britons, who had attacked individually, with no plan or tactic

389

other than ferocity, fell back. Some of them ran off in search of easier prey, while the rest simply shouted taunts and insults from a safe distance.

"That's the stuff, lads," Sdapezi told his men. "Just hold out until help arrives."

"If help arrives," someone muttered.

Togodumnus shared the speaker's concern. Sdapezi and his men had shown that the Britons would struggle to defeat a well prepared defence, but most of the Legion had been caught unprepared. He could only imagine what carnage was being wrought among the legionaries. There seemed to be thousands of Britons in the fort, and even the best troops would eventually succumb if they were surrounded. He dared not think what was going to happen to Sdapezi's small band of soldiers. All they could do was stand and hope.

A squeal of alarm from Thenu made him turn. He saw Venutius holding her, one arm clamped around her slender waist, the other hand holding his ornately-jewelled dagger to her delicate throat.

"What are you doing?" he demanded.

Venutius gave a wild stare as he replied, "If they break through, she is my bargaining counter."

"Let her go!" Sdapezi snapped, looking back over his shoulder.

Venutius ignored him, and the Centurion was distracted by another warning shout from Daszdius.

"There are more of them coming this way!"

Togodumnus took a hesitant step towards Thenu, barely able to move in the confined space at the centre of Sdapezi's troop. The other hostages, the two older men and the young Prince from Hibernia, were looking on with resigned expressions, clearly unwilling to become involved.

Venutius twitched the dagger.

"Stay back, boy."

"If you kill her, your bargaining counter is gone," Togodumnus said, trying to sound calm and confident in the midst of the panic that was rising all around him.

He could sense the tension among the troopers. Their heads were turning, looking for danger. The men furthest from the approaching Britons were half turning, breaking their wall of shields in their anxiety to see the threat. Their nervousness had affected Venutius, whose eyes held a wild, desperately calculating look.

"Killing her won't do you any good," Togodumnus asserted, keeping his voice steady.

Venutius snarled, "That's true, but it doesn't mean I can't cut her up a bit, just so you can hear her scream."

"You bastard!"

Venutius gave a half-hearted sneer.

"So like your father, aren't you? Always concerned about other people. You should learn, boy, to look after yourself first."

"Like you do?" Togodumnus retorted. "That's why people hate you."

"You think I care about that?" Venutius snarled, his eyes darting around wildly. "I will do whatever I need to do, boy. Let people hate me if they wish. Their feelings mean nothing to me."

Togodumnus wanted to lash out, to pound more punches into Venutius' face, but the man's dagger held him back. He knew he would never be able to reach it before Venutius could plunge the blade into Thenu's throat. She was swallowing nervously, doing her best to remain calm, but he could see the fear in her expression. She was helpless, just as he was, because they both knew that Venutius would have no hesitation in using his knife.

Togodumnus bunched his fists in impotent rage, not knowing what to do. All his attention was focused on Venutius, so much so that he did not turn his head when he heard Sdapezi shout, "Here they come again!"

Togodumnus saw Venutius stiffen, his eyes fixing on something beyond the cluster of Sdapezi's troopers. For an instant, the knife in Venutius' hand wavered, then he recovered and tried to shrink down out of sight.

Togodumnus took a cautious half step towards the Brigante, but he stopped when he heard Sdapezi gasp, "Oh, Mars save us! It's Calgacus himself."

Togodumnus whirled. At first, all he could see was a horde of shadowy figures looming out of the darkness, swords, shields and spears held ready. They came at a slow, steady run, keeping together in a compact group while other barbarians hooted and yelled as they ran on either side of the main group. Then his eyes made out the giant figure at the head of the approaching warriors and he knew who it was. The way the man moved, the way he held his huge longsword, were so familiar that he had no doubt who it was.

He was not sure how to react. He had known his father must be here, but he had not considered the possibility of seeing him in person. For a long moment he stood, immobile, wondering what to do.

Venutius did not delay. Fear galvanised him into action. The gasp of surprise from Thenu did not warn Togodumnus in time. He had barely registered her call of warning before he felt Venutius' arm clamp around his chest and the tip of the Brigante's dagger prick his neck.

"I think I need a better bargaining counter," Venutius hissed in his ear. "One move, boy, and you'll be joining your ancestors."

Chapter XXXV

Calgacus held up an arm, calling a halt less than ten paces from the huddle of Roman soldiers. His men obeyed, although some of them growled that they were ready to attack. He knew that giving the signal would result in slaughter, because the Romans were surrounded, outnumbered and fearful. He could see the scared look in the eyes of the soldiers who were staring at him as if he were some spectre come to steal their souls, but he was stopped in his tracks by the voice which called out to him from behind the wall of shields.

"Keep away, or he dies!"

It was a voice that Calgacus had not heard for many years, but which he could not mistake.

He hesitated. It was not only the surprise of learning that the Governor had left the hostages here when he had moved his Headquarters to another camp, it was the sight of his oldest and most dangerous foe which left him momentarily speechless. Venutius had haunted his steps for years, always managing to escape Calgacus' vengeance. Now he held a dagger to Togodumnus' throat, rendering Calgacus helpless.

For a long moment, nobody moved. In the dim light, Calgacus could not make out his son's expression, but the dull glint of the blade was unmistakable, and it held Calgacus in place.

Then he saw a flash of white as Venutius bared his teeth in a triumphant sneer, and the spell was broken.

"Venutius!" he barked. "Come out here and face me."

"You are as stupid as ever, Calgacus," Venutius sneered. "Leave us, or your son dies."

393

"He is not my son," Calgacus replied. "He says his name is Cingel, and he wants to be a Roman. Tell me, why should I not order my men to kill you all?"

Venutius hesitated for a moment before answering, "I think you are bluffing. You were always too soft. You won't stand there and order your own son's death. Not to mention these other hostages the Governor has so kindly provided."

Calgacus' own warriors were standing still, waiting for his command, but other men were streaming past, darting further into the camp or prowling round the circle of Sdapezi's tiny clutch of soldiers, surrounding them.

The troopers braced themselves, their faces grim beneath their helmets. The warriors made threatening gestures, pointing with spears and swords, but there was a momentary lull as both sides weighed up the other. The Romans dared not break out of their defensive circle, and the Britons waited for Calgacus' order.

That order did not come. Calgacus could see the dagger at his son's throat and he could not think of any plan that had any hope of saving him. Yet he could not hold his men back forever. They had come to kill Romans, and they were growing increasingly angry.

Desperately, Venutius called, "If your son's life is not enough for you, let us make another bargain. I will give you the name of a spy who has been sending us information about your plans. Wouldn't you like to know who it is? Is that name not worth my life?"

"I don't need your help to find him," Calgacus stated.

"I think you do. The man has instructions to send assassins after you. Wouldn't you like to find him before one of them kills you?"

Calgacus had a sudden vision of Algarix and his dying threat. From Runt's soft exclamation of outrage, he knew his friend had made the same connection.

Calgacus hesitated. All around him, men were keyed up, eager to lash out. It would take very little to spark a vicious fight to the death. He had no fears for himself, and he would back his own warriors against the Romans, but Togodumnus would die, and he could not allow that. He also knew that dawn was not far off, and they were running out of time.

Reluctantly, he said, "All right. We didn't come here for you anyway. Tell me the name of the traitor and we will leave you alone."

"Not good enough," Venutius spat. "Swear on your sword's blade that you will not kill me, nor order anyone else to harm me. Swear it twice, once in Latin, so these men know."

Runt hissed, "Let me kill him, Cal."

"How would you reach him before he kills Togodumnus? Do you want to go back and tell Beatha how her son died?"

Runt subsided into angry curses.

Adelligus warned, "The sky is growing lighter behind us. We need to go soon."

Calgacus nodded. Already, the outlines of men and tents were becoming clearer.

He gripped his sword, holding it upright with both hands, the flats of his palms on either side of the thick blade.

"I swear I will not harm you, nor order anyone else to harm you if you give me the name of the spy, and if you let my son live."

He could sense the frustration among his men, but he held them by the force of his will as he repeated the vow in Latin so that the troopers could understand.

Venutius replied, "You are known as a man of your word, Calgacus, so I will trust you on this. The name of the traitor in your camp is Drust, King of the Caledones."

An angry growl sounded from the throats of the warriors as Venutius continued, "I tell you, Drust is the man you seek. He wants peace, but he is too afraid of you to defy you openly."

Runt hissed, "And he's got Bran to speak for him. That's why he kept arguing with you."

Calgacus nodded grimly, "It's plausible, but I wouldn't trust Venutius to tell the truth even now."

"So, what do we do?"

Still Calgacus delayed. Time had almost run out, he knew. The attack had succeeded but it had not yet destroyed the Legion. He could still hear the sounds of frantic, desperate battle from the far side of the camp. He should be there, he knew, should be leading the attack on the bulk of the Roman forces. But his son was here, and Venutius, who had haunted his life for thirty years, was here.

"Leave them," he decided. "We need to finish the Legion off before dawn."

The warriors were about to obey when the strident, wailing call of a great carnyx, a war horn, echoed through the greyness of the pre-dawn.

Swearing under his breath, Adelligus warned, "We must go. That signal means more Romans are coming."

Calgacus nodded. With a savage curse, he waved a hand, barking the order.

"Everyone get out of here! Return to the horses. Now!"

The warriors turned and ran for the gate that they had so recently stormed. Only Calgacus' own men remained with him, determined not to leave him alone.

Triumphantly, Venutius called, "Goodbye, Calgacus. Remember that vow you made."

Calgacus stared at the man, wishing him dead, but knowing the Brigante had beaten him again.

Then another voice growled in Latin, "I swore no vow, and I am sick of you."

Calgacus watched in amazement as the dagger at Togodumnus' throat was yanked aside. The Roman Centurion who commanded the troop had seized the Brigante's arm and flung him around. With a savage thrust, the soldier buried his own dagger in Venutius' belly, driving the blade deep, twisting it viciously.

Venutius screamed, his face contorted with shock and agonised despair. Almost unbelieving, he looked at the Centurion in horror, then he was shoved roughly backwards and fell, vanishing from Calgacus' sight behind the ranks of soldiers.

For a moment, nobody moved. The Roman troopers seemed shocked, frozen by the violent justice meted out by their commander, and Togodumnus was staring down at Venutius' dying body, blinking in astonishment.

With a gruff word, the Centurion ordered his men to make way for him. He stepped out from behind their protective shields, holding his bloodied dagger like a vindication.

"You probably don't remember me," he told Calgacus. "But you spared my life one day, when that treacherous bastard ran away and left me and my friends to die."

"I remember," Calgacus told him. "I will never forget that day."

"Now I have given you that life back," Sdapezi said. "We are even, are we not?"

"We are even," Calgacus agreed.

Togodumnus had shaken off his shock. He edged out from between the wall of shields, leading a young girl by the hand.

Speaking in their native language, he told Calgacus, "This is Thenu. Take her with you."

Calgacus asked, "What about you? Are you coming back with us?"

Togodumnus shook his head.

"I can do more good for our people if I stay here. You might have need of me if you ever want to negotiate with the Governor."

"I will not negotiate," Calgacus told him firmly.

"Nevertheless, I am not a warrior. I can do more good if I stay here. You know that. But I am not a Roman, Father. Do not forget that."

"I will not forget," Calgacus assured him. "You are a man now, and you must make your own decisions."

The two of them exchanged a look of understanding, then Calgacus held out his hand and beckoned Thenu.

"Come, girl. We will take you home."

Sdapezi frowned, but before he could voice any objection, Thenu turned to Togodumnus.

She said, "I will only go if you go. If you are staying here, so will I."

Frowning, Togodumnus shook his head.

"I cannot go. I must stay."

Grabbing his arm and clinging to him, Thenu declared, "Then I am staying, too." Turning to Calgacus, she added, "Have mercy on my grandfather. He has lost everyone except me. That is why he betrayed you. He was afraid of losing me, too."

"You are Drust's granddaughter?" Calgacus asked with a puzzled frown.

Togodumnus said, "No. Venutius lied about that. Drust is not the spy."

"Then who is?"

Togodumnus said, "Her grandfather is Ebrauc, King of the Damnonii. His messenger is named Dwyfel."

Calgacus felt his blood run cold. He knew the identity of the man who had betrayed their plans, but it was another name that filled his thoughts.

"Beatha!"

Chapter XXXVI

Beatha had sat with the aged King of the Damnonii through the long, silent eeriness of the night. They were virtually alone, with only the great herd of tethered horses for company. Beatha's women and a few men had been left to watch over the animals, but Broichan had taken most of these to the top of the hill where he had ordered them to build bonfires that could be lit to guide the warriors back if the attack on the fort failed.

"We will also watch out for any signs of other Romans coming to the aid of the fort," he declared, gesturing at one of his acolytes who held a long, curved carnyx horn, the head of which was shaped in the design of an eagle's head. Small, moveable metal flaps within the wide beak allowed the player to adjust the sound of the horn and could be used to create unearthly, wailing calls that could be heard over great distances.

When the druid led the handful of warriors away, Beatha and Ebrauc sat on the rear of the platform of his chariot, talking idly. Anhareth, Beatha's self-appointed guard, sat on a tussock ten paces away, giving the pair some privacy, but watching carefully in case Beatha needed anything. The young woman pulled up her hood and wrapped her cloak tightly around herself to keep her bare arms and legs warm and dry.

The fine drizzle continued, making the night air damp and miserable, but Ebrauc seemed in the mood to talk. Beatha guessed that he had wanted to take part in the battle, but his aged body was long past the time when he could wield a sword.

"I have lost everything," he told Beatha sadly. "My land, my sons and daughters, my grandchildren. My strength is almost gone, too."

"You still have your mind," Beatha told him. "You can guide your people because you are wise and experienced."

"Experienced, yes," he sighed. "I am less sure about being wise. I fear I have made many mistakes."

"Calgacus says we all make mistakes," she replied, trying to reassure him. "All we can do is deal with the consequences in the best way we can."

"I cannot argue with that," Ebrauc nodded wearily.

"Have you no family left at all?" she asked.

"I am told one of my granddaughters still lives. I had hoped she would marry young Dwyfel, and that he would become King after me."

"Dwyfel?"

"One of my closest and most trusted men. He is the son of a chieftain, very strong, a mighty warrior."

"And he was to wed your granddaughter?"

"Yes. He loves Thenu almost as much as I do."

"What happened to her?" Beatha asked. "You said you thought she is still alive."

"The Romans took her," Ebrauc explained, his voice thick with loss and grief. Tears glistened in his old eyes, and he wiped them away with the back of his hand.

"I am sorry," he sighed. "I have become an old woman instead of an old man."

"It is right to grieve for those we have lost," Beatha assured him gently.

"I live in hope that Thenu will be returned to me one day," he said.

Beatha did not respond. She knew enough about Rome to know that Ebrauc's granddaughter was probably a slave somewhere far to the south. She would not have been surprised to learn that the girl had been taken across the sea,

400

perhaps even to Rome itself. Whatever dreams Ebrauc had for the future of his dynasty, Thenu would not play any part in the reality. She might be alive, but she would never return.

"The rain has stopped at last," Beatha observed, holding out one hand, palm upwards.

"It is still a miserable night for this attack," Ebrauc sighed. "I fear it is doomed to failure."

"Not if Calgacus has anything to do with it," she replied proudly.

A sudden roar filled the night, the sound they had been listening for even while they had been speaking. When it came, Beatha's heart surged, knowing Calgacus would be at the forefront of the fighting. She offered a silent prayer for victory and his safe return, but she could not shake off a sense of mounting dread.

A flicker of flame from the top of the ridge caught her eye. Broichan had lit the bonfires, beacons that would guide the warriors back to their horses. Then she gave a start as a rider appeared, coming from the east, his horse lathered and snorting with exhaustion.

"It is Dwyfel," Ebrauc told her.

The young man dismounted, leaving his tired pony and striding towards them. Beatha saw a tall man, broad in the shoulder, slim at the waist, a sword on his back. She could make out little of his features except a firm jaw and deep-set, watchful eyes. When he spoke, his voice was deep and powerful.

"I have done as you commanded," he informed Ebrauc.

The old King gave another tired nod. He indicated Beatha.

"This is the wife of Calgacus. I promised to take care of her."

Her nerves on edge because of the distant sound of battle, Beatha gave Dwyfel a brief, distracted welcome. She wondered what he had done for Ebrauc, and why he was not with the other warriors, but she was too preoccupied with trying to interpret the sounds of the battle to pay much attention to the young man.

He, in turn, had other things on his mind. Speaking urgently, he told Ebrauc, "There is a problem."

Sighing, Ebrauc pushed himself to his feet, saying to Beatha, "Excuse us a moment."

The two men walked a few paces and held a hurried, whispered conversation before Ebrauc hobbled back and sat down beside Beatha again.

"Is something wrong?" she asked.

"No, everything will be fine," he replied. "You know what young people are like, seeing problems where none exist. I have asked Dwyfel to keep your woman company until the warriors return."

She saw Dwyfel walk over to where Anhareth was sitting watching them, but her thoughts were still on the unseen battle raging beyond the ridge. She could hear shouts and screams like a muffled roar of the sea pounding on rocks, and her fear for Calgacus returned. Trying to force out her growing concern, she watched as Anhareth cautiously rose to her feet to greet Dwyfel. From the sly smile on Anhareth's young face, Beatha guessed the woman was weighing up her chances of snaring the powerfully built young warrior in an amorous embrace. She smiled to herself. Even within earshot of a battle for the survival of the free tribes, Anhareth had no shame.

"I wish there was something else I could do," Ebrauc said, jerking Beatha's attention away from the shadowy figures of Dwyfel and Anhareth.

"What do you mean?" she asked, thinking she had missed something that the old man had said to her.

The King placed a hand on her arm, his thin fingers pressing into her flesh. His grip was cold and clammy, sending an involuntary shiver through her.

402

Then his other hand had seized her arm, and she heard a dull thump, followed by a stifled gasp from Anhareth. She looked up to see the young woman crumple to the ground, and Dwyfel run towards her. Ebrauc's grip was tight on her arm, holding her. She could have broken free, but she was too stunned.

"Anhareth?" she shouted, but there was no response.

Then Dwyfel was in front of her, holding a knife to her face.

"She is not dead," he told her in a low, urgent voice. "At least, I do not think I hit her too hard. Now, be still."

Ebrauc snapped, "Hold her. I have ropes and a cloth we can use as a gag."

"What are you doing?" Beatha gasped, uncomprehending.

Dwyfel seized her, clamping a strong hand over her mouth to prevent her calling out. Ebrauc bustled to the front of the chariot, returning with two short lengths of rope and two strips of linen.

"Gag her and bind her," the King ordered.

Beatha tried to scream for help, but Dwyfel was too quick for her. He hit her on the back of the head with the hilt of his knife, then, while she tried to recover, he had stuffed one piece of linen into her mouth, almost choking her. In a matter of moments, the second cloth had been tied around her mouth, holding the first gag in place, and her wrists and ankles were bound tightly. Roughly, Dwyfel grabbed her and heaved her onto the platform of the chariot.

"Tie her to one of the posts," Ebrauc ordered, gesturing towards the front corner of the chariot.

Dwyfel took the end of the rope that held Beatha's wrists and knotted it around the thin post that was used to hold the reins when they were not in use. Lying on the wooden boards of the rectangular platform, her hands were in front of her face, her feet towards the rear edge, with her back jammed against the wickerwork side panel of the chariot.

Satisfied that she could not move, Dwyfel untethered the two ponies who were still yoked to the chariot's long cross-pole, then he jumped aboard and took the reins.

"Slowly," Ebrauc told him. "Do not arouse anyone's suspicion."

"They will all be too busy trying to see what is happening down in the fort," Dwyfel replied, flicking the reins to spur the ponies into motion. He turned them, driving between the lines of tethered horses, heading eastwards, keeping to the left of the long, low ridge where Broichan's fires burned.

Beatha, lying bound and gagged on the platform, listened in disbelief as Ebrauc told her, "I mean you no harm, but Calgacus has forced me into this. He led me to believe that Venutius and Thenu were with the Governor, but Dwyfel has learned that they are in the camp that Calgacus is attacking."

The old man's voice was full of despair, but Dwyfel's response was harsh and uncompromising.

"The Governor is on his way. He should be here very soon. With luck, Calgacus will be trapped. The Roman I spoke to was confident that the walls of the fort could not be breached."

"May the Gods grant that he is right," muttered Ebrauc fervently.

"If he is not," Dwyfel rasped tersely, "If Thenu is harmed, everything we have done, everything we are doing now, will have been for nothing."

"She will not be harmed," Ebrauc insisted, although his words sounded more like a prayer than conviction.

With an edge of desperation in his voice, he went on, "We have no choice. The Romans must take us into their protection now. We will give them Calgacus' wife. They want her, so we shall use her to gain Thenu's freedom."

"What about Calgacus?" Dwyfel asked. "Venutius demanded his death."

"He will be dead soon, if he is not already," Ebrauc replied coldly. "I sent that disgraced Taexali, Algarix, to kill him. It was fortunate that he chose to hide among our tribe when the Taexali were hunting him. He hates Calgacus, so it was a simple matter to persuade him into working for us."

"Then the war will be finished, and we can return home," Dwyfel said in a satisfied tone.

"That is all I want," Ebrauc agreed. "My days are numbered now, but I wish to end them in peace, knowing that my granddaughter is safe. Thenu will marry you, and you will be King."

"Our people might not consent to that," Dwyfel complained sourly.

"The Romans will ensure it happens," Ebrauc told him. "They will reward you for what we have done."

Dwyfel did not sound overly enthusiastic as he grunted, "I hope so, because nobody else will."

The chariot picked up speed as they left the broad valley behind. Bounced and jostled, Beatha closed her eyes. All she could do was pray that Calgacus would find her before Ebrauc handed her over to the Romans. But Calgacus was in the fort, and a killer was stalking him. What hope did she have?

The chariot ploughed on through the night, moving slowly because Dwyfel was not a trained driver and struggled to control the vehicle. Under his inexpert guidance, the iron-rimmed wheels bounced over obstacles, or became stuck in patches of boggy ground, while the ponies often floundered in swampy puddles.

Ebrauc, clearly exhausted by the constant buffeting of their passage, asked plaintively, "How much further must we go? I can no longer hear the fighting."

Dwyfel retorted angrily, as if the King's complaint were an insult.

He said, "The ground has not been suitable for chariots. We have been forced too far north. But it is growing light. As soon as we can see, I'll turn south and we can meet up with the Governor's relief column."

Beatha, bruised and aching, lay on the boards, struggling to breathe, her mouth dry and choked by the rag that was tied firmly in place. The rough journey had added to her misery, and her inability to move meant she was plagued by thoughts of what was going to happen to her.

Her fear was that she would be delivered to the Governor, Julius Agricola, who would use her as a hostage against Calgacus. When that failed, as she knew it must, Agricola would probably send her south, to be returned to her brother, Cogidubnus, King of the Regni, a loyal ally of Rome.

It was, she thought miserably, a ridiculous fate. She was a mother, a grandmother now, wife of a mighty chieftain, yet her brother still regarded her as his property. She had run away from the marriage he had arranged for her, and he had never forgiven that insult. Grown woman or not, he would treat her as a disobedient child, administering beatings and other cruel punishments to demonstrate that he, as head of a Roman family, controlled her. Cogidubnus had always been a vindictive bully, she recalled. Too weak to stand up to powerful rivals, he had turned to Rome to keep him in power, and had become more Roman than many who lived in the imperial city. He was a petty despot, she knew, but that would not make her predicament any easier to bear. She resolved not to beg, not to cry, not to show any weakness. She would adopt the detached, insolent obedience she had employed during the dreadful years she had been married to a Roman Centurion. Cogidubnus might beat her, but she vowed that he would not break her.

She became aware of growing daylight, of faint warmth from the rising sun. Dwyfel was cursing again, having been required to dismount and heave one of the wheels out of another deep patch of marshy ground. Now, though, he clambered back onto the chariot, his boots spreading muck and mud across the boards, some of it splattering over Beatha.

"Now we can see where we are going," he declared, snapping the reins to encourage the ponies into a slow walk.

Their progress was only a little faster as Dwyfel picked a cautious route across an empty landscape, making frequent detours to avoid patches of woodland and marsh. Eventually, they turned to their right, climbing a low hill, skirting a thick forest, then heading down into a wide area of undulating ground that was relatively clear. By twisting her neck, Beatha could peer between the legs of the two men, out beyond the rumps of the ponies with their docked tails, to catch a restricted view of their surroundings. She could see nothing except grass and trees, a dull, grey sky above, but Dwyfel let out a cry of triumph.

"A cavalry patrol!"

He flicked the reins, urging the ponies on. The chariot gained speed, rumbling across the ground, taking Beatha ever closer to her doom.

She felt the vehicle slowing as Dwyfel pulled on the reins.

"Better stop here," he advised. "We don't want them to think we are hostile."

The chariot drew to a merciful halt, easing the pummelling on Beatha's aching body.

"Best get out," Dwyfel suggested, nudging at old Ebrauc to make him move back. The aged King did not object, and Beatha sensed that something in the men's relationship had altered, that Dwyfel was now the one in command. They clumped past her, stepped down, and she

407

saw them walk to the far side of the chariot. They stopped, and Dwyfel shouted his rehearsed Latin greeting.

"I am a friend," he called at the top of his voice, raising his arms wide to show that he offered no threat. "I have come to speak to Venutius of the Brigantes, who is a guest of the Governor."

Now Beatha could hear the dull rumble of hoofbeats. Craning her neck, trying to push herself up, she caught sight of a line of more than two dozen horsemen spreading out as they approached at a fast canter. She saw from their cloaks and helmets, from their bare legs, and from the long javelins they held, that they were Roman horsemen.

As they drew near and reined in, spreading out in a long line, she also saw that they were nervous and angry. These were men who had recently been in danger, or who had witnessed violence, and their mood was ugly, their nerves on edge.

Dwyfel repeated his greeting, saying the words over and over again, almost pleading, and she knew he had recognised the danger they were in. To the Roman cavalry, they were Britons, and in these untamed lands, all Britons were enemies.

A voice snapped irritably, "Who are you?"

Dwyfel did not understand. He repeated the words he had memorised, almost shouting them as if saying them loudly would make the Romans understand.

Another Roman said, "Sir, there's someone hiding in the chariot."

"Bring them out!" the first voice ordered. "And be careful. They could have been with the barbarians who sacked the fort."

Beatha heard someone coming towards the rear edge of the platform. Over the rim of the side panel, she saw Dwyfel turn, moving to block the soldier.

"Venutius!" he shouted, as if the rebel Brigante's name were a talisman.

Beatha caught sight of the helmeted face of a soldier at the rear of the chariot. Then Dwyfel was grabbing at him, trying to prevent him climbing aboard, and the soldier was shaking him off, shouting back angrily.

She wanted to yell her own warning, to tell Dwyfel to stand back, but the young man had pinned all his hopes on exchanging her for Ebrauc's granddaughter, and he did not want anyone else to take her from him.

"I must give her to Venutius!" he shouted, shoving the Roman back.

It was a mistake, and Beatha knew it. The Roman horsemen were keyed up, their nerves raw, their blood pumping with a deadly mix of fear and excitement. Dwyfel's angry response was enough to trigger a violent reaction. Several men urged their horses closer, closing in around the chariot.

Ebrauc yelled a strident warning, but one of the soldiers stabbed his long lance into Dwyfel's back. Dwyfel gasped, arching his body, then collapsed as the soldier yanked his lance free.

The killing sparked the other riders into action. They crowded in, lances thrusting as their horses snorted and jostled for space. Ebrauc screamed as his aged body was pierced by three sharp blades.

Beatha closed her eyes, but she could not shut out the dying cries of the two Damnonii.

The officer's voice was barking at the men to make room, demanding to know what they were doing.

"He was going for his sword," a man explained sulkily.

"Well, it's done now," the officer sighed, clearly not unhappy that the Britons had been killed. "Now, check that chariot and let's get out of here before any more barbarians turn up."

The chariot jerked as a man stepped onto the platform.

"Immortal Gods! There's a woman here!"

Beatha tried to speak, but her voice was stifled by the gag. She saw a man in a plumed helmet join the first soldier. Both men's eyes were bright with menace and the lust for more blood.

"Get her out of there," the officer commanded.

Rough hands tugged at Beatha. The cord binding her to the chariot pole was cut, but her wrists and ankles remained bound, and they did not remove the gag from her mouth. Instead, the officer prised the golden torc from her neck and yanked the rings from her numbed fingers.

"A rich woman!" he grinned malevolently. "It's my lucky day."

Staggering, unable to stand, Beatha saw that soldiers were already stripping the two dead Britons of their valuables. Her own cloak fell away as a man ripped her brooch away.

"It really is my lucky day!" the officer leered when he saw Beatha's close-fitting tunic and trousers, the war outfit she had worn with such pride.

"What do we do with her?" the soldier holding her asked, his tone making it clear that he could make some suggestions.

Beatha struggled in his grasp, frantically trying to speak, to let them know she could understand them, but they had no interest in listening to her. She was, she realised, nothing more than a prize, and she could see their intentions in the hungry way they looked at her. With Ebrauc and Dwyfel dead, these men would probably murder her, too, but only after they had raped her.

The officer, a coarse, unshaven man with dark, sunburned features, gave her another appraising look, but his words were cut off by a warning shout from one of the mounted men.

"Sir! There's more of them!"

All heads turned. Beatha twisted, catching sight of a group of horsemen who had appeared at the top of a hill several hundred paces to the north. She could not make out any details, but she guessed they had been following the tracks of the chariot. Which could only mean it was Calgacus.

But he was too late.

She saw the Roman officer's cold, hard eyes and knew that he was considering killing her on the spot. She closed her eyes, determined not to show fear, waiting for him to draw his dagger and end her life.

The blow did not come.

"Bring her!" the officer snapped.

She was dragged to a horse. One of the soldiers helped the officer into the saddle, then she was hoisted up over the animal's back, jammed between the front of the high saddle and the horse's neck, lying face down, dangling precariously.

"They're coming!" someone yelled.

In response, the officer clamped a hand on her back, kicked his heels and shouted at his men to ride.

The troop set off at a gallop. Beatha was bounced mercilessly, adding to her mounting tally of bruises. Only the Roman's firm hand kept her in place, her face dangerously near the pounding legs of his horse. It was a nightmare ride, a barrage of pain and discomfort that she could only pray would come to an end before she fell or passed out.

"They're following us!" a soldier called over the thunder of hooves.

"How many?" the officer demanded.

"About thirty, I think. We could turn and drive them off."

"There might be more behind them," the officer decided. "Keep going. Back to the fort. Our task was to search for signs of the barbarians, and we've done that."

Beatha clung on desperately. She briefly considered trying to fling herself off the charging horse, but the Roman was holding her firmly in place and, even if she could somehow wriggle free, she knew she would be trampled by the horses who were galloping behind them.

Through her pain, she knew there was no escape. Calgacus could not save her now. Nothing could save her now.

Chapter XXXVII

As the sun slowly rose over the fort, the carnyx was still sounding its warning cry, calling the warriors back. Calgacus ran towards the gateway, dodging through the detritus of the ruined fort. The ground was strewn with dead and wounded men, with discarded weapons, with cooking pots, shattered pottery, pieces of armour, swords and shields. Flapping sheets of leather from fallen tents fluttered in the morning breeze, ropes and pegs threatened to trip him, but he kept moving, knowing that his warriors were slowing their pace to allow him to keep up.

His legs ached, his neck was stiff where Algarix's knife had cut him, and he could feel dried blood caking his skin. Worse than that, though, was the anguish in his mind. His son had decided to stay with the Romans, which was hurt enough for any man, but his fear for Beatha overrode everything else.

"Keep moving!" he gasped, saying it more for his own benefit than anyone else's.

They reached the gate, where Bridei was waiting with a handful of warriors. The Boresti King's face was a mask of dried blood, his hair was matted, his clothes and bare arms streaked with mud and blood, but he was grinning like a madman, and he held his sword aloft in greeting when he saw them.

"I thought you'd got lost!" he beamed. "That was a bonnie fight, was it not?"

"What's happening?" Calgacus asked breathlessly as he staggered to the gate.

"Buggered if I know," Bridei replied cheerfully. "But everyone's clearing out, and the Romans are gathering again, so we'd better not hang around."

413

They ran north, along the edge of the fort's outer ditch. It was almost full daylight now, the sun spilling its glare over the eastern horizon. As they reached the corner of the fort, Calgacus could see thousands of warriors climbing the slope to the ridge where the carnyx player was still calling his warning. Most of the warriors had made their escape, and there was no sign of pursuit from the Romans inside the fort.

His relief was short-lived, dashed by a warning shout from Adelligus.

"Horses to the right!"

"Romans!" Bridei yelled, apparently delighted.

"Keep going!" Calgacus urged.

He ignored the protests from his aching limbs as he pounded towards the slope. The distance seemed much greater than it had been on their night-time advance, and he kept turning his head to watch the approaching horsemen.

"They're going to catch us!" Runt gasped as he ran.

The Roman cavalry had seen them and had urged their horses into a gallop. They came with lances outstretched, banners flying, and a loud shout of triumph.

"Stand here!" Calgacus yelled. "Close up!"

They had little chance of escaping, he knew, but at least they would be able to kill some of their enemy. Running men were easy targets for horsemen, but a solid phalanx of swords and spears could inflict some damage.

Now that he had stopped running, Calgacus had time to see that there were only around fifty horsemen charging at them. Hope flared in his mind, a desperate hope that they might be able to drive off the attack, but then he caught sight of more horsemen in the distance, hundreds of them following behind the leading group.

Around him, the warriors skidded to an exhausted halt, the foot of the hill less than a hundred paces away, but too far to run before the horses caught them. They clustered together, standing shoulder to shoulder, gripping their swords and spears to form a hedge of bristling iron blades, waiting for the charge.

"I knew you'd get me killed one day," Bridei chuckled.

"We're not dead yet," Calgacus growled, "Just let me get my breath back, and we'll take a few of them with us."

The galloping Romans were a hundred paces away, but instead of charging at the knot of warriors, they suddenly veered off, turning towards the fort.

The carnyx blared again, and Adelligus shouted, "It's Bran!"

Calgacus twisted his head to look up the slope. Hundreds of horsemen had appeared, coming over the ridge, threatening to charge down on the Roman's right flank. Fearing a trap, the Romans made for the safety of the fort.

Scarcely believing their luck, Calgacus saw Bran waving to him from the ridge.

"Go!" he shouted.

They ran for the hill again. As they reached the lower slope, Bran led the Caledones down to meet them.

"I thought you could do with a spot of help," he grinned as he wheeled his horse beside Calgacus.

"I told you to get away from here as soon as it was light," Calgacus wheezed. Then he, too, grinned as he added, "But I'm glad you came back."

"My pleasure," Bran nodded. "Come on, before the rest of the Romans get here."

With the Caledones forming a protective screen, they scrambled up the wooded ridge, heading back to where their own horses were waiting. As they hurried across the boggy ground, Calgacus asked Bran what had happened during the battle.

"Drust is dead," Bran said with a shrug. "He charged into the gateway and practically threw himself on the Romans' swords."

In answer to Calgacus' enquiring look, he went on, "I think he was tired of life. He made a good ending, though. He killed two Romans and broke their line for us. We got into the fort because of him."

"What about the others? Gabrain and Muradach?"

"I don't know about Muradach, but Gabrain is as happy as I have ever seen him," Bran replied. "He and his men took the western gate. We had the Romans penned between us and would have killed them all if we had had enough time."

With a nod, he concluded, "It was a great victory, War Leader."

"I hope it was enough," Calgacus grunted.

The wide field where the horses had been tethered was a riot of noise and excitement. Bran had led several hundred men back to help the last of the warriors escape, but thousands more were jostling around, grabbing for horses, arguing over who had killed the most Romans, and struggling to load their booty onto the skittering ponies.

Some men carried Roman heads they had hacked from the bodies of the men they had killed, others had contented themselves with bringing away helmets. Some carried cooking pots of iron, or Roman armour. Some had found jugs of Roman wine, while one or two had snatched up entire tents, somehow managing to drag them away from the fort but now puzzling over how to carry them on horseback. The more sensible men had merely gathered as many coins and rings as they could carry. Yet whatever plunder they had collected, all of them were jubilant.

Gabrain was waiting for them, animated and bouncing from foot to foot in his excitement.

"We did it!" he yelled excitedly. "We killed thousands of them!"

"You did well," Calgacus told him, not wishing to point out that it was impossible to know how many Romans

416

they had killed. "Now, get out of here. Take everyone back to Cingel's tomb before the other Legions arrive."

Gabrain shouted his agreement, running off to find a horse, but Bran, more insightful, asked, "Are you not coming with us?"

"Not until I find my wife."

He returned to the spot where he had left Beatha with Ebrauc. There was no sign of her, but he found Anhareth, nursing a large lump on the side of her head, with the other female warriors who had accompanied Beatha standing close by, their faces angry and full of outrage.

"It was Ebrauc," Anhareth said, wincing as she dabbed a hand at the bruise under her long, wild hair. "He took the Lady."

Calgacus growled, "I know. Where did he go?"

The young woman waved a hand eastwards.

"That way, I think. They were gone when I woke up, but I think I heard the chariot." She gave him an apologetic look as she explained, "I was a bit groggy. The King's man hit me quite hard. I am sorry."

"It is not your fault," Calgacus told her. "Don't worry. We will get her back."

Anhareth gave him a weak smile of thanks. Indicating the other women, she declared, "We will come with you. The Lady was in our care."

"If you are able to ride, you are welcome," Calgacus replied. "Fetch your horses quickly."

Adelligus and the warriors had already rounded up some horses. Calgacus mounted one, checked that everyone was ready, then set off across the field. While the vast host of the allied war band flooded northwards, he led eighteen men and six women in pursuit of a traitor who had kidnapped his wife.

The field was trampled, destroying all trace of the chariot's tracks, but they spread out and Adelligus soon located the faint marks of the wheels.

"He's going east, right enough," the young man observed. "But he has a good head start on us."

"We'll catch him," Calgacus insisted.

They galloped towards the sun, their eyes constantly scanning the ground for signs of the twin trails that marked the passing of the chariot. It was not a difficult track to follow, because the ground was still damp with dew and the rain of the previous night. Whenever they did lose sight of the trail, they were soon able to pick it up again.

They rode for nearly an hour before the tracks turned south, climbing a low ridge. Wheeling their mounts, they charged up the hill.

Runt was in the lead, some ten lengths ahead. When he reached the top of the ridge, he yanked on his reins, curbing his horse roughly. The others gathered beside him, looking down on a wide vista of open ground.

"Roman cavalry!" Runt pointed. "And they've found the chariot."

Calgacus felt his heart lurch. The Romans had seen them, and were mounting up, wheeling away. The ponies yoked to the chariot, with nobody controlling them, followed their instincts and chased after the Roman horses.

"They have taken her!" Anhareth exclaimed.

"Are you sure?" Calgacus asked her.

"She is bound across one of their saddles," the girl insisted.

"Let's get after them," Runt urged.

There were nearly thirty Romans, roughly the same strength as their own band, but that was not enough to deter them. They pushed their tired mounts down the slope, stopping briefly to examine the two bodies that lay abandoned on the ground.

"Ebrauc has got his reward," Runt spat.

418

"I suppose that must be Dwyfel," Calgacus said, indicating the second corpse. "Come on, they're getting away."

It was a forlorn chase. Their ponies were tired, having been pushed hard for too long. The larger Roman horses soon outpaced them, but still they would not give up. They overtook the chariot, whose ponies had at last stopped, tired out by their exertions, but the Roman horsemen slowly increased the distance between them.

Still Calgacus continued the chase, feeling his horse tiring beneath him, but determined to pursue Beatha as long as he could. Only when he saw the troopers approach the devastation of the Roman fort did he reluctantly rein in. Watching helplessly from a rise in the ground, gazing past the stand of trees where he and the Boresti had sheltered only the previous night, he saw the Roman horsemen reach the ditch and rampart.

He stared as if he could will Beatha to escape, but he could not make her out among the milling figures that swarmed around the camp. Soldiers were everywhere, digging more ditches, planting more stakes, creating additional earthworks to defend the gateways that had been so recently breached. Others were building a great funeral pyre, while dozens more were laying bodies in long lines at the edge of the ditch.

"Gabrain was right," Adelligus remarked. "We did kill thousands of them."

Calgacus did not care. He barely saw the ruin of the camp, the stacked corpses, the piles of discarded weapons and armour. None of that mattered to him.

He had won a great victory, but he had lost Beatha.

Chapter XXXVIII

Anderius Facilis had witnessed death in the past, but even after a major battle, he had rarely seen so much slaughter in such a confined space.

The north and west gates of the Ninth Legion's fort were almost choked with bodies, Roman legionaries and half-naked barbarians, lying tangled and piled atop each other. Within the camp it was almost as bad, with piles of dead packed so closely together that some of the men seemed to be standing upright because they had not had enough room to fall. Others had been crushed by the press, trampled into the mud where, if they had not died from their wounds, they must have suffocated.

Caught completely unawares, the legionaries had run from their tents, straight into the bloody slaughter at the gates. There had been no time to establish order, with soldiers simply charging into the melee individually. When the Britons had broken in, the Legion had tried to rally in the open ground at the north-west corner of the fort, where they had stood back to back, hemmed in on two sides while the Britons poured in to surround them. The fighting, Facilis could see at a glance, had been desperate and vicious, but the soldiers who were engaged in that struggle were the lucky ones. Many of their comrades had been caught when the barbarians who had breached the eastern gate flooded through the tent lines, massacring anyone in their way. Unarmoured, barely awake, hundreds of Romans had been cut down before they knew what was happening.

Licinius Spurius, the Legate, was sitting on the ground, his face streaming with tears, gazing at the hundreds of dead.

"My Legion," he sobbed inconsolably. "We have been destroyed."

A grim-faced Agricola had organised a roll call, quickly establishing that, of the understrength Legion's four thousand men, nearly two thousand had been killed or wounded. The auxiliary troops who had been stationed with them had lost over seven hundred dead. It was a devastating blow, and Spurius, supported by Aulus Atticus and the other Tribunes, was already advising the Governor to withdraw the entire army south of the Bodotria before they were all slaughtered.

Agricola, of course, would not be rushed into making such a drastic decision, but Facilis could tell from the shocked expression on the Governor's face that his usual confidence had suffered a severe blow. The night attack, so unexpected, was little short of a catastrophe for the Governor's invasion plans.

"It should not have been possible," Agricola breathed, scarcely able to believe that the fort had been stormed.

The Governor, though, was a true Roman, and not one to dwell on disaster. He quickly mastered his shock, and began restoring some sort of order.

He set the surviving legionaries to securing the camp, tending to the wounded and gathering the dead for a massive funeral pyre.

"Burn all the bodies," he commanded. "Including the barbarians. I want no plague breaking out."

Nobody knew how many Britons had died. Hundreds, certainly, and the wounded who had not been able to escape were soon added to that count as the legionaries took bloody revenge for the death of their comrades, hunting through the fallen and dispensing swift justice with the points of their swords.

The Roman wounded were carried to the south section of the fort, where there had been less fighting. There were, though, so many of them that the medical orderlies could not cope and Facilis knew that many of the wounded would not survive their injuries.

Facilis had seen disaster before, and he had seen how men reacted. In the midst of the devastation, Agricola soon demonstrated that he was a truly great leader. He did not panic, did not shout or vent anger on anyone, he simply cajoled and encouraged, even congratulating men who had displayed bravery during the battle. He walked around the camp, talking calmly, and masking his inner feelings with an air of confidence.

Yet one burning question still troubled him.

"Find Venutius," he told Facilis. "I want to know how this could have happened."

Facilis went in search of the Brigante. As he walked through the camp, he noted the destruction, and grimaced when he saw the mutilated, headless corpses. It was a sight he hoped never to see again.

He found the man he was looking for near the centre of the camp, where the Centurion, Sdapezi, was standing over Venutius' corpse. Alongside the Centurion was Togodumnus, who had a young woman clinging to his arm, an incongruous sight in the midst of so much carnage. Facilis realised she must be the hostage Venutius had been using to extort information from the Britons.

"What happened?" Facilis asked when he recognised the dead man.

Sdapezi replied, "We were attacked by Calgacus himself."

Facilis glanced enquiringly at Togodumnus, who confirmed, "That's right."

"But you stayed here? You did not leave with your father?"

"I told the Governor I wanted to help him," Togodumnus explained with a shrug. "I do not go back on my word."

Indicating the young woman beside him, he added, "Thenu wishes to stay as well. With me."

Facilis looked at the young woman, noticing the sparkle in her eye when she looked at Togodumnus. He nodded his understanding.

"I'll explain it to the Governor when I get a chance. He's rather busy at the moment." Turning to Sdapezi, he asked, "How many men did you lose?"

"None, Sir. We were very lucky."

"Venutius was the only casualty?"

"That's right, Sir."

The Centurion's tone was convincing, but something in his manner gave Facilis the impression that he was, if not lying, certainly not telling the whole truth. Frowning, Facilis took a closer look at the blood-soaked corpse.

"The wound doesn't look as if it was inflicted by a barbarian longsword," he observed softly. "He's been stabbed, not slashed."

"It was a spear," Sdapezi explained a little too easily and promptly.

Facilis stood up. There was a mystery here, and a secret, but it was not one that he cared to investigate further.

"What about his spy?" he asked.

Togodumnus informed him, "My father knows who it is. There will be no more messages."

"Then that is an end to it," Facilis sighed. "Have him burned along with the other dead."

"Yes, Sir," agreed Sdapezi.

Wearily, Facilis reported to the Governor, who dismissed the matter with a curt shake of his head.

"Much good his spy did us anyway," Agricola sighed. "Calgacus used him to trick me."

Facilis was tempted to say that Agricola was not the first person who had been fooled by Calgacus, but he thought better of pointing that out. It was never wise to remind a

423

senior officer of his mistakes, even if he had already acknowledged them.

Facilis asked, "What do you want me to do now, Sir?"

"Send messengers to the Twentieth Legion," Agricola ordered briskly. "Tell them to rejoin us as soon as they can. And find out what has happened to the rest of the Second Legion. Make sure they are on their way here."

"Very good, Sir."

Facilis made his way to the north gate, passing the long lines of stacked, naked bodies that were already attracting a horde of flies, while carrion birds were circling overhead, seeking chances to feast.

Making his way through the eerie bustle of the grisly work details, he walked to the short section of free-standing earth wall and ditch that was supposed to have protected the entrance to the fort. A small group of legionaries stood there, keeping a nervous watch.

"Where are the cavalry?" he asked them.

"There's a patrol just coming in, Sir!" one of the soldiers reported. "They must have important news, because they're coming in a hurry."

Following the soldier's gaze, Facilis made out a *turma* of legionary horsemen galloping towards the camp. They were bunched together, but clearly anxious to reach the fort quickly. He could see the riders using the butt ends of their long lances to beat the horses' flanks, urging the tired animals to keep going.

Facilis went out to meet them, holding up a hand to halt their headlong charge. The horsemen reined in, coming to a halt in a welter of mud, murmurs of relief, the jingling of harness, and the smells of leather and sweat.

"What's happened?" Facilis asked.

To his surprise, he saw that the commander of the cavalrymen had someone draped across his horse in front of the saddle. All he could see were long legs encased in woollen leggings, with the ankles lashed together, but it was evident that the prisoner was a woman.

The officer, a swarthy man with a cruel face, dismounted, slinging Facilis a cursory salute as he reported, "Publius Fabius Aramantus, Centurion of the Third Turma, Second *Adiutrix*."

Facilis took an immediate dislike to Aramantus. Legionary cavalry always adopted a superior attitude, considering themselves better than the Auxiliaries who made up the bulk of the Roman cavalry force. Each Legion had an *Ala* of around one hundred and twenty citizen horsemen, a mere handful when compared to the thousands of legionary foot soldiers. Rome's strength had always been her heavily armoured infantry, yet the men of the cavalry Ala tended to strut and swagger like peacocks, never slow to remind everyone that the cavalry were the elite of the army. In Facilis' experience, the Auxiliary horsemen, raised from allied barbarian tribes, were far more effective than the Legionary *Alas*, and he was instantly wary of Aramantus. He realised, however, that his own abrupt greeting had irritated the officer.

"Anderius Facilis, Tribune on the Governor's staff," he said, formally introducing himself to let the cavalryman know that Facilis outranked him. Then he gestured towards the figure slumped over Aramantus' horse.

"Who have you got there?"

Aramantus grinned, "A prisoner. We ran into some barbarians. They chased us all the way back here, but we killed a couple and took this one. Wait till you see her."

The men of Aramantus' Turma had clustered around their officer, most of them still on horseback, the beasts panting and snorting after their long gallop. They almost obscured Facilis' view, but he peered beyond them and caught sight of another group of riders silhouetted against the skyline where they had stopped to look down on the fort.

"Ignore them," Aramantus said with a barely concealed sneer, "they won't attack. There aren't enough of them."

He grinned at his men as he added, "We gave them a good run, didn't we, boys?"

The riders chuckled, echoing their commander's delight in having outpaced their pursuers.

Facilis nodded. There was no immediate threat, but there was an immediate question that required an answer.

"So, who is your prisoner?"

"No idea," Aramantus shrugged. "But she's no ordinary woman, that's for sure. Look at the way she's dressed."

At last, the officer heaved his captive down to the ground, holding her tightly to support her, and leering in triumph as he displayed her to the Tribune.

Facilis froze. The woman could barely stand, almost collapsing. Even if her legs had not been tied together, she would not have been able to support herself. She looked exhausted, barely conscious, dishevelled, and disoriented. Her wrists were bound in front of her, and her mouth was gagged, the tight cloth making her grimace in a rictus smile, but he could not fail to recognise her.

For a moment, he could not speak. All he could do was stare at her in disbelief.

"She's a bit old for my taste," Aramantus grinned. "But she'll do. And I might get a decent price for her when I sell her."

"Put her down!" Facilis barked, his anger jerking him from his momentary stupor.

"What?" The cavalryman frowned.

"Lie her down. Now! Do you know what you've done?"

Aramantus grew defensive. He retorted, "I've taken a prisoner, and killed some of our enemies. That's my job."

426

"You've taken the wrong prisoner," Facilis shot back. "Put her down and let me talk to her."

Reluctantly, the soldier lowered Beatha to the ground, while Facilis ordered the other riders to back away and allow him some space. They did as he commanded but, intrigued by his reaction, they remained in a circle around him, watching curiously.

Ignoring the horsemen, Facilis knelt down beside the exhausted woman. Speaking in Brythonic, he asked, "Beatha? Are you all right?"

Her eyes fluttered open, blinking weakly. It took a few moments for them to focus on him. When she recognised him, she sagged with relief.

"Say nothing," he warned as he untied the knot that held the gag in place and pulled the cloth free.

He need not have worried about her saying anything he did not want the soldiers to hear because it took her several moments to recover from the stifling gag. She retched and spat, trying to remove the taste of the linen rag.

"Water!" he demanded as he took his dagger and cut her bonds.

One of the soldiers handed him a small waterskin which he held to Beatha's lips. Her own hands were too numb to grasp anything and she leaned against him for support as she drank.

"Thank you," she whispered.

He smiled. Even in her distress, she had the sense to speak Brythonic.

"Do they know who you are?" he asked.

"No."

"Good. Now, tell me what happened to you? How did they catch you?"

Her voice hoarse, taking frequent sips of water, Beatha told him about Ebrauc and Dwyfel, about their betrayal of Calgacus, their death and her capture. By the time

427

she had finished, she had regained some strength and composure, and there was more colour in her pale cheeks.

Facilis muttered, "Thank Jupiter that our cavalry have less sense than their horses. They killed the wrong men."

Beatha gave a wan smile as she said, "I would disagree, but what will happen to me now?"

"I'll think of something," he told her.

"I hope you can think quickly," she sighed. "I don't want Venutius to get his hands on me."

"Venutius is dead," he informed her.

She gave a tired nod, but asked another question.

"What about my son? Where is Togodumnus?"

"He is alive and well. I have spoken to him."

"Can I see him?"

"Best not," he advised. "That would give away your identity. Stay silent. Let me deal with this. I have an idea. Say nothing. Don't let them know who you are."

She gave a tired nod, not understanding what he intended to do, but trusting him.

He helped her to sit up. Wincing with pain, she began kneading her wrists, keeping her head lowered so as not to meet the eyes of the curious soldiers who were still watching them.

Facilis stood up, turning to face the cavalry commander. His idea was born of desperation, a wild notion that could easily fail. But time was against him, and he had no alternative.

"You have made a serious mistake," he informed Aramantus, doing his best to copy the arrogant stance of Aulus Atticus and the younger Tribunes.

Aramantus gave a worried frown.

"What do you mean?"

"Stay calm," Facilis told him. "I think I can get us out of it."

"Get us out of what?" the cavalryman demanded with mounting agitation.

Facilis explained, "She is from one of the tribes Venutius had bribed to become allies of ours. The men you killed had kidnapped her, hoping to use her as a hostage to persuade her people to change their allegiance."

The officer frowned, "I didn't know there were any friendly natives around here."

Sternly, Facilis asked, "Do you think the Governor has time to tell you everything that is going on?"

Aramantus flushed, angry at being rebuked in front of his men, but Facilis gave him no time to protest. He needed to keep the man off balance, to deflect his questions about his hastily concocted story. Aramantus may have been slow of wits, but even he would be able to identify gaps in Facilis' story if he were allowed sufficient time.

"Did the men you killed say anything?" Facilis demanded.

Looking faintly guilty, Aramantus shrugged, "We didn't have time for a cosy conversation, you know. Besides, they didn't speak much Latin. They shouted something but it made no sense."

Seizing on a justification for his actions, he added, "They were barbarians, and they were hostile, so we killed them. I wasn't going to take any chances, considering what happened here last night. You can't blame me for that."

"I understand," Facilis replied. "The men you killed may have been enemies, but the ones who chased you are supposed to be our friends. That was your mistake, although I appreciate your position. Unfortunately, you may have seriously damaged a potential alliance the Governor has been working towards for months. So, I suggest you forget all about this and leave it to me. I need to make the best of this bad situation."

"How?" asked Aramantus, his gaze flicking nervously down at Beatha.

Facilis explained, "You were correct in thinking she is an important woman. If we want to avert another disaster, I must return her to her people."

Aramantus declared, "You can do that on your own, then. I'm not taking my lads out to face a bunch of savages."

Facilis said, "Don't worry. I'll go alone. But there is one other thing. She had a torc."

"A what?"

"A neck ring made of gold. Shaped like a circular horseshoe. I know she had one. I can see the marks on her neck where it was snatched from her. Give it to me."

The cavalryman hesitated, not willing to surrender his plunder, and clearly considering claiming that the torc had been stolen before he had found Beatha.

Facilis held out his hand, snapping, "Give it to me! If we don't restore her to her people safely, her tribe could join the war against us. Things are bad enough as it is, without you and your men creating more enemies for us. Do you want me to tell the Governor that you were responsible for turning a friendly tribe against us?"

"All right," Aramantus conceded with a scowl. He went to his horse, pulling the precious circlet of gold from his saddlebag. Stomping back, he thrust it into Facilis' outstretched hand.

"Thank you," Facilis nodded, softening his tone slightly, but still playing the part of an angry Tribune. "Now, I want two horses. I will take her back to her people. While I am doing that, I want you to send some of your men to find the Second Legion. They should be close now. Tell them the Governor wants them here quickly. Take the rest of your men to the Twentieth Legion and tell them to come here. I'll write you a message to deliver."

"Our horses are tired," the cavalryman objected.

"Better tired than dead," Facilis retorted. "The Governor wants all the Legions to gather here today, so I suggest you do as I say. And don't say anything to anyone

430

about this woman. If I can pacify her people, nobody needs to know what you have done."

Aramantus gave a reluctant nod, admitting defeat.

Calling for a writing tablet, Facilis scribbled a hasty note to the commander of the Twentieth Legion, handing it to the officer with a reminder to deliver it as soon as possible. Then he helped Beatha to one of the horses the soldiers had set aside.

He supported her as she pulled herself into the saddle. She was still weak, hardly able to walk, but the saddle was designed to keep a rider firmly in place. Its high front and back, with four sturdy pommels, one at each corner, provided a secure seat for even the worst horseman.

"Here is your torc," he said as he handed her the golden neck ring.

"Thank you," she said with a weak smile.

She clutched the torc in one hand, not bothering to put it back in place around her throat.

Facilis mounted the other horse.

"Come on," he told her. "We need to go before the Governor finds out you are here. Will you be all right?"

"I will manage," she nodded weakly.

They wheeled away, urging the horses into a trot, leaving Aramantus to organise his men and deliver his messages. Facilis was not convinced they would keep Beatha's capture a secret, but he hoped that sending them off would delay any rumours spreading.

"Why are you doing this?" Beatha asked as soon as they were clear of the fort. "Your Governor will not be pleased if he finds out."

"Aramantus and his men don't know who you are," he replied. "If the Governor does hear some rumours, I'll think of something."

"But you do not need to do this at all," she said.

431

"Yes, I do," he insisted. "You let me go when you could have kept me as a prisoner. That is a debt I intend to repay."

"You are a good man, Anderius Facilis. Thank you."

He found that he could not speak. Up ahead, he could see the waiting tribesmen, could make out that one of the figures was a giant of a man, so large that his feet dangled just above the ground even though he was on horseback.

Calgacus was waiting for her, and Facilis was letting her go. He could have kept her, he knew, could have taken her as a hostage, a captive of war, perhaps even held her as a slave. But he knew she would hate him if he did that, and he could not bear that thought.

Finding his voice at last, he said, "I know we are at war, but I would like to think that we are not enemies. Not personally, I mean."

"You will always be a friend," she smiled.

"But the war will continue," he said sadly. "Calgacus has won today, but one thing you must know about Rome is that she always avenges her defeats. This victory of yours will not end the war."

"I understand," she sighed. "The war may go on, and you will be a part of it, just as Calgacus and I will be, but that does not mean we must hate each other. There must be room for friendship in the world."

"It is difficult, though," he sighed. "As for me, I do not think I want to be part of this any longer. Soon, either Rome will be humbled or, more likely, your people will be conquered. I don't think I want to witness either of those things."

"Then what will you do?"

He gave a tired shrug.

"I am not sure. Perhaps I will ask the Governor to find a civilian post for me, somewhere in the south of Britannia. Or I might return to Rome. I have a wealthy uncle. If I work for him, he might leave me an inheritance when he

432

dies. It will not be pleasant to work for him but, for the first time in my life, I think it might be better than staying here."

"Then I wish you well, Anderius Facilis. May the Gods smile on you."

"That would be a welcome change," he said with a wry smile.

They were nearing the top of the slope where Calgacus was waiting. Facilis reined in, drawing to a halt.

"I will go back now," he told her as she curbed her own horse and drew alongside him.

"Calgacus will want to thank you," she told him.

"This is hard enough as it is," he said. "There have been too many goodbyes in my life. It is better if you just go."

She hesitated, then leaned towards him holding out her golden torc. She placed it over a pommel of his saddle.

"A gift," she told him. "From one friend to another."

He gaped at her, then at the precious object she had given him.

"I cannot take that!" he protested.

"It is a gift. It would cause offence if you refused it."

"But I have nothing to give you in exchange," he said, acknowledging the importance of gift giving among the Britons.

"You have given me your friendship," she smiled. "That is worth more than a mere piece of metal. Keep it, and use it wisely. Perhaps you will not need to work for your uncle, after all."

Facilis could find no words. He merely swallowed, nodding his thanks.

"Goodbye, Lucius Anderius Facilis," Beatha said.

Turning away, she jabbed her heels into her horse's flanks and rode up the slope. Facilis saw Calgacus nudge his pony to meet her. He watched as the two of them met, leaning towards one another to embrace.

Facilis sat there, a lump in his throat, tears stinging his eyes, and memories crowding his thoughts. Faces and names flashed across his mind's eye, people he had known and loved, people he would never see again. Just as he would never see Beatha and Calgacus again. Watching them embrace one another, he felt an almost overwhelming sense of loss.

The emotion was so powerful that, for a brief, mad moment, he considered going with them, leaving the Empire behind and living among the Britons.

He fought the desire, knowing it was an irrevocable step, and one that he should not even contemplate.

Then he saw Beatha give him a wave of farewell, and Calgacus, sitting astride his small pony, looked at him, giving a nod of thanks before thumping his massive fist to his chest and extending his arm in a Roman salute that would have delighted even the most demanding of Centurions.

That gesture reminded Facilis of who he was. The ghosts that had been tormenting him were not banished, but they faded into the dark recesses of his mind, no longer haunting him.

The impulse to leave also faded. That was an impossible dream, born of his loss, and of his secret love for Beatha. He could not go with them. He was a Roman. He belonged in the Empire. More than that, he belonged *to* the Empire.

Smiling through his inner pain, Facilis returned the salute, his sense of identity restored.

He waited until Calgacus and Beatha had rejoined their companions and disappeared over the ridge, leaving him alone on the hillside. For a long moment he sat there, unmoving, while his horse bent its neck to crop at the lush grass.

He took a deep breath, filling his lungs with cool air, then slowly exhaled. For the first time in many months, he felt at peace within himself.

Turning the horse, he looked down on the bustle within the wrecked fort, where the grisly work of gathering the dead and tending to the wounded continued. The Roman army had suffered a terrible blow, but he knew the war would not end. Far off to his left, lost somewhere in the distance, the Second Legion was marching to reinforce the remnants of the Ninth. Twenty miles to the west, the twentieth Legion would soon also be adding its might to the Governor's invasion force.

No. The war was not finished. Julius Agricola and Calgacus were too similar in nature for there ever to be peace. Neither of them would contemplate defeat. Neither of them would negotiate.

The war would continue, but Lucius Anderius Facilis would not be a part of it.

With a wry smile, he nudged his horse, taking the first steps on the long journey to the rest of his life.

Author's Note and Acknowledgements

The attack on the Ninth Legion's fort is one of the most baffling incidents reported by the Roman writer, Tacitus. He was, of course, writing a eulogy to his father-in-law, Agricola, not recording what we would regard as a history. This approach has, however, left some fascinating omissions and contradictions in his account.

Tacitus claimed that Agricola was such a superb general that he always chose the sites for his army's camps, and did this so well that none of the forts were ever breached. Yet only a short while later, Tacitus admits that the camp of the Ninth Legion was attacked and that the Britons broke through the gates. Perhaps Tacitus had forgotten his earlier claim. Despite his assertions that they were driven off, it seems that the Britons came close to achieving almost total victory, only being denied by the arrival of a hastily despatched relief force led by Agricola himself.

Tacitus claims that the Britons fled in panic, seeking refuge in swamps and forests, but this, I think, can be taken as pure propaganda. Tacitus cannot conceal the basic facts that the Britons struck, stormed the camp, and escaped without being caught by the relief force.

What is not at all clear is why Agricola divided his army into three parts in the first place. Tacitus says that he learned the Britons had divided their forces, so the Governor decided to do the same. The most intriguing question is how Agricola learned what the Britons had done. In the various civil wars that often wracked the Roman Republic and Empire, desertions were common, with men changing sides and selling information to save their own lives. Would the same temptation have persuaded some Britons to collaborate with the enemy?

While Agricola's scouts could have brought him information on the Britons' movements, it seems unlikely that he would divide his army unless he was absolutely certain of his opponents' moves. Could his scouts have been that certain? I think a more logical explanation is that some Britons must indeed have gone over to the Romans.

However he came by this information, Agricola was deceived, because the Britons suddenly combined their forces and stormed the Ninth Legion's camp at night.

This raises another question. Military operations at night are notoriously difficult and prone to mishap. Even the great Duke of Wellington was badly caught out on his first attempt to fight a battle in the dark. How, then, did an army composed of undisciplined barbarians locate and attack a Roman fort at night? The answer will probably never be known but, however they achieved this remarkable accomplishment, they caught Agricola completely off guard.

We do not know the full extent of the damage they caused in terms of casualties or destruction, but the Ninth Legion was rarely mentioned by Tacitus after this night attack, so I have interpreted this as meaning the Legion suffered considerably. Tacitus does report that some of Agricola's senior officers were so dismayed that they urged him to abandon the advance. This, of course, may simply be a literary device to show Agricola in a favourable light, as he insisted on continuing his campaign despite the pessimistic views of his advisers. That, however, is for the next instalment of Calgacus' adventures.

Returning to the storming of the Ninth Legion's camp, another mystery is how Agricola learned of the attack in time to bring a relief force. Tacitus claims that he was following the Britons' movements, but this seems unlikely seeing as the attack took place at night and ignores the obvious objection that, if Agricola had been aware that the enemy were approaching one of his Legion's camps, he would have sent warning to the Ninth, which he failed to do. There must be another explanation.

Unfortunately, we do not know how far apart the Roman forces were. It is just possible that they were within signalling distance, or perhaps had signalling stations, although I think this is unlikely. The mystery does, fortunately, lend itself to the plot of my story.

A brief word of explanation is required about the Roman Legions involved in this campaign, particularly references to the Second Legion. Confusingly, there were two Second Legions based in Britain during the Roman era. These were differentiated by names, each Legion having a name as well as a number. So, Agricola's advance into what is now Scotland involved the Ninth *Hispana*, the Twentieth *Valeria Victrix*, and the Second *Adiutrix*. This last was a relatively recently formed Legion and had only been in Britain for a few years, having taken part in the conquest of Brigantia where it was involved in putting down the rebellion of the real-life Venutius.

There was, though another Legion, the Second *Augusta*, which was also based in Britain. This is the Legion that has featured in previous Calgacus adventures, having been defeated by the Silures of South Wales, and having refused to march to join the battle against Boudica. This Legion remained in the south, where it was latterly based at Caerleon. The remains of the Second *Augusta*'s fort can still be seen and are still being excavated. This Legion does not seem to have taken part in Agricola's campaign in northern Britain.

I should also make some comment about the number of combatants involved in this campaign. We know that Agricola had three Legions, plus auxiliary troops. Allowing for casualties, sickness, the need to leave some troops in the already conquered regions of the island, etc, it seems likely that his army numbered somewhere around twenty thousand men, a figure I have inflated slightly for dramatic purposes. Tacitus claims that some of Agricola's officers were concerned about being outnumbered, and in a later passage describes the famous battle of Mons Graupius where the Britons, according to Tacitus, greatly outnumbered Agricola's army.

I believe these claims should be treated with caution. Tacitus was trying to glorify Agricola's achievements, and what better way to do that than to portray him battling against seemingly impossible odds?

So, how many fighting men could the Britons put in the field? That question is almost impossible to answer with any degree of certainty. Estimates of population are notoriously difficult to judge, but the general view is that the population of Iron Age Britain was somewhere between one and two million. Assuming that the situation then was, as now, that the majority of these people lived in the southern part of the island, the population of Britain north of the Forth-Clyde line must have been very low, perhaps little more than one hundred thousand people. Bearing in mind that this included women and children, the number of men of fighting age could not have exceeded forty thousand at most, and was probably considerably less than this.

Another argument against a huge force of Britons is that the logistics in feeding an army of that size must surely have stretched the native population to breaking point. To my mind, it seems much more likely that the Britons could muster no more than twenty thousand fighting men at the very most. I must stress, however, that this is a guess on my part.

We must also bear in mind that a man with a spear is not necessarily a warrior. The Romans had a professional army, but their opponents, with only a few exceptions, would have been men who had left their farms to fight off the invaders. Only the elite classes would have trained for war.

And yet Roman accounts, from Julius Caesar onwards, insist that the Britons were very warlike and later accounts of the Picts stress their constant raiding and plundering. This raises yet another question about the culture of the Britons. Were they similar to the later Vikings of Scandinavia? Was it a warrior culture, with every man expected to fight? Did they live more by plunder and raiding than by farming and raising livestock? We shall probably never know.

However many men the Britons had at their disposal, they were certainly very mobile and highly effective. Roman sources claim the Picts had "very many cavalry" which would help explain how the British army managed to evade Agricola's army and attack the Ninth Legion's camp. All in all, it was a remarkable achievement, and a testament to the commanders of the British army. Unfortunately, we do not know the names of the tribal leaders involved. In fact, depending on which Roman source you consult, we do not even know with absolute certainty where the various tribes were based. All we do know is that they resisted the invaders with all the force they could muster.

For the background to this story, I relied heavily on Tacitus, who recorded an account of the Usipi and their ill-fated voyage around Britain. This same tale is told by another Roman historian, Cassius Dio. The problem is that the two accounts do not exactly match. Tacitus states that the Usipi murdered their Centurions and stole three ships, but he is vague on which direction they took. Whether they began on the west coast or the east, Tacitus states that they were eventually captured and treated as pirates by some continental Germanic tribes. Dio, on the other hand, claims that they murdered a Tribune before stealing the ships and that they sailed from the east coast, round the north of Britain, then down the west coast, before being caught by the Roman Navy when they returned to "this side" of the island.

It seems to me that, if the Usipi were based on the east coast, they would have tried to sail south to get home rather than take the much longer route around the north of the island. I have therefore made them voyage from west to east, because that fitted where I wanted poor old Facilis to end up. I have, though, retained Dio's account of them being captured by the Romans.

For the information on Pompeii, I am indebted to Mary Beard's excellent book, "Pompeii – The Life of a Roman Town., (Profile Books, 2009), and to the account of Pliny the Younger, who was an eyewitness to the eruption.

The rest of the story is all invention, including the myth of Cingel, although legend claims that the founder of the Picts was a man named Cruithne or Cruidne, whose father was named Cinge. For the rest of Cingel's story, I have borrowed and adapted from other ancient legends, many of which do abound with magic cauldrons and cunning heroes.

As for Calgacus, he has, at last, seen the end of his nemesis, Venutius. This is probably the place for me to once again apologise to the shade of the real Venutius, the King of the Brigantes who opposed Rome vigorously during the earlier years of their conquest of Britain. Sadly, every hero needs an enemy, and it fell to Venutius to play that role in these stories.

Calgacus' tale is not quite finished yet, though. Agricola's army is still largely intact and, despite this significant setback, the Governor's desire for total victory is undiminished. The final confrontation is imminent and will be covered in the last of the Calgacus series, "Last of the Free".

As always, I am indebted to friends and family for their support and help in creating this story. Moira and Stuart Anthony, Ian Dron, Stewart Fenton and Liz Wright for reading the first drafts and making their usual helpful

441

suggestions, Philip Anthony for his work on the cover design, and my wife for putting up with my daydreaming while I puzzled over the plot. I also owe a debt to modern historians Alastair Moffat and Tim Clarkson for their excellent books on early British history. I'm afraid I have plundered Tim Clarkson's work for names for many of the characters in this story. In addition, I must thank the contributors behind the excellent website www.romanscotland.org for the information on Roman marching camps in Scotland.

GA
April, 2017

Other Books by Gordon Anthony

All titles are available in e-book format. Titles marked with an asterisk are also available in paperback.

In the Shadow of the Wall*
An Eye For An Eye

Hunting Icarus*
Home Fires*

A Walk in the Dark (Charity booklet)

The Calgacus Series:
World's End*
The Centurions*
Queen of Victory*
Druids' Gold*
Blood Ties*
The High King*

The Constantine Investigates Series:
The Man in the Ironic Mask
The Lady of Shall Not
Gawain and the Green Nightshirt
A Tale of One City

ABOUT THE AUTHOR

Born in Watford, Hertfordshire, in 1957, Gordon's family moved to Broughty Ferry in the early 1960s. Gordon attended Grove Academy, leaving in 1974 to work for Bank of Scotland. After a long but undistinguished career, he retired on medical grounds in 2008 without having received any huge bankers' bonuses.

Registered blind, Gordon had more time on his hands after retiring so, with the aid of special computer software, he returned to his hobby of writing and had his debut novel, "In the Shadow of the Wall" published in 2010. Gordon's books are now being read by a world-wide audience. As well as his historical adventure stories, he has ventured into crime fiction with some spoof murder mysteries in the "Constantine Investigates" series. He is also kept busy with speaking engagements, visiting libraries, schools and community groups to talk about his books.

In addition to his novels, Gordon devotes some of his time to raising funds for the RNIB. As well as visiting schools and social clubs to talk about his sight loss, he has self-published a charity booklet titled, "A Walk in the Dark", a humorous account of his experiences since losing his eyesight. The booklet is available free from Gordon's website www.gordonanthony.net . All Gordon asks is that readers make a donation to RNIB. This booklet can also be purchased from the Amazon Kindle Store. Gordon will donate all author royalties to RNIB.

Now completely blind, Gordon continues to write stories and, in his spare time, attempts to play the guitar and keyboard with varying degrees of success.

Gordon is married to Alaine. They have three children and one grandchild. The family lives in Livingston, West Lothian.

You can contact Gordon via his website or by sending an email to ga.author@sky.com

18817805R00254

Printed in Poland
by Amazon Fulfillment
Poland Sp. z o.o., Wrocław